# THE
# DARTMOUTH
# MURDERS

# THE
# WAILING ROCK
# MURDERS

# THE
# DARTMOUTH
# MURDERS

# THE
# WAILING ROCK
# MURDERS

## Clifford Orr

COACHWHIP PUBLICATIONS

Greenville, Ohio

*The Dartmouth Murders / The Wailing Rock Murders*, by Clifford Orr
© 2016 Coachwhip Publications

*The Dartmouth Murders* published 1929.
*The Wailing Rock Murders* published 1932.
No claims made on public domain material.

ISBN 1-61646-323-6
ISBN-13 978-1-61646-323-6

Cover: Baker Library, Dartmouth College [(CC) BY-SA, Šarunas Burdulis],
    with modifications.

CoachwhipBooks.com

# CONTENTS

# INTRODUCTION
## CURTIS EVANS

CLIFFORD ORR WAS BORN on November 19, 1899, in Portland, Maine. The son of a Portland business advertising agent and grandson of a Maine sea captain, Orr rose to a considerable height from his provincial roots, ending his days in 1951 as a "Talk of the Town" columnist for the *New Yorker*. As a high school student he had shown great literary aptitude and at Dartmouth University he distinguished himself in the school's drama club, the Dartmouth Players, writing the books and lyrics for a series of musical comedies. After leaving Dartmouth (without a degree, though he attended the school for the full four years), he continued to write occasional song lyrics, scoring a hit with the ironically-worded "I May Be Wrong (But I Think You're Wonderful)," sung by Doris Day in the 1950 Kirk Douglas film *Young Man with a Horn*. Orr also worked for several years at the *Boston Evening Transcript* and later managed publisher Doubleday, Doran's Wall Street bookshop. Perhaps it was his exposure to popular mystery novels in the latter capacity that persuaded him to launch his career as a mystery writer.

Orr wrote much of his first detective novel over the summer of 1929 while lazing at Ogunquit Beach, Maine. Published in November of that year under the title *The Dartmouth Murders*, Orr's debut work of fiction quickly won fame for its novelty as a murder mystery with a college setting. Today Kenneth Harris, the student narrator of *The Dartmouth Murders*, sounds quaintly naïve as he speculates on the reasons for the rarity of violent killings on campus: "One hardly, in college, murders for jealousy, for revenge, or even in sudden anger." But murder most certainly is done in *The Dartmouth Murders*, three times.

The first unnatural death is that of Ken's roommate, Byron Coates, whom Ken on a "damp, foggy, chilly morning" discovers hanging from the rope ladder fire escape outside his and Ken's room in North Massachusetts Hall (the real life living quarters of Orr when he was a student at Dartmouth), "his wet pajamas sticking to his skin." What first appears the suicide of a moody college student, however, soon proves a most diabolical murder. On hand to investigate the mysterious affair is Ken's officious father, an attorney and the author of two detective novels. In evident deference to the recognized Golden Age detective novel chain of authority, the local police essentially make way for Mr. Harris to manage the investigation, with help here and there from his son. Two more students will die before an intricately-plotted puzzle turning on old sins casting long shadows is untangled.

Proclaimed "sensational" by the *New York Herald Tribune* and blurbed as *The Great College Mystery* by its publisher, Farrar & Rinehart, *The Dartmouth Murders* was filmed six years later, under the title *A Shot in the Dark* (1935). Although it was a poverty row production, the film, which is mostly faithful to the novel, still has admirers today among aficionados of Thirties cinematic mystery. It is recommended viewing to those who read and enjoy this edition of *The Dartmouth Murders*.

While *The Dartmouth Murders* is a good though conventional example of the Twenties whodunit, Orr's second detective novel, *The Wailing Rock Murders*, is an altogether more original work with a strong element of terror, resembling eerily atmospheric Thirties detective novels by locked room mystery master John Dickson Carr like *The Three Coffins* (1935), *The Burning Court* (1937) and *The Crooked Hinge* (1938) and even Joel Townsley Rogers' surrealistic masterpiece of horror and mystery, *The Red Right Hand* (1945). Readers of *The Wailing Rock Murders* likely also will be reminded of the "old dark house" thriller popularized at the time through books and such hit films as *The Bat* (1926), *The Cat and the Canary* (1927) and, of course, *The Old Dark House*

(1932). Additionally, much of the plot of the well-regarded 1946 noir film *So Dark the Night* appears to have been adapted from *The Wailing Rock Murders* (though unfortunately without acknowledgment of the author).

The events of *The Wailing Rock Murders* take place over one hagridden evening and morning on an isolated stretch of Maine coast near Ogunquit Beach, where are found a rock whose wailing foretells death and two identical neighboring cliffside houses, Victorian monstrosities described with distaste by the narrator of the novel, Spaton "Spider" Meech, who shares the rationalist disdain, so typical of Golden Age detective fiction, for the romantic excesses of mid- to late-nineteenth-century architecture. Nearly seventy-six years old, Meech is a sleuth of long and esteemed repute who in *The Wailing Rock Murders* encounters his most challenging and personal case.

We learn in the opening pages of the novel that Meech's ward, Garda Lawrence, invited the eminent detective to a weekend house party at the Maine country mansion of Creamer and Vera Farnol. On the very night of his arrival at the perilously rock-perched Farnol abode, Meech discovers Garda slain in her locked bedroom, her throat "most horribly, most hideously slit." Before his investigation into Garda's savage murder is over, two more people will be dead, with every promise of a another death soon to follow—a resolution that is a long way from the "restoration of order" which is said to characterize Golden Age mystery and makes *The Wailing Rock Murders* something of a tour de force, as English author and crime fiction reviewer Charles Williams suggested in his review of the novel. "Too good a book may undo a writer as well as too bad a one," Williams ironically observed, "and what Mr. Orr is going to do for his next climax I cannot think."

Perhaps Clifford Orr could not think either, for his next detective novel, said in 1932 to be in preparation under the title *The Cornell Murders*, never appeared. Giving up a career as a mystery novelist, Orr for the next two decades worked as a columnist at the *New Yorker*, where his duties also included answering letters to the editor (including those from the many people puzzled or outraged by the ending of Shirley Jackson's famous short story "The Lottery," originally published in the magazine in 1948). With his wavy red pompadour and large, light-green eyes, "Kip" Orr, as he was known, was remembered by colleagues as a wickedly catty homosexual and alcoholic who could so quickly and surreptitiously down Manhattans at lunch that people unacquainted with his ways assumed he was still on his first drink when he was actually guzzling his fourth. Unhappy in his personal life, Orr passed away in a nursing home in Hanover, New Hampshire, home of Dartmouth University, in 1951, five weeks shy of his fifty-second birthday. It was a sad end to a life that once had held much promise of personal fulfillment, of which the two fine detective novels collected herein give strong evidence.

# THE DARTMOUTH MURDERS

TO
FRANKLIN MCDUFFEE

# CHAPTER I
## SATURDAY: FIRST DEATH

I SHALL NEVER AGAIN hear the night wind pushing at the windows without thinking back against my will to another night and another wind when I lay staring before me in the dark, listening to that muffled, slowly repeated thump against the pane.

There have been times, since, when a wind has arisen in the dark and blown a tiny twig to tap at the glass, and always I have awaked from a sound sleep, to sit half upright in bed, to listen and shiver, and then to lie down again and stay very still thinking the whole thing over, afraid to shift my position lest I bring myself even wider awake to think longer. And naturally, in these nights of remembering, I have imagined, by going over the events that immediately preceded the awful happening, that I can find a hundred portents of what was coming which should have given me some sort of warning.

That morning, for instance, Byron said, "If I die, for heaven's sake don't ship my letters home to Mother without sorting them first."

That afternoon, at the football game, when the first chill November wind swept down from the mountains and brought with it, not the usual autumn tang, but a damp, uncomfortable cold, Professor Bostwick remarked, "There's death in that wind."

And that night, while Father and I were taking the drive that I must promptly tell about, I pointed to the rising full moon and said, "The Hunter's Moon, Dad." And Father answered, "The Murder Moon, you mean."

Of course, in my saner moments I can see that Byron's remark was perfectly natural in one who never could throw away a single letter, however incriminatingly feminine. Professor Bostwick has sworn that he never made any such remark at the game, and meant nothing if he did. And Father, who never was a sportsman and never will be, declares that he used the phrase months before in one of his meddling letters to the game commissioner. So in full daylight my portents pass, but after dark they rise again and I clench my fingers because I failed to heed them. . . .

Byron Coates and I were seniors together at Dartmouth, and roommates. We were roommates by chance as freshmen and by choice the rest of the time.

We were good companions, careless friends, and happy enemies when anything small enough arose to fight about. His claim to undergraduate fame lay in his really excellent baritone voice. Mine lay in a facility with the piano and an ability, after a fashion, to write dancy tunes for the annual musical shows. He was more of an athlete than I and dabbled a bit as a sophomore in both track and swimming, and he was also more studious, though his grades almost always fell slightly short of mine. Mine was the quicker wit, his the greater doggedness. We took to each other's friends as easily as we did to each other's clothes. He was apt to be moody and go into fits of silence in which there was no ill nature nor (I thought) any particular depression, and for which, as far as I could see, there was no particular cause.

One of these moods struck him right after the football game that cold Saturday afternoon. And although it was the last game we should see Dartmouth play as undergraduates, and although we were badly beaten in a ragged, dull game in weather which was far from inspiring, he was not football enthusiast enough to let the afternoon's performance throw him very far into the dumps. Yet, as we walked back from the field he begged Professor Bostwick to excuse him from the tea we had planned at the Bostwick house, nodded good-bye to the rest of us, and plodded across the campus to North Massachusetts Hall, our dormitory.

Jean Coates, Byron's sister, was with me. She had come from Vassar for the game and week-end at her own invitation and with Byron's grudging consent, and was handed to me as a companion. I was neither pleased nor displeased. She was, I thought, a nice girl, quite good-looking in a dark, slim way, but a little strange. And she had brought with her the angular Miss Case, some sort of part-time companion and secretary to Jean's mother, as week-end chaperon—a needless procedure which she said her mother deman-ded. With us, too, at the game and at the tea was Charlie Penlon, who lived two floors below Byron and me in North Mass. and had recently become one of my intimates.

And as for Professor Bostwick, Byron and I had long ago selected him as by far our favourite among the faculty. Tall, slightly stooped, and blondly bearded, he had arrived at college when we were freshmen. He was in the Department of Music, and besides teaching the rudiments of its appreciation and composition, he puttered on the side with glee-club-training, oratorio presentation, and my musical comedies. The same musical bond that held Byron and me together drew us to Bossy, as we called him, and we found him excellent company. He was a bachelor and had the epicurean taste that so often accompanies bachelorhood so that the innumer-able meals that By and I had eaten at his house stood out as quite exciting milestones in our college course. Three evenings a week, at the very least, saw us playing his piano, pawing over his scores, eating the steaming dishes his housekeeper delighted in prepar-ing for us, burning his fireplace wood, listening to his tales of Munich, Fontainebleau, the Sorbonne, and the Quartier, and drink-ing his wine. By the time I was a senior I should no more have omitted Bossy from a social gathering of any size than I should Byron. He was host, guest, companion, and father confessor.

But at the tea that afternoon I was somehow uncomfortable. Byron's leaving it seemed so unnecessary it vaguely troubled me. Bossy played his part as elder all too well and devoted practically all his attention to Miss Case, while Jean and Charlie bantered with each other over the teacups, ignoring the rest of us entirely. And when, as was seldom, the conversation did become general for a moment or two, it was merely to recall a particularly poor try for a field goal that Dartmouth had made, or a certainly unnecessary appreciation of how good the fire felt after the chill of the stadium. And it was somehow with relief, though with great surprise, that I heard myself summoned by Bossy's housekeeper to the telephone.

"Long distance," she said, "for you, Mr. Harris."

I was completely surprised to hear my father's voice: "Is that you, Kenneth?"

"Father!" I cried. "Where are you?"

"In Barre, Vermont. I had to come yesterday on that corporation case and I'm through earlier than I expected. How's the car? Is it in condition? Can you run over and get me? I'll spend the weekend with you."

"To-night?" I asked.

"If it's at all convenient. I've got to have dinner with a man, but if you can get over here in the middle of the evening, everything will be fine. How far is it?"

"I don't know exactly," I said. "Somewhere between fifty and sixty miles, I think. Good two hours run, anyway. . . . Oh, Father, it's fall house party, you know, and I've got a girl up—Byron's sister. I may have to bring her along."

"Oh! Sure you want to? Hadn't you rather dance? I can hire a car."

"Not at all. Don't think of it. I'll be there sometime, somehow. At the hotel?"

"At the hotel. Bundle up warm; it's cold as Greenland."

"Right. See you soon."

"Good-bye, Ken."

I broached the subject as soon as I got back to the living room. "Father's over in Barre, Jean, and wants me to come and get him. Had you rather have me find you someone to take you to the dance, or do you want to come along with me? We'd start after dinner, probably about eight."

Jean showed more interest and animation than I'd seen her show the entire week-end. "Oh, Barre by all means! By says it's a beautiful drive, and there's a full moon to-night. Can Miss Case come along?"

"I'm afraid," I said, "that the car'll only hold three, and bringing Father back—"

"Don't mind about me," said Miss Case. "I trust you two implicitly."

Shortly afterward we said our thanks and farewells to Bossy and started toward the Inn where Jean was staying. On the way we dropped Charlie at North Mass., and while he was giving his final whispers to Jean I called from the portico up to Byron, suggesting that he come to dinner with us. He leaned out of the window and begged to be excused, saying he'd snatch a bite somewhere and go to bed early. I recognized his mood and didn't press the matter, told him I'd see him later, spoke too brusquely to Charlie, and piloted the women toward the Inn.

All the way, and all through dinner, Miss Case chatted incessantly, trying to draw me out on the subject of music, of which I found she knew practically nothing. Jean sat silent, eating busily for a few moments and then staring ahead of her with a curious, far-off expression. Every now and then she shook her head as if to get rid of a disturbing thought and for a moment or two seemed to take an interest in our conversation. I remember thinking, "Queer family."

It was nearly eight when we were through, and as we rose I said, "Put on something warm, Jean. We've got four hours of cold ahead of us."

She put her hand on my arm. "Ken," she said, "would you mind awfully if I didn't go with you?"

"Why—no," I began, "but—"

"I think I've started a sore throat or something sitting on those damp seats. I'll talk with Miss Case for a while and then go to bed."

"Why, just as you say," I told her. "Only hadn't you rather I'd get someone—Charlie or someone—and let him take you to the dance? It seems a pity—"

"No, Ken, really. I'd much rather not. You run off, and I'll meet you for breakfast. About ten?"

And after further remonstrance I left her standing in the lobby, adamant to the last, but looking after me, her hand clutching the skirt of her dress. And it was at that moment that I thought, "Gosh, if she were only more human, I'm afraid I'd fall for her."

The drive to Barre was lonesome, I'll admit, but I had the rising full moon behind me to make fascinating if bewildering shadows on the rocks and fields, and the Vermont roads twist and turn enough so that no driving upon them is ever really dull. But it was cold and there were mists in the hollows and I was glad when the first lights of Barre shone ahead.

I found Father in the hotel lobby, deep in conversation with a gray-moustached gentleman. Father greeted me affectionately and told me he'd be through in ten minutes. But while I waited, still in my overcoat and gloves, the conversation continued, and it was after eleven when Father rose, made his goodbyes, and dispatched a bellboy for his bags.

"Sorry," he said, "but it couldn't be helped," and told me no more.

"Where's the girl?" he asked almost at once.

I told him.

"H'm," he grunted. "Like her brother, isn't she?"

I flared a bit. "What do you mean by that?"

"Why, moody—strange."

"By's not moody," I exclaimed, lying, as usual, in his defense.

"Well, strange then," said Father. "I never liked him, what little I've seen of him. Strange bringing up, I think's the matter with him. What do you know of his father?"

"Nothing," I confessed. "He died when By was very young and Jean was only a baby. I don't think I ever knew what he did, but he left plenty of money."

"And his mother?" asked Father. "In Boston, isn't she, and yet you've never been asked there, even though you've had Byron to Detroit a couple of times."

"Well," I confessed again, "I guess she is sort of queer. Likes to keep to herself anyway. But By's all right. And I'm sure Jean is, once you give her a chance."

Conversation lapsed then, and save for Father's inquiry about the health of Bossy, whom he had met several times, and his remark about the Hunter's Moon, which I have recorded before, we spoke very little all the way back to Hanover. Father has always been difficult to me. He is clever, I know, and extremely observant and canny. There are those who say that if he had taken up criminology as a profession instead of as a hobby he would have made a remarkable success. But sons can't judge, and certainly his corporate and contract law failed to interest me. When, in a group, he told of some famous criminal case in which he had assisted as an unofficial expert, I was always fascinated, but between us the common barrier of father and son was almost always reared when we were alone.

However, a Dartmouth man himself, he loved Hanover and came as often as he could. Moreover, he almost always put up with me, sleeping on the couch that By and I kept for guests in our study, and so it was directly to North Mass. that I drove him.

"Go right in, Father," I said, "and go to bed. I'll skip the car down to the garage. You know the room. Top floor, number 39. By'll probably be asleep, but the door is always unlocked. I'll be up in ten minutes."

But I wasn't. After I'd put the car away I dropped into one of the restaurants for a cup of coffee to take the chill out of my bones, and there joined several who were eating after the dance, chatted with them for half an hour, and then walked with them to the Psi U House for another half hour before the fireplace. And the clock on Dartmouth IIall was just striking three across the campus when I reached the dormitory.

I found the door to the room locked. Strange! By and I never locked the door except when we were both away on week-ends. I rattled the knob, and fished for the key I knew I didn't have. Damn Father for locking the door! I knelt and called in a whisper through the letter slot. "Father! Father!"

No answer.

"Father! It's Ken!"

Still no answer.

And then I peered through the slot. The moon was high, and shone through the south window directly on the couch, and it was empty, and the room, save for the white rays, was dark.

So now I banged louder and called, "By! By!" But still no answer came, and I suspected that the door from the study into the bedroom was shut and By in his usual sound sleep. Then I cursed the fact that we lived on the top floor, else I could have gone into the room above us and tossed out the rope fire escape with which each college room is supplied, and clambered down it into our bedroom. It was often done, though the coiling of the rope again was a nuisance.

I rattled the knob again, and thought. . . . Jay Corey, Charlie Penlon's roommate, was away for the week-end, I knew. If his door was unlocked, I'd swipe his bed for the night. They lived directly underneath us, two floors below, and—thank heaven!—I found the door unlocked and the room dark. But I swear that as I opened the door I saw the light in Charlie's bedroom suddenly switched off, and I heard the click. But when I tiptoed in, and whispered, "Charlie! Oh, Charlie, are you awake?" I got no response, and saw Jay's bed empty and Charlie's sleeping form in the other bed, his head turned to the wall and the bedclothes pulled tight around his neck.

I threw off all but my underwear and climbed into the empty bed, shivering in the wind which whirled in through the window until I had closed the door to the study. For half an hour, perhaps, I lay awake, wondering about Father and watching the tops of the trees waving in the wind above the old, old cemetery that lies almost below the rear walls of North Mass.

I suppose I slept. I know I slept, but it couldn't have been long, or the light thump on the window would not have awakened me. But it came, a decided thump—muffled, uncanny.

I opened my eyes and stared at the window. The moon was already nearing the west, and I could see as plain as day. The window was open at the bottom, and the shade was pulled down some ten inches from the top, but there was nothing there. And yet—

Thump! Muffled. Dull.

Two stories up. What could knock, even softly, on the window? What the hell!

I slept again.

And again I woke. It was faintly dawn, and I could see and feel that the clear cold night had given way to a damp, foggy, chilly morning. I lay, for some reason, wide awake, cursing the unusual luck that stopped my sleep so early on a Sunday. And the Dartmouth Hall clock struck a cold, damp six.

Thump!

It came again, muffled as before, but clearly something rapping at the window.

I jumped from the bed, grabbed the string of the window shade, and ran it up.

And there, against the dawn, swaying so that even as I watched they came against the window with a dull impact, were two bare feet!

I think I made a guttural noise. I'm not sure. I know that in a moment my head was out of the open lower sash and I was looking up. And from our room, hanging on the rope fire escape, with his wet pajamas sticking to his skin, was Byron.

# CHAPTER II
## SUNDAY: ROPE

"Charlie!" I yelled, and shook wildly at the foot of his iron bed. "Byron's killed himself!"

He opened his eyes to stare at me, bewildered, made a slight motion as if to throw the clothes from him and leap out of bed, but instead clutched the clothes tightly about his shoulders and let his head sink into the pillow again. "Hello, Ken," he said.

"Charlie!" I cried, "Don't you hear me? By has killed himself!"

This time he sat bolt upright. "Killed! What do you mean? How?"

"Hung himself. Look! Look there!" I pointed to the window where the feet, revealed now by the raised blind, still swayed grotesquely and dripped the morning damp.

Charlie was all action at once, and leaping from the bed, he leaned out and looked up, as I had done. And then I noticed for the first time that, except for his coat, vest, and necktie, Charlie was fully dressed, his trousers and shirt badly wrinkled. But there was no thought of mentioning it.

Charlie drew in his head. "Whew!" he whistled. "When did you discover him?"

"Just now. Just this minute. I was here all night. I couldn't get into my room. The door was locked. I don't know where Father went." I rattled off excited sentences, hoping he'd catch the drift. "I came in about three. I heard the thump, but I didn't look until now."

Charlie looked out again. "Thumped all night, did he? Funny I didn't hear it. But as a matter of fact, I didn't hear you come in."

Charlie always was cool, but his coolness now exasperated me.

"But what are we going to *do?*" I cried.

"Get the doctor," he said, and started toward the corridor.

"No, Charlie! Not yet. We must pull him up first. There may be a spark of life in him yet."

Charlie stopped and thought. "You say your door is locked? How can we get in?"

"Get the key from the janitor. He comes early."

"He doesn't come at all on Sunday."

"Break the door in. No, it's too strong, and we'd wake the whole dorm." He paused and thought again. "I'll go up to Bill Smart's room and climb up the rope."

Bill Smart lived on the third floor, just below my room on the fourth, and just above Charlie's on the second. The rope that Byron was swaying on would pass Bill's bedroom window.

"Up—up the *same* rope, Charlie?" I asked him. Mentally I could see By's limp body dangling and dancing as Charlie climbed above him.

"Sure, no harm. You go up and wait outside your door. I'll open it from the inside in half a shake."

But it seemed an eternity before I heard, inside my room, the bedroom door open; and a second later the outer door was opened and Charlie let me in. "Bill didn't even wake up," he said. Then, motioning toward the bedroom, "Come on, give me a hand. He'll be heavy."

At the bedroom door I stopped. "Look, Charlie!" The rope, attached to its usual bolts beside the window, was drawn inside the room to the farther end and run through the head of Byron's bed before it traced its way back to the window again and disappeared out of it. "Look, he caught it up so that it wouldn't reach the ground."

"Yes," Charlie remarked, "he calculated it nicely so that the fall would be long enough, yet he'd land just between two floors and wouldn't be found too quickly. He must have thought a bit about it. . . . Here, give me a hand."

I was glad that Charlie took the foremost position during the hauling. He leaned out and brought it up hand over hand. I stayed behind him, gathering up the slack and keeping the tension. But when Byron's dark curly head appeared at the sill, with the dew in little drops all over it, I stepped forward, and leaning out with Charlie, caught underneath one arm as Charlie caught the other, and together we lifted him in and carried him to the bed.

Charlie's next remark was unnecessary, but I was glad he made it to save my doing it. "He's dead all right," he said. "Cold as ice, and stiff. Poor By! What do you think made him do it?"

"I don't know," I said, as slowly and with as much expression as if I were saying something of great wisdom. But then I brightened. "Charlie! Perhaps he's left a note!" I dashed into the study and searched rapidly around, but there was nothing but the usual clutter of books, paper, ashes, and neckties, with By's clothes draped as usual over the back of his desk chair. When I stepped into the bedroom again, Charlie was bent over Byron, searching, it seemed, his face, which in death was hardly whiter than it was in life, and no less handsome.

"Nothing, Charlie," I said.

Charlie straightened up. "Which had you rather do, Ken," he asked, "stay here, or go 'phone Dr. Preable?"

"'Phone," I answered. "But don't you think, Charlie, we ought to—to cover him up?"

"Hell, no!" said Charlie. "That's movie stuff. There aren't any squeamish females here."

As I grabbed some small change and ran downstairs to the telephone in the lower corridor, I repeated his phrase. But Jean was there—that is, just a couple of minutes away at the Inn, and she had to be told. It was not yet half-past six. Might as well let her sleep, at least until the doctor had come. There was nothing she could do, anyway. But Father must be found. And Bossy—he must be told at once. He seemed, suddenly, much more like one of By's family than Jean did.

I got Dr. Preable with difficulty and stammered to the poor man my name and room number, and I know I used the words "hanging" and "suicide." He told me he'd be there in half an hour, after asking me carefully if I was sure By was dead. Then I called Bossy, getting his startled housekeeper first and having to plead with her to wake him when she recognized my voice. "God's love!" he cried, and said he'd hurry right over. No, he said, my father hadn't been there. Try the Inn.

I tried the Inn, grudging the dime I had to sacrifice for lack of nickels. Yes, Mr. Joseph Harris was registered. "Hello," said Father, "where on earth did you go to? I waited outside your door half an hour and then gave you up. I got the last room they had here."

I told him the news, articulate after two repetitions.

"The devil you say! I'll be right over."

On the way upstairs I stepped into Charlie's room and pulled on the rest of my clothes. And when I reached my own room again, Charlie was seated in the armchair in the study, gazing at the floor. He looked up at my entrance.

"Luck?"

"The doctor'll be here soon. I 'phoned Bossy, too, and found Father at the inn. They're both coming over.

"Lord! A crowd. I suppose you told Jean, too."

"No," I said. "There's no need yet. She was going to breakfast with me at ten. No need to wake her yet awhile."

There was silence for a minute. Then Charlie: "I've looked around carefully. There's no note, or anything out of the ordinary. I didn't think there would be."

I stared at him. "Why not? It isn't like By. I'm sure he'd want to explain."

"Think so?" Charlie asked. "I never thought he was particularly communicative."

"Oh, but he was, Charlie! He gave me almost all his letters to read, and we'd talk for hours and hours, about everything. Oh, Charlie!" I cried, slapping the arms of my chair, "why do you think he did it?"

"I don't think he did," said Charlie.

Bossy arrived, then, punctuating Charlie's remark with a rap on the door, and immediately Charlie said he'd dash down and finish dressing. His statement rang in my ears, but I was promptly engrossed in a detailed narration to Bossy. I poured it out whole-heartedly, for the first time being on the verge of tears as the horror of it began to wear off and the knowledge of the loss made itself realized.

"Poor kid," said Bossy, and I don't know if he meant Byron or me, although by that time I was ready for sympathy from any source.

And then my father came, and promptly upon his heels came Charlie, and my tale was told again while we crowded in the bed-room door, staring at Byron's body.

"You say, Penlon," Father began, addressing Charlie, "that you went to bed some time before Kenneth did?"

"Yes, sir," said Charlie. "Shortly after twelve, I think."

"And you didn't hear any of these thumps that Kenneth speaks of, even before you went to sleep?"

Charlie was silent for a moment. "I've been thinking it over, Mr. Harris," he said. "When Ken first told me of them, I could have sworn I didn't hear anything at the window. But now I'm not sure; I couldn't swear to anything. If I try to think hard, I can faintly remember some sort of noise, at not very frequent intervals. But I shan't swear to it, mind you, because as like as not I'm imagining it from hearing Ken's story."

"Were you particularly tired?" Father pursued. "Did you go to the dance?"

"I was at my fraternity house," Charlie answered. "There was dancing, but I didn't dance. I took a couple of drinks upstairs with two or three of the fellows, and started home, as I said, about mid-night. My roommate's in Northampton for the week-end, and I went straight to bed."

And then Bossy broke in. "Did you change the window at all, Charles? Raise or lower the shade, or open the sash. The shade, Ken tells me, was down about ten inches from the top, and hid the—er—hid Byron's feet." He looked a bit apologetic at asking the question, as if it somehow implied that Charlie had manoeuvred the whole transaction and hounded By on to hang himself.

"I didn't touch the window," Charlie assured him. "I doubt if it has been touched in a week. We almost always leave it open, keep the bedroom door closed, and undress in the study."

"And you deviated last night from the usual in no way?" asked Father, with the slightly patronizing air of counsel conducting direct examination.

"Not that I can think of," Charlie answered. "I went to bed as usual and went to sleep as usual. That's all I'm really sure of."

For the first time since Charlie's leap from his bed, I remembered something, and from the window, out of which I had been staring at the old graveyard, I turned on him. "Charlie!" I almost cried. "You didn't undress. You had all your clothes on when I woke you up this morning."

I was sure he changed colour, but he laughed coolly enough. "So I did. In the excitement I guess I didn't notice. I must have had more drinks last night than I realized."

I shifted my glance from him immediately, but I saw Father and Bossy almost simultaneously lower their brows at him, and I heard Father mutter, "Well, of course, if you'd been drinking, your account is of no value whatsoever."

Then the doctor entered, nodding gravely to us all and peering around for, I suppose, the body. I motioned toward the bedroom, but Charlie blocked his way.

"Before you go in, doctor, I'd like to ask a question, just to see if I am right."

"Yes?" said the doctor.

"Has anyone here ever seen a hanging? An execution, I mean. Have you, Mr. Harris?"

"Distinctly not," Father said.

"But you have read about them, haven't you?"

"Of course. Criminology, or anything that's attendant upon it, has always been one of my hobbies, as Ken will tell you."

"Then tell me—in every detailed account you've read, and in every drawing you've ever seen of a hanging, weren't you surprised at the smallness of the rope that the man was hanged by?"

"Well," said Father, "come to think of it, I suppose I was. I know that hangmen's nooses are made of very thin cord indeed."

"Exactly!" cried Charlie. "But the popular impression, however, is that the rope is full-size—regular rope, in fact."

"Charley's right," I put in, and Bossy added, "I doubt if I've ever seen even a picture of an execution."

"In fact, doctor," Charlie went on, "I doubt if a rope the size of these fire escapes, which must be large enough for a hand grip, would cause instantaneous death—instantaneous enough, that is, so that any sane person would trust a well-planned suicide to it— do you?" He reached inside the bedroom and drew out a slack length of rope which he handed to Dr. Preable.

The doctor fingered it and then looked up. "I think you're right, Penlon," he said. "It is large, and very unwieldy."

"Charlie!" I cried.

"Just what are you getting at, Penlon?" Father asked.

"Why this," said Charlie, coolly. "I looked Byron over while Ken was 'phoning, and you all should do the same. I think that if the doctor postpones cutting the rope for a moment, he'll show you that the knot someone has tied is hardly loose enough to slip at all. And I think that he'll find, once we've given him a chance at examination, that the bruises under that rope look darn' funny, and that By was dead before it was even tied around his blessed neck!"

The doctor pushed his way to the door and stopped on the threshold. "I can see at a glance," he said. "The boy did *not* die by hanging."

# CHAPTER III
## SUNDAY: BLOOD AND LIGHTS

IT WAS JUST AFTER NINE when I knocked on Miss Case's door at the Inn.

"Come in," she said. "I haven't seen anything of Jean yet. I suppose she's still asleep. It isn't very proper, I know, to have a young man caller before the bed's made, but come in just the same."

"I've got to tell you something, Miss Case," I said as soon as the door was closed, "that I'm afraid you'll have to tell Jean. It's this—her brother is dead."

She took it much more calmly than any of the others had. "Hm!" she grunted. "Tell me about it."

"I found him hanging early this morning on the rope fire escape outside of the window. The doctor says he died about midnight."

"Hm!" again. "Suicide, eh?"

"We thought so at first, and we're not sure yet. But we think the way the rope was knotted that it couldn't have been. And the doctor says that the bruises it made on his neck were made after death—about fifteen or twenty minutes after. Before we had him moved, the doctor made a slight examination, but he can't find any other wounds on the body yet. He's going to perform an autopsy this afternoon, and then we'll know."

"Hm!" I wished she wouldn't grunt, but I was glad she didn't chatter.

"I think you'd better be the one to tell Jean," I went on. "And do you want to wire Mrs. Coates, or shall I?"

"I'll 'phone her," she said. "She'll probably have some instructions, though if I know her, they won't amount to a row of pins." She snorted a little. "A useless female if there ever was one. I'll wire Vassar, too. Jean'll probably want to go home, and I'll go with her. It's a terrible mess. . . . Hm! Murder, you think!"

It was the first time the actual word "murder" had been spoken by any of us, and I shuddered.

"Let's not say that yet, Miss Case, until we really know."

She stiffened a bit. "Well, I'm only going on your say so. And if it's true, there'll be a rumpus in the college all right."

"I know," I said. "And Bossy—Professor Bostwick, that is— offers to give us all meals up at his house, beginning this noon, so we won't have to hang around with crowds too much. Will you tell Jean? And tell her I'll come for you both about one."

"I'll see to everything," she assured me. "You run along and don't bother yourself about us. I'll wake her up now. She's slept quite long enough, if she came in when she said she was going to."

"Came in?" I repeated. "Did she go out? She told me she had a sore throat and was going right to bed."

"Well, I don't know about that," Miss Case answered. "But just at nine, while we were still sitting around the lobby, she said she thought—why, she said she thought she'd walk over to North Mass. and see if Byron was in, and that she'd be back by ten anyway, and go right to her own room without disturbing me. She went up and got a coat, and that's the last I saw of her. I didn't hear her come in, but that's not strange. . . . Heavens, man!" she suddenly exclaimed. "What if she's—"

She leaped from her chair and dashed to the telephone. "Miss Coates's room, please," she ordered. And then, in a voice that showed her relief. "Oh, good-morning, Jean. Up? Good. I'll come in in a moment. Have a long sleep? . . . That's the girl." She hung up the receiver. "That's that," she said. "Says she was in bed by ten-thirty."

I left then, after hearing her advice to "buck up." I met no one I knew on the way back to the dormitory, and I was glad of it. More than anything else, I wanted to avoid having to talk about it to any of the fellows, particularly as it would be some hours before the doctor could give a final verdict. But coming down the dorm. stairs was Bill Smart, out of whose window Charlie had climbed to ascend the rope.

"Ken," he said. "I've just been up to see you. Charlie told me the news, and I'm terribly sorry. Is there anything I can possibly do?"

I liked Bill. He was plump and good-natured and was one of few in college that Byron knew before he came. They were in prep school together. "Yes," I told him. "Come upstairs and talk to me a few minutes. There's no one there, is there?"

"I don't think so," he answered. "The door's locked."

I had not forgotten my key this time, and Bill sat on the couch while I took the armchair. It became immediately apparent from his first words that Charlie had not told him of our suspicions, and I determined not to say a thing about them. Bill was comforting. He was almost cheery in a kind sort of way. "Good old By!" he said. "He was a prince. He liked you an awful lot, Ken."

"I liked him, Bill."

Then suddenly: "Why, for Pete's sake!" he exclaimed.

"What is it, Bill?"

"I damned near forgot. I saw By and talked with him at about half-past eleven last night!"

"You did!" I cried. "Where?"

"Why, here. You see, it was this way. I was in all the evening, almost, and about nine or a little after I leaned out the window and called up to By to see if he didn't want to go down street and eat. He said he guessed not, that he was half undressed and was going to bed in fifteen minutes or so. So I fooled around, reading and writing a couple of letters and wondering if I was hungry enough to go down street alone, and then I heard your door open and close and footsteps in the room. I thought of course it was you, and I looked at my watch to see if it was too late to eat. That's how I know it was just about eleven. So I leaned out and yelled up, calling for you this time. But By came to the window and said you were out, driving somewhere. 'Thought you were in bed,' I said.

'So I was,' he said, 'but I got up again. I've got a visitor.' And I said, 'Ask him if he doesn't want to go down and eat.' And he laughed and said, 'Not a chance. Good night, Bill,' and shut the window."

I knew this was important and couldn't refrain from telling Bill the whole story—all that we knew, and what we feared. He gave a long, low whistle. "Cripes!" he said. "Then his visitor may have been his murderer."

"He may," I agreed. "You're sure, Bill, that By didn't tell you his name?"

"Positive. It was really only in a joking way that I asked him to suggest that the visitor eat with me. I might not have known him from Adam."

"And was By in his pajamas when he came the second time?"

"Yes, I'm sure of that; with his bathrobe on over them. I saw the gray of his robe and the stripes on the collar of his pajamas."

I sprang to my feet. "The stripes, Bill! You're sure you saw stripes?"

"Sure? Yes, very sure. Why?"

"You're not confusing yourself, just because you happen to know that By had some striped pajamas?"

"I'm positive, I say. And I didn't know that By did have striped pajamas. But what's up?"

"Why this, Bill," I cried. "When I found him this morning, he had on blue—plain blue!"

In silence, and with one accord, we both started into the bedroom. We ransacked every drawer in both bureaus; we looked through both closets, By's and mine; and we dived into the laundry bags, overstuffed and ready to go to the wash. The striped pajamas were not there.

"And I remember distinctly, too," I said, "though it wouldn't ever have entered my head unless you'd mentioned it, that By wore striped ones the last two or three nights, probably all week."

"Here's the gray bathrobe," Bill broke in, "hung in By's closet." He tossed it to me.

"That's not his usual habit," I remarked. "He almost always leaves it over the foot of his bed at night." I held it up. "It was his pet. He wore it all the time. Used to say he couldn't study without it. . . . Look, Bill! Look!"

On the back of the gray silk shawl collar was a spot of crimson.

"Blood," said Bill in a low voice. Then, after a moment's pause, while I stood motionless with my finger still indicating the splotch, "But he probably cut himself shaving."

I narrowed my eyes. "Funny place to cut yourself shaving—back of the neck." It was the first bit of reasoning, tiny though it was, that I had contributed to the case at all, and I thrilled at it. "Bill," I said. "All of us—Father, Charlie Penlon, Jean, her chaperon, and I—everyone that knows anything at all about the business—are eating up at Bossy's about one. You've got to come too, and tell them what you know, Father particularly. If I know him at all, just as soon as the doctor reports that it wasn't suicide—if he does— he's going to be hot-foot after all clues, and revel in them."

"All right," said Bill.

I sent him off to breakfast then, hardly realizing and certainly not caring that I'd had none myself. And then I went carefully over both rooms once more. Distinctly, the pajamas were not there. I locked the bathrobe into my handbag and put it in my closet. And then I went out to walk, leaping the back railing of the portico and wandering into the old cemetery. The chilly morning mist was burning off, and the sun, almost warm, was shining through. I sat on the iron rim of a silent rusty fountain and let the full purport of the thing run wild in my thoughts.

Byron dead. And murdered almost beyond doubt. And in college! And at Dartmouth! Why, the place would be wild when it became known! And the moment the doctor gave his verdict, the police would come in. And the Boston papers would be at us, with the New York papers following. Detroit would come, too. "Dartmouth Man Slain. Roommate of K. D. Harris, Detroit Boy, Found Dead." There would be pictures. It was incredible. Why, college men don't kill each other. They don't even fight, seriously.

And they don't have enemies. Not real, deadly enemies. And By had none that I knew of. There was John Meseraux, whom By always said he detested, but that was quite easily explained. People said that John resembled By uncannily, save that Meseraux was much blonder. But as a rule By, like myself, either liked or ignored. It was a puzzle.

I sat, I think, for about half an hour, and then kept on into the cemetery, coming out at the farther end and cutting diagonally across the fields to Tuck Drive. I climbed the gully at the bend and gained the height over the river almost in front of Bossy's little white house. It was nearly noon.

Father was already there, seated in front of the fire, with Bossy scribbling at his desk in the corner of the living room. Bossy stood up when I came in. "We've been wondering where you were," he said. "How's the nerve? Bearing up?"

"So-so, Bossy," I answered. "I've been walking, and sitting in the cemetery."

"Hardly the place, I should think," he remarked.

"It never entered my head."

"Kenneth," said my father. "I've just been to see the president. The doctor reported, it seems, almost immediately, and the president called me at the inn. He's tremendously upset and he's postponing a trip to Boston he was going to take this afternoon. He's staying at home until the examination is completed, and he's asked the doctor to 'phone him at once. He says that if the verdict is what we think it is, he's going to conduct chapel to-night himself, and announce it to the college."

"Oh!" I cried. "Is that necessary?"

"Not necessary, perhaps, but admirable, I think. It can't be hushed up, and if the undergraduates got it all by rumour, or from to-morrow's papers, it would make a terrible mess."

"Yes, Ken," said Bossy, "it's an undergraduate affair, whichever way you look at it, and information must come first-hand."

"I suppose you're right," I said.

Charlie arrived, asking again after my state of mind, and saying, "I've had the very devil of a time. Met everyone I ever knew, it seems, and, naturally, if I talked with any of them at all, I had to tell them about By. I dodged questions, though, and I didn't say a word about foul play. I don't think anyone guessed, however, except possibly Sam Anderson. He's shrewd, you know, and brought up the bigness of the rope question right off. I tried to stall him off, but he looked sort of funny."

Sam Anderson lived right across the hall from me, in number 40, with big, slow-going Jerry Dawes. Sam was big, too, but with none of the stodginess that went with his name and Scandinavian ancestry. He had a booming bass voice and sang in the glee club and choir, and By knew him more because of that than because we were neighbours. Bossy, of course, who trained the choir, knew him, too.

"Sam won't talk too soon," he said. "He's got a lot of sense."

I told them that Bill Smart was coming, and I told them that together we brought news, but Father agreed with me that it should wait until Bill came. "For the first time," he pointed out, "we'll have everybody interested, except the doctor, all together, and we'll tell our stories in turn and see, by fitting them together, if they make sense."

Charlie, at that moment, suggested that he take the burden of fetching the two women from the Inn off my hands, and I readily consented. I felt that if I could face Jean, supposedly the most affected, against the background of a larger company than Miss Case afforded, it would be much easier. And so it proved. She came in, dressed in her traveling suit, obviously the darkest clothes she had. There was a surprising bit of warmth in her handclasp. "Poor Ken," she whispered. "I know how you feel."

I introduced Father and Bill to them, and imagined I saw a curious sudden flash in Father's eyes when he took Jean's hand. A moment later, as the others moved toward the dining room, Father drew me back. "You told me," he said, in a very low voice, "that Miss Coates was going to bed very early last night, and therefore couldn't drive with you."

"Yes," I answered. "And so she did. She says she was asleep by ten-thirty."

"She lies then," Father said grimly. "I saw her come in while I was registering at the desk about two in the morning."

"Impossible!"

"It's true. And furthermore, she looks strangely familiar to me. I'm sure I've seen her before, or someone very like her."

"You see her resemblance to By, probably."

"Nonsense: She doesn't resemble Byron in the least. You know that. But come, we'll hear her story."

We couldn't keep Byron out of the conversation during dinner, try as we might. But none of the gruesome details were mentioned. Instead, Bossy related one or two pleasant things By had done or said, and Miss Case told a few anecdotes of his prep-school days.

Neither Jean nor Father said a word.

After the meal, around the fire, with Father taking the lead, we each told all we knew. For the first half hour there was nothing that we all didn't know before. Then, when Bill told his tale of the conversations from window to window, and I followed it up with a telling of our inability to find the striped pajamas and of our discovery of the blood spot, Father leaned forward and tapped the arm of his chair.

"It's our first step," he said. "It's little, but it's clear. The murder—we'll call it that—was bloody. The guilty one had to do away with the pajamas if his suicide hoax was to hold at all. The spot on the bathrobe was an oversight." He shook his head. "Careless, most careless."

Then Jean told her story. She had sat with Miss Case in the Inn lobby until nine, rather regretting that she hadn't ignored her sore throat and driven to Barre with me. As Miss Case had said, Jean thought she'd walk over to North Mass. and see if Byron were in. "I'd seen so little of him," she said, "and we didn't even sit beside each other at the game. I knew it would be all right for a sister to go into the dormitory, but I didn't want to walk up through the corridors alone, so I went around in back, intending to call up at his windows, but they were dark. So I went right back to the Inn, and as I couldn't find Miss Case downstairs, I went right up to bed. I read awhile, I heard ten o'clock strike, and I was asleep by half-past."

Father leaned forward again. "About what time, Miss Case, did Miss Coates leave the Inn, saying she was going to Byron?"

"I see what you're driving at," Miss Case said, "but I don't think there's anything in it. It was just about nine."

"So that, even if you did go upstairs after your wrap, Miss Coates, it wasn't very much past nine when you looked up at Byron's window?"

"Not much after," Jean agreed.

"Yet *you* say, Smart," pursued Father, turning to Bill, "to use your own words, that it was 'nine or a little after' when you looked up and talked with Byron. The lights were on then, I presume?"

"Yes, sir," said Bill.

"And Byron said, I believe, that he was going to bed—again I quote—'in fifteen minutes or so.' Leaving out, for the moment, the obviously conceivable possibility that Byron switched out his lights and went to bed at once after talking with Smart, there is inconsistency in your two stories."

There was silence.

"I stick to my time," Miss Case snapped out. "It was practically on the dot of nine that Jean said she was going out. I heard it strike, and I was waiting for it, as a signal to go upstairs. It could have taken her not more than two minutes to get her coat."

"And I stick to my time, too," said Bill. "It was the striking of nine which made me think of eating. I might have waited three minutes, or five or six, before I called. By, as he said, was half undressed. He was not yet in his pajamas. Of that I am certain."

"It is certainly strange," Father mused, "that not more than a minute after that his room was dark." He leaned back in his chair and rested his gaze on the ceiling. "One of you is wrong," he said sternly, "or lying."

Another silence followed, a tense one, during which I didn't dare look at anyone. It was broken by Bossy's housekeeper calling Father to the phone. "It's Dr. Preable," she announced.

No one spoke while he was out of the room, but each one tried to listen to Father's voice in the hall. All we could make out was the phrase, "Tell the president," and then Father came back. He stood in the doorway, one hand on his lapel.

"The autopsy is not quite finished," he announced. "But it has gone far enough to report. Byron was killed by some small sharp instrument piercing the brain from under the back of the skull. The doctor thinks the instrument is still there. He is calling an assistant and they are about to open the cranium."

"God!" cried Miss Case. "We're in for it now!"

# CHAPTER IV
## SUNDAY: SECOND DEATH

JEAN, WHEN I DARED TO LOOK AT HER, was sobbing; not violently, but with her head down and her handkerchief at her lips. And Miss Case, after glaring suddenly and silently at each one of us in turn, as if to make a row of exclamation points in punctuation of her last remark, rose and crossed to the girl. "If you have a room where we can go, Professor Bostwick," she said, "I think Jean and I will retire for a while."

Bossy told them that they were welcome to the guest room, and went with them to the foot of the stairs. Jean looked at no one as she left, and said nothing.

All of us, I believe, had thought that when the doctor's verdict finally came our tongues would loosen, and that our restraint and uncertainty and the fear of saying too much would vanish. But it was not so. Bossy made a few inconsequential remarks, mostly expressions of pity for Jean; both Bill and Charlie murmured sentences somewhat after the order of "It beats me!"; and I wondered audibly what the small sharp instrument of death might be. For half an hour there was nothing done and nothing said which was of the slightest importance, nor, in retrospect, the slightest interest. All of us, I think, were somehow mentally kow-towing to the silence into which Father had fallen ever since he regained his seat by the fire.

Finally he spoke, looking at Bill and Charlie. "If Professor Bostwick will excuse me for dismissing his guests," he said, "I wonder if you two boys would mind leaving Kenneth and me alone for the time being. Kenneth, as Byron's roommate, is necessarily both deeply grieved—I'm sure we all are that—and deeply involved. Presently he will have to face the police. There are a few points of conduct there which I think I can give him—both as a lawyer and as a father. It will be made easier if—"

There was always this one good point about Father's sentences: they gave you time to be about your business long before he finished. Bill and Charlie were already risen and ready for their thanks to Bossy. I walked with them to the door and heard their expressions of anxiety to be called on if there was anything they could possibly do. "I'll see you both to-night," I told them.

I returned to the living room just in time to hear Bossy say that he would be upstairs in his room if he were wanted.

"Tut," said Father. "I didn't mean that literally. I have nothing to say that you can't hear. Sit down." I was immensely relieved. A second person has always helped me to bear the brunt of Father's pomposity.

"I was merely anxious," Father went on, "to muse aloud for a minute or two without a great crowd of listeners. The women, I think, will be upstairs for a little while yet. And by way of introduction, I might say this: I don't know how much Kenneth has told you, Professor Bostwick, of my delvings into criminology, but they have been quite considerable, though I have performed them solely as a hobby. I have read thousands of cases and reports, become acquainted with several of the better detectives and investigating experts, and generally done about as much as an amateur can do to probe the subject and its practice. I have also, as you may have heard, amused myself with the writing of two books of fiction, so-called detective stories."

"I have read them both," said Bossy. It was kind of him not to add that he never would have heard of them if I hadn't lent them to him.

"You rather astound me," said Father. "They had no sale to speak of. The critics called them ingenious but dull from lack of action. I admit," he added, a little bitterly, "there was no shooting."

"I enjoyed them thoroughly, Mr. Harris," said Bossy, rather weakly.

Father waved his remark aside by raising his hand and wiggling it. "No matter," he said. "Thank you, sir, but no matter. What I was getting at was this: I saw the president this morning, as I say, and we talked the matter over. He knows of my hobby—my extra-curriculum work, as he put it—and has read both my books. And he told me that if the doctor should announce, as we were practically sure he would, that murder had been done, I was to consider myself retained by the college to putter with investigation. Unofficially, of course," he hastened to add, as if he were afraid we should consider his hobby degraded if put to official uses, "and entirely without recompense. I am to work, as it were, under cover. That is why I presumed to be rude enough to dismiss those two excellent young men."

Bossy caught Father's formality. "Pray don't mention it," he said. "It was obviously the thing to do."

I can't say that I had ever been much informed or even much interested in Father's tiptoeing around after things criminal. I knew we had a large library of such matters at home, but I'm afraid my type of mind cares little for that sort of thing. I have always been a good observer and, I hope, a fair recorder, but I never could make deductions. I felt, naturally, a thrill of pride that the president, who was nothing if not thorough, should see fit to intrust so important a college matter to my father, but I must admit a certain annoyance at the realization that Father would now stay on in Hanover indefinitely. Father was clever, but he was an almighty bore. And, son-like, I couldn't seem to find words for congratulations. But Bossy came to my rescue.

"Fine, sir," he exclaimed. "It's a great honour. And you must live *here*. For a long stay, it'll be much more comfortable than either the Inn or Kenneth's room. And the living room is yours for any conferences you care to hold."

Father inclined his head importantly. "Thank you, Professor Bostwick. It will be a pleasure, and I accept."

Immediately, like a visitation, the entire weight of the case seemed to fall upon his shoulders, and his brow was deeply wrinkled. "My problem is a tremendous one," he said. "You see it?"

I forget what we murmured. It was unimportant.

"I'll show you," he pronounced. "How many of us were there at dinner? Seven, I think. Well, any one of us might have murdered Byron Coates."

"Father!" I cried, "please don't—"

"It's quite true," he interrupted. "Myself, first. No one, I believe, but the hotel clerk can actually testify to seeing me between my leave-taking of you, Kenneth, at the dormitory door, and the finding of the body. And you, yourself, Kenneth, cannot prove your absence from the scene from the time you left the Psi U House until you woke Penlon."

"But—"

"No 'buts,' please, just now. Since Professor Bostwick is a member of the faculty, he very naturally was not seen in the vicinity of the dormitory."

"It is only by chance I was not seen," said Bossy. "I did not go down to the campus last night. But the college is slightly different, I imagine, from what it was in your day, Mr. Harris. The faculty and students are much closer together. Many of the instructors, the bachelor ones particularly, call on the undergraduates as frequently as they do on each other. I have been to Kenneth's and Byron's room any number of times. If I hadn't been occupied with orchestrating some of Ken's tunes, I might easily have dropped in on Byron last night just for a casual talk."

"I certainly am not asking you for an excuse why you were *not* seen there," remarked Father. "Neither of you sees my point. I'll make it in a moment." He paused. "Penlon's plea that he was at his own fraternity house earlier in the evening has not yet been substantiated, and his excuse for rising the next morning, fully dressed, was lame, to say the least. He, so far as we know now, could have killed Byron. Smart's story of being alone for so many hours in his own room is, I admit, convincing in its naturalness, but not yet proven. We have only Miss Case's own story that she was in her own room from nine last night until Kenneth called upon her at nine this morning. And as for Miss Coates—we can assume that either she or Smart was lying about the lights in Byron's window, and I have already caught her in another lie, which I have told to Kenneth. I am waiting only for the best opportunity to confront her with it."

"But Father," I argued, "why pick on just us seven? There's a whole college to suspect in the same manner?"

"There, Kenneth," Father cried, "you've anticipated my point, and I'm glad you see it. It is what I meant by the enormity of my problem. Each one of us can be embroiled. In the same manner, without any doubt, practically every last undergraduate or teacher in Dartmouth could be embroiled, and, for that matter, every last townsman of Hanover. But you object, and say that in every death such a supposition might be made; that, for instance, in the case of a murder in New York City, the entire millions of population, by my interference, would fall under suspicion. . . . It is not so. At least, it is certainly not so to so great an extent as it is here. Hanover is a unique place. It is possible, though not probable, that everyone in town knew Byron by sight, yet there are upward of four thousand people here. It would be an important city resident indeed who could be recognized by so many. And furthermore, here, in a college, there are not the motives that the outer world calls forth. One hardly, in college, murders for jealousy, for revenge, or even in sudden anger. It couldn't be for money, for though I believe the Coateses have plenty, there is none here who could profit by his death. Byron's intimate character I admit I do not know at all, and presently I shall ask both of you, and many others, for as much information as you can give me. But he was obviously not in business, and not seeking power. We can't look for enemies among his underlings. And a college senior rarely has a murderously serious past where love affairs are concerned. There is practically nothing in the concentrated but care-free life of a collegian that we can put our finger on and say, 'Here, given cause enough, is motive.' . . . You see, Professor, my point, and my problem?"

"I do," said Bossy, "and I appreciate it."

The two women came in then, with Miss Case in the lead, saying that if the men didn't mind, she thought they'd better go back to the hotel. "I want Jean to rest," she said. "She'll undoubtedly have to do a lot of talking with the police before long."

Bossy said he was sorry and Father excused them with more grace than I had ever seen him exhibit, and the three of us went to the door with them. I was surprised to see Charlie Penlon coming up the path.

"Oh, Ken," he said. "Glad you're still here. Can I speak with you a moment?"

I went down the steps and stood beside him on the gravel walk. Immediately conversation in the doorway ceased, and I knew they were all listening, but Charlie didn't seem to mind.

"It may be tremendously important," he began, "and it may amount to nothing at all. But I met Sam Anderson in the dorm. again, just now. He was on his way down to the Junction to see his folks off on the train, but he stopped and asked me, quite anxiously, it seemed, about the development of this business. I told you I thought he guessed that something queer was afoot—something besides suicide, I mean. So I told him the doctor's verdict, seeing that everyone will know it in an hour or so. You know what good sense he has. Well, he told me that he'd been waiting to hear just that, and he asked me to tell you to meet him right after chapel so that he can tell you something. Says he'll be tied up with his folks and choir rehearsal until then. He says that last night, just after eleven, he heard someone going into your room. He knew you had a girl in town and, just for fun, he thought he'd peek out and get a look at her, if you were by any chance sneaking her in. So he put out his light and opened the door just a crack and looked—and he saw who By's late visitor was."

"Who?" came from two or three of the listening group on the steps.

"Think he'd tell me?" said Charlie. "Not Sam. I tried to get it out of him, but he was mum. He said he hadn't told anyone, and he wouldn't tell anyone but Ken or the police, if he was asked."

We all buzzed frantically for a minute or two, and Father ordered, "Don't fail to keep the date, Kenneth. It is all-important."

Charlie again offered to take the women off my hands and escort them to the Inn, and again I consented. But before they left I spoke to Jean. "If you feel like it, Jean, I'd like to see you sometime this evening. May I come to the Inn?"

"By all means," she said. "I want to talk to you very soon."

They left, and Father and Bossy went a moment later, Bossy to conduct his choir rehearsal, and Father, as he said, to jot down something in his room and to pack up his bags. "Call for me on the inn porch," he said, "just before chapel. I want to go and hear the president. The attitude of the crowd will be not only interesting but important to watch."

Attendance at chapel, in the year of which I write, was compulsory, although it is not so now, and the Sunday service was held late in the afternoon, ending just a few minutes before six if the sermon was not too long-winded. It was almost dark, then, when, after an unrefreshing nap on Bossy's divan, I walked down and met Father on the steps of the Inn. As we crossed the campus toward the chiming of the bells, Father swept the scene with his arm. "Beautiful," he said, "all these hundreds of boys streaming through the dusk. All confident, all happy, all eager—"

There was no doubt about it; Father *was* a bore!

"—yet in half an hour they will know that murder has come among them."

The chapel was crowded when we entered, and I thought I caught a glimpse of Miss Case coming in through another door in a group of female left-overs from the week-end, but I was not sure. Father and I found that the only seats left were near the front, on the aisle, among those reserved for my own senior class. I wanted to look around for Charlie and Bill, but I didn't care particularly to have to give a smile to many of my classmates. Instead, I looked at the choir loft.

In those days, before the chapel was remodeled as it is at present, the choir and the organ console were placed in a balcony almost overhanging the pulpit. The balcony was composed of four steep steps with the console in front. And standing on the top step, his head shining almost as gold as the organ pipes a few inches behind him, was Sam Anderson. He caught my eye and raised his eyebrows. I took it to mean, "Meeting me right after the service?" and I nodded. He nodded, too, and jerked his thumb back over his shoulder in the direction of the dormitory. I presumed he meant, "In North Mass."

Bossy was already at the organ where he could both accompany and direct the choir, playing a prelude. And then the president came in, the assemblage rising to greet him and waiting until he had laid his notes and Bible on the pulpit and taken his chair before it rumbled into its seats again.

We sang a hymn in unison. I don't remember what it was, but it affected me strangely. Then the president read a prayer. I listened intently, half suspecting that he might make some reference to what had occurred, but there was nothing. After that the choir sang an anthem, during which I kept my eyes glued on Sam, towering above the others, and I fancied I could hear his great bass voice louder than the rest. Who on earth, I asked myself over and over again, was By's visitor?

Then the president rose and fiddled for a moment with the things on the desk. "Men of the college," he said, "it is not the policy of the administration to use the chapel services for other than that for which they were originally intended. It is not even the custom to make announcements from the pulpit, however brief. But something has occurred to-day which by its very nature is so unusual and so important that there is no choice but to drop tradition and lay it immediately before the entire college group.

"One of your number," he went on, after a pause, "last night met death, here, in one of the dormitories. I cannot of course, in this place, go into details, and those you will find in to-morrow morning's *Daily Dartmouth*. But circumstances and evidence which is indisputable point to the fact that that boy met death at the hands of another. He was, we are now certain, *murdered*."

There was a sudden but low sound from the congregation, and another, slightly louder one, as the president told Byron's name.

"Now," he continued, "a murder is a terrible thing. If there can be any degrees of it at all, it seems more terrible when it is found in a college where youth and the highest of ideals are supposed to prevail. Such an occurrence is practically certain, for a time at least, to propel the name of the college into undue and possibly unmerited publicity—an event which is bound to be a great obstacle in the progress of an elemosynary institution such as you know Dartmouth to be. But Dartmouth, I can certainly say, will attempt to cover nothing. It will do everything it can to solve what now is a mystery and bring about justice. And the college not only requests but requires that, after you have read the details, each one of you shall come forward and tell all you know that is relevant."

There was dead silence. I half expected someone to rise behind me and shout the truth, when from the organ loft came an uncanny yell.

The congregation jumped as if a shock had passed through it. Looking up, with the rest, I saw the tall Sam Anderson reel forward, lose his balance, and fall, pushing those in front of him out of the way. He crashed down the steps and against the balcony railing and came hurtling over to land with a dull thud before the pulpit.

He lay face downward, not five feet away from me, and in that breathless second, before anyone moved, I saw the blood trickling from the back of his neck.

# CHAPTER V
## SUNDAY: GHOST

FATHER PUSHED ROUGHLY BY ME and in one stride reached Sam and bent over him. He was, I think, the first one to move in the entire chapel, but immediately afterward everyone was moving, pushing forward, crowding from behind, with a thousand voices mingling in a low roar. I found myself beside Father, standing over Sam's sprawling form, helping to hold the crowd back. It was utmost confusion for three minutes and then someone, though I don't know whether it was the president, Father, or an undergraduate volunteer, shouted from the pulpit and by degrees calmed the hubbub so that four or five of us could lift Sam and carry him into the tiny little anteroom.

The next few minutes are extremely confused in my mind and I cannot report actually what occurred. But shortly Father, Bossy, the president, and I were crowded into the room with Sam.

"The boy is dead," said Father, "and I call you all to witness this little bleeding hole at the back of his neck. Such a mark, we presume, the doctor has also found upon Byron Coates."

We stared in silence. The president and Bossy, still in their black robes, gazing down at Sam, looked as if they were standing at prayer.

"I have sent for the ambulance," said the president. "Don't you advise, Mr. Harris, that he be taken at once to the undertaker's, where undoubtedly Dr. Preable still is, rather than to the hospital or his own room?"

"Undoubtedly," said Father. "It is the thing to do." And then, as we entered another silence, he continued, "It is tragic. It is most lamentable. But it simplifies my problem immensely."

We all wanted to ask, but Bossy voiced the question. "How so?"

"Why," Father explained, "Byron's murder, we think, has been repeated. It becomes like two simultaneous equations—the unknowns are restated. Their values, by adding, subtracting, and transferring, are much more easily determinable. We now, if you choose, have a second death, undoubtedly at the same hands as the first, and we can check one against the other. At present, of course, we know as little about this young man's murder as we do about Byron's, or the causes for it, but in time, if—"

"Father!" I broke in. "Don't you realize who this is?"

"Why, no," Father said. "He seems a—"

"It's Sam Anderson! It's the fellow who was going to tell about last night!"

Father turned suddenly from me and stared down at the body. "Blue hell!" he muttered. "That's an entirely different matter."

I turned to the president and rattled off an explanation of Sam's message to me. He looked extremely grave and thought for a moment.

"The motives for the two then, Mr. Harris," he said, "can hardly be coordinated. This one is entirely clear. It was for the sake of silence. I think your problem is as obscure as it was before.

Father, who had bent down and turned Sam's face upward, now rose again and looked squarely at the president. "On the contrary, sir, it is lightened a hundred times!"

"How so?" Again it was Bossy.

But a rap came at the door and the ambulance was announced. Immediately Father sprang into action. "I'll go with it," he said. "Meanwhile, Professor Bostwick, I am going to ask you if you will kindly round up four or five men who were in the choir with you when this occurred and ask them if they'll go to your house with you and talk it over. Be most particular, please, that you get the men who were standing near Anderson—most important of all, those who were on either side of him in the back row. You'll have no difficulty finding them. The whole college is outside and I doubt if the choir has yet unrobed. You, Kenneth, hunt for Charles Penlon and take him to Professor Bostwick's. I'll be there shortly."

He strode out, and I followed after him. If Charlie was in or near the chapel I knew that, by virtue of his connection with the case, he would be in or near the front row of the great crowd which was filling the vestibule and overflowing onto the green outside. But I couldn't spot him, so I pushed through, taking advantage of the temporary pathway that the men carrying Sam had made, feeling sure that if Charlie saw me, though I couldn't see him, he would follow me. A score of fellows tried to speak to me and ask a dozen questions, but to them all I replied, "Tell you later," and kept on. I had to cross the street before I was out of the mob and, then, twenty paces farther, I looked back. The ambulance was threading its way out of the crowd, a dozen or more undergraduates running along beside it, but there was no one coming in my direction, so I continued straight on toward North Mass.

Down the narrow path that leads to Mass. Row from the campus, a hatless figure was running toward me with no coat on and his white shirt shining through the dark. I recognized him and held out my arms to block his way. "Charlie!" I cried.

He stopped, panting. "Ken! That you? What in hell has happened!"

"You weren't at chapel?"

"No. Took a nap and woke up when the ambulance, or patrol, or whatever it was started clanging and the fellows began to run out of the dorm. What's up?"

I slipped my arm through his and began to lead him back toward our rooms, and on the way I told him. "And Father wants us up at Bossy's in a few minutes," I concluded, "to talk it over."

"God," said Charlie, "what a mix-up! By and Sam! It isn't possible, that's all!"

"I'm afraid the impossible has happened," I said lamely.

We reached Charlie's room and he began to put on the rest of his clothes. "Was Jean there?" he asked.

"I don't think so. I didn't see her. Doubt if she'd have gone."

"Was Miss Case?"

"I don't know. I thought I saw her as I was going in, but I'm not sure."

"Bill?"

"I didn't see him."

"Bossy, of course?"

"Yes, he played the organ. And Father sat with me."

"Neither all present, then, nor accounted for," said Charlie.

"What do you mean, Charlie?"

"Nothing. Let's wait until we get to Bossy's."

We did the walk in almost complete silence and I am afraid I started at shadows along the way. It was a comfort to have Charlie take my arm so tightly.

The housekeeper let us into an empty living room, but I had hardly built up a new fire in the fireplace when Bossy arrived with six boys, two of them still bearing their chapel robes on their arms. I didn't know any of them by name, though by sight they were all familiar and I tried to greet them cordially without being introduced. Charlie and Bossy pushed forth chairs.

I heard the noise of a car outside and, stepping to the window, saw Father descend from the ambulance, say a word to its driver, and dismiss it with a wave of his hand. "What a man!" I thought.

I have never seen anything like the absence of fuss and ceremony with which he made his entrance. He waited for not a word from any of us, but entered brusquely, glanced around the room, and took a stance with his back to the fire where he could survey us all.

"Hanover, gentlemen," he began, as if he had rehearsed his speech mentally, and doubtless he had, on the way up in the ambulance, "possesses a police department which is thoroughly adequate in times of—shall we say—peace. We cannot expect it to operate with metropolitan efficiency in such a crisis as this. Just now the entire department, numbering, I believe, two, is conferring with Dr. Preable in the undertaking rooms. The chief informs me that the sheriff and his men are on their way here, but they can hardly arrive for some hours yet. Having had legal training and being closely connected with this case because of my parenthood to Kenneth, roommate of Byron Coates"—I saw a slight movement among the six choir members as if they were glad that this rather frightening gentleman had explained his presence—"I have suggested to your chief that I save a bit of his time and the sheriff's by making an attempt to clear the ground a trifle. And I suggest that you six men who were present in the balcony during the service select a spokesman from among you and let him tell, as fully as he can, what he saw and heard, and that any or all of you ask to speak afterward if a single detail differs from what you individually witnessed."

There were, naturally, embarrassment and shiftings in the chairs until Bossy came to the rescue. "Suppose you tell what you remember, Jeffers," he suggested, and indicated a slight, blond fellow sunk into one end of the divan.

Jeffers sat up, and in a voice obviously tenor said: "There isn't much to tell as far as I am concerned, Professor Bostwick. I am in the front row, you know, and I was directly in front of Anderson, with just one man in between us. I was listening to the president, as I suppose we all were, and I heard Sam yell behind me, and almost immediately, even before I had time to look behind, he came crashing down the steps. He fell against my shoulder, but kept on, and I saw him disappear over the railing. I don't see that there is anything more to tell."

"Nor do I," said Father. "But which of you were in the back row? Were any of you standing beside Anderson?"

"I was," said a deep voice from the armchair. "I was on his left."

"And I was on his right," said another voice, coming from a young giant crouching on a footstool.

"Did either of you see any more than Mr. Jeffers has described?" Father pursued.

"Only," said one them, "that I heard a little click and felt him give a violent start almost simultaneously with his yell, and that I think I put up my hand to break his fall, but it did no good. He hurtled down those four steps like a plunger."

"I can't add a thing," said the other. "It was sudden and terrifying and awful. I have never heard such a yell. I do know, however, that the whole choir was absolutely quiet until Anderson cried out. It was so still, and we were so fascinated by the announcement the president was making, that the slightest movement on the part of any of us would have attracted the attention of us all."

"And is there absolutely nothing that any of you can add to that?" Father asked, after a pause.

They all shook their heads. I pitied them. Moreover, it was impossible not to believe them. They were all underclassmen, that I knew, and all of that stolid type which is, on the face, so difficult to move, yet in reality so easily unnerved. There was embarrassment, but nothing more. I believed them implicitly and evidently Father did, too, for he dismissed them kindly and asked me to show them out.

When they were gone he turned to Bossy. "It's what I expected," he said, "but it had to be done. And now, Professor, let us hear your story. You were at the organ. . . ."

"I'm like the rest," Bossy said. "I was at the organ, and facing the whole choir, but I saw no more than they did. However, I was listening intently to the president and staring at the music in front of me. Either of those two men beside Anderson might have raised his hands to him, and I'm not sure that I would have noticed, but I can't be positive even of that."

"But you believe their stories?" asked Father.

"I think I do," Bossy answered. "They are honest boys, both of them, and I'm sure that neither of them knew Anderson at all well."

"I think," said my father, "that they were telling all they knew, . . . And now, Fenton," he went on, in a new tone of voice, "I should like to ask you a question or two."

"Certainly, sir," said Charlie.

"When Anderson told you that he wanted to see Kenneth and hinted at his message, did he convey the impression that he had told no one else?"

"Entirely, sir," Charlie answered. "As I said before, he waited until he had heard from me a definite statement that Byron was murdered before he mentioned a thing. Furthermore, he was shrewd and silent by nature, and if it hadn't been for seeing his

folks of and his choir rehearsal, I'm positive that he wouldn't even
have told me to make the appointment with Kenneth."

"Then you don't think he might even have told his roommate?"

"I'd be willing to swear that he didn't. They never were particularly good friends."

"Now, if you don't think me offensive, I'd like to ask this: Whom
did you tell afterward that Anderson had an identity to reveal to
Kenneth after chapel?"

"No one," he said.

"Are you sure?"

"Oh," said Charlie, "Bill Smart, of course. He was with me when
I met Sam Anderson, but he walked on ahead while I was talking
to him. Naturally I told him. He was in on all the rest of the evidence, if you can call it that."

"Ah!" said Father, and a moment later: "You have been indis-
creet, Penlon," he added.

"Perhaps I have been," Charlie replied, "but if so, it never entered my head. I certainly made no bones about giving Ken Sam's
message in public, but there again it was because it didn't occur to
me to do anything else. We are all equally interested, aren't we?"

"Not necessarily, Penlon," Father remarked, seriously. "As a
matter of fact, I fear we are not. For some person who heard of
Anderson's discovery from himself or from you hastened to bring
about his death before chapel was over and Kenneth should learn
it all!"

Charlie was silent as we all were, and Bossy stirred up the fire
before any of us spoke. Then it was Father again: "I think that's all
for this time. Each of us will have to prove, to our mutual satisfaction, our whereabouts during the chapel service. Professor, is there
any cold chicken left from lunch?"

Charlie excused himself before the three of us went to the
kitchen and hurriedly munched things from the ice-box. Father,
during the stand-up meal, asked a few questions of Bossy concerning Anderson's attitude that afternoon at choir rehearsal, but Bossy
could remember nothing out of the ordinary. Yes, he said, Sam had
talked with several of the boys, to his recollection, but he didn't

seem to be in particularly long or earnest conversation with any of them.

Then, "Kenneth," asked Father, "have you a flashlight in your car?"

I told him I had.

"I'll walk down with you and get it," he said. "In an hour or so, Professor, I'll have Kenneth drive me up with my bags and I'll accept your hospitality. Meanwhile, I wonder if you can lend me the keys to the chapel. I presume, as organist, you have them."

"Why certainly," said Bossy. "This is it," and he pulled a large, old-fashioned one from his ring. "But if you're going inside to-night you'll find it spooky. Ken, I think, knows where the switches are."

As soon as we were out of the house I asked Father what he meant to do, but instead of answering, he asked me a question.

"Is there a way of getting into the organ—among the pipes, I mean?"

"Yes," I said. "There's an entrance from either side. I've been in, watching the men tune it."

"There is some sort of passageway, isn't there, just behind the big pipes that form a background to the choir loft?"

"Yes," I said again. "There's a quite spacious one."

"And how far, Kenneth, would you say it was from the organ pipes to the—to the neck of a person standing in the back row of the choir."

"Not more than a foot," I answered. "Less if anything."

"Then it is perfectly possible," Father went on, "for someone to hide, unseen, in that passageway behind the great pipes and still reach, let us say, Sam Anderson."

I stood still in the road. "Yes," I said.

"There is nothing in particular that I hope to find to-night," Father said, "but before things are mussed up, or even dusted, I want to go in."

"Am I to go with you?" I asked.

"I'd rather you wouldn't," he answered. "I can think better alone. You go to your room and I'll come there immediately. Then you can drive me to Professor Bostwick's."

I got him the flashlight from the car at the garage and saw him started up the street with it, toward the campus. I decided to save time later by taking the car out now, and I drove it up to North Mass., parking it outside the dormitory.

My room looked singularly lonesome when I opened the door. It was strange not to find the lights on and good old By sunk in the arm chair, with pipe and gray bathrobe, ready to throw aside his work, however important, for an evening of chatter.

I sank on the couch and glanced at my watch. It was ten minutes past eight. Just twenty-four hours before, I thought, I was starting out of Hanover with the rising moon behind me, to bring Father back to a quiet, even dull week-end. And now, in that short space of time, although it seemed an age to me, there had been two murders. And both victims were my friends and classmates.

So I mused on for, perhaps, half an hour, when suddenly the door was thrown open and Father stood on the threshold, breathless and with his hat in his hand. There was a look in his eyes that was half terror, half sheer amazement. I sprang to my feet as he slammed the door behind him.

"Kenneth!" he panted. "Kenneth, do I look insane?"

"Why," I stammered, "Why—why—no."

He ran his fingers through his hair.

"Were you in the chapel?" I asked. "Did you go into the organ?"

He drew a few quick breaths before he answered.

"I did," he said. "And in the organ—inside—I turned my flashlight full on Byron Coates—alive!"

## CHAPTER VI
## SUNDAY: ORGAN NOCTURNE

THE HUMAN MIND is a queer contraption. At times a single innocent little remark will set it leaping from association to association, lightning-quick, until in a fraction of a second it reaches a logical but distant goal. At other times it can't be budged one mental millimeter from a fixed idea. Excitement and terrific surprise, I know, have something to do with it, but I am on the whole cool-headed and I should have been able to explain, almost immediately, what Father had seen. My mind would have had to leap back a bit and forward again and chase around a circle or two in order to land at the correct and now obvious explanation, but it should have done that instead of standing stock still and repeating to itself over and over again some such nonsense as, "Byron dead but alive, Byron dead but alive."

A hundred times these last few years I have pretended that I did grasp immediately what I think I should have grasped and, thinking on, have built the story from there. And I have a hundred times decided that Father and I should at once have dashed out of the dormitory and driven with all speed a few miles east to the little village of Etna and almost surely have cleared up within half an hour the entire mystery of the two horrible murders.

If only Father had been somehow calm and had made a normal entrance and had said, "Ken, the strangest thing has happened. Don't be alarmed, but just now, in the chapel organ, I thought I saw Byron," I think I should have pooh-poohed him, questioned further, grasped at the truth, and rushed him downstairs. Instead, I merely stood there, staring at him as he leaned against the door.

"Byron dead but alive, Byron dead but alive," was all I thought.

It probably was not more than ten seconds before he suddenly whirled around, jamming his hat on his head with one hand and yanking the door open with the other.

"Come on, quick!" he said, and started at a half-run down the corridor.

I waited for neither hat nor coat; I didn't switch out the lights nor shut the door, but ran after him. Once, in our rapid descent of the three flights of stairs, I called "Dad!" but got only an impatient upward fling of his hand in reply.

Outside, with me about ten paces behind, he made for the car, opened the door and held it open, motioning for me to jump into the driver's seat. And in a twinkling he had leaped in beside me saying, "North. What's the first town, Lyme?"

I had the engine roaring. "Lyme!" I shouted.

We were off. We turned into Main Street, crossed the head of the campus, and headed north. In less than a minute we were actually out of the town. Father leaned toward me.

"How much will it do?" he asked.

"Sixty-five," I said. "Seventy in a pinch."

Father leaned back. "Let her out."

I let her out. We roared down the gully that the beginning of the Vale of Tempe forms. We roared up the hill and over the flats past the golf links and the towering ski-jump. We barely missed a car turning in toward Hanover from the road that leads to the reservoir. We shot up steep hills, whirled around corners, and dashed down again. Now and then, when the headlights of another car twinkled in the distance, I had to slacken speed a bit, but I passed them all at fifty. I don't remember that I thought of safety. That's the pity of it: I don't remember that I thought at all.

Once, shortly after we had passed the entrance to the River Road, on which still stand the pillared ruins of the old Revolutionary inn, we sighted ahead the red tail light of a moving car. Father gripped my right arm and drew back on it. I assumed he meant for me to slacken speed, and I did so, passing it at not more than thirty or thirty-five. Father released his hold on my arm and we shot ahead again.

It was a mile or so farther on that he leaned over and shouted, "That was a Buick. He was in a Ford."

I let that sink in a moment. Then, "Who?" I asked.

"Pay attention to the road!" said Father.

We rushed on in silence for the remaining miles, and I rather felt amazement at myself for daring to penetrate the inky darkness of the twisting way at such a speed, even though I knew the road as well as I knew any road that led out of Hanover. And so we climbed the last hill, turned sharply to the right, and came upon the Lyme village green. I slowed up.

"Turn around," said Father. "We'll go back."

I circled the green and started back toward Hanover, pressing the throttle again the moment we were clear of the town. Father laid a restraining hand on my arm and I brought us down to a natural traveling pace.

"No hurry now," said Father.

There was a pause, as I waited for him to speak, and during that pause the moon, an hour high, came breaking through the horizon clouds and turned the black road silvery gray.

"If he came this way," Father said, "in a Ford, we should have caught up with him before Lyme easily. How far is it? Ten miles?"

"Nine or ten."

"Easily." Father turned up the collar of his coat. I did the same to mine, thinking, "We haven't felt the cold until now."

"I suppose you want to hear about it, Ken."

"Tell me from the beginning."

"Well," said Father, "it's all very strange. I left you at North Mass. and cut directly across the campus to the chapel. It was dark, of course—the chapel I mean. Two boys were standing on the corner in front of it and for no reason in particular I decided to wait until they'd moved on before I entered. I don't know why, but I walked on past the chapel for a moment, almost to Wheeler Hall. Ahead of me, just beside Wheeler, a Ford was parked in the street.

The top was down, there was no one in it, but its engine was running. That's the only reason I noticed it.

"I turned around and saw that the two boys were moving, one up over the hill toward Fayerweather and one along the sidewalk toward me. I began walking in his direction, passed him, and got to the chapel steps. I waited a second to see that he didn't look back and that no one else was in sight, and then I took out the key Professor Bostwick gave me. But as I was putting it in the keyhole the door swung open. It was unlocked and the latch wasn't caught. It was all done in complete silence.

"Silence is funny, Ken. It's the hardest thing in the world to break, voluntarily, and particularly in the dark—and more particularly in a dark church. I certainly expected to find no one there, even with the door unlocked, and yet I tiptoed, and I have rubber soles. I tiptoed through the entry and into the pitch blackness of the chapel. And I hadn't taken more than four steps into the chapel itself when I heard a faint noise—oh, very faint—above my head, in the organ loft.

"I stood stock still. And in a few seconds I heard it again. And then softly, even more softly than before, I crept forward until, by turning around and looking up over the pulpit, I could see in the direction of the choir and the faint, almost phosphorescent glow of the big organ pipes."

Father paused, and just at that moment the car hit a rock and I wrenched the wheel around quickly. I knew that Father was dramatist enough to feel that the involuntary interruption rather spoiled the suspense of his story. He was silent, I think, for about half a mile.

"And while I stood there," he continued, "someone lit a match inside the organ."

He said it slowly, and despite my coatless chill a flush of warmth crept over me. It tingled and for a few hundred yards I went full speed. We rounded a curve and I dropped to normal again.

"I could see the glow," Father went on, "and the pipes in silhouette and a figure behind them, and then the match went out. I shrank back at once into the blackness under the loft. It was a useless movement, but I rather fancy I had a momentary thought that whoever was there might look out between the pipes and see me against the faint glow of the windows. I stayed still for almost a full minute. A minute is a very long time."

He paused again, as if to show how endless a minute may be, and then kept on.

"You don't know how silently I moved. I doubt if a cat could have heard me tiptoe, step by step, out of the auditorium into the entry again. It was slow going. I even made my hand move through the air inch by inch when I reached it out to feel through the dark for the newel post of the choir stairs. And I started up them like a snail, ever, ever so slowly. On the way up I heard two more matches being struck, and as I crept along the narrow corridor beside the organ I heard another. Its flare still showed through the cracks when I reached the little door into the passageway behind the big pipes. There I stopped until the glow died down and I heard a breath blow the last flame out.

"Then I crouched a bit. The door isn't tall enough, you know, to let you enter when you're standing full upright. And I felt with my fingers for a knob. I couldn't find one, but I got a slight pur-chase with my thumb on the edge of the door. . . . It creaked and I heard a quick movement inside as if someone, straightening up suddenly, had scuffed the floor. And instantly I flung the door open, still crouching, and switched on your flashlight. And I heard a faint ring of something metal, but something small, perhaps a coin, strik-ing the floor."

Once more Father paused. He was waiting, I knew, for the ques-tion I was bound to ask, "And it was Byron?" But I didn't ask it. Instead I asked, "You saw him clearly?"

"Clearly, yes. Full in the light. But only for a second. He turned quick as a flash, ran for a few yards, stooped, and banged out of the door at the other end of the passageway. I should have called, although calling would have done no good, and I should have backed out immediately and run down the stairs I had come up with a good chance of confronting him in the entry when he reached the foot of his stairs on the other side of the loft. But I didn't. Not, that is, on that very second. I was dazed; I confess it. I was startled. . . . To find—to find—Byron! . . . The first thing that leaped into my mind was 'Ghost!'

"It wasn't until I realized that I was hearing his footsteps racing down the stairs that I made a movement. I ran, too. Just as I reached the entry the outer door banged behind him. I had to fumble a few seconds with the latch, for it had caught, and by the time I was out of the portico he was racing like mad down the sidewalk toward Wheeler Hall."

"The Ford, Dad!" I cried.

"Yes," said Father, "he got in the Ford—jumped in, without opening the door, and in a moment, with a terrible roar, he was off toward Lyme.

"I had sense enough not to chase him. I flatter myself that I whirled around at once to see if there was any car coming from the campus that I could commandeer, but there wasn't a one. And I began to run immediately toward North Mass., taking the short cut behind Webster and the White Church and past Chandler. . . . Don't ask me what I thought during that three-minute run. I don't know. If I thought at all of anything but speed and getting you and the car and how much start he would have on us, it was just incoherent things about Byron. I do remember that as I reached the top of those endless three flights of stairs I had a flash of a thought that I might have imagined it all and that I was going mad."

"Those were your first words, Dad," I said. "You asked me if you looked insane. I said you didn't, but you did."

He lifted his hat and ran his hand through his hair.

"It couldn't have been more than six or seven minutes," I went on, "before we were after him. And we should easily have been able to catch him before he got to Lyme if he didn't turn off. He might have ducked into the River Road, or up toward the reservoir. Or he may not even have left town at all. Perhaps he switched west at once a block farther on, over toward the hospital."

"Perhaps I should have stood and watched," said Father.

The lights of Hanover, then, twinkled before us, and in another moment we were down the hill into the gully and up the other side to the outskirts of the town.

"Now where?" I asked.

Father turned his coat collar down. "The chapel," he said.

As I drew up before the ugly old steps I couldn't resist a rather grim jest. "Shall I leave the engine running?" I asked. I got nothing but a grunt and a banging of the car door in reply.

I mounted the steps behind Father slowly. My blood had suddenly gone cold although my heart was pounding like a machine gun. Father stopped outside the door with his hand on the great iron latch. "Let there be no silence," he said, and lifted it with a loud clang. As the door swung open he turned the flashlight on the wall of the entry and moved it to the left until the circle of light fell on the foot of the stairway. "Those are the stairs he ran down," he said. He switched the light rapidly to the corresponding position on the other side of the entry, illuminating the foot of the other stairs. "Those are the ones I used. You go up those. Don't be afraid. There's surely no one here. Whistle if you want to."

But I couldn't have whistled even if I had wanted to. Once the light was moved away from me and centred on the stairs that Father was going up, I shivered and clutched the stair rail and saw, in the blinding darkness, a thousand faces, all Byron's, and the sound of Father's footsteps seemed like the thunder of armies rushing down on me. The narrow corridor beside the organ seemed blacker still until I caught the gleam of Father's flashlight on the other side. He called across.

"Find the door, Ken?"

I fumbled a moment, failed as Father had to find the knob, but caught my thumb in the edge of the door.

"O. K." I called, and could hear the echo.

"Then go inside. Be careful of bumping your head. Go in about six or seven feet and stand and face my door. Don't be frightened. I'm going to bang this door open and turn the flashlight on you."

He didn't need to explain. I knew when he first suggested going to the chapel that he would try something of the sort. There might be some shadow there, or something queer, that would give a face and figure the momentary look of Byron's.

I pulled open the door, crouched and entered, and let it swing to behind me. I shuffled forward, feeling the cold of the gilded pipes beside me as I guided my way with an outstretched hand. It was a ghostly place and Father had put his light out. What, I thought, if suddenly the great pipes should sound—some awful chord. I should go mad!

I stopped.

There was a full minute's terrible silence.

Then the door at the other end burst open and I was blinded by the glare of the light. I stared at it, too excited to blink, and the light was lowered.

"You're as natural as life, Ken," spoke Father gruffly.

His door slammed behind him as he entered the passage, and with the light still pointing at the floor, moved to within a few feet of where I stood. There he stopped and made a pool of light about my feet.

"There you are, Ken," he said.

I looked down and saw on the floor the stubs of five or six burned matches, the yellow paper kind. Then Father stooped, picked something up, felt of it a moment, and stretched his hand forward, laying it in my palm and turning the light on it.

It was a thin steel needle about three inches long.

# CHAPTER VII
## SUNDAY: THE LAW

MY HAND SHOOK AND THE NEEDLE ROLLED OFF it. Its ring, as it hit the floor, was high-pitched and musical.

"It's the same sound," said Father. "That's what he dropped when I surprised him." He bent down and let the light play around until he found it again, and then, handing the light to me, he took an opened letter from his pocket and placed the needle inside the envelope. Then he looked at me.

"You know where we're going now?" he asked.

"I can guess," I answered. "The undertaking rooms to find out if—"

"To find out two things," he interrupted. "Come on." He started for the door he had entered by, but as he was about to stoop to push it open he stopped and moved aside against the pipes, keeping the circle of light fixed on the red wood of the door. "It's silly," he said, "but I want to try it. Go out to the choir loft for a second, Ken. I'll shine the light out between the pipes so it won't be too dark. Stand as nearly as you can where Sam Anderson stood, facing the congregation. Just for a second."

I went, not too willingly, not too hurriedly.

I had to feel my way around the corner into the open loft. Beyond me the great empty chapel seemed to stretch for miles in the darkness. I shivered again. Suddenly Father's light shone through the pipes and the fat shadows of two of them moved across the back wall of the auditorium, far ahead of me. I was glad. It defined the distance. I climbed the steep steps to the last row where Sam, four or five hours before, had stood and nodded to me before the services began. I moved to a position just beyond the centre and turned my back to the organ. Those few steps *were* steep. Given a push from behind, I thought, even with control of my muscles as Sam had not, and I too might go hurtling down to crash against the low rail—or topple over.

"I'm here, Dad."

The light was moved until it struck the back of my head and I saw my tremendous shadow for a moment far ahead of me. Then, with a click, it disappeared.

Suddenly, momentarily, as the blackness came, I thought: "Father! What if Father were the killer! What if in the back of my neck, up under my skull, should come the jab of something infinitely sharp—that needle—like Sam—like Byron—and a fall forward in the darkness—and a crash—and Father laughing inside the organ—and—"

There was a prick at the back of my neck. Tiny. I yelled and the dark chapel rang with it as I lost my balance and stepped down one high step, reached blindly out for something to hold, found nothing, but checked my fall and stood trembling and panting. And within the organ Father chuckled.

I lost my temper. "Damn you, Father!" I shouted.

He switched the light on and I heard him hurrying out the little door. I groped my way along the step and met him at the end of the loft. He turned the flashlight on the gilded pipes and the diffused glow fell clearly upon us. He laid his hand on my quaking shoulder.

"I'm sorry I scared you. It didn't enter my head. I just wanted to gauge distance and I touched you with this." He reached his hand inside his coat and drew out a long, sharply-pointed yellow pencil. "It's an easy reach. Hardly more than a foot."

"I might have fallen," I said bitterly, though it seemed foolish now to take that tone.

"I'm sorry, Ken," he said, as sincerely as he knew how. "Come on." He turned and led me down the stairs.

The moonlit street was chill and lovely, and as we climbed into the waiting car the clock in the Dartmouth Hall tower struck ten.

Twenty-four hours ago, I thought, I was speeding toward Barre over the winding Vermont roads. I took the driver's seat and it was in silence that we glided through the quiet town to Rand's undertaking rooms. They were run, as always in small towns, by the local furniture dealer. The doctor admitted us.

"I've been trying to find you," he said, "and so has the sheriff. He arrived from Woodsville some time ago."

Father looked up quickly. "Is he intelligent?" he asked.

"He's not bad," the doctor answered. "You needn't fear friction if you treat him right. He's not a blunderhead."

"Good," said Father, and then, assuming the official tone he seemed to have put aside for the entire evening, he addressed Dr. Preable: "I suppose you have something to report to us, and very probably something to show."

"I have," said the doctor, and went to a table from which he lifted a fold of white paper. "We've completed the autopsy," he went on, "on both bodies. The results are exactly as we expected. Each was killed by a violent, beautifully placed piercing of the brain up under the back of the skull. Death was, in each case, practically instantaneous. In the brain of each boy we found one of these."

He turned again to the table and on its top opened the folded paper, revealing two steel needles. "Dad!" I cried. "Do you see? They're exactly like—"

He interrupted me quickly. "Yes," he said. "They're exactly alike. They're exactly identical. . . . They're slightly discoloured, I notice, Doctor."

"I made no attempt to clean them," said the doctor. "They have dried just as extracted."

"Tell me, Doctor," Father pursued, bending over the table, "could I, seizing one of these and plunging it into your brain—always supposing that I caught you napping, of course, and that I had time to aim as carefully as the murderer of Sam Anderson had—could I, in your opinion, kill you instantaneously?"

"Holding the needle in your bare hand?" asked the doctor.

"Yes," said Father.

The doctor thought a moment. "I doubt it. It might be possible but not probable. The needle is hardly long enough to allow for the finger grasp and the thrust."

"Then your theory is—"

"I fear it's more than a theory," the doctor pursued. "The needle was propelled into the brain with terrific force—more force that the thrust of a hand. It was totally imbedded in the brain and we had to cut to extract it."

"Could it have been hurled?" asked Father. "And then some sort of handle pulled away afterward?"

"No," said the doctor. "The blunt end would still protrude."

"Then your verdict is—"

"That it was *shot* in. There is no other possible explanation."

"And the instrument used for firing?"

"I haven't the remotest idea," finished the doctor. He folded up the paper and put it in his inside pocket. "I'll keep these," he said, "until the inquest tomorrow. I've arranged for it to be held at ten in the morning, upstairs in the Davison Block. Of course, you'll both be there. Either you," he said, looking at me, "or his sister will have to identify Coates. I am calling Anderson's roommate, Jerry Dawes, for the other identification." He reached for his coat and hat.

"One moment, Doctor," said Father. "Just to satisfy one little whim of ours, may Kenneth look at Coates now? For only a second."

The doctor stopped and stared at me. "It won't be an official viewing," he said.

I was trembling. "I know it," I said. "I'll do it again to-morrow. But I'd like to satisfy myself that—"

"As I said," Father put in, "it's just a little whim. If you could allow it."

The doctor nodded, laid down his coat, and opened a door to another room. Father put his hand on my back and gave me the slightest possible push. "Look closely," he whispered. "I'll stay here."

I walked straight ahead, just as the doctor switched on some lights, much brighter, I was glad to see, than those in the room we had just left. I saw two sheeted figures, lying side by side.

"Coates only?" asked the doctor.

I nodded and he crossed the room briskly. I followed more slowly and he had already raised one of the sheets by the time I got to his side.

I leaned forward and looked.

It was not so bad as I had anticipated. Byron was beautiful.

Father was standing, hat in hand, just outside the door as I returned to the outer room. I met his gaze steadily and nodded.

"I was satisfied before," I said, almost in a whisper. "It's no one but By."

The tears welled in my eyes and I was glad that Father turned at once and made for the door. As we went out I heard the doctor click out the lights behind us.

"Now what?" I asked when we were in the car again. "I told Jean I'd see her sometime to-night and it's getting rather late."

"She won't be sleeping yet," said Father, "and I shall probably want to see her with you." My heart sank. "But just now I rather fancy the sheriff is waiting for us in your room. Drive to North Mass. He won't keep us long."

The door to my room was still open as I remembered to have left it and the sheriff and his man were inside, the sheriff in By's desk chair, swung around so that it faced the centre of the room, and the other man on the couch, holding his hat down between his legs. They both rose as we entered.

"Mr. Harris," said the sheriff, and shook Father's hand. "How do you do?"

"My son, Sheriff," said Father, and I shook hands with him.

"Ab Barker," the sheriff announced, and jerked his thumb in the direction of the man on the couch. We nodded that way and then all sat down. I looked at the sheriff. I couldn't remember ever having seen one before. He was about as far removed from the long-moustached, hip-booted, two-gun movie sheriff as I could imagine. He was a medium-sized man, slightly gray, with an intelligent face, smoothly shaven, and was dressed in a cheap but well-made business suit of oxford. There was no visible badge or gun and I felt a trifle cheated.

"This is a sad case, gentlemen," he said, and Father and I nodded in silence. I could feel that Father was preening himself for a speech, but the sheriff went on: "I saw the president and he told me that you had been retained—"

"At no compensation," said Father.

"Naturally," the sheriff continued. "That you had been asked to take charge of the investigation of the two murders."

"Nothing has been said about the death of Anderson," Father put in.

"That's a small matter. Solve one and you solve the other."

"I'm not so sure," mused Father.

The sheriff straightened up. "What's that?"

"Nothing. Nothing's certain. I was merely thinking a possibility aloud. As a matter of fact, it was the first time it had struck me."

The sheriff leaned back again. "I have seen Dr. Preable, the coroner, too, and he told me the main things—about the discovery of young Coates, at least. And then I went up to Professor Bostworth's—"

"Bostwick," I corrected him.

"Professor Bostwick's. The doctor told me I'd probably find you there. And the professor told me more about the morning affair and a great deal about the death of Anderson in the chapel. It all beats me."

"At present," said Father, "it seems to beat us all."

"There's one thing I want to say," continued the sheriff. "I'm just a sheriff, Mr. Harris, and elected more or less out of a clear sky, at that. I'm in the hardware game, privately. And I've never done much fooling around with mysteries one way or the other. Grafton's a quiet county, take it all in all, and what keeping of law and order there is is mostly done easy and quick. I've got some good men and some pretty handy deputies, but none of them are what you might call sleuths and none of them are very deep thinkers. And always before, though it's only been once during *my* service, we've called in a man or two from Boston—county expense, of course—to do the brain work of investigating. Now I hope you won't take offense, Mr. Harris, because none is intended, but I suggested such a course of action to the president this afternoon."

I could see Father stiffen.

"But naturally enough he told me that the case was in your hands so far as the college was concerned, and that while he wouldn't presume to dictate to the county, he would suggest that we hold our horses for a few days at least. 'Harris is a clever man,' he told me, 'and he may work more quietly and more efficiently than a professional detective.'"

Father stiffened again, but this time it was to bow slightly from his chair.

"It puts quite a burden on you, Mr. Harris. Barker and I will stay in town, ready to help you, and we'll make as many moves on our own part as we can think of, but we're not the quickest of wits, are we, Barker?"

Barker dropped his hat and picked it up again, between his spread knees.

Father was glowing by this time. "It's an intelligent man, Sheriff, who knows his own limitations," he said. "I hope that you both will be called upon to act with warrants—and maybe revolvers before long." He paused, and I could see good nature radiant in his face. "You're a strange sheriff," he added.

"Well, you see, sir," the sheriff said, hitching a bit forward in his chair. "I've always read detective stories and I still do read them, and while I don't think they're true to life, not a bit of it, nor accurate reports of what the police do or how they act—no, nor the detectives either—I've always sworn, since I was an arm of the law, so to speak, that I wouldn't be the blundering up-country constable that the investigators from Scotland Yard seem to have to put up with. Cards on the table and cooperation is what I think, and nothing else will do. You've got a magnifying glass and I," he slapped his hip, "figuratively speaking, have got a gun."

Father cleared his throat. "I congratulate you, Sheriff. We shall work perfectly together. I, too, have read detective stories. Indeed, I've written two of them—nothing you've ever read. And I have

always sworn that I'd be as far as possible from the fictional investigator—at least where my relations with the police are concerned.
I shall not work in the dark and send you on false clues and nod
knowingly when there is nothing to nod at. I do not take opium
nor play the violin, nor have I an Oxford accent and a deep knowledge of porcelain figurines. Instead, I am quite ready to tell you
all I know, but I must warn you first that all my knowledge in this
particular matter is entirely factual."

"Just the same," said the sheriff, "I'd like to hear your version
of it. Start from the beginning, will you, and make believe I'd never
heard any of it before."

Father did it well. He began with his telephone call to me from
Barre and told of his arrival at the dormitory, of my going off with
the car and of his finding the door to 39 North Mass. locked, neces-
sitating his registering at the Inn when I failed to come back in
decent season. But he said not a word about seeing Jean come in,
so late. And from then on I was on the alert, watching for every
single omission and trying to understand the reason. He told of
my seeking a bed in Charlie Penlon's room, but he did not mention my discovery of Charlie fully clothed in the morning. He told
of Bill Smart's timing of Byron's visitor and his preparations for
bed, but he failed to speak of Jean's conflicting evidence of her
visit to the dormitory. Indeed, although he told the whole tale, he
omitted, I decided, practically everything which could throw suspicion, even momentarily, on any individual. He even skipped (and
I thought this decidedly wrong) all mention of his first visit to the
chapel and his sight of Byron in the organ. Nor did he tell of the
finding of the needle, though he said that he and I had been in
among the pipes and that we had discovered that the murder was
most feasible from there. In fact, despite his high words of fairness, he told the law nothing at all.

"And you don't suspect anybody?" asked the sheriff, when he
had finished.

"I accuse no one," Father evaded. "But I'd like to listen to any
of your theories." I detected a slight note of scorn.

"I haven't any," the sheriff said. "But I think I can ask a question or two which may put one in your mind. It concerns the second murder only."

"Do ask them."

"You've talked with the doctor, I take it?" We both nodded. "And you've seen the two steel things that caused the death?" We nodded again. "And you've heard the doctor say that no hand alone could have done it, but that the needles must have been propelled into the craniums?" For the third time we nodded in unison. "That they must have been—well, the doctor said *shot* in? Well, from what I gather from the professor as to the evidence of the boys that stood near Anderson in the choir, they didn't hear any *shot*—any real gun, that is."

"No," I cried. "But they heard a click! Don't you remember, Dad, that one of them claimed to have heard a funny click?"

"Exactly," said the sheriff, beginning to get excited himself. "Something mechanical, but not a regular gun. A silent gun of some sort. And of course the first thing that enters our heads is compressed air."

Father stood up.

"And when we think of compressed air," the sheriff went on, "what strikes us first in this case? The fact that the whole thing was done in an organ, which is air from first to last!

"Now, despite my hardware, I'm not mechanical-minded and I don't know what clever contraption a man knowing just where a certain member of the choir might stand, might or might not rig up inside a pipe. Something that might release and shoot a needle when a certain note on the keyboard was pressed. Or he might not even use his hands but press one of the big pedals with his foot."

There was a dead silence.

"Who," asked the sheriff, "was at the organ?"

I felt my face go dead white.

"Bossy," I said, dully. "Professor Bostwick."

# CHAPTER VIII
## SUNDAY: SKELETONS

FIVE MINUTES LATER the sheriff and Barker had left us and I turned to Father very nearly in tears.

"You don't think there's anything in it, do you?" I begged. "It couldn't possibly be Bossy, could it?"

"Whether it could be Bossy or not," said Father calmly, "is not the sheriff's point. He advanced an extremely interesting theory—he put it into words, that is. Of course, it had been in the back of my mind for some time. But it is a theory that's easily tested and either strengthened or broken down entirely."

"How, Dad?"

"I know a way, and I'll do it the first thing in the morning. Just now, we must go to the Inn and see Miss Coates."

I spoke to him pleadingly. "Dad," I said, "I really think Jean would like to see me alone. She must be frightfully upset and she hasn't had a word of comfort from either of us. The only words you've spoken to her, yourself, were harsh ones when you were practically calling her a liar."

"It's no time to stand on sentiment, Kenneth," said Father, picking up his hat. "Half an hour, now, with Miss Coates and Miss Case, just talking, will do a great deal toward furthering our understanding of what's in back of all this mess. There will be times aplenty in the future for you to talk to her alone. Just now, I insist on being present and directing the conversation."

There was nothing to do but give in. However, I extracted one promise from him: that he would make no insinuations or attempt any browbeating, and that he would not confront Jean, to-night at least, with her appearance at the Inn so late the night before.

"I'll take the car to the garage," he said, "and you can go directly in. That will give you five minutes or more alone with her for any whispering you care to do."

"There will be no whispering," I said tersely.

Jean was in Miss Case's room, curled up on the bed, and Miss Case was reading to her from a magazine. She sat up when I entered and held out her hand.

"Kenneth! Thought you weren't coming at all! This is a nice time of night, really!"

I took her hand. "I'm awfully sorry. You've been terribly neglected, both of you, but Father has kept me chasing all over creation, and he isn't through yet. He's coming here."

"Oh, Lord!" cried Miss Case, and Jean sprang to her feet and began to shake out her wrinkled dress. She turned to me, her eyes half smiling, half serious. "More inquisition?"

"I don't think so," I said. "He'll be pompous, of course, but I think he's planning something different from the third degree to-night."

"I suppose he'll stay forever," Miss Case complained. "Not that we could sleep even if he did go, but Jean can't stand much talk. Charlie Penlon was here for ages to-night and they talked and talked, and I finally had to send him packing when Jean began to get hysterical. I was reading her some Temple Bailey to quiet her nerves. I hoped she'd drop off."

"The attempt at hysterics," said Jean, "was supposed to be a secret. Charlie and I went over the whole thing, again and again, and we made all sorts of wild guesses about the chapel affair and poor Anderson. Neither of us was there and I haven't had it told to me by an eye witness yet."

I turned to Miss Case. "Weren't you there? I thought I caught sight of you as I was going in."

"Yes," she said, "but I had to sit 'way over in the back of the transept. I couldn't see the choir at all and I didn't happen to be looking when he fell. And as soon as the crush began, I slipped out the side door and came back here. . . . Smooth the bed, Jean; here's Mr. Harris."

Father was grand. He was kind and cheerful and solicitous, and I noticed with pleasure that both the women were immediately at ease. Jean even perched on the bed with her legs drawn up under her and gave her black hair a punch into comfortable and attractive disarray.

"It's not the present nor the future," began Father, "that I want us to discuss for a while now. I want you all to talk to me about Byron, as if I'd never met him, and in half an hour or so try to make me understand what he was like, from the very beginning. Imagine, now, that I should be called upon to investigate some man's death. I should immediately have to find out as much as I could about him—his habits, his family, his income, perhaps even his opinions, and certainly his friends before I could find his enemies. Byron's case is different, but I can't find a motive until I know the boy himself. . . . So talk to me, won't you? Just ramble on. Everything you say will be of some value. . . . Miss Coates, tell me as much as you can about your home life."

Jean stared at a ring on her finger for a moment and then raised her head. She talked for Father but she looked mostly at me. There was no hesitancy in her voice; she was completely at ease.

"Byron and I have had a beautiful home life," she began. "It has never been conventional, but it has always been happy. Mother is lovely, isn't she, Miss Case? Have you ever seen her, Ken?" I shook my head. "I'm supposed to look like her, superficially, but I haven't got her radiance. It's astounding, even now. People still turn to look after her when we're dining out or in a theatre. Both Byron and I grew up simply adoring her, never getting very close to her, perhaps, in the old-fashioned way, but thinking that she was just about perfection itself.

"Byron and I, as kids, were great companions. We moved a lot and we didn't make friends with many other children. You see, my father died when I was only a year and a half old and Byron wasn't quite three. I don't remember him at all, of course, and I don't believe Byron really did, although he used to say he thought he could faintly remember rubbing his cheek against someone with a face that scratched."

"You have pictures of him?" Father asked.

"Yes, several. One of the few really old-fashioned things about our house is the big heavy album that Mother still keeps in the living room. The actress's scrapbook habit, I suppose."

"Your mother is an actress!" Father exclaimed.

"I never knew that, Jean," I said.

"She used to be," Jean answered, "and a good one, evidently, but she left the stage when Byron was born. Byron got his voice from her, you know, and his love of music. She was a singer, but not a concert artist; more a *chanteuse* or a *diseuse* or whatever you call it. She was a favourite abroad. In fact, I think it was in Paris that she met Father. They were married in London, anyway."

"Did Byron look like your father?"

Jean laughed merrily. "Heavens, no!" she said. "Excuse me for laughing, but if you could see Father's pictures! He was short and quite fat and had a stubby nose and a big moustache, vintage of 1903. Byron takes after his grandfather, Mother's father. We have pictures of him, too. He was handsome. But Father really wasn't good-looking at all, and of course all the pictures are funny. Byron and I always said that we thought Mother married him for his money. He was much older."

"Do you remember ever living anywhere else but Boston?" Father asked.

"Oh, my, yes! When Father died we had an apartment in New York. I don't remember that, of course, but we've had one there several times since. And we've lived at hotels in the South, and two whole years we were abroad—living, you know, not just traveling—one whole year in Paris and another year at Sorrento. But we've lived in Boston for the last ten years, except for going abroad for a few months now and then." Her voice grew more serious. "You see, there's something very curious about my darling mother. She has an awful ambition to be conventional, and she really can't be. And sometimes, lately, I've had a feeling that she's afraid of not being. I suppose when Byron and I got to be school age, she felt she ought to settle down, and she chose the most respectable place in the world, Chestnut Street in Boston, and bought an old house. And so, you see, we've always been rather lonely."

"Lonely?" asked Father. "Why?"

Jean bit her under lip. "Well," she answered, "Mother's not Boston, not old Boston or new Boston. The old Beacon Hill people, of course, wouldn't look at her, and she hasn't any interest in the new. We would go for months and months without any visitors, and then suddenly we'd have a gang there, actors and artists mostly, but nobody important."

"I see," said Father. "And what was Byron like as a youngster?"

"He was adorable. Simply adorable. Of course, he was always the best looking thing! I worshipped him. In fact, we liked each other so much that we more or less cut out all other friends, even when we had chances to make them. He went to the Latin School before St. Paul's and I went to a private place, and it seems as if we rushed home alone right after school hours to be with each other. We never brought any of the other kids home. But all that changed when we went away to college. He found outside interests, you see, for the very first time in his life. And of course we were growing up and our ideas changed. I've hardly known him at all of late years. He even stayed away a great many vacations."

"He spent two vacations with us, you remember, Dad," I said, "and went to Europe with me one summer."

"Did he write you often from college?" Father asked.

"No. Not much. Not more than once every two months or so. Our intimacy really stopped three years ago."

"But he wrote your mother?"

"Oh, yes, all the time. Every few days. Wonderful letters. Mother used to send them to me sometimes. He adored Mother. He really and truly worshipped her. He thought she was absolute perfection itself. You should have seen him sitting and feasting his eyes on her when she was at the piano, singing to him. I used to get awfully jealous."

Miss Case spoke for the first time. "If we're telling secrets," she said, "and we seem to be, I can tell you something. It sprang into my head this morning when Mr. Kenneth told me Byron was dead. Jean hasn't put Byron's devotion to his mother strongly enough even yet. It was more than just plain worshipping; it was almost insane adoration. I remember that shortly after I was engaged by Mrs. Coates, six years ago, she told me to be very careful indeed about Byron's relations with her, that he was awfully sensitive and that he would detest me for life if I said anything to him against her. And I could see she was right, too. And then, when he was about sixteen, this thing happened. . . . You have never heard it, Jean, and perhaps you shouldn't, but it won't do you a mite of harm.

"It was one night during the Christmas holidays when Byron was home from St. Paul's. He'd gone out in the afternoon and got tickets for some concert, to take his mother. He bought them as a surprise for her, and she told him she couldn't go. I've never seen such disappointment as he showed, and I was rather surprised at her, for generally she gave in to him on every single point. But he went alone, just the same, didn't even ask either Jean or me and I doubt if he even turned in his ticket. . . . Well, he came home about eleven o'clock and let himself in with his latchkey, quietly, so that he could go right up to bed without disturbing his mother—punishing her, I suppose, by not letting her tell him good-night. And—remember this was a long time ago, Jean—he saw his mother through the open door, on the couch in the arms of a strange man."

Jean didn't move a muscle. "It doesn't surprise me. Go on."

"His mother didn't see him that night, but the next morning she went in his room early to waken him, and I suppose make up with him, and he wasn't undressed, but was lying on the bed in his shirt and trousers, and a revolver was lying beside him, near his hand. She ran from the room and screamed for me, and I went in with her, but he was only sleeping. He hadn't quite had the courage and had fallen asleep. . . . But he had written a suicide note. She found it after he'd gone back to school, among his things."

We sat in silence for a moment and then Jean spoke. "I never knew it at all. But I remember ages ago By telling me that if Mother ever married again he'd shoot me and then shoot himself. But he was only a kid then."

"I wish you'd go on for a bit, Miss Case," suggested Father. "Tell me more about the household."

"Well," said Miss Case, "except for the points that Jean has brought out, it's not so awfully different from most households. There's a cook and a maid, and I more or less manage them and keep Mrs. Coates's accounts and pay her bills and act as sort of companion, too, though Lord knows I'm a funny person to be a companion to her. I rather think," she smiled grimly, "that it may be another gesture of hers toward respectability. I suppose, to her, I seem to sort of go with Chestnut Street."

"And do you mind telling me," Father asked, "what the financial conditions are?"

"There's plenty of money," Miss Case replied. "Just how much, I don't know, but much more than is spent. I do know that. Mr. Coates, I've heard several people say, was an extremely wealthy man, but I've sort of gathered that the greater part of it, perhaps all of it but the income, is held in trust for Byron and Jean. Mrs. Coates has now and then dropped a hint to that effect, saying such things as 'when Byron comes into his money.' . . ."

" Family skeletons. That's another thing I never knew," said Jean.

"You have an allowance, Miss Coates?" asked Father.

"No," replied Jean. "I just write and ask when I'm getting broke."

"Jean *has* an allowance," corrected Miss Case. "Thirty-five hundred a year, and I deal it out."

"I'm really learning an awful lot about myself," said Jean.

"Byron had four thousand," I put in. "He told me. He had full charge and an account of his own. He told me just a few weeks ago that he had saved quite a bit."

"That doesn't sound as if he expected any great sum of money when he came of age," Father remarked.

"I don't think he did," I said. "If so, he never gave any hint of it. He certainly was making all sorts of plans for earning his living. He was going to Harvard Law next year, any way."

"I am very sure that Byron had never been told," said Miss Case.

Father turned to me. "Have you anything to add, Kenneth?"

"About Byron, you mean? No. Hearing Jean and Miss Case has made me know Byron better, but it doesn't change him at all. He was always just the same—awfully sincere, awfully steady-going. He took his likes and dislikes tremendously to heart, and he was easily worried and upset. I never knew, much, what was going on inside him, but I never cared much, he was such a prince of a chap outside and such a perfect friend. I can understand, in a way, his actions over his mother, he felt things so very deeply. I suppose, after all, that was the reason for his moods."

"He inherited his moods," said Miss Case. "Sometimes his mother won't speak to me for days."

"Thank heaven I'm not talented!" said Jean.

"How much older was he than you?" Father asked.

"About a year and a half," answered Jean. "A little over. I was born in June."

"And Byron was how old?" Father pursued.

Jean and Miss Case looked at each other in surprise. Jean turned and looked at me, but I'm afraid I returned her look blankly.

"Why, don't you know?" exclaimed Miss Case. "To-day is his birthday. He would be twenty-one to-day!"

# CHAPTER IX
## SUNDAY: LETTERS

BYRON'S BIRTHDAY had slipped my mind entirely. It was silly of me to forget, for earlier in the week we had talked vaguely of some sort of celebration. But Byron and I never gave each other presents, so there was not the impulse of gift-buying to keep it in my mind. Now, in the hotel room, we talked more sentimentally of his death, and Jean even disappeared into her own room for a second to return with a gold-linked wrist-watch bracelet she had brought to him. As Father and I left, she stood with it slipped halfway on her own hand.

"Oh, one thing more," said Father, as we were already out the door into the corridor. "I'd like to ask you, Miss Case, how Mrs. Coates took the news."

"She was utterly distracted, of course," Miss Case replied. "I 'phoned her in the middle of the morning, long before we'd heard the doctor's verdict. I tried to be vague and I think I succeeded. She jumped to the decision of suicide right off and I let her think so. I could hear her scream over the 'phone, and she let me hold onto the receiver for almost fifteen minutes without anything but silence. I think perhaps she fainted. . . . Later in the day I 'phoned again, but got only her maid. She said that Mrs. Coates had been in hysterics and had had the doctor but that at last she was sleeping a little. I didn't say anything more."

We left then, and I walked with Father beside the dark and sleeping campus to Bossy's. We went a while in silence, but finally Father spoke, slowly and seriously:

"Although it may not seem so to you, Kenneth, we have made more progress toward solution in this last half hour than all day."

"I don't see, Dad."

"To me, it's clearly revealed that the secret lies somewhere inside the family, and whether or not the murderer—or murderess—is part of the family, the key to it is in the same door that conceals the family skeleton."

"But you can't suspect Jean!" I blurted out.

"I suspect everyone," he replied. "Or rather," he went on, "I free no one from suspicion who stood on Professor Bostwick's steps this afternoon and heard Charlie Penlon give Sam Anderson's message to you. If we can somehow get further into the heart of this family and by combined hard work and intuition see that one of that group, or some intimate of that group fits into the scheme, we shall have gone a long way toward finding the guilty one. It was not a murder of the moment. It had been planned. And furthermore, it was marvelously timed."

"How do you mean, timed?"

"It took place a few hours before Byron, by coming of age, received a large inheritance. . . . Somewhere, someone wants that money."

By that time we had arrived at Bossy's house. He had gone to bed, but the little verandah light was burning, and one shaded lamp was shining through the windows of the living room.

Father paused on the lower step. "You'd better sleep here, Kenneth. Your room will be lonesome."

"I shan't mind," I said. "I think I'd rather be down there. When'll I see you in the morning?"

"When are your classes?"

Classes! I hadn't thought of them. I couldn't go and be stared at. I couldn't go, anyway, and sit with my mind on the murder.

"I've got plenty of cuts left," I said. "And even if I hadn't, I'm sure the dean would fix it up. Besides, the inquest is at ten."

"Well, then," said Father, "suppose I come to North Mass. at eight-thirty. You be up and all through breakfast. I want to spend half an hour in the chapel, just after morning service. In that time

I'm sure I can clear up, one way or another, what the sheriff hinted at to-night. By half-past eight I'll be with you. And from then until the inquest, we can make our first stab at Byron's papers."

"Byron's papers?" I asked. "What do you mean?"

"It's absolutely necessary. We must go through his mail. And his diary if he keeps one. And to-day was his birthday. We must see his birthday letter from his mother. Twenty-first birthday letters are likely to reveal the past. Good-night, Kenneth." He turned and let himself into the house.

I walked rapidly toward the college. Father, or anyone else, should *not* see Byron's mail! Why, looking through another person's mail was worse than robbery! And what good could it do? His mail was just ordinary average mail, and he'd read me a lot of it anyway. And then, suddenly, I remembered his remark of the morning before that I have already quoted: "If I die, for heaven's sake don't ship my letters home to Mother without sorting them first."

I stood stock still in the road while I reconstructed the scene: It was about eleven o'clock. I had just come in from an English class and he was seated at the desk, with the chair swung around facing the room. I spoke to him—nothing in particular, but he didn't reply. He shifted his face and stared out the window toward Middle Mass. "Better hurry up," I said. "It's after eleven. You've got eccy, haven't you?"

He turned around slowly in the chair and picked his black leather notebook from the desk. "Suppose so," he said—wearily, I thought now. "I'd like to cut." And then, after a moment of silence, "Ken, if I die, for heaven's sake don't ship my letters home to Mother without sorting them first." He got up and walked to the door.

"What's the matter?" I asked him. "What did you get in the mail this morning?"

"Too damn' much," he said, and banged the door behind him.

Now what did that mean? I began walking again. . . . Was Father right? Did some clue lie in those papers that always cluttered Byron's desk as if a small hurricane had been shut into the drawers? Had he really got something disturbing in that mail? And was it, somehow, a portent of death? Or perhaps even a threat of death!

Whatever the explanation, one thing was clear: Father should not see those papers until I had been over them first. I couldn't do it thoroughly, I knew, unless I stayed up all night, and that I mustn't do. But I could make a stab at sorting them to-night and then, for an hour or so in the morning glance over them. It wasn't that I wanted to prevent the discovery of anything important, I assured myself again, but it was just that I didn't want strange eyes reading words that were meant for Byron alone—and now for me by his own request.

I took the stairs of North Mass. three at a time. There was no need to waste time fumbling for my key. I had slipped back at once into my usual habit, and the usual dormitory custom, of leaving the door unlocked.

The room was dark and ghostly and I hurried to switch on the light. Things suddenly became cheerful and familiar. Except for the fact that the bedroom door was standing open, I might merely be coming in late from the fraternity house, and Byron already gone to bed. Even the coat to his gray suit was still draped on the back of the chair where he had put it when he undressed Saturday night, just a little more than twenty-four hours ago. Its lapels were wrinkled now, from the weight of the sheriff's back.

I began with the coat itself. In its inside pocket was an envelope, dated on Friday. It contained a receipted bill from Campion, the haberdasher, for $51.80. There was nothing else there but a check book, long and red, from the Dartmouth National Bank. I peeped at the last stub. It showed a cash balance of $473.00 and the last check was made out, on Friday, to "Cash" for $25.00. I had gone with him to the bank Friday noon while he cashed it, for pocket money.

I put the things back in the pocket, and lighting the bedroom light, hung the coat on a hanger in By's closet. Then I threw off my own clothes and donned my dressing gown, shut the bedroom door, and sat at Byron's desk.

It was in a terrible mess. The top of it was littered with books and papers and two or three black leather notebooks. There was an ash tray, half full, and a grinning plaster skull into which he had stuck, stems upward, his three pipes. There were papers everywhere—but all useless papers I discovered by turning them over. Much of the paper was blank. Some of it had been scribbled on—penciled notes and assignments. There were returned quizzes in economics, political science, and philosophy. There was a bit of musical manuscript, with a melody half harmonized. Under the blotter were some dusty filing cards with some notes on the Federal Reserve System and Chateaubriand. I gathered them all up and swept them into a lower drawer, which was almost filled already by two pairs of skates and one battered volume of Havelock Ellis. The other lower drawer contained nothing but a scattering of blank paper and some used fillers for loose-leaf notebooks of various sizes. The top flat drawer was a mess of pencils, clips, erasers, rulers, a couple of broken Ingersoll watches, some blank glass slides for a microscope, and a few thin isinglass cover plates. The only other thing of interest there was Byron's bill fold, slipped into his top drawer, evidently, when he was getting ready for bed. But on examination that revealed nothing out of the ordinary. He had spent, I noticed, seven dollars of the twenty-five he had drawn from the bank, and he had collected half a hundred useless calling cards and cards to six or seven Boston and New York speakeasies. His Massachusetts driving license was there, and a useless Pullman berth receipt stub. Nothing else.

But the two upper drawers on either side, I knew, were jammed to the brim with letters. I pulled them open and had to hold my hand on the top to keep the bulky, wrinkled envelopes from spilling all over the floor. There were hundreds, it seemed, on paper of every colour and in every colour of ink. Twice, since I had known him, Byron had had a fit of neatness and order and had attempted to sort things out, but each time he had got discouraged and taken one armful and thrown it away and stuffed various other handfuls back into his desk—"For future reference and fun during the long winter evenings," he had ruefully said.

I worked quickly. Those that bore postmarks of the past month or two I placed in piles on top of the desk, arranged as to handwriting. There were many from his mother, a few that I recognized as being from Jean, and scattered feminine ones from Wellesley and Northampton. There were bills and notices and circulars from Hanover and Boston and New York. All those that were older than October first, I tossed into an empty wastebasket. It was rapidly done.

And then, selecting from those on the desk, I began to skim the contents of a few. They were nothing at all but the most ordinary of letters. His mother's for the most part began:

> Dearest Byron:
> It was so good to get your letter this morning. I was all ready to scold the postman if he didn't bring it. . . .

and went on in narration of what she had done in the last few days, and what she had tickets for, and what Jean had written from Vassar, and what Miss Case had said. That was all.

Jean's were briefer. They began:

> Dear By:
> You're a good egg to take all that trouble for me. Thanks loads. I'm busy as the very devil. Mother has probably told you all the news. . . .

And those from his female admirers were the usual thing, either beginning, continuing, or ending some sort of petty squabble:

> By Dear:
> I loved your letter, of course, but I can't possibly see how you think I'm to blame. After all, I told Peggy what to expect and what more could you ask, I ask you, especially on a blind date. . . .

They were absolutely harmless, and when I had skimmed a dozen or more, I decided that if Father wanted to pry into such a blameless mass of correspondence, he was welcome, but I was going to bed. I put the sorted letters into the upper left-hand drawer and dumped the contents of the wastebasket into the right-hand one, jamming the letters down in order to shut it. Then, for no particular reason, I turned the key that locked all the drawers at once and dropped it into the pocket of my bathrobe. Then I switched out the light.

At once the room seemed full of ghosts and I shuddered.

Perhaps, after all, I thought, I'd better go down and sleep in Charlie's room. I wasn't exactly afraid, but I knew I should lie awake if I slept so close to Byron's bed, and start at the tiniest sound. My clothes I'd leave up here until the morning.

So down the two flights I went, without turning the light on again, and found Charlie's door unlocked, as usual. He was asleep, but he wakened as I was getting into the other bed, asked me how I felt and what time it was. I told him it was about two. Yet for half an hour we talked.

He told me the college was wild with excitement and rage and that all sorts of rumours were flying about, one of the most absurd of which was that all classes were to be suspended for the next few days until the murderer was caught and that armed posses of students were to be sent out into the hills to beat the woods and track the culprit down. "Anyway," Charlie said, "they're at fever heat and I wouldn't give a snap for the life of anyone who was arrested in the next day or two. This crowd could lynch as well as it can talk."

I told Charlie of the finding of the needle and how it matched those taken from Byron's and Sam's brains, but I didn't tell him of Father's vision in the organ. I told him of the letters, though, and my futile attempt to hide anything I chose to from Father's eyes.

"And are you positive," Charlie asked, "that there wasn't anything there that came Saturday in the mail—except the Campion receipt?"

"Positive," I assured him. "And, furthermore, there was hardly anything for the whole past week, and nothing at all that amounted to a damn."

We stopped talking then, and I lay staring at the window—the same window at which the thumps had come.

I tossed. It was useless to try to sleep. Everything at once came rushing through my head—bare feet and steel needles and great organ pipes and a gold bracelet around the hand of a dark-eyed girl.

I shifted my position again.

Let me think this out. It's the first moment I've had to myself at all, except for those few minutes in the cold cemetery. Perhaps if I think. . . .

One of us, Father believes, who heard Charlie give me Sam's message! But that includes Bill Smart, because Charlie said that Bill was with him when Sam spoke.

One of us did it, Father thinks, or knows who did it.

Did Charlie? He might have. He had the opportunity. He didn't go to his fraternity at all, perhaps, but went up to Byron, and somehow, with some diabolical needle machine, killed him as he lay in bed. And then had a stroke of terror at what he'd done, and in a feeble attempt to make it look like suicide, tied him on the rope and lowered him from the window. What he did between then and the time I came in, I don't know, but he was still up when he heard the door click, and he dived into bed with his clothes still on. And then the next day—did he have time to run from the chapel after the murder of Sam and be seen by me as he appeared to be coming, coatless and out of breath, down the walk from Mass. Row? But Charlie, next to By and Bossy, is my best friend, and Byron's too!

Could Bossy have done it? He could get in to the dormitory all right without suspicion. He often came. And he knew I was to be away until late, because the 'phone call from Father came to his house. But so, too, did Charlie. So did all of them. But Bossy—did he do it? And then, as a dodge and a blind, did he offer his house for conference purposes and sit in on them all, silent and sure? And some time, between Charlie's message and chapel time, even with choir rehearsal intervening, did he have a chance to rig up some diabolical mechanism so that, during the president's speech, he could press a key of his organ, in the clear view of more than a thousand people, and send Sam to his death?

And Bill Smart—oh, it isn't worth thinking about Bill. He has the clearest slate of any of us and is only in it at all because he happened to get hungry at nine o'clock last night. But still, the same opportunity was open to him as to the rest of us.

Jean? I can't think that she is in it at all? Yet where was she all night, up until two o'clock? And why did she lie about Byron's lights? And most of all, isn't it highly probable that on Byron's death the money is hers?—particularly as he hadn't received it yet and she, under her father's will, was probably next in line. But if he *had* received it, legally. That is, if it had been one day later when he had died, wouldn't it possibly have gone, not to her, but to his mother if he died intestate. I don't know law. I wish I did. . . . And is Jean possibly strong enough to haul Byron's body from the bed and lower him out the window?

Miss Case could do it. She's as strong as an ox. And no one saw her after nine at night, or really knows where she was during chapel, although she says she was in the transept. Perhaps, somewhere, she's caught up in the family in some other way than just by being companion. Father *is* right. There's more, much more, to be found out about them all.

And Father! Does that mask of his conceal more than his secrets of investigation. Did he for some unknown reason plan all this, and commit the murder while I was taking the car to the garage, locking the door after him and going to safety in the Inn, and perhaps cooking up the story of having seen Jean somewhere before, and noticing her coming in late? But he sat with me in chapel! Has he got an accomplice that murdered Sam? Or did he somehow find out where Sam usually stands, and fix some automatic compressed air instrument that shot the second needle?

These are absurd thoughts. They're wild and not logical or mechanical.

But Father insisted on going alone to the chapel this evening, with the flashlight. Did he go to remove traces of his machine? Wasn't he, perhaps, disturbed while at it and so came running back to me, out of breath, with a spur-of-the-moment story about seeing Byron there, and chatter about a Ford and the sound of something dropping in the organ? And then taking me back with him to retrieve the needle he had dropped in his haste, and making me stand there, while, in maniac glee, he satisfied himself by partly doing the crime over again, using my neck for Sam's and Byron's!

Why do I think this way?

But did he really see Byron? That's impossible, and I braved the undertaking rooms to satisfy myself.

What did he see, then? A ghost? *Or someone that looked like Byron?*

It came like a flash! It was what had been knocking at my mind since early evening. It was what I should have pounced upon when Father first told me, if I hadn't been so startled.

I sat up in bed.

"John Meseraux!"

I cried the name aloud.

*"John Meseraux, of course!"*

## CHAPTER X
## MONDAY: SANS SOUCI

THREE MILES OR SO EAST OF HANOVER, on the outskirts of the practically negligible village of Etna, there had been established, for the last three years, a roadhouse called "Sans Souci." It was a fairly good place, an easy hike and an easier ride from college, and was well patronized by the undergraduates. They served good steaks on short notice, and their fireplace was large and blazing for winter evening talks after a heavy meal and before the hour's walk through the snow back to the town.

But what gave the place its real popularity was the fact that the proprietor was not averse, when he knew his patrons, to serving wine with dinner. And, even more, it was known that now and then he would furnish a private party with cocktails before and highballs afterward.

For a year and a half the place ran quietly enough, but during Winter Carnival of its second school year of operation, one of the fraternities staged a rather brilliant brawl there, drinks on the house, and one Wellesley and one Vassar and two Smith girls were brought back to their chaperons rather stiff and incoherent.

There was a great to-do when it was reported to the various girls' colleges, and although Sans Souci was not completely closed, it took to serving drinks only in the sanctity of its kitchen. But the other colleges demanded that the Council on Student Organizations forbid, henceforth, any parties, private or public, at the roadhouse during any official Dartmouth function. And furthermore, each of the three girls' colleges prescribed immediate expulsion for every girl seen there. And Dartmouth followed by prescribing the same for every Dartmouth man found there with a girl during fall houseparty, carnival, or prom.

The proprietor objected to the college, crying his innocence, but he accomplished nothing. He had a French accent and his name was Pierre Meseraux.

His son, John Meseraux (I presumed it originally was Jean), was a junior in college, a colourless sort of boy and not generally well liked. I have already recorded his name and told of his resemblance to Byron. It was rather astounding, sometimes. He was slighter, and whereas Byron was dark, John was almost sandy-haired. But their features were almost exactly like, and except for their colouring they might easily have passed for twins. John was older, by a year, although he was a class behind Byron and me—kept back, I presume, by less intensive schooling than Byron had had.

He was, I say, not well liked. He was a non-fraternity man and hardly active at all about the campus. If it hadn't been for his looks, we should have gone for three years without realizing his existence, save, perhaps, as an underling and an infrequent sight around the verandahs of Sans Souci.

But if I remember correctly, it was Bossy who first called our attention to him by declaring, one night at the beginning of our sophomore year, that a dead-ringer for Byron had tried out for the glee club that day. "He won't make it," he said, "but he'll probably make the choir."

Others soon began to notice the resemblance, and Byron had it thrown at him continually, until he began to detest John's very presence. But later that same year he did swallow his rather unreasonable prejudice long enough to allow the Dartmouth Players, taking advantage of the likeness, to put the two of them into *Twelfth Night*. Byron played Sebastian and John, being slighter, did Viola. Never on any stage, I truly believe, were the Shakespearean twins more convincingly played.

During rehearsals the two of them got acquainted for the first time, and although Byron, after talking with John, admitted that he wasn't half bad after all, he did it grudgingly. It was never an active hate, anyway, but more of a silent scorn which Bryon had more and more of a chance to indulge himself in as John, lonesome individual that he was, began to look us up and call on us, apparently taking the dramatic acquaintance as a newly found friendship. Byron would either sulk all through these visits or find some excuse for leaving—at any rate, throwing the entire duty of entertaining on my shoulders. I often lectured him on it, but it did no good. "I just don't like him, Ken," Byron would reply. "Probably the only reason in the world is because he looks like me and I get kidded for it. I rather enjoy my face, but I don't care to see it spread around."

"He's older than you," I would counter. "He owns the copyright."

"That's no reason why he should come sneaking up here and sit around and talk, looking like a damn' mirror."

During the past year John had practically ceased his visits to us and had almost dropped out of our thoughts, but that was no reason why I shouldn't have pounced upon him, six hours before, as the only logical explanation of what Father saw in the chapel. Yet now, in the dark of Charlie's bedroom, it came swiftly and clearly, and I cried his name aloud:

"John Meseraux, of course!"

Charlie started and sat up. "What's the matter? Is that you, Ken? What's the matter?"

"Charlie!" I cried. "I've got an idea! I think I've got the key to the whole business!"

"What is it, Ken? What's the matter? What did you yell that way for? You scared the life out of me."

"Are you really awake, Charlie?" I asked. "Can you listen sanely?"

"I'm wide awake. Go ahead."

I got out of bed and switched the light on, and then got in again, lying so that I could see Charlie.

"Listen, Charlie, and see if you come to the same conclusion I do. It's simple enough, only it just struck me now. . . . I didn't tell you a while ago, but early this evening Father borrowed my flashlight and went into the chapel organ alone—to see if by chance there was something tell-tale left around. This was an hour or so earlier than the visit he and I paid together. I stayed in the room and waited for him, and in less than no time he was back, all out of breath and in a great stew. He had crept into the passageway behind the big pipes—crept in, because he heard someone in there, and saw them scratching matches. And when he burst the door open and turned the flashlight on, he thought he saw Byron standing there!"

"Good God!" cried Charlie. "Is the old man going crazy? What was it, a trick of the lights?"

"No, Charlie. He really saw someone. There was really a fellow there, and he turned and ran, dropping that needle we found. It really was someone—*who looked like Byron!*"

Charlie was silent.

"Do you see, Charlie?"

He sat up and threw the clothes from him. "Great God! John Meseraux!"

"Yes!" I cried triumphantly. "That's what I yelled when I woke you up."

"He ran, you say?"

"Yes, and Father chased him, but he got away."

"How? In that old Ford of his?"

"Yes, *of course!* And even the Ford didn't give me a clue until now. Lord, what a dumb-bell!"

Charlie slowly got back into bed again, but stayed half sitting-up, supporting himself on his arms.

"But what do you think it all means, Ken?" he asked.

"It means that John damn' well killed By and Sam," I answered.

Charlie whistled. "That's rushing things, Ken."

"Well, he was there in the organ, wasn't he, caught with the goods—the needle, I mean, which he had to go and drop? And who else but the murderer would know it was there?"

"It sounds reasonable," said Charlie. "But tell me. Where did he go in the Ford?"

"We chased him," I answered. "Our car was parked in front of here and he only had a few minutes start out the Lyme Road. We simply tore, all the way to Lyme. But he must have turned off, or we'd have caught him long before that."

"What he probably did," said Charlie, "was turn up the road to the reservoir, cut over in back of Balch Hill, and strike the Etna road that way."

"He probably didn't know he was followed anyway," I added.

There was silence for a moment.

"Charlie," I said. "I think it's up to us to go to Sans Souci."

"When?"

"Now."

"Why?"

"Well, John is there, isn't he?"

"He may be," said Charlie, "and he may be a hundred miles away. It's all according to whether he thinks he was recognized in the organ—or whether, in the first place, he's really guilty. Or what his defense is anyway. But one thing's certain. If he's home now, he'll be home in the morning, or here in his Ford again, for classes."

"I suppose you're right," I said, rather ruefully.

"And exactly what would we do if we found him there at this time of night, or rather morning?"

"Nab him," I said weakly.

"We haven't a warrant in the first place," Charlie said. "And we aren't armed. And we can't go yelling at people's windows that they're murderers."

"I suppose you're right," I said again.

"The thing to do," Charlie went on, "is to get what sleep you can now, and in the morning, when your father comes to see the letters, tell him the whole business and let him act as he wants to. It's either much too late already, or else there's all the time in the world."

"But I don't believe I'll be able to sleep."

"You have to. It's awfully late, and you only got about three hours last night. Now, forget things until you see your father." Charlie put the light out and I lay back on the pillow.

But I couldn't sleep—not for a long time, tired though I was. I lay there, sometimes with my eyes closed, sometimes with them open, staring at the window through which, before I really slept, the faint dawn came.

I tried over and over again to fit John Meseraux into the scheme somehow or other. I tried, by every means I knew, to find some faint motive for his murder of Byron—if, indeed, he really did it.

Suppose, for instance, that he was a highly sensitive boy. Suppose that he, too, had been as much affected by his likeness to Byron as Byron had, only in a different way. Suppose that the resemblance had made him feel like a despised under dog, that he had seen Byron go up and up in college activities, society, and popularity, while he, outwardly the same person, had got nowhere at all. Suppose that his attempts at making friends with Byron, which had been so coldly repulsed, were genuine and warm. Could he, by a stretch of the imagination, be eventually brought to such an active state of mad jealousy that he would kill? And then kill again to prevent discovery?

It was feeble, but everything else that I thought of was much more fantastic—that John was some long-lost brother of Byron's, trying for his heritage—that somehow there was a mix-up in bodies, even though I had looked again at Byron in the morgue and satisfied myself—that Byron was somehow killed by mistake for John and that John knew it—or that somehow John had killed Byron, intending to dye his hair and take Byron's place. . . . My brain went round and round and the dawn was cold. . . .

Father was shaking me.

"Ken, wake up! Kenneth!"

I sat up, blinking.

"I thought you were to be up and dressed and breakfasted. It's after half-past eight. I've been up and doing for two hours, and I've accomplished much."

"I'm sorry, Dad. I talked with Charlie until late." I glanced around and saw Charlie struggling out of sleep. He blinked his eyes at us and murmured a smothered "hello," sank back again for an instant, and then sat up, asking the time. We told him.

"Missed my eight o'clock," he said, "or isn't this Monday?"

"It's Monday, all right," said Father. "I had an appointment with Kenneth upstairs at eight-thirty, but when I went there I found his bed unslept in and his clothes all over the place. I guessed he was here."

"It got creepy upstairs," I explained.

"Nonsense!" said Father, and walked over and shut the window.

"Father," I said, "before we do another thing, I want to tell you something. Charlie and I talked it over last night, and that's why we're so late this morning. Sit down."

He sat on the edge of my bed and I talked. I told him of the sudden flash I had about John Meseraux, the only logical explanation of the chapel scene. And then I told the whole story, much as I have set it down here, of his place in the college and of his relations with Byron. Father listened silently until I related how I had tried to get Charlie to drive with me to Sans Souci at three o'clock and how Charlie had refused.

"And you were quite right, Penlon," Father said. Then he turned to me. "Just think, Kenneth, what trouble you might have got into if he proved to be innocent and cared to make any disturbance about it."

"But how could he be innocent, Dad?"

"Well," said Father, "let's think a minute. . . . From what you say, he evidently was extremely fond of Byron. At least, he liked him enough to try to seek his company, time and time again, even though he was discouraged from the first. He undoubtedly sensed, too, that you were more or less sharing Byron's opinion of him. So, when he heard of Byron's death and saw Sam's death in the chapel, and heard rumour linking the two, he didn't care to come directly to you and offer his sympathy and his help. For the past year, you say, you have had nothing to do with him at all. But, because of the resemblance which probably has meant much more to him than it ever did to Byron, and which in more ways than one has moulded his college career, he felt somehow caught up in the case. It was personal to him.

"So, at the first opportunity, he drives to the chapel, thinking, perhaps, that no one else will hold the same theory he does, that

Sam's death might have been accomplished from inside the organ, yet fearing that you, with your Coatesian manner, might laugh at whatever suggestion he might make. So he sneaks into the organ, and examines the place, inch by inch, back of where Sam stood, and he finds the needle and picks it up.

"But just then, out of the silence, I burst open the door and blind him with the light. He drops the needle in his fright, stands stupefied for a second, and then flees in terror. . . . You see, Ken, it can be explained—innocently."

I was thoughtful. I was also disappointed. "I see. And what do you plan to do about it?"

"Why, nothing just now," Father answered. "He may be guilty and may have fled town. He probably is still here. We might, on a technicality, have him arrested and questioned, and it might do some good. On the other hand, it might not. I highly favour letting him go his own way, closely watched, particularly in his attitude toward you as you meet him on the campus. Are you in any of his classes?"

"I'm not," said Charlie.

"I am," I replied. "I have English with him at eleven on Mondays, Wednesdays, and Fridays."

"Then go to English to-day," Father said.

"Damn' right I will!" I answered.

I leaped out of bed and found my dressing gown. "Come on, Dad," I said. "Let's go up. You can start on the letters while I'm dressing. Come up when you're ready, Charlie."

We walked down the corridor and up the two flights of stairs. Two boys that I knew to speak to moved silently back against the wall to let us pass. I was a celebrity, I thought bitterly.

Father seated himself at the desk immediately and I took the key out of my pocket and tossed it to him.

"You'll find that I've done some sorting already," I said in as nonchalant a tone as I could assume, fearing his wrath. "All the later ones are in the upper left."

Father took the key and bent to the left-hand drawer.

"But this isn't locked, Ken," he said.

And then suddenly he made a violent movement and pulled drawer after drawer open until all five stood gaping.

"Look here, Ken!" he cried. "Look!"

I strode to his side.

The wood at the top of each drawer was splintered. They had all been jimmied open!

# CHAPTER XI
## MONDAY: OIL AND A WIRE

"Forced open!" I cried. "Every one of them!"

Father bent to the drawers again. "How did they lock?" he asked. "Not each one separately?"

"No," I answered. "See, there's only one keyhole, in the centre one. It manipulates a metal catch at the back of each of the others. Not very strong. It would be an easy matter to force them open. . . . What do you suppose he used?"

"This, probably." Father reached down and lifted a skate from under the desk. "Undoubtedly this."

It was one of mine, I could see, taken from the shelf of the closet. Byron's were still plainly undisturbed in the lower drawer. Father was holding it up, examining it minutely.

"Fingerprints, Dad!" I cried. "Have the sheriff or someone examine it for fingerprints!"

Father turned and gave me a cold glance. "I can take fingerprints as well as any country sheriff," he said. "But our robber is cleverer than that. He's wiped it clean. It couldn't shine more if it were rubbed with silver polish." He tossed it on the floor again and faced the desk.

"Before I touch a thing, Kenneth," he said, "look and see what has been disturbed. Tell me everything that is at all disturbed."

I looked. It was impossible to tell a thing about the upper right-hand drawer. I had poured the papers in in such a mess that a small hurricane might have hit them without visibly rearranging any of them. But the upper left-hand one had surely been pawed over. I had made neat piles the night before, but now they had toppled onto each other and were turned askew. Someone most evidently had taken them out, one at a time, searched rapidly through them, and replaced them hastily, caring nothing for their order. The other drawers looked untouched.

"Then it is clearly a letter that our thief was after," said Father.

"Absolutely," I agreed. "And though I'm rather reluctant to admit you're right, Dad, if any one of those piles is disturbed more than another, it's this one." I pointed. "And those letters are from his mother. . . . And look!" I took them in my hand. "Here are a couple pulled out of their envelopes and one only half stuffed back. I swear I didn't leave them that way!"

Father took them from me and laid them on the desk, and then swung the chair until it faced the room. "Tell me exactly what you did last night."

"Why, nothing much. I suppose it was rather a sneaky thing, but it didn't amount to anything. . . . On the way back from Bossy's I had the idea of going over the letters first, just to see if Byron had any secrets I could hide from strange eyes. Nothing to do with the murder, of course—I shouldn't have hidden that—but little personal things that I'd hate to have a stranger see. So I made a half-hearted attempt to sort them out. I admit I got discouraged when I saw how many there were, and I ended up by reading only about a dozen, but I'm sure they're all the same. There isn't anything in any of them. . . . But I did sort out the late ones. Unless the envelopes have been switched, those in the left drawer are all he's received since the first of October. All the rest are earlier—last year mostly, and this summer."

"What date was the latest?" Father asked.

"Except for a receipted Campion's bill, there was nothing for the last two days."

"You can swear to that?"

"I can swear to it. You can look for yourself."

"When was the last letter from his mother?" Father swung to the desk again. I bent over his shoulder and pawed through the pile until I found it.

"Here," I said, and opened it for him. "Just a correspondence card. Dated on Wednesday."

He read it, and I read it with him:

> Byron Dear:
> Just the shortest of notes on an awfully busy day. I have a dressmaker here and I'm having the library done over. New paper and ceiling. You never saw such a mess. You haven't told me yet what you want for your birthday. Think hard and decide on something you *really* want. It's your most important day since twenty-one years ago, you know.
> Lovingly,<br>Mother.

"And they're all like that, Dad," I said, "really. There isn't a thing. If there ever was anything important, I'm sure it's gone now."

"I'm afraid so," said Father, fingering the splintered wood.

"I don't mean last night," I said. "I mean before that. Byron must have destroyed whatever there was, if there was anything at all. Though I admit he was the least destructive mortal I ever met. He never threw away a thing."

Father was silent for an instant, rubbing his forehead.

"Why didn't you lock your door last night?" he asked.

"I didn't think of it," I said. "I never lock the door. I've told you that before. I should have, I know, but it didn't come natural, particularly just skipping down to Charlie's room in pajamas and a dressing gown."

"Then why did you lock the drawers?"

"I don't know," I answered truthfully. "It was just mechanical, I guess. The key was there, and I'd spent some time putting things in shape, so I just turned it."

"You were afraid I might get here ahead of you and you hoped to do some more sorting and eliminating." Father's voice was accusing.

"Subconsciously, perhaps," I said. "Not intentionally, I promise you, Father. I simply can't account logically for locking them, and that's all there is to it."

Father laid his hands on the ends of the chair arms and gripped them. "Look at me, Ken," he said.

"Do you swear on your honour that you're telling the truth and that you did not take any letter from that drawer?"

"Great heavens, Father!" I exclaimed. "Do you think I swiped one and then pried the drawers open for a blind? Do you accuse me of that?"

He shifted in his chair.

"I'm accusing you of nothing. I'm simply asking you to swear you're not keeping anything from me."

I looked him straight in the eye. "I swear," I said.

"I believe you." Once more he turned to the desk. "Better get dressed, Ken," he said, in an entirely different tone. "I asked Bostwick to come down and pick us up here on the way to the inquest. We've got three quarters of an hour yet, but you'll want breakfast."

Something flashed into my mind. "Oh, Dad," I said, "did you go to the chapel? What did you find out about that fool theory of the sheriff's?"

"I'll tell you when Bostwick gets here," he replied. "You dress. I agree with you that it's useless now, but I want to go through a few of these."

When I had come back from shaving in the bathroom, Bossy was already there, seated beside Father at the desk and reading letters with him.

He looked up with a smile as I entered. "Isn't this foolish, Ken?" he said.

"Highly," I answered. "Particularly as—"

"Particularly," Father interrupted, "as Kenneth went over them last night and reported this morning that they were as blameless as a new-born babe. But I don't always trust Kenneth. He's sincere, but not always logical."

I turned with a grunt and pulled on the rest of my clothes. From the bedroom I could hear Father and Bossy crinkling papers, and I was more than glad that I had, after a fashion, read the letters, at least enough to taste of their tone. When I had tied my tie (it was curious, the little pause I made before I selected a dark one) and slipped on my coat I went back to the study and was met by a wave of Father's hand. He was on his official behaviour again. He waved me to a seat on the couch.

"Sit down, Kenneth," he said. "And you, Professor Bostwick, stop reading for a few moments. I have something that will interest both of you."

Bossy folded the letter he held in his hand and stuffed it back into its envelope.

"Professor Bostwick," Father began, "we have met the sheriff. He knows his place and will not, I am sure, interfere, police-fashion, with the work of the official investigator. Yet I don't deprecate him. He is an intelligent man, to a certain degree, and his words are not to be disregarded entirely. I feel bound, inasmuch as he is proving so genial, to listen to all of his theories. And last night he advanced one."

"Yes?" said Bossy. I could see he was prepared to be bored.

"Yes," echoed Father. "And the theory was this: that you are the murderer!"

Bossy turned deathly pale. I wondered, for a second, if he wouldn't rise and strike Father. I could see his hands twitching in his lap. But in another moment he was calm again and his colour had come back.

"Please go on, Mr. Harris," he said.

"His theory was this," Father continued: "that you had placed some cleverly contrived machine in among the organ pipes, so regulated that in front of the whole congregation you could press a key at the console and shoot, by the air of the organ, a steel needle into Sam Anderson's brain."

"A steel needle!" exclaimed Bossy.

"Yes," answered Father, "such as this." He fumbled in his pocket and laid the needle bare on the desk before Bossy. "Needles such as this were found in the brains of both boys."

Bossy bent over the needle for a moment and then straightened up. "Go on," he said again.

"I went to the chapel this morning, directly after the service. I didn't see you."

"No," said Bossy. "My assistant played this morning."

"I didn't go into the auditorium but sought out the janitor. He is a genial soul. The name, I believe, is Gresham and he also does the janitor work in Dartmouth Hall and rings the swinging bell for classes. He has, if you are interested, five children. The possession of children has not made him unobservant of small details. His heart is evidently in his work."

Bossy spoke. "He knows the organ well," he said. "He was a good one to go to."

"He was the obvious one," Father corrected. "But I admit that I was in luck. He had planned, yesterday afternoon after the chapel service, to oil the motor that creates the organ's air in the basement."

"Ah!" said Bossy. Evidently he saw what Father was getting at, but I didn't.

"I asked him about the motor, and I learned what I expected to learn, that it was electric; that not a lever could move or a breath could stir within the organ unless that motor was running; that when that motor was stopped anyone could press a hundred keys on the console or pull a dozen stops without as much as a squeak from the pipes or the moving of a hair's breadth of one of the valves. And that that motor is always turned off the moment the organist finishes a piece of music because the sound of its whirring is slightly audible from the chapel proper."

"Gresham is quite correct," said Bossy.

"As I say," Father went on, "he was planning to oil the organ directly after the service. He was in the basement, getting his oiling kit together all through the service, after he had assisted in ringing the bells. He is able to hear the singing from down there. He knows the service thoroughly and from years of experience has timed it so that he knows when each hymn comes and when the motor will spark and start to revolve as you turn it on in the organ loft. After the hymn, "O Love That Will Not Let Me Go" (which he named to me and which I have verified), the motor did not stir! He was waiting, before commencing his oiling, for the final hymn and postlude. It never came. The motor was silent. And instead he heard the tramping of feet overhead and went up to meet the excited crowd. The motor did not move during the president's address!"

"I could have told you that," said Bossy, ingenuously.

"You were not the one to ask," Father replied. "Indeed, I even tested the good Gresham. I offered him spot cash of five hundred dollars for the truth, if he were concealing the truth. His mouth watered but he stuck to his story and I gave him fifteen. And I consider it settled. It is obviously impossible for you to have caused the death of Anderson."

It seemed for a moment as if Father were going to add the words, "and I congratulate you," but he was silent.

Bossy was calm and sincere. "I'm relieved," he said; "relieved, of course, that I'm free from suspicion. I don't think you understand, Mr. Harris, what your words meant to me when you first accused me, through the sheriff, of being Byron's murderer. I took it for Byron, anyway. The murderer is obviously the same for both. Only Kenneth can realize how infinitely dear Byron was to me. You have a brutal turn of phrase, Mr. Harris."

Father bowed. "I'm more than sorry. Will you forget it?"

Bossy shook Father's proffered hand.

"Now," I thought, "if I can only get him to clear Charlie and Jean likewise!"

Father's manner, now that he considered his official duties over, immediately became easy. "Well," he sighed, "I can't say that I regret it, but it really leaves us not very much more advanced than we were before. It rules out the chapel, I'm sure, as far as holding the key to the mystery is concerned. Kenneth will tell you that it's my theory that these letters hold—or once held—clues toward solution. Kenneth himself thinks that we should all go driving at once toward Etna."

Bossy looked at me in great surprise. "Etna! How's that, Ken?"

I turned to Father. "I can tell him, can't I?"

A knock came at the door. An impatient knock. "It's Charlie," I said. "Come in, Charlie!"

I was answered by another knock, and I rose and strode to the door, throwing it open.

Miss Case stood there, with Jean just behind her.

I stood aside for Miss Case to enter and then reached out and took Jean's hand, pressing it and leading her into the room. Father and Bossy rose, and bowed to Miss Case. "Good-morning," Father said. "We were going to call for you both at the Inn on our way to the inquest, but we've got twenty minutes yet. Do sit down."

I sank on the couch beside Jean and Miss Case took the chair Bossy had been sitting in, while he perched on the edge of the desk. Father remained standing.

"I've got business," said Miss Case, in her usual brisk voice. "And shady business too. Shady, that is, because I'm afraid that I'm supposed to keep the telegram I've just received a secret. But I've talked it over with Jean and she agrees with me that I should show it to you, letting you," she was addressing Father who stood before her, "take the responsibility."

"You are right," said Father. "Whom is it from?"

Miss Case reached in her handbag and drew out a yellow paper. "It's from Mrs. Coates," she said. "It came half an hour ago, addressed to me," She handed it to Father.

I rose and looked over his shoulder at it. It read:

I CHARGE YOU TO DESTROY UNREAD LETTER
BYRON RECEIVED FROM ME SATURDAY.

# CHAPTER XII
## MONDAY: INQUEST AND A MISSION

"MAY I SEE IT?" ASKED BOSSY. He asked it of Father, but Father looked up at Miss Case.

"I think that's up to you now, Mr. Harris," she said. "I've broken confidence already in giving it to you. It's in your hands."

Father passed the telegram to Bossy and stood looking at him thoughtfully as he read. Bossy read it at a glance and handed it back. "I don't see, Miss Case," he said, "how you're exactly breaking a confidence by showing it to anybody. Mrs. Coates hasn't asked you to keep the existence of the letter a secret."

"No," answered Miss Case, "but naturally she implied it. If I held to the exact wording of her telegram, I might consider that I could ask Mr. Harris or Kenneth for the letter and let them read it, or anybody else, so long as *I* didn't read it before burning. As it is, I'm going to lay myself open to Mrs. Coates's anger, and probably discharge, by saying to you, Mr. Harris, that the decision rests with you whether or not anyone reads the letter. But if you want to know my thoughts on the matter, I think it ought to be read. There's my disloyalty in a nut shell."

"It's sensible disloyalty, though," Jean put in. "I'm ready to stand against Mother with you, though I think perhaps I might be chosen as the one to do the first reading. Then, you know, if there *were* something which is too much family, I might—"

She was interrupted by the snap of the letter slot as the morning mail fell inside on the floor. I turned to get it, but Father brushed hurriedly by me, strode to the door, and opened it. Steps were going down the corridor.

"Postman!" he called. "Postman!"

The postman came back.

"Did you know Coates?" asked Father abruptly.

"Sure," said the postman, "and I'm sorry to hear what's happened." He looked at me and nodded. "Sorry, Harris."

"I want you to try to remember something," said Father. "Try hard now. Can you possibly recall how many letters Coates received on Saturday? I know it's difficult, but it's important."

The postman shifted his heavy pouch a trifle.

"It isn't difficult at all, sir," he said. "I've already told it to one person to-day."

Father stepped forward as if he were going to grasp the man's shoulder. "Who?" he cried.

"My wife," he answered. "We read the morning *Dartmouth* at breakfast and talked about the murders. 'Did you know 'em?' she asked, and I said, 'Sure I knew 'em; they both lived on the top floor of North Mass.' And then I told her that just Saturday morning I had talked with young Coates. He was standing at the top of the stairs, waiting for me, probably'd heard my step, because the boys tell me they'd know my step anywhere. Just while I was coming up the stairs he said, 'Hello, Julius. I know you've got something for me this morning.' 'How do you know?' I asked, sort of kidding him. 'I feel it in my bones,' he said, 'and besides, it's my birthday.' 'Happy New Year,' says I, still sort of kidding him. I looked through my stack and found two and said, 'Campion's wishing you many happy returns by sending a bill.' He laughed and said, 'I guess that's a receipt.' And then I gave him both of them and that's all there was to it. I've always liked young Coates. He's been on my route for four years. Always lived somewhere in Mass. Row."

"And this other letter—besides the one from Campion. Can you possibly recall where it was from?" Father pursued.

"Sure." The postman grinned. "Boston. Gray envelope. He's had two or three a week for four years. His girl, I guess. I used to kid him about them. Didn't I, Harris?" He grinned at me.

I nodded.

Father dashed into the room and took a couple of letters from the top of the desk. He came back with them and held them up to the postman. "Like these?" he asked.

"Exactly," said Julius.

"Are you sure of it?"

"I'd swear to it."

"Then thank you, my man," said Father, and bowed him away.

The moment the door was closed he stooped down and picked up the mail, running hastily through it. There was a surprising lot of it, fourteen or fifteen letters. "All for you, Ken," he said, and handed them to me. At a glance I saw that they were practically all from Hanover. Letters of sympathy, I supposed.

"But why all this rigmarole?" demanded Miss Case. "We know from the wire that Byron got a letter from his mother on Saturday, and probably on her usual gray stationery."

I dropped my mail on my desk and looked at Father. He stood in the middle of the room and clenched his hands behind him.

"I shall tell her, Ken," he said. "Because, Miss Case, the letter has never been seen by any of us, not even Kenneth. And it cannot be found anywhere."

"Have you looked everywhere?" Miss Case asked.

"We've searched the place thoroughly. The only place that hasn't been gone over carefully is Kenneth's desk, but it would hardly migrate there in a few short hours."

"All his pockets?" asked Bossy.

"Everywhere," said Father.

The door opened and Charlie Penlon appeared, nodding to us all and sinking on to the couch beside Jean, silent when he saw that Father was standing and in charge.

"And, furthermore, I might as well tell you, this room was entered last night and Byron's desk drawers forced open. If anyone"—I fancied he glared at Miss Case—"realized that an important letter had arrived Saturday, that one certainly made a thorough search for it sometime before eight-thirty this morning."

"Great God!" said Charlie.

Bossy whistled.

Jean tossed her hair back. "You're staring at Miss Case, Mr. Harris, as if she were the culprit." Then she had noticed it, too! "I wish you'd look at the time on the telegram. The time of receiving, that is."

Father reddened slightly. "It isn't necessary. I certainly am not accusing Miss Case."

"I'd really like to know," Jean went on. "When did Mother send it? Was it a night message?"

Bossy picked up the yellow paper from the desk and scanned it. "It is dated at Boston at 8:20 this morning. It was received here at 8:39."

"We got it just as we were going down to breakfast," said Miss Case, "about a quarter of nine. And we came here immediately afterward."

"I'm certainly glad you did," said Father.

"So am I," said Miss Case, "as things have turned out. I felt that it was more than important, and now we know it is."

Father looked at his watch and announced that we had only five minutes in which to get to the inquest. "I assume, if we get separated," he said, "that I'll see you all at lunch—that is, if Professor Bostwick's generous offer of meals still holds good."

"Until the case is solved," said Bossy.

The inquest was brief and to the point. It was, of course, my first, but after the thrills of the past twenty-eight hours it was curiously unexciting. I had expected a throng of undergraduates, trying to get in, at least, but there were none there except those of us directly connected. Indeed, there were no visitors at all. I believe a few did try to get in, but the coroner and the sheriff's man kept them out.

I viewed Byron's body and Jerry Dawes viewed Sam's. It proved to be cold-blooded, unsentimental business without any of the horror of the evening before.

Back again in the room in Davison Block I gave evidence as to the finding of the body and its recovery. Charlie corroborated it.

Then Dr. Preable's assistant gave a detailed account of the autopsy. And the jury, composed partly of faculty and partly of townspeople, returned immediately a verdict of death by the hand of person or persons unknown. Nothing else, of course, was possible. The doctor's statement showed conclusively that Byron was dead before the hanging, and both Charlie and I testified to the fact that no means of shooting the needle into his brain was found.

The moment that was over, the second inquest was begun and the same jury sworn in to sit on the death of Sam Anderson. Both Bossy and Father described his toppling from the highest step in the chapel choir loft, and the same doctor gave the same autopsy findings. The verdict was death at the hand of person or persons unknown. It was all curiously informal and uninteresting. To me it seemed like useless retrogression to matters which we had known long ago and almost forgotten. We were far beyond North Mass. and the chapel now, I thought, and were facing Boston—or Etna— or both.

The moment it was over I heard the Dartmouth Hall bell swinging for a change of classes and Father came toward me, watch in hand.

"It's eleven," he said. "I want you to go to English class."

Charlie walked with me across the campus and I was glad of his company and moral protection. I was stared at. I felt myself being pointed out. Three times I was stopped and given sympathy, but Charlie had to leave me at the door of Dartmouth Hall and I entered my classroom alone.

The professor was already there and summoned me to him.

"You shouldn't have come," he said.

"It'll occupy my mind. There's nothing else to do," I lied.

The class was small, not more than twelve, and eight of them, at least, shook my hand or laid their hands on my shoulder and said variations of "I'm sorry, Ken," or asked questions that I tried not to answer directly.

It was just before class began that John Meseraux entered. I gave a perceptible start. He dared to come!

He gave one glance in my direction, but I could read nothing from it; and as, in the classroom, we were seated alphabetically, which brought him a row behind me, I couldn't study his expression during the interminable hour.

I knew the professor wouldn't call on me, but I tried my hardest to give my utmost attention, though I admit I found it hard. For ten minutes at a time, I am sure, I didn't hear a word that was being said, either from the desk or from the floor, but every now and then I would collect my thoughts and bring them back to the room and listen intently, too intently, to what was going on. But I find that for the life of me I can't remember what was being discussed. Once, I know, John Meseraux was called upon to answer some question. I didn't hear the question; it was only the calling of his name that brought me out of a reverie. He failed, saying he didn't know.

Immediately I was off again. Of course he wouldn't know! How could anyone study with two murders on his hands—and ranging the countryside at night in a roaring Ford!

There were bells, and the class was over, and John was coming toward me. I felt him before I left my seat, or before I had turned around to look at him. I knew he was going to speak.

I got up, looked at no one, and slowly made my way out between the chairs. The rest of the class, from embarrassment, perhaps, went out ahead of me, and John was still behind. I felt his hand on my shoulder and turned.

"I have to speak to you, Ken," he began. I turned toward him. His face, always whiter than Byron's, was pale, and I either saw or imagined sleeplessness in his eyes.

"I want to tell you how terribly sorry I am about Byron."

I kept my face as impassive as I could.

"I know he never liked me, but just the same, I liked him. Perhaps better than anyone else here. It's horrible to think he's gone."

"Thank you, John," was all I could think to say. He reached for my hand and I shook his. It was hot and dry, and I wanted to blurt out, "What were you doing in the chapel last night?" but I didn't dare. I merely dropped his hand and watched him go out the door ahead of me and become lost in the crowd outside in the corridor.

"Now, Miss Case," said Father when lunch was over and Bossy had taken us into his living room before he went to his one-o'clock class, "tell us your plans."

"They're simple," she replied. "Jean and I will take the afternoon train to Boston. It goes about three. Byron's body will be on it. I've arranged for that. Jean will stay at home, probably, for the rest of the week, and then go back to Vassar."

Jean stared into the fire. "I've decided not to go," she said quietly.

"What?" snapped Miss Case.

"I've decided not to go."

"But what about your brother's funeral, young lady?" asked Father harshly.

"I can answer that easily," said Miss Case. "There will be no funeral. Mrs. Coates is not religious and there are no friends of the family to judge and talk. Byron will go directly to the undertaking rooms where his mother may see him if she chooses—I shall advise against her seeing him—and then, tomorrow, to the cemetery. . . . But just the same, Jean, what do you mean by not coming with me?"

Jean still kept her eyes fastened on the flame. "I want to stay here," she said, "until things are cleared up, or until we know definitely that they can't be cleared up. I won't be of much comfort to Mother—I'm not sentimental enough—and I may be of help to Mr. Harris and Ken."

"But unchaperoned—" began Miss Case.

"I should like to break in on this for a moment," interrupted Father, "and turn the conversation for a second, and I think it will settle itself."

We all looked up at him eagerly.

"Just listen, please," he went on. "The centre of the investigation is necessarily here, you'll all agree, even though, for the moment, it seems to have shifted, through this business of the letter, to Boston. Kenneth and I could tell you, though we'd rather not just at present, that there are definite suspicions resting on at least one person here in Hanover, and the work must be done here. And while I am not in any position to order that no one connected with the case shall leave town, I should like to so order it. Instead, I request that neither Miss Coates nor Miss Case go for the next day or two."

Miss Case was silent. "I like that request," said Jean.

"Someone," Father continued, "must accompany Byron's body, of course, but I think I have an idea for that." He paused for a moment. "I should like to. I can't, but I should like to interview Mrs. Coates."

"No!" cried Jean. "Excuse me, Mr. Harris, but you wouldn't get a thing out of her. You'd scare her to death."

"I fear I realize that," replied Father. "I have an unfortunate habit of being forbidding. But Mrs. Coates has got to be interviewed at once."

"Why?" I asked.

"The secret of Byron's death," Father answered, "is probably unknown to Mrs. Coates. Just the same, she wrote him a letter which reached him on the day he died. And now she wants that letter destroyed."

"It was a birthday letter," said Miss Case

"It was more than that," corrected Father. "It was a twenty-first birthday letter, and more than likely it unlocked the family cupboard and revealed the skeleton."

"If any," put in Jean.

"And I think," Father pursued, ignoring her remark, "that Kenneth is the logical one to conduct the interview."

"Oh, Father!" I cried. "I couldn't, really!"

"You don't know Mrs. Coates, I realize," said Father. "But on the other hand, you're the one stranger (and it must be a stranger) who is close to the family. You are Byron's nearest friend and she will talk to you if she will talk to anyone. You must tell her that Miss Case faithfully tried to carry out the orders in the wire, but, finding nothing, took you into her confidence and asked for your help in finding the letter. But that it had disappeared. You must ask her, somehow, for its contents. And every other means failing, you must tell her that it was murder and not suicide."

"Suicide!" I exclaimed.

"Yes," said Father. "Don't forget that Byron's mother still thinks, if they have kept the morning papers from her, as I suppose they have if she is hysterical, that Byron committed suicide."

"That's right," said Miss Case.

"And what's more," Father went on, "considering her 'phone message and her telegram to Miss Case, and the incident of Byron when he was still at St. Paul's, she believes that the contents of her birthday letter drove her son to kill himself. And we must know what she dared to tell him!"

# CHAPTER XIII
## MONDAY: A MOTHER

BOSTON, WHEN I ARRIVED shortly after eight o'clock that night, was damp and cold and bathed in November fog. The ride down had seemed interminable even though I had tried to occupy my mind by going over, a hundred times, the things I was planning to say to Byron's mother. But even with all my thinking I couldn't decide definitely what tone to take—whether to be cheery and comforting, or sadly reminiscent, or formal as Father would be, or even downright forbidding and accusing.

I took a cab directly to the Hotel Bellevue, choosing it for its position on Beacon Hill and therefore its nearness to the Coates home. I was hungry but it was getting late and I decided not to eat until afterward, so I merely washed the railroad dust from my face and hands, asked the way to Chestnut Street from the desk clerk, and went out onto Beacon Street.

A cold wind was sweeping up from the river, rattling the bare limbs of the great trees on the Common, and the State House rose beside me like a huge white ghost. I found the entrance to Walnut Street and climbed its steep incline, and there, dipping sharply down to the left, was Chestnut Street with its double row of charming old houses, their front windows all cheerfully aglow.

I found the Coateses number and stepped off the sidewalk to look at it in the light of an inadequate street lamp. It was a lovely little house. I remember Byron telling me that it was a genuine Bullfinch, one of the very few private buildings left in Boston which are authenticated. There was a light in the hall, streaming out into the fog from the fanlight over the dark door with its glistening brass knocker, and there was a light in an upstairs room. Otherwise the house was dark, though for a moment I thought I caught the gleam of a fire under the half-drawn shades of the living room. But I knew I should be admitted. Miss Case had 'phoned when, after much more talk than I have recorded, it was finally decided that I should be the envoy.

I rang the bell. I wanted to use the knocker but didn't quite dare, and almost immediately the light over the steps was switched on, revealing the brass plate with the name "Coates." A maid let me in—not a trim and young little thing, but a middle-aged woman whose white hair ruffle looked a bit incongruous.

"Mr. Harris," I said. "I think Mrs. Coates is expecting me."

"Yes," she said, and ushered me into a charming white hall from which one of the most graceful staircases I have ever seen went curving upward. "You are to come in here," she said, leading the way into the living room and switching on two table lamps. "Mrs. Coates apologizes for the formality but the library is being done over and the fire in here sometimes smokes."

"Is Mrs. Coates well?" I asked.

"No," she said, "but she wants to see you. The nurse will let her come down for a little while. And the nurse asked me in private to tell you not to excite her. I'll tell her you're here." She went out and I heard her going up the stairs.

It was a beautiful room, white, high-ceilinged, furnished in perfect taste with either genuine antiques or perfect reproductions; and the glow of the fire and the two graceful lamps made every-thing delightfully soft and warm. But there was one incongruous note which caught my eye the moment I was seated. Sprawling in the angle of a Sheraton sofa was a great crimson and green doll, thoroughly jazz, with its long stuffed arms and legs tied into the most grotesque of knots. It most obviously said, "I am Marion Coates. The rest of the room is a very expensive decorator."

I heard a soft voice and the rustle of silk on the staircase, and I rose to face the door. She came and stood in it and posed. I am sure she posed.

She was one of the most beautiful women I have ever seen, even though I instinctively felt that brighter lights would have showed lines at her eyes. Her hair was raven-black and knotted low at the back of her neck. She had Byron's eyes, I saw, but it was Jean's face with the pertness gone and much more beauty added. She was dressed in some sort of formal negligee—a *peignoir*, I supposed—of close shining black with a ruffle of bright green about the low neck. She carried a tiny green silk handkerchief, edged in black.

"Kenneth Harris," she said, and came toward me with an outstretched hand. I took it, somehow feeling that she intended me to kiss it. Instead I pressed it and murmured something.

"You're like your pictures," she said, "but handsomer." She flashed a smile that showed teeth as even as Byron's. I saw in a moment that she was playing, and that evidently, despite her grief, she had a desire to keep Byron out of the conversation as long as possible.

We sat down then, I near the fire, and she on the sofa where she slipped an arm about the hideous doll and hugged it to her side.

I don't remember, really, how the conversation began, but it was not easy. It was mostly, I think, questions from her about my family, such as, "Byron, I remember, told me you had a sister. How old is she?"

It was fifteen minutes or so before Byron's death was directly mentioned by either of us, and then she gave a genuine and convulsive sob into her handkerchief and turned back to me with tears standing in her lovely eyes.

"Tell me about him," she said. "Where is he?"

"At Waterman's funeral rooms," I said.

"I shan't see him," she sobbed. "I couldn't stand it."

I watched her for a moment in silence while she dabbed at her eyes. Then she spoke in a new tone, deeper than the other and more reserved.

"I'm going to try not to be sentimental. You are kind to come and you have enough grief of your own. I want you to tell me, in detail, how he died. The nurse wouldn't let me see the papers all day and I know nothing. But I'm much stronger to-night. I'm always stronger at night."

What should I tell her? The truth? Or should I wait until I saw her attitude toward the letter when I could bring it gracefully into the conversation. I made up my mind quickly.

"He was hanging, Mrs. Coates," I said, in as gentle a tone as I could assume, "on the rope from our window that is used as a fire escape. I found him."

She paled and turned her head away. "What a terrible death!" she breathed. "And how awful for you. And for Jean," she added, facing me again. "Did Jean see him?"

"No," I answered. "We thought it better not to let her."

She switched the subject for a moment. "Jean is well?"

"Very well," I replied. "She thought that her coming home now would only make it harder for you. We talked it all over and Miss Case finally agreed that they should stay on for a few days."

"They are right," she said. "This house is no place for a young girl. The reporters ring the bell constantly and they have been taking pictures outside. We wouldn't let anyone in."

How to broach the subject! It was constantly on my mind.

"Byron was such a happy boy," she said, after a short pause. "He was a funny little thing as a child. Have you ever seen his pictures?"

I shook my head.

"Then do get that book, the big black one on the table there, and bring it over here. I must show you." She was actually vivacious.

It was the album, the one Jean had spoken of, heavy and leather-bound. I carried it to the sofa and sat beside her while she took it in her lap and let the crimson doll fall head first and sprawling on the floor at her feet. She opened the book and began to point pictures out to me.

Byron at the age of three on the beach with a pail and shovel. Byron squinting at the sun in a sailor suit at the age of seven. Byron and Jean on the backs of donkeys in some formal-looking park. Byron embarrassed in what were evidently his first long trousers, with an antedated collar and a stringy tie and a hat set on the back of his head. We turned the thick leaves. It was Byron, Byron, Byron. Now and then Jean, but nowhere near so often. We went 'way up to Byron's college days and I saw pictures of myself and the one I liked best of all, of Byron and me seated, apparently in earnest conversation, at an outdoor table in Munich with two foaming steins of beer before us.

We went back again, to Byron's baby pictures, and I noticed that now and then half the picture would be either cut away or inked out. I asked Mrs. Coates about them. "I was there originally," she said, "but I looked awful and disposed of myself."

"But if you want to see me," she went on, flipping the pages to the very front of the book, "look at these."

They were evidently professional photographs, mostly with foreign imprints, showing her radiant—sometimes arch and cute, sometimes studiedly pensive, sometimes in costume, and once naked, clutching a white fur to her bosom—but always overwhelmingly beautiful.

"Wasn't I charming?" she asked. "Would you have loved me?"

"You were lovely," I agreed, and immediately regretted the past tense which I didn't mean at all. She was just as lovely now and there was a perfume about her which was going to my head. "Jean looks like you, in a way," I said.

" Jean lacks femininity," she answered. "All modern girls do."

"And Byron," I went on, "takes after his grandfather, Jean tells me."

"Yes," she said, "my father. I have only one picture of him, taken when he was nineteen." She turned the pages again and showed it to me. It was stiff and formal and taken with the young man leaning on a marble-topped photographer's table, but it was Byron to the life, the same curl of hair, the same sensitive mouth. She let me look at it for a long time and then she turned to the picture of a short, stubby man with a walrus moustache and a choker collar. "This was Mr. Coates, Byron's father."

I couldn't suppress a chuckle. It was even funnier than Jean had said. "He didn't leave his imprint on the family at all," I remarked.

"No," she said, "the children were all Morrison."

"That was your name?" I asked. "Marion Morrison?"

"Not on the stage," she said. "My stage name was Marie Fleuron. It was a gesture toward the French managers, and it helped here, too."

"Byron used to hum and sing all sorts of foreign songs," I told her. "I suppose they were yours. There was one in particular—"

She jumped up and the album crashed to the floor. "It was this one!" she cried. "I bet it was this one." She pulled back the curtains over the wide door into the room beyond and disappeared into the darkness.

I bent down and picked up the album. The leaves whirled past me and I caught a tiny fleeting glimpse of a face I knew—a full-sized portrait, terribly familiar, yet I couldn't place it. I turned some pages over and turned them back again, but I couldn't find it, and she was calling me.

"Come in here, Kenneth Harris," she called, and struck a chord.

Reluctantly I obeyed her, and stood in the bend of the great piano. She hadn't put the lights on, and all I could see in the glow from the living room was the white of her face and her moving hands.

She sang the song I had heard Byron sing a score of times, a tripping little French marching song with an interval of sentimental serenade. . . . "*Un soldat vient à la porte.* . . ." She sang it marvelously, in a rich contralto with a perfect accent and a dozen little tricks of voice that showed her to be an actress of ability. But when she came to the final verse, where the barmaid sings the slow waltz that despairs of her lover's return (just before the march begins again and another soldier comes to the door), she broke into sobs, stopped playing in the middle of a measure, and laid her beautiful head on the piano.

"He liked it best of all," she sobbed. "I taught it to him and he loved it. . . . And then I killed him!"

I went to her and took her gently by the shoulders, trying to lift her and take her back into the light. "Please, Mrs. Coates," I said. "Please! You know that you're not to blame at all."

She raised her head. "But I am!" she cried. "You don't know! You haven't any idea!"

"How?" I asked. "Tell me how?"

She wiped the tears from her eyes, not by dabbing at them as she had before, but with a quick firm movement. Then she rose and stood with her back to the piano, her hands shutting the keyboard behind her.

"By being a sinful woman!" she said, and her tone dared me to contradict her. Immediately she brushed by me and walked into the living room, the silk whispering about her. I followed, and together we stood in front of the fireplace.

"I don't understand, Mrs. Coates," I said quietly. She must, if possible, be made to mention the letter herself.

"You couldn't understand, Kenneth," she replied, "because you don't know how Byron worshipped me.

"Yes I do," I told her, but I didn't tell her how recently I had found it out. "You were perfection in his eyes."

She began to cry again, but not harshly, and she stared at the fading fire. "Once, years ago," she said, "Byron caught me in a slight indiscretion—very slight—and he almost took his life in the disappointment and the shame."

"I know," I said.

She looked at me, startled. "How do you know?" she demanded.

"Byron told me," I lied. "He told me everything."

There was almost terror in her eyes. "Did he show you my letter, then?" she cried.

"What letter?" I tried to be calm.

"His birthday letter! The one he got Saturday: Did he show you that?" She caught at my shoulders.

"No," I said. "Should I have seen it?"

"No one should have seen it!" she cried. "I should never have written it!" And while I waited in silence she went on: "But I thought he was a man now and could understand things, and forgive things." She began to cry again, "Instead, he paid me back by killing himself!"

I led her to the sofa and sat beside her, holding one of her hands in mine.

"Tell me about it," I pleaded. "I was very close to Byron, and I'm just his age. Tell me, and let me see how it affected him, if I can."

She shook her head violently, "Never," she said. "It shall never be told again. The letter has been destroyed now. I wired and saw to that."

I tried once more. "It might help to relieve your mind."

She shook her head again. "Nothing can ever relieve my mind."

I knew then that I should have to tell her everything, and the decision brought a curious cruelty with it.

"I have to tell you something now, Mrs. Coates," I began. "The letter has not been destroyed unless Byron destroyed it before his death, which would not be like him."

"What do you mean?" Her voice was dead.

"Miss Case tried to honour your telegram but there was no letter to be found. The desk was broken into the night before it was searched."

"Who wanted it?" she cried. "Tell me that! Who wanted it?"

I caught her other hand and held both of them tightly.

"I don't know," I said. "None of us knows and we wish we did. Because—take this quietly, Mrs. Coates—Byron did not kill himself. He was really—murdered. And the murderer wanted the letter!"

She shrieked and cried out, but it was not the news of the death that affected her, because the word that she cried was "Blackmail!"

There was the sound of running feet along the corridors upstairs and I knew I had to hurry.

"Quickly, Mrs. Coates," I said. "Don't you see it's all important that we know what was in the letter so that we can know who could have wanted it? Tell me. I'll see that the newspapers don't get hold of it."

It was an unfortunate choice of words.

"The newspapers!" she screamed, and then she pushed me away from her and lay face down on the sofa in a fit of violent sobbing.

The footsteps raced down the stairs and the nurse came rushing in, followed by the maid. They paid no attention to me but hurried to the woman who was crying terribly, in hysterical shrieks and gasps and trying to talk at the same time.

I could catch a word here and there: "Byron" . . . "built us all a quiet home" . . . "newspapers."

Slowly the two women raised her from the couch and led her, still crying and talking and moaning, from the room.

I stood in the door and watched their slow ascent of the stairs, and for a long time afterward I still stood there, trembling all over, my mind racing madly, until the maid came down again.

"I'll 'phone for a taxi," she said.

I was not sane enough to tell her that my hotel was only five minutes' walk away, and I let her 'phone before I realized, and then I heard her 'phone the doctor.

"Will you let yourself out, please?" she asked as she passed me, "I have to go up again. Mrs. Coates is in a terrible state."

I nodded and she hurried up the stairs.

Slowly I put my hat and coat on. Defeat! I thought. I had learned nothing except that the letter seemed more important than ever.

I walked into the living room and sat on the sofa waiting until I should hear the arrival of the cab. And then suddenly I grabbed the album and turned the pages rapidly.

It was in the front of the book that I caught the glimpse of the face I knew. It shouldn't be hard to find.

There it was! I passed it and had to turn back again.

Head and shoulders of a good-looking young man, old-fashioned and a bit laughable. And familiar—so very familiar. But who was it?

In the lower right-hand corner were the words: "To Marie from Joe. Paris, 1899."

I knew! We had the same picture in an album at home.

It was my father!

# CHAPTER XIV
## TUESDAY: SLAUGHTER

THE TELEPHONE WOKE ME the next morning. "It's eight o'clock," said the operator.

"Thank you!"

Still half asleep, I was staring down from my window at the gray Common lying under the gold of the State House dome when the telephone rang again.

"Is this Mr. Kenneth Harris?"

"Yes."

"This is Dr. Fernald, Mrs. Coates's doctor."

"Yes? How is Mrs. Coates?"

"She had a very bad night but is much better this morning. However, I'm calling you to ask you not to try to see her to-day at all. Both she and I think it would be unwise."

"Are you calling at her request, Doctor, or on your own behalf?"

"Why," hesitated the doctor, "she asked me to 'phone, but I am firmly of the opinion that she should see no one."

"How did you know I was at the Bellevue?"

"Mrs. Coates asked her maid to call the various hotels until she found you. Mrs. Coates knew there was a nine o'clock train north and thought you'd like to take it if you knew early that she wasn't well enough to be seen."

"Thank you. Good-bye. Tell Mrs. Coates I shall take the nine o'clock."

So she was anxious to make sure that I left town and couldn't corner her again. Perhaps she was wise in 'phoning me. Before I went to sleep I had thought of trying to see her again, not so much to hound her again on the subject of the letter as to put the murder aside and satisfy my curiosity about Father's picture. Why was it there, and what connection did it have with the terrible events at Hanover?

I caught the nine o'clock easily enough and found a Pullman seat, loading myself down with every newspaper I could buy. Although it was the second day of the news, they were all still screaming with the Dartmouth Murders. All of them carried pictures of Byron and Sam and the *Herald* printed mine: "Roommate of the murdered Coates who found the body hanging outside the window." It was, I noticed, the picture I had recently had taken for the *Ægis*, the senior yearbook. There were pictures of North Mass. Hall and the chapel and diagrams of our rooms. But the material was scanty. Father, I judged, had talked a bit with reporters, but most of the facts, essentially correct, seemed to have come from the sheriff. No personalities, I discovered with relief, were dragged into it at all, nor did Jean's picture appear. Mrs. Coates was referred to, but nothing was said of her past life. She was called "honoured resident of the fashionable Beacon Hill district," and I hoped she would see it. It would please her tremendously.

At Concord a fellow I knew by sight but not by name got on and took a chair diagonally from me. I saw him turn around and look at me once or twice, and finally when he caught my eye, I nodded. He came over and stood beside me.

"You're Ken Harris, aren't you?" he asked.

"Yes," I said.

"I'm Sid Campbell. Sophomore."

"I've seen you around," I said, and shook hands with him. "What house?"

"Chi Phi," he answered, as I motioned for him to sit on the arm of my chair.

"I had a girl up for the game," he said, "and brought her down to Concord Sunday afternoon. I cut Monday and I'm just getting back. We left Hanover before," he paused to swallow, rather embarrassed, "before Sam Anderson died. I didn't know it until I saw the papers. I didn't even know about By Coates."

"I've just come from taking By to Boston."

"I'm awfully sorry, Harris," he said.

"Thanks," I replied.

"It's making an awful stink," he went on. "It won't do the college any good."

"I guess you're right," I said. I wished he would go back to his own chair and let me alone.

"By Coates's sister was up, wasn't she?" he asked.

"Yes," I answered. "She's still there."

"Cute kid."

I said nothing.

"What is she, pretty fast?"

I looked at him quickly and then turned away. "I don't know her very well."

"I don't know her either," he said, "but I saw her Saturday night. She seemed to be having a great old time."

Saturday night! Where was Jean Saturday night?

I made believe chuckle a bit. "Where was this?" I asked. "At the Inn?"

"Hell no!" he laughed. "Peggy—that's the girl I had up—and I went looking for excitement and skipped the crowd at the house. It was an awfully dumb bunch. We got a car and went out to Sans Souci." He grinned with one of those knowing grins and I detested him. And I knew what was coming and was trembling a little, but all I said was, "That's pretty dangerous during house party."

"Yeah," he said. "We knew it, but we wanted excitement. There was quite a gang there, anyway. They wouldn't have fired the whole bunch."

"They would if they caught you," I put in.

"Well, there hasn't been any rumpus so far. And Peggy isn't in school, anyway, so it didn't make a hell of a lot of difference to her. But it certainly was lively. Lots of liquor and pretty good music. Radio. And I noticed this dark-haired kid that was stepping out quite a bit, and I asked somebody who it was. He said it was By Coates's sister."

Bang! So that's where Jean was!

"Who'd you ask?" I inquired, as calmly as I could. "Mind telling me? I didn't know many people knew her."

"I asked John Meseraux. Said he was going to try to get a dance with her later."

I was silent for so long that he finally got up to go. "Glad to have seen you," he said, shaking my hand. "Drop down to the house some time."

"Thanks," I replied. "I will."

He went back to his own seat, and I settled back to stare out of the window. But five minutes later I rose and crossed the aisle. "Oh, Campbell," I said. "Do you happen to know who Jean Coates was with at Sans Souci? I'd rather like to know who was rushing her."

"No," he said, "I don't. She was dancing with a lot of different guys. I didn't make out who had brought her."

"You never got a dance with her?"

"No. I missed out."

"I suppose Meseraux did, though!"

"I don't know. He might have. I didn't watch her much. Peggy and I went out for a ride and when we came back the Coates girl had gone."

"Had Meseraux gone, too?"

"I don't remember. At least I don't remember seeing him around after that. But why all the details?"

"Oh, no reason in particular," I said. "Just inquisitive."

Now there, on top of the discovery of Father's picture, was something more to think about. It was silly, I knew, to fasten upon every single act that any one of us did, and to try to link it up with Byron's death, but I couldn't help it. And I leaned my chin on my hand and stared at the passing hills and tried to think. I decided, eventually, that I shouldn't confront Father with the presence of his picture in the Coates album. If it meant anything at all, and I was sure it didn't, though I was curious to the bursting point, it would be much better to wait and watch his actions. Perhaps more carefully than I had before. Perhaps even to try to connect that pin prick he made through the organ in the back of my neck with the fact that he was somehow in Mrs. Coates's past, and therefore in Byron's.

And what was Jean doing at Sans Souci, pleading a sore throat and rushing off to that notorious place? Vassar, strictest of all, would fire her in a minute if the authorities learned. But that wasn't the point. What was she doing in the house of John Meseraux? I decided to confront her with it at the first opportunity, on the plea that I was merely entreating her to be careful.

Charlie Penlon met me at White River Junction, as I had expected he would, and in my own car. I was glad to see him and glad, too, that Campbell disappeared as soon as the train was in. I had no desire to be compelled to ask him to ride those last five miles to Hanover with us, and to listen to his chatter on the way.

Charlie looked around the platform as I greeted him. "Mrs. Coates didn't come with you?" he asked.

"Why no," I answered in surprise. "You didn't expect her to, did you?"

"I didn't," he replied, "but your father gave a guess last night that she would. Miss Case disputed him, though. How did you come out with her?"

I told him how fruitless the whole journey had been, except for the knowledge I had obtained of her character and her curious selfish devotion to Byron.

"What news here?" I asked, as we swung out of the town and started to follow the river to the college.

"Little or none," said Charlie. "I dined up at Bossy's with your father and the women, and nothing much was said."

"Was Father decent to them?" I asked, wondering if he had yet found the opportunity to question Jean on her coming in late.

"Awfully decent," Charlie replied. "Quite jovial, in fact. Full of rather weak wise-cracks. We talked mostly about how you were faring in Boston, and then he made the remark about your bringing Mrs. Coates back with you. The whole table looked worried, or else I imagined it."

"How is Jean?"

"Well. She's a great kid."

"And Bossy?"

"Bossy left this morning for a couple of days."

"Left!"

"Yes. I was up there quite early, just as they were finishing breakfast, and a wire came asking him to play at some sort of concert at Mount Holyoke tonight. The regular organist disappointed them or something like that. Anyway, he left on the late morning train. I drove him to the station. So," Charlie went on, "Jean and Miss Case have moved up to his house. It was silly of them not to in the first place. And now there's plenty of room."

"No other news? No developments? How about Meseraux?"

"Nothing there," Charlie answered. "Your father got a report this morning from the sheriff. He's had Meseraux practically shadowed all the time. Meseraux went right to the Coffee Room for lunch after English class, and then to biology, and then worked for an hour in the lab, etherizing and counting banana flies. Then he walked down to the gym and watched football practice for a while, went in swimming for about ten minutes, and finally got in his Ford, parked in back of Dartmouth Hall, and drove home. He didn't leave the house again until this morning. That's all."

"I'm afraid that's the way it will always be," I said. "Lots of thinking on everybody's part, and no action, and no solving."

"Well, I don't know," said Charlie. "Your father's got some sort of clue, and it concerns me, I think."

"What, Charlie!"

"I can't quite make out. But last night he and I were sitting in Bossy's living room after dinner. Jean and Miss Case had gone back to the Inn and Bossy was off somewhere. Your father took something out of an envelope in his pocket and stared at it for a long time while I kept silent."

"It was probably the needle," I said.

"That's what I thought," said Charlie. "Anyway," he went on, "at last he looked up and said, 'Penlon, do you happen to know any acquaintance of Byron's who comes from Chicago or Kansas City?'

'Why yes,' I said. 'Why?' He looked at me very sternly and said, 'I asked you a simple question, Penlon. Never mind why!' I looked at him squarely and said, 'Well, Mr. Harris, I come from Kansas City and Jerry Dawes comes from Chicago. There are two.' He didn't say a word but put the needle or whatever it was back into his pocket and got up and switched the light off. 'Good-night, Penlon,' he said, and went away leaving me in the dark."

"And what did that all mean?" I asked.

"I haven't the faintest idea," Charlie answered, "but I rather wish you'd try to find out. There's something on his mind. That's sure."

We climbed the last long hill and entered Hanover, speeding up Main Street toward the campus.

"Where to?" asked Charlie.

"North Mass.," I said. "I'll leave my bags and then try to find Father."

Father was in my room, standing with his hands behind his back and facing a gentleman who sat in the desk chair, looking at him. I recognized the gentleman as Professor Brand, Byron's instructor in economics.

Father glanced around as I entered, saw who it was but without a word of greeting, motioned for me to sit down, and then turned to the professor:

"Describe this instrument, please, Professor. Listen carefully to this, Kenneth."

I listened, wondering wildly what it was all about.

"It's a complicated thing and rather difficult to describe," said the professor. "It looks a bit like one of the old-fashioned horse pistols, except that there are many more bits of apparatus around the trigger—and it is made of nickel, or polished steel. Silver-coloured, not dark like a revolver. It shoots, by means of tremen-dously powerful springs, thin steel needles. Some models, I under-stand, use compressed air, but this is worked by springs."

My eyes widened. What had Father found? I couldn't suppress a cry: "What is this?"

"Would you mind telling again, Professor, for Kenneth's benefit?"

"Not at all," said the professor. He looked at me. "I have been away for the weekend and just now got back. I came to see your father after I'd been to the president with some information I thought might be valuable. From the descriptions in the press, as well as something that happened in class, I rather connected the needles found in the brains of the two dead boys with those which I displayed in class Saturday morning."

"Saturday morning!" I echoed.

"Yes," he continued. "We, as perhaps you know from your roommate, who is in my class, have been studying some of the larger industries in the country, as completely as possible. And lately we have been dealing with meat-packing and the slaughter houses."

"I know that!" I cried, seeing light.

"As it happens, I have done a bit of humanitarian work among the slaughter-house men—S.P.C.A. stuff mostly, articles on this and that method. And last week one of the big Kansas City houses sent me a new invention that they have adopted in the killing of cattle, hoping, I suppose, I might write an article that would give them publicity. It has superseded, with them, all the old methods—the hammer, the axe, the vein-cutting—even the modern steel pin and driving hammer. I was describing it as you came in. It is much like a large pistol, only it shoots with terrific force thin steel needles, by means of springs, into the brain of the animal, up under the skull. Death is instantaneous—and, they claim, therefore painless."

"You took it to class!" I cried.

"Yes," he said. "On Saturday. I was talking about the older methods and explaining the new. And I demonstrated. I even inserted a needle and shot it into the wood work, before the class."

I stared at Professor Brand in silence, but Father, in his cool, even voice, said:

"Go on Professor. Tell the rest."

"Well," said the professor. "I had just finished telling your father that after the class Byron Coates came up to the desk and asked me if he might borrow the instrument for over the week-end. He said he was interested in such things and would like to make drawings, and perhaps write something about it. I let him take it."

"And how many needles?" asked Father.

"Three," said Professor Brand.

## CHAPTER XV
## TUESDAY: BYRON'S DAY

FATHER REACHED IN HIS POCKET and from an envelope took the bit of steel we had found inside the organ. He handed it to Professor Brand. "And is this one of them?" he asked.

The professor examined it only for a moment, and then gave it back. "Yes," he said. "It is either one of the three needles I displayed in class, or it is another of the very same kind. There is no doubt of that."

Father turned on me. "I was right, Kenneth, after all."

"What do you mean, right?" I asked.

"I concentrated last night on this needle. I pictured every possible means by which it might be projected under a man's skull with force enough to kill—and yet remain embedded deep enough to be invisible, showing that some handle, permanent or removable, had been used. I knew, or at least I guessed, that no one would take the trouble to make such an instrument just for murder's sake, when there are a dozen easier ways. Such an instrument was already made, and somehow obtainable. But what was it legitimately used for? Death, naturally, to something, but not to man. . . . And so I thought of the slaughter houses, and somewhere from my memory I dug the recollection of having read that such a machine was in process of being patented—quick, sure, practically painless because of its swiftness. I even went so far as to imagine the possibility of some undergraduate whose father, perhaps, was a meat-packer, sending for the instrument under some pretext and using it on the two boys. I asked Penlon, just as a test question, if he knew anyone from Chicago or Kansas City."

"He rather got back at you there," I said. "He told you he was from Kansas City himself."

"I know," said Father. "But there is no need for suspecting him on that score any longer."

"Professor Brand," he continued, "do you happen to remember young Coates's attitude in class Saturday morning? What I mean is, did you happen to notice anything out of the ordinary?"

"Nothing out of the ordinary," remarked the professor, "but I do remember his attitude. It was serious and attentive. I noticed that he was one of the very few in the room who were taking notes when I was talking about the older methods of slaughter. I happened to remark, when I saw him and one or two others writing, that there was no need for note-taking, that I had just brought the subject up for its interest's sake and that it was distinctly a side-line to the course. I merely thought the class might be as fascinated as I was by the presence of the needle-gun. They were. And I noticed that all of them stopped taking notes when I spoke. We discussed the various methods back and forth and I answered a few questions."

"Did Coates ask any questions?"

"Yes," said the professor. "Let me see if I can remember what he asked." He laid his fingers to his forehead. "Oh, yes, I remember. He asked if the spring was strong enough to propel the needle through the skull of cattle. I told him I didn't believe so, but that the report I had received with the gun told of shooting it up under the skull, through the neck. I don't remember that he said anything else until he came up after class and asked to borrow the gun. I gave it to him, naturally, without any questioning."

"Would you have given it to anybody who asked you?"

"No," the professor replied. "I thought of that afterward. There are two or three in the class, irresponsible sort of boys, that I probably should have refused. But Coates was serious and steady-going. I didn't hesitate at all."

"Did he carry it away with him immediately?" asked Father.

"Yes."

"Wrapped up?"

"In a box which was made for it. And inside was a smaller box, such as a fountain pen comes in, containing the three needles."

When Professor Brand had gone, Father and I stood looking at each other.

"What did Byron want it for?" I asked.

Father didn't answer but turned to the desk. "Find me Byron's notebook," he ordered. "The one he took to economics class Saturday morning."

I found it immediately. It was still lying on top of his desk. It was loose-leaf, bound in black leather, and I knew that shiny brown cardboard pages separated the notes of one course from those of another. I turned rapidly to the section on economics and flipped the pages open until I came to the end. At the top was written: "Sat. Lect. Meat Industry."

A few notes followed, not more than seven or eight lines, listing the older methods of slaughter, and then the item:

> Newest method, adopted by some leading houses. Gun which shoots sharp steel needle. Worked by powerful springs and trigger. Sure instantaneous death if used by expert. Under cranium into brain. Practically bloodless.

"Sane and direct enough," I remarked. "He was paying attention all right."

"He was fascinated, very likely," said Father.

Suddenly he grabbed the notebook and held it close to his eyes. Then he rubbed a spot on the page with his finger, very lightly. He put the notebook, flat open, on the top of the desk and turned to me.

"Do you remember Byron's early decision on suicide, Kenneth?" he asked.

"Of course," I said.

"He wrote a note, didn't he?"

"Yes. His mother found it later."

"I have found another," announced Father. "See," he pointed to a spot on the notebook page, on a line which looked blank to me. "It's written in pencil and then erased, but the impression is left. Bend down and look."

I followed his directions. Plainly I could see that something had been written in hard pencil—probably his silver one—and then rubbed out.

"Can you make it out?" Father cried.

"There's a capital G," I said. "And the other word is K something."

"That's right," said Father. "It's *'Good-bye Ken'!*"

I looked again. He was right, and I could make out the letters plainly.

"It is!" I cried. "It is the beginning of a suicide note!"

"Tell me how you think it fits in," said Father; "fits in with the economics class, I mean."

"That's easy," I replied. "Byron's whole last morning is quite clear now. His whole day, in fact!"

"Piece it together, Kenneth. We'll see if we agree."

"It was the day before his birthday," I began, "and he was expecting, naturally, that the letter from his mother would come that day instead of Monday. He was anxious for it, of course, and a little bit excited. He didn't wait in the room for the mail to come, but went and met the mail man at the top of the stairs. He got the letter—"

"He received two letters," Father interrupted.

"One was just the Campion receipt," I said.

"Leave out nothing, Kenneth. Go on."

"He took the two letters back to the room, and opened them both. One was the receipt. One was from his mother. What was in it we don't know. But it had to do with family affairs. It concerned both himself and his mother, probably."

"How did it concern himself?" asked Father.

"About his money, probably," I answered. "We have every reason to believe that on the next day he would come into quite a good deal."

"And how did it concern his mother?" Father asked.

"We don't know exactly how. But we are pretty sure it did, and that it concerned her rather scandalously."

"How do you know that?" Father's sentence was an exclamation and he dropped the routine tone in which he had asked the other questions which were merely Socratic.

"Because," I said, "I discovered in Boston that what was affecting Mrs. Coates more, perhaps, than the death of Byron, was the fear of the papers and the public getting hold of that letter."

"But she told you none of the contents?"

"None at all. Not a hint. But she was dead sure that the letter had driven Byron to suicide until I told her the facts."

"And then what?" Father was tremendously interested.

"Then hysterics," I said. "But not until I had told her that Miss Case had not destroyed the letter and that it was nowhere to be found."

"But she gave you not a single clue?" Father pursued.

"Not one."

"Then go on. Go back to Byron."

"Byron read the letter," I continued. "It *was* upsetting, tremendously so, and it did somehow show his mother in a disappointing light—perhaps very much the same light as the one in which he had seen her some years ago when he came back from the concert. And it affected him in very much the same way. It threw him into the dumps, hard. He dropped into his desk chair and stared at the floor. And he stayed there, thinking and thinking until I came in. I asked him if he wasn't going to economics class and if he had any mail. He growled, 'Too damn' much,' and grabbed his notebook and went."

"Keep on, Kenneth. This is splendid."

"He went to class. Already, perhaps, while he was sitting in the chair, he had thought a little about suicide. How much, I don't know. But it had entered his head, because his mother had disappointed him again, and he remembered what he did the last time. But I don't think he thought of it seriously until Professor Brand displayed that needle-gun. He was fascinated. He followed it closely, taking more notes, perhaps, than were necessary because he wanted to bend over his paper and not show what he was thinking."

"That's stretching the imagination a bit, Kenneth," cautioned Father.

"It's logical, anyway," I said, and went on: "I don't know whether, during the class, he actually decided on suicide or not, but at least he saw the possibility. He inquired of Professor Brand how the thing worked—whether, that is, it was shot through the skull, and then he sat in silence, just listening. He had put his fountain pen away when the professor told him that notes were not necessary. Suicide, either definitely plotted or hastily considered, ran through his head, and his mind went back to that other time when he had taken a revolver and lain on the bed. And he had written a note. So now he reached in his pocket and took out his pencil, remembering that I should probably be the one to find the body. And he penciled on his page, under the notes, the beginning of a suicide letter: 'Goodbye, Ken.'"

I felt tears coming to my eyes and had to stop a minute.

"Almost immediately he rubbed it out. It was a little foolish. It was just a sentimental moment anyway. But the idea was still in his mind, and after class he went up to Professor Brand, asking to borrow the gun. Perhaps he even asked that question earlier in the class to make his interest in borrowing it seem more natural. He had no trouble anyway, and took it away with him."

"Where did he take it?"

"To this room, undoubtedly. And put it, box and all, into his closet or under his bed or in any one of a dozen places."

"You didn't see anything of a large, unfamiliar box?"

"No," I answered. "If I had I should have noticed it particularly and asked Byron what it was, thinking it was a birthday present."

"Go on. What time did you come back to the room?"

"Soon after twelve. Byron had come in and gone out again. I knew he'd come back from economics because I saw his notebook on the desk. So I went and ate and met him down town. Together we went and got my car and drove down to White River after Jean and Miss Case."

"What was Byron's attitude? How was he feeling?"

"He was slightly in the dumps," I answered. "I've mentioned that before. We gathered Charlie and Bossy and went to the game. All through it he wasn't very merry, and immediately afterward, as we were walking back to the campus, he asked to be excused from the tea we had planned at Bossy's. And he went right to his room. He was still thinking of the letter and all it meant. I suppose he couldn't stand our chatter."

"He didn't even join you at supper, as I understand it," said Father.

"No. I never saw him again, except when we were on our way to the Inn after the tea and I called up to him from the North Mass. portico. He stuck his head out of the window and said he guessed he wouldn't come with us at all."

"You're sure it was he?" Father asked.

I looked at Father sternly. "Are you still thinking of that?" I asked him. "Yes, I'm sure it was he. And after supper I started right off for Barre. My driving coat was in the car and I didn't go back to the dorm. at all."

"Keep on with Byron," said Father. "What about his evening?"

"It's vague. He probably went out and got himself a bite to eat somewhere and then came back to the room alone. Aside from the fact that at nine o'clock or a little after he told Bill Smart that he was going to bed in fifteen minutes, and that he had a visitor about eleven, after he was in his pajamas, we don't know a thing save that he died about midnight. And that's all."

"I think, though," said Father, "that we may be able to hazard a rather good guess as to what he did. Let me try a moment and you see what you think of it. Give me one of your cigarettes." I handed him one eagerly. It was the first time I'd ever seen him smoke anything but an after-dinner cigar. He leaned back and puffed thoughtfully for a moment or two.

"He read his letter over and over again—over and over again. He got the box out and looked at the needle-gun. He thought alternately of suicide and of living it out, knowing that disappointments are short-lived. But still, he somehow wanted to make the gesture. Think how his mother would feel! He wondered about the gun. Could he work it successfully, on the first try. Wouldn't it be hard—almost impossible—to do it himself? He welcomed the interruption of Smart's calling up from the floor below, but he wasn't courageous enough to leave the room and go down town with him.

"At last he went to bed, putting on his striped pajamas and throwing his bathrobe, as usual, over the foot of his bed. He took the gun into the bedroom with him, possibly even lying on the bed with it in his hand as, years ago, he lay with the revolver. The lights were out and he stayed awake for a long time, wondering if he dared and if it was worth it. It probably wasn't worth it. It probably was just a little thing in his mother's past, but his mother was his world, and it hurt more than you or I can realize. And still wondering, he fell asleep. . . . Filthy habit, cigarettes." He crushed it out in the ash tray on Byron's desk.

"About eleven o'clock, we know from Bill Smart, a visitor came. Sam Anderson heard the footsteps and thought it was you and a girl, so he peered out and saw the visitor. And the visitor either knocked or walked in. If he knocked, he walked in when there was no response. Byron was asleep. He switched the lights on in the study and opened the door into the bedroom and called, "Byron!" And Byron woke up with a start and asked who it was, just as the visitor switched on the bedroom light. Byron greeted him in embarrassment, because the weapon was in his hand or beside him on the bed, and the visitor exclaimed in surprise at the sight of it. Just then, or soon after, Bill Smart, hearing the footsteps above him, called up from his window again and Byron slipped on his bathrobe and went to the window, saying that he *had* been to bed but that he had a visitor and had got up again. Bill asked him if the visitor didn't want to eat and Byron laughed and said, Not a chance,' and closed the window.

"Then what happened? Did the visitor demand to know what the gun was for? Probably, and Byron told him how it was used. He perhaps even demonstrated it by holding it to the back of the visitor's neck, pointing up, under the skull. Did he hint at suicide or did his manner show it? I think he didn't. I'll tell you why in a moment. Did he tell the visitor that he was depressed because of a letter? We don't know because we think that the visitor and the letter were somehow connected, as is evidenced by the forcing of the desk the next night. But they talked at any rate.

"And then, let us say, there came a moment when, in fun (or so it seemed to Byron), the visitor handled the gun and made believe demonstrate it on the back of By's neck, getting just the right angle and possibly asking By to guide his hand. . . . And pulled the trigger which worked those powerful springs and sent the needle crashing into Byron's brain!"

I shuddered violently. "Father! You're imagining more than you have any right."

"I don't think so," said Father. "It's imagination, I admit, but it fits all the facts."

"Why," I asked, "do you think, for instance, that the visitor 'demonstrated' on Byron? Why not a sudden attack?"

"It was too accurate an aim," Father replied. "It was done slowly. I doubt if an amateur with the machine could leap forward the moment Byron's back was turned and plunge the needle home so correctly unless Byron had stood still and posed—just as Sam Anderson posed, unconsciously, in the choir loft, when the same gun was shot out between the pipes while Sam was tense and motionless, listening to the president's speech."

"All right," I said. "I grant you that. Then what?"

"Where, in the two rooms, Byron was killed we have no way of knowing, but it makes little difference. The blood flow was negligible. What little did spill, the visitor wiped up at once. Because already in his mind was the idea that he might manage to fake it as a suicide. I don't think Byron had mentioned it, or the visitor would have left the gun, hoping that the angle of the needle might be one that Byron could have achieved himself. But that hardly entered his head. He was, we must realize, in a panic of fear, even though he had premeditated it. We don't, of course, know that it was premeditated that very night, although we think it highly likely on account of the birthday. At any rate, he did a lame thing. He thought of the rope.

"But if it was to be death by rope there must be no blood of the spurting kind that the needle had loosed onto the collar of Byron's pajamas. So he rummaged in Byron's drawer and took out the plain blue ones. He stripped the body and redressed it and, not noticing the blood spots on the collar of the gray bathrobe, hung that up in what he thought was its accustomed place, the closet. You say it always lay over the foot of the bed.

"It was a hard job, but he managed finally to knot the rope, inexpertly, around Byron's neck and lower him out the window. One thing he did nicely. He calculated the fall of the rope and hitched it first through the head of Byron's bed, far from the window, so that the rope wouldn't fall its full length and dangle in front of the windows on the lower floor. It fell between two stories, Bill's and Charlie Penlon's, or almost between. It was a little low, but as luck would have it, the feet were hidden from Charlie's sight by his window shade being pulled down a foot from the top.

"As soon as that was done, the murderer fled, taking with him the deadly instrument and the pajamas, probably in the same box. He didn't know then that the instrument would be used again the next afternoon in chapel. He merely knew that if his suicide hoax was to hold, he must get the gun out of sight. It was a shoddy trick. He was unskilled. Death he had planned, but not that sort of death.

"He turned out the lights, locked the door, and went away. Where did he go? Just downstairs? Or to the Inn? Or to Etna?"

# CHAPTER XVI
## TUESDAY: DISCOVERY

WE WERE A LARGE PARTY AT DINNER that night: Miss Case, Jean, Charlie Penlon, Bill Smart, the sheriff, his man, Father, and I. Bossy's housekeeper did her New England best and put on style enough to serve us our coffee in the living room before the fire. While we were eating, a telegram came from Bossy in Holyoke, wishing us well and regretting his absence.

"A host," said Father, "should always go away if his going would inspire his cook as Professor Bostwick's housekeeper was inspired to-night." He was in genial mood. He had been genial all the afternoon, ever since he traced Byron's evening for me. He seemed pleased with himself and pleased with the progress that had been made, although I couldn't see that we had learned anything more than the kind of weapon by which the two boys had died.

Now, in the living room, the talk was general, always keeping the murders to the fore, but circling around them rather vaguely. Charlie and Jean sat together on a little settee by the fireplace, looking very handsome and surprisingly happy. I wondered that I felt no jealousy.

Father noticed them too. "Comfortable, Miss Coates?" he asked. It was mean of him, but Jean looked up with a brilliant smile.

"Entirely," she said.

"Miss Coates," Father went on, in a more serious but certainly not a stern tone, "Kenneth tells me that I frighten you. I don't want to frighten you. Kenneth tells me that I would bulldoze you if I got

146

the chance. I don't want the chance. Here, while you have the support of six neutral people, may I ask you a question? Then no one can accuse me of anything."

Jean's smile faded. "Why, of course, Mr. Harris," she said.

Father left his seat, flicked a cigar ash in the fireplace and then sat down again.

"Where were you the early part of Saturday night?"

There was well-feigned surprise in her face. "Why, I told you, Mr. Harris!" she exclaimed. "Haven't we been all over that ages ago?"

"Not thoroughly enough," Father replied. "Where were you?"

"Well," she began, "I was sitting with Miss Case in the lobby until about nine when I said I thought I'd—"

"Just a moment," interrupted Father. "Tell whatever you choose as long as it is true. But I'll give you a hint. You didn't come in until two o'clock in the morning!"

She stared at Father and changed colour a trifle. "How do you know?" she demanded.

"You were seen."

"By whom, please!" She was ready to be defiant.

"By me," said Father quietly.

Jean glanced hurriedly around the room, looking at me, at Miss Case, and finally at Charlie. I saw him, or thought I saw him, take her hand under the folds of her dress.

"Perhaps you did," she acknowledged.

"I'm sure I did," said Father. "Where had you been?"

There was absolute silence in the room.

"Had you been to Byron's room?"

"No!" she cried.

"Or at the dormitory!"

"No!"

"Not at all the whole evening?"

"No!"

"Not even at a few minutes after nine as you told me before?"

Jean's eyes fell. "No," she replied. "I made up that story. It was a poor one."

"Then will you tell us where you were?" Father pursued.

Jean looked at him again. "I'd rather not, if you don't mind. I don't see what difference it makes anyhow. I don't see what it has to do with Byron."

"I'm afraid you *don't* see, Miss Coates," said Father. "But I'm afraid I'll have to ask you to prove that you were elsewhere between nine and two."

Miss Case, I could see, was trembling a little, but she said, "I think it would be better in the end, Jean, if you told now. Mr. Harris is quite fair in asking you in public. There's no third degree."

Jean glanced once at Charlie and then turned to me. "I'm a fool, I suppose, Ken," she said, "but my first lie was really to spare your feelings. I didn't think it would get me into a mess."

"Don't mind me, Jean," I put in. "I know you were at Sans Souci."

I said it deliberately. Inasmuch as Father had gone so far, I wanted to go the rest of the way and watch the effect, and the effect was startling. Everyone, the sheriff included, leaned forward. Father's mouth dropped open and the sheriff cried: "That's the Etna place!" Jean and Charlie didn't move, save that Jean looked at me in mild surprise.

"How did you know that?" she cried.

I tried to reassure her by my tone and show her that I suspected nothing wrong of her, although I didn't know what to think. "Oh," I said laughingly, "I have my scouts."

"Then why didn't you tell me before and have this over with?"

"I didn't know it myself until to-day and I didn't see you until now."

"Please explain, Miss Coates," said Father sharply.

Charlie leaned forward. "I'll explain, Mr. Harris," he said, "and apologize to Ken at the same time. It's really on account of Ken, as Jean said, that we haven't spoken before. . . . Saturday afternoon, when Ken got that 'phone message from you during Bossy's tea, Jean said she'd go with him, even though he gave her the choice of going or staying and dancing. I was disappointed, and on the way back to the Inn we walked together and I asked her if she wouldn't reconsider and stay in town and dance somewhere with me. She said 'no,' but I argued and finally she said that she'd see, that she'd really like to, but that she felt she ought to go with Ken after she'd said she would."

"I changed my mind," said Jean. "It was a mean trick but I did it. I thought all through dinner." "That's why you were so quiet," said Miss Case.

"I suppose so. And right afterward I pleaded a sore throat to Ken and he went off alone. Almost at once I was sorry I did it, but I called up Charlie and told him to get me at nine. And at nine I left Miss Case in the lobby, got my coat, and Charlie met me out in front of the Inn."

"The rest was entirely my fault," said Charlie. "I had borrowed a car and we drove around for a long time. And while we were over near Etna I suggested, more or less jokingly, that we drop in at Sans Souci. Jean took me up and I was game. Of course, we considered the possibilities first—of being caught and kicked out of college—but we went just the same—and stayed until almost two o'clock. So you did see Jean, Mr. Harris."

"Then your story, Penlon, about drinking at your fraternity house was made up, too?" asked Father.

"Yes," admitted Charlie. "And now you see why I had my clothes on when Ken came in. I was in the bedroom getting my pajamas when I heard his steps in the corridor and recognized them. I didn't want him to find out that I'd not only stolen his girl but had taken her to Sans Souci, and I was afraid I couldn't lie well on the spur of the moment so I just doused the lights and crawled into bed. I didn't have an idea that he was going to pop into the other bed and spend the night. And I fell asleep and didn't know a thing until he yelled in the morning and we found Byron."

Everyone was looking at Father to see if he was going to believe the tale, but the sheriff broke the brief silence:

"I'd like to ask Mr. Penlon," he said, "if—"

"You needn't," interrupted Charlie. "I know what you're going to ask. The boy who lives at Sans Souci doesn't come into our story at all. He was there from shortly after midnight until we came home."

"What boy?" asked Jean, innocent and wide-eyed.

"I believe you both," said Father. "Let's change the subject."

I beamed at Jean and Charlie and they beamed back at me. In my eyes they were both vindicated entirely, and as far as I was concerned there were no hard feelings. I tried to show it in my smile and I think they caught it.

Father was talking again.

"You will be interested to know that this afternoon Kenneth and I for the first time were able to piece out, bit by bit, Byron's last day. Would you like to hear it?"

They all expressed great interest and I was rather amazed that Father, hitherto reticent even before the sheriff was going to tell everything, or practically everything we knew. And although I listened closely, I detected no omission. Now and then he had to stop and explain certain points, but he concealed nothing, not even the letter—not even the identity of the needle-gun. Those two points caught the listeners' fancy more than anything else, and when he had finished, the questions were upon him. Most of them were easy to answer, but one, which came from Bill Smart, was this:

"But, Mr. Harris, you haven't mentioned anything about Byron's disposal of the letter you know he received. You say he was reading and rereading it all the evening, or you imagine he was, and it's good imagination. What did he do with it? And if he did do anything with it, *when* did he do it?"

"I confess I can't imagine," said Father. "Some of you help me. Let's talk and think, and see what he would do?"

"Couldn't the visitor have taken it?" asked the sheriff's man.

"You forget, sir," answered Father, "that he made another visit, the next night, to get it. Whether or not he knew of its existence on Saturday night, I can't say. But on Sunday he did know, as we did, *when* we did—or at least when we suspected it—and came for a search. Luckily, through Ken's uncontemplated sorting, we know he didn't succeed."

"What about the wastebasket?" asked Miss Case. "Didn't he do the simplest thing and tear it up?"

"No," I said. "I can vouch for that. There is no waste emptied in the dorm. on Sunday. And Sunday night the wastebasket was empty as it had been since Saturday morning. I used it to dump letters into when I was sorting."

"Burn it?" suggested Jean.

"There's no fireplace," I said. "He could have done it out the window or in an ash tray, but I'm afraid you're all wrong. You must understand that it would have been the strangest thing in the world for Byron to burn a letter. It just wasn't in him. I doubt if he'd burn even a proof that he had robbed a bank."

"Knowing his character then," suggested Father, "you try to tell us what would be his natural action when he finished reading it for the last time and decided to go to bed."

"Easy," I said. "He'd merely slip it into his pocket. It would stay there until he had his suit pressed the next time, then it would be taken out with a dozen others and thrown into a drawer and there it would stay for a year or more."

"But this letter," said the sheriff, "was the cause, we think, of thoughts of suicide. Wouldn't he have acted somewhat differently in this case?"

"I don't know," I said. "Very possibly. But on the other hand, I shouldn't think it strange. Byron was almost insanely careless about such matters."

"And there's the possibility," put in Miss Case, "that he really wanted it to be found, as further revenge, we'll call it, on his mother."

"But the letter isn't there," said Father. "It isn't in the rooms. Ken pictures him slipping it into the inside pocket of his suit. The suit he wore has been searched. So have all the others."

I jumped to my feet. "By Jove!" I cried. "I believe I've got it." And I started for the door.

Father rose. "What is it, Ken!"

"The dressing gown. Byron's gray dressing gown! He'd have it on in the evening, of course. I told you he always wore it in the room!"

"But the whole room has been searched," said the sheriff.

"Not the dressing gown!" I cried. "Bill Smart and I locked it into my suitcase when we discovered spots on it, and forgot about it. Father and I didn't search there."

I started for the door again and Charlie yelled, "I'll come with you!" but I called back, "Don't bother!" and slammed the door behind me.

I drove like mad to the campus and tore up the three flights of stairs. The key to the bag was in my vest pocket and I fished it out as I ran along the upper hall. I turned the study light on and pulled the bag from the closet. For one awful moment I thought it felt light and empty. But there was the robe, wrinkled as we had stuffed it in.

I held it up with one hand and felt in a pocket. A handkerchief and a paper of matches. I felt in the other.

It was a letter!

I dropped the robe and held the letter to the light. Yes. Gray stationery. Boston. Postmarked on Friday.

It was thick, and I pulled it from its envelope and snapped open the folds. A check fell out. I picked it up and read it. Made out to Byron for a hundred dollars and signed by his mother. And I caught a glimpse of the first words of the letter itself.

> Dearest Byron:
> Happy Birthday to you! . . .

I switched the light out, and folding the letter as I ran, sped down to the car again and roared back toward Bossy's house.

Everyone there was standing, all eyes, facing the door.

I stopped and held it up. "Here it is!" I cried. There were exclamations as they all stepped forward, but then I drew back and held the letter behind me.

"Just a moment," I said. "Father, I wish you'd tell me what to do!"

"I think your judgment is as good as mine, Kenneth," said Father.

"But this is the point," I said. "Mrs. Coates wants it destroyed unread. Yet—"

"Yet I could prevent that," said the sheriff. "I could demand it as evidence."

"I could grab it and run," said Miss Case, "but I think it's gone beyond that now. Someone should read it. Not all of us, I think, but someone."

"Shall I, Miss Case?" asked Father. "Or will you? I agree that because of Mrs. Coates's order we should limit the readers to a very few until we know, at least, what it contains."

"It seems to me," said Charlie, "that Jean is the one. If it's a family matter, the family should have it."

"That's it!" cried Miss Case, and Father nodded, but I could see his disappointment and I felt my own.

"All right," said Jean. "I tell you what I'll do. I'll go upstairs and read it alone. If it's merely a family skeleton, I ask the right to tear it up and keep my mouth shut. If it has any possible bearing on the case, I'll come down and let you read it, Mr. Harris, and you, Ken, and you, Miss Case, and the sheriff. The others—"

"The others shouldn't see it at all," Charlie interrupted. "Bill and Barker and I will go out and stroll around. In half an hour or so we'll come back, and if there's anything to tell, you can tell it. If not, never mind."

The tension was cleared as soon as they had left the room and I walked over to Jean and gave her the letter. Then Miss Case excused herself and took Jean into a corner and whispered for a moment. I knew she was telling her not to let whatever she was about to read affect her, as perhaps it had Byron, for I saw Jean shake her head and laugh a bit, and I heard her say, "I'm not that kind."

"Good luck to you," said Father as Jean started up the stairs, and she waved the letter at him. "I'll be down in ten minutes," she called.

Miss Case and the sheriff and I sat down again before the fire, but Father said he knew where the ginger ale was that the housekeeper had set out for us, and disappeared through the dining room to get it.

It was perhaps three minutes before anyone spoke, and then the sheriff leaned forward in his chair. "Give a guess, Miss Case," he said. "What's in it?"

"I haven't the faintest idea," she answered.

"Is it a family skeleton?"

"Without a doubt."

"Does it bear on the murder?"

"That," began Miss Case . . .

Upstairs we heard Jean's sudden footsteps running across the floor. There was a shot—and Jean's piercing scream!

# CHAPTER XVII
## TUESDAY: THE LETTER

EVEN THE SHERIFF STOOD STOCK STILL for a few seconds until we heard the thunder of rapid footsteps running downstairs. We jumped into the hallway, the sheriff with his revolver out. But there was no one there.

"The back stairs!" I yelled. "The back stairs!" and at the same moment, while the sheriff ducked through the dining room, I started up the front, hearing as I went what I recognized as the banging of the back door.

The upper hall was dark, but even as I ran, my fingers found the button and pushed the lights on. I rushed directly to Bossy's study and pushed the unlatched door open.

Jean was lying in a crumpled heap in the middle of the floor.

Miss Case, not a second behind me, pushed by and knelt beside her. "Bring water!" she cried. "Hurry!"

I dashed into the hall again, toward the bathroom, and caught sight of Father leaping up the back stairs. "In there!" I cried, pointing to the study, as he tore past me. I filled a glass and started back. Charlie and the sheriff's man were running up the front stairs.

"Go back!" I called. "Out the back door! Go after the sheriff!"

They crossed the hall and dived down the back stairs and I heard the back door bang behind them.

Miss Case was slapping Jean's wrists and Father took the water from me and dashed it in the girl's face, handing the glass back to me and motioning for more. I ran again to refill it, and when I got back, Father had raised Jean so that she leaned against his knee and I could see that her dress was torn at the shoulder. None of us spoke, but Miss Case dipped her handkerchief in the water and bathed Jean's face with it.

"Is she—is she alive?" I managed to whisper at last.

In answer Jean opened her eyes, just a bit at first, and then widely.

"Jean!" cried Miss Case. "Are you hurt?"

She shook her head weakly. "Not at all. I just fainted. Help me to the couch a minute and I'll be all right."

Father and Miss Case lifted her and carried her to Bossy's couch, where she lay back and closed her eyes. I knelt beside her and Miss Case sat down in a chair Father drew up, and began again rubbing Jean's wrists.

"Miss Coates," said Father, "can you speak? Can you tell us what happened?"

Jean opened her eyes. "In just a minute. I'm all right, but just wait a second until I stop trembling. Feel under this pillow, please, that my head is on, and see if you find anything."

I reached my hand under the red cushion and drew out some crumpled sheets of paper. "It's the letter!" I cried, and Jean smiled and nodded.

"I foxed him," she said. "I thought I did."

I folded the letter and held it tightly in my hand. Jean had closed her eyes again, but now she opened them and propped herself up on one elbow. "I'm fine now." Then she looked around. "Did you catch him?"

"Who?" demanded Father.

"I don't know who it was. Oh, did he get away!"

"They are chasing him," I told her. "Charlie and the sheriff and his man. He got out the back door and they're after him."

"And you didn't see who it was?" asked Father.

"No," Jean answered. "I'll tell you the whole story." She sat up, piling the pillows behind her.

"I came up here, in the study," she began, "and sat just about as I'm sitting now, here on this couch, with my back to that door there." She pointed to the door into Bossy's bedroom which Miss Case was occupying while Bossy was away. "The door was either closed or slightly ajar," she went on. "I didn't open the letter for a minute or two, but just sort of sat here, holding it and wondering about it. You know the way you'll do. But finally I did open it and began to read.

"I had read, I think, about a page and a half when I heard or thought I heard a faint noise behind me. I turned around—not suddenly because I wasn't frightened—and saw that the door was open a crack and that the barrel of a revolver was pointing right at me, through the crack."

"Was the light on in the other room?" asked Father.

"No. It was dark. I couldn't see anything but the revolver. I didn't have time to scream. It didn't affect me that way anyhow. It just struck me dumb and I stared. And then a voice came, in a whisper—a hoarse sort of whisper."

"What did it say!"

"It said, 'Put that letter down on the couch. Put it down.' I didn't move. 'Put it down on the couch,' he said, 'and walk into that closet.' The end of the revolver moved until it pointed at that closet over there."

"Good God!" cried Miss Case. "Why didn't you scream then?"

"I don't know," said Jean. "I was getting a little calmer. I knew he wouldn't shoot. And I kept my eyes on the revolver and slowly, very slowly, folded the letter and made believe lay it on the couch, but really I only laid the envelope down. The pillows hid my hands from his view and I slipped the letter under one of them, and let the envelope stay in sight. 'Now, get up,' he said, 'and walk into that closet. Shut the door and stay there three minutes.'

"But I had made up my mind. And instead of doing what he said, I grabbed the envelope and dashed for the door—the door that leads into the hall. And then he shot and I screamed. It didn't hit me. He must have been too surprised at my sudden movement.

"But then he ran after me—like a flash—and caught me by my shoulder. And I fainted. I guess he got the envelope, but that's all. And that's all I know."

"Then you saw him!" exclaimed Miss Case. "Did you know him?"

"I only caught a flash of him. He had a cap on, and the usual handkerchief tied around his face. And an ordinary dark suit. I don't know who it was."

"What height?" asked Father.

"Heavens, I don't know!" said Jean. "Just average, I guess. Your height, or Byron's."

"And his whisper?" I asked. "You couldn't tell anything from that?"

"Not a thing. It was just low and hoarse. Probably disguised. He fired, you see, in excitement, and he knew that immediately you would all rush up. So he merely dived for the letter and then ran, I suppose."

"Back through the bedroom," I said, "and out into the hall and down the back stairs. I heard the door bang."

"I heard it too," said Father. "The housekeeper evidently forgot to leave the ginger ale out, and there wasn't any in the ice chest, so I had to go down cellar to hunt for some. I was down there when I heard the shot, in the far end of the cellar where the cold closet is. I didn't really think it could be a shot so I was just standing there listening when I heard the steps running down the back stairs. And I was halfway up the cellar stairs when the back door banged."

Just then we heard the front door open and Charlie's excited voice called my name up the stairs. I dashed out of the room. Charlie was standing in the lower hall.

"Throw me the keys to your car!" he said. "The sheriff's out in his and I'm going to scout around in yours. We think we lost him. He had a car of some sort parked down on Tuck Drive and he dashed down through the bushes and got away in it. Look!" he exclaimed gleefully. "I've got a gun! The sheriff gave it to me."

I threw him the keys and he fled out the door. "I'm afraid he's got away," I said when I got back to the room.

"That was Penlon?" asked Father, and I nodded. "Where was Smart?"

"I don't know," I answered. "He went out with the others when Jean started upstairs. I didn't see him come in again."

"It's peculiar," said Miss Case, meaningly, "that all of them except Kenneth and the sheriff and I were out of sight while all this business was going on."

Father looked at her keenly. "Yes," he said, "even I."

I tried to think of the element of time. Could either Charlie or Bill leave the sheriff's man, sneak around to the back of the house, slip noiselessly up the stairs into Bossy's room, and be ready at the bedroom door when Jean had finished the first page and a half of the letter? And then dash down the back stairs again, out the back door, and around to the front by the time I was running for water? It was possible. There was plenty of time.

There was time for Father, too, to go directly upstairs instead of into the kitchen, do the shooting, and then run down again, banging the back door just as a decoy, but really slipping into the kitchen until the sheriff had passed and then running up again before Jean had recovered consciousness. Why did Father keep creeping into the case? Why should my mind keep running in that track?

I attempted to forget it for the time being and held out the letter. "What about this now?" I asked Jean.

"We'll take no more chances," she said. "Read it at once. Read it aloud. What do you say, Miss Case?"

"I agree," said Miss Case. "It's gone beyond even Mrs. Coates's jurisdiction now."

"Shall I read it?" I asked. "Or will one of you?"

"You read it, Kenneth. And I suggest that we don't interrupt once while you're reading. Wait until the very end for any comments, no matter how important you think they are."

My fingers trembled as I opened the folds. It was closely written in Mrs. Coates's round, legible hand. I read quietly and slowly until I reached the very end:

Dearest Byron: Friday.
Happy Birthday to you! And many many more of them! And so much love that I can't write it!
You will get this the day before your birthday, really, but if you *will* have it fall on a Sunday, that's

your look-out. Anyway, you always did like to have your presents early. And here is a check enclosed. *Spend it now.* Before you get through with this letter you'll see why I say that.

You are twenty-one, Byron! Do you realize what that means? It means that I have only one child now—Jean. And that you are a man. And that you are really at the head of a fatherless family.

But it means more than that, Byron dear. It means that suddenly, and (I think) as a surprise to you you are *rich!* Not a millionaire, Byron, but very close to it. In a Boston bank, waiting for you to come and sign papers and such things, is a lot of money from your father—very nearly $750,000!

Why haven't I told you this before?

Well, one reason is that I was afraid the knowledge of it would hurt you when you were young, and that you wouldn't take your studies seriously, and that you would consider yourself far above some of the less fortunate fellows in college and thereby miss their valuable friendships.

That's one reason, Byron, but that isn't the real reason. The real reason makes a rather long story, and the money is so much a part of it that I should be telling only half the story if I told you of the money alone. And until now you have not been old enough, officially at least, to hear it all.

Byron, dear! I'm going to hurt you awfully, I'm afraid. Do you remember how, some five or six years ago, when you were at St. Paul's and home on a vacation, I shattered your beautiful illusion of me? And how hard you took it? Well, I'm going to do it again. And even more harshly this time.

Why don't I wait and tell you this when I see you Thanksgiving? Because I can't bear to have you look at me while I talk. Your clear eyes would make me lie.

I've planned this letter for years. But now, when I come to write it, it's nothing like my plans. You are to read it carefully and then think it over for two or three days. You are to do nothing rashly, Byron. That's all I ask of you. You may write me or not when you have thought it over, just as you feel. *But you are to do nothing rashly!*

So listen, dearest, to your beautiful mother. Tell me I'm still beautiful to you. . . .

You've asked me, now and then, about my childhood and my family, and I've always told you the truth. My mother died when I was young and my father had eloped with her and never became reconciled with her family. We never knew them and I don't know them now. My father was an only child and I was an only child, and so we have no relatives at all. I say this to show you that never, in all my life until I had a family of my own, was there any hampering influence on me. My father was a writer, a careless free-lance with no money at all. We roamed the world, finding the pennies where we could—just Father and I. And when he was thirty-five and I was fifteen, he died and I went on the stage.

I shan't tell you again, as I've told you before, of my early struggles to make something of myself, and how I studied with my little chorus earnings, and all that. You know, and remember, even though the world has forgotten, that I finally became a star. All alone, and through nothing but hard work. And more than that, I became an international star, and I conquered Paris and Berlin and Vienna and London as well as New York.

Listen, Byron, and try to see clearly and understand.

Every star has a thousand admirers. Somewhere, back in your past or down in your present, you've

probably written a mash note to a movie person or
an actress or a concert singer yourself. I got hundreds, of course. But for every hundred letters a star
receives, she meets one admirer in the flesh. And
can't you understand that out of every hundred men
she meets, there must be at least one who attracts
her—particularly on the continent in the late 'nine-
ties and the early nineteen hundreds when things
were gay and dashing and men still had romance left
in them?

I fell in love.

I was young, Byron—not yet your age.

I fell in love, not once but many times—with this
man who took me driving in the Bois—with that man
who took me to supper at the Savoy, or, if it were
Paris, to Maxime's. I collected their pictures and they
autographed my slippers, and once, I remember, I
started making a collection of wisps of hair from
their moustaches. Moustaches were moustaches in
those days, Byron. I went mad on the continent. I
thought I had only to snap my fingers, and there
would be a Petit Trianon for my own.

Are you listening, Byron? I know you're listening, but can you understand?

And then, suddenly, I fell really in love. *Really*
in love. Please remember that, Byron. And where I
had known the others only for a day or two, this man
I knew for three months. I shall tell you his name,
though it doesn't matter now, and I wish I could forget it. It was Joseph Baird. He was an Americana
student in Paris, brought behind the scenes at the
Casino by a wealthy friend of his with whom I had
often dined.

We fell in love, I say, and I had the courage to
give up my place at the hotel and go to live with him
in his crowded little quarters in Montparnasse.

It was a happy time, Byron. Whatever you think, and you'll think a lot, you must not forget that I was happy with him. Whatever has happened, I am still able to think that I was happy with him.

But it didn't last forever. It couldn't.

One day I told him I was going to have a child. And I never saw him again.

That's love, Byron.

The child was going to be born in October. In June I was still appearing nightly at the Casino, terrified. Afraid to tell anyone. Knowing nothing, really, and with no real friend to talk to. And in that same June I met John Coates.

You've never asked me much about your father, Byron. Did his picture tell you everything, or have you always been instinctively wise? In this day you might have called him a butter-and-egg man. In that day, to me at least, he was a blessing from heaven. He was rich and homely and a widower and older than I and comforting. And three nights after I had met him, he proposed.

Don't misjudge me, Byron. I told him about Joey Baird and about the child. And he proposed again and I accepted. I cried more that night than anyone has ever cried before or since. We were married the next day.

I left the stage three weeks afterward, and I haven't set foot on it since.

But we stayed on the continent, and in Switzerland, in October, my child was born. There was no legalizing to be done, for John accepted him as his own, and loved him as if he were. And save for his sandy hair, he thankfully didn't look like Joey Baird at all, but like Peter Morrison, my sainted father.

No, Byron, it was not you. It was a brother that you never knew you had, a year older than you, and we called him John.

In January the baby was old enough to travel and we sailed for America. And there, in New York, the next November, my second child was born—and we named him Byron, which was your grandmother Morrison's maiden name.

And I became domestic. You don't *know* how domestic I became, and devoted myself to you and John and to my husband, who was really a perfect dear. I married him for his money, Byron, and his protection, which came in the nick of time, but I grew to love his funny, faltering ways, and his loyalty to me because of my first child, and because his family cut him off when he married a notorious actress with a heathenish French name. But his money came from his grandfather and we certainly didn't have to live in poverty.

And then Jean was born, looking, for the first time amongst the three of you, like me. Again, you had taken after my father, but you had caught the black hair, this time, of *your* father.

And four months afterward my husband died, of pneumonia which developed from a cold he caught (and this characterized him) swimming at Coney Island. Imagine a man with a house on lower Fifth Avenue swimming at Coney Island!

Shall I tell you about the will now, or shall I wait and tell you about your brother John, first. It's hard to decide. The will, I think. As long as possible I postpone your judgment of me.

Your father left all his money in trust for his children. His *three* children, for he recognized John as one of his own. Share and share alike as each becomes of age. More than half a million apiece, the income to be mine until they all had received their share. He didn't dare to leave it all to me, because he knew my extravagance.

I haven't used all the income, Byron. Each year I've turned back the residue, and to you and Jean, on reaching the age of twenty-one, comes, apiece, what now amounts to almost $750,000.

And to John should come the same!

Byron, dear, how can I make you see the inside of a feminine mind?

After John Coates had died, I tried to find Joey Baird. I tried, through friends of mine, to tell him that I would love him if he came back and that his son—*his* son—was standing heir to a fortune. And all that I heard was that Joey Baird had taken to drink, or that he was married, or that he had become a millionaire himself. Rumours from Parisian friends flew thick and fast, and all I learned was either false or true, but certainly that he cared no more about either of us.

And as you children grew (you can't understand this, Byron) I came to love you and Jean more and more and more and like little John less and less and less. And through terrible long nights of loneliness wondered why he should share the money and the care that really were yours and Jean's alone. And the thought grew until it became an obsession.

And one day we all four of us sailed for Europe again, and shortly afterward I had John given to an innkeeper and his wife, good, clean people by the name of Meseraux, and settled enough upon them to allow them to fulfil their hearts' desire and migrate to America. I did it anonymously, and I lost John, and all memories of Joey Baird, forever, and I saved the money for you.

But—and this is the devil in me, Byron—I couldn't resist, afterward, dropping a brief note to Joey Baird, in care of his university, hoping against hope that they still had his forwarding address, to tell him what I had done. But nothing ever came of it. Years and years later, during the war, I saw that Lieutenant Joseph Baird was killed at Château Thierry.

So now you know, Byron dear. And now your mind is going round and round in great circles. And for the moment you hate your mother. But just because she is not like other mothers.

I have made it all up to you, Byron. I have built you a home—a respectable home. I have seen to that. I have loved you as no mother ever loved a son, and you have loved me. You must think and think and think, and justify me at last.

And just to-day I saw our lawyer. Some day, the money that was falsely John's will be divided between you and Jean. It can't be quite yet, even though your father provided for such a division in the event of the death of either of the others, and I have told the lawyer, time and again, that John died in infancy. But there are still things to be arranged, and you must help.

Byron—you will help! You will love your mother now as much as you did before, won't you? You will bury her past with her! You will *do nothing rashly*, but you will still call me

Your ever loving,<br>Mother.

# CHAPTER XVIII
## TUESDAY: THIRD DEATH

FAR AWAY, AS I FINISHED, the Dartmouth Hall clock struck eleven. We all counted it to ourselves and were silent until the last bell had sounded. Then it was Father who spoke.

"Is that enough, Miss Case," he asked, "to drive Byron to suicide?"

Miss Case shook her head, not in negation, but as if she were shaking off something ugly. "It's enough," she said, "to make him think of it, as a parallel, to that other time years ago. But not quite enough, remember. He never really did it."

"Poor Byron," said Father.

"Poor Mother!" exclaimed Jean. "Poor, pretty mother! Making an early mistake and then blundering along, making a worse one and thinking she was doing her legitimate children good by getting rid of the illegitimate one."

"He was not illegitimate, Miss Coates. Don't forget that. Your father legalized him and treated him, really, as his first-born."

"Father, I'm afraid," said Jean, "must have been sentimental. In Mother's eyes the child was illegitimate. And think of her courage! And her courage in telling Byron!"

"That had to be done," said Father. "Byron was entitled to know and she told him well. She tried to make him see it in her light. It was not her mistake that she failed, although I truly believe if Byron had lived until morning he would have come to his senses."

My thoughts were in different channels. If Father wasn't going to speak of the important thing, I was.

"John," I said. "John, his name was, and given to Meseraux. John Meseraux."

"Yes," said Father. "It's all perfectly clear now. I should have gone with you to Etna yesterday morning, as you suggested."

"What's all this?" exclaimed Jean. "What's all perfectly clear?"

I told the women everything, even about Father's adventure in the chapel and our chase of the Ford to Lyme and of my viewing Byron's body to satisfy myself that there had been no mistake. I told how John's name struck me Sunday night as I lay in bed and how he had been watched all yesterday.

"He wasn't watched to-night," said Father. "The sheriff called his man off after Meseraux was found to be living such a normal, uninteresting life."

Miss Case had been listening intently, narrowing her eyes. "Then Meseraux was Byron's visitor. Why? Did he know who he was?"

"He must have known," said Jean.

"How?" asked Miss Case.

Father shook his head. "I can't imagine. Perhaps he didn't know. Perhaps nothing was planned at all. Perhaps he merely knew that it was shortly to be Byron's birthday, and liking him so well, came to the dormitory merely to offer congratulations—one more gesture to get into his favour. And Byron, knowing the truth, for he must have read clearly that John Meseraux was the lost son, blurted it out to him, telling him that he was his half-brother— trying at last to rectify the wrong that his mother had done. But probably doing it bitterly because John was so despised. And per- haps then John saw his chance for claiming not only his third of the money, but Byron's too—a tremendous sum—even more tre- mendous to a poor boy. Perhaps he thought he could remain as Meseraux for some time afterward, years if necessary, while plan- ning how to reveal his real identity and claim his heritage. Per- haps, after he had killed Byron and blundered with the fire escape, he even considered, sometime in the future, the possibility of effecting your death, Miss Coates, and becoming a millionaire indeed."

Jean shuddered. "It's all too real," she said, "now that we know. And it will kill Mother. She will never laugh again."

"You're really satisfied, Mr. Harris?" Miss Case asked Father.

Father nodded. "Yes," he said. "There are obscure points, of course. How did Meseraux learn what Sam Anderson had to tell Kenneth? How did he know the psychological time to rifle Byron's desk? How did he happen to be upstairs here to-night, of all nights?"

"How did he get into the organ?" asked Jean.

"That's easy," I told her. "He was a member of the choir any-way. He could have gone upstairs with the rest of the choir when they took their places and could have slipped into the organ unno-ticed—"

"Probably," Father put in, "with the needle-gun concealed un-der his choir robe."

"He knew where Sam stood," I went on. "And afterward, in the terrible confusion, he could have joined the whole gang outside the chapel. The whole choir still were robed."

"And he," said Father, "still with the gun under his robe. But he had left one needle in the organ. He had taken two out of the box, ready to jab another one in if by any chance the first failed. In his excitement he forgot it. That night he had to go back and get it, and I surprised him. He fled in terror. But these last two days of inactivity have shown him he wasn't recognized. Yes," he turned to Miss Case, "I'm satisfied that the mystery is solved. All that is left now is capture—and justice."

Outside we heard the roar of a motor and the slamming of a car door and then, downstairs, the opening of our front door.

"Who's here?" called a voice, and all four of us rushed to the top of the stairs.

It was Bill Smart.

"Quick!" he cried. "Where's the sheriff?"

"Out," I said, running down the stairs with the others follow-ing. "Out on a chase."

"Damn!" cried Bill, and stood looking bewildered.

"What's up, Bill? Tell us!"

"I've got somebody!" he fairly shouted. "I've got somebody cor-
nered!"

"Where?" Father and I both demanded.

"In the old ruined inn. Out on the River Road."

"Who?" we both cried.

"I don't know," said Bill.

Just at that moment we heard my car and the sheriff's coming
up the drive.

"Thank God!" cried Bill. He opened the door to admit the sheriff and his man and Charlie, all looking a bit disgruntled.

"Quick," said Bill. "Everybody listen. I'll talk fast because we've
got to get going. I left Charlie and Barker outside and said I thought
I wouldn't wait but would go back to the dorm. and do some work.
For some reason or other I cut down through the gully and came
out on Tuck Drive, intending to walk up that way. But I'd just gone
up the hill a few steps when a car came along and stopped, and
someone called to me. It was Jerry Dawes and he said he was just
out for a ride. Said he couldn't stay alone in that dorm. without
Sam. Asked me to ride along with him. And we were still standing
there talking when we heard noises up at this house and suddenly
somebody came crashing down through the bushes and jumped into
a car we hadn't noticed before; it was parked up under the trees
with the lights out. He drove off, hell-bent. I thought something
was up and I yelled to Jerry to follow him, and jumped in."

"What kind of car?" asked the sheriff.

"Ford," said Bill. "Old Ford, but how that thing could go! Jerry's
old bus was full of carbon and we couldn't keep up with it. We lost
it five or six times. He went across the bridge to Vermont and up
that side of the river. Way up to Thetford and then crossed the
bridge toward Lyme. And started down the river again on the New
Hampshire side. And then we lost him.

"But by a stroke of luck, when we came to the place where that
old dirt road leads off—you know, the one that runs down close to
the river—Jerry said we'd take that and try to head him off. He
thought that, even though it was rough and narrow, he could cut
off a couple of miles instead of taking the regular highway. We

thought the fellow in the Ford had taken the highway, see? But he hadn't!

"But we didn't know it until we got 'way down and passed that old ruined inn. And just as we were driving past, hell-bent, I saw a flicker of light upstairs, and I yelled to Jerry to stop. But by the time he had stopped we were into the woods again on the other side of the clearing. I told Jerry to stay there, in the car, and I'd sneak back. And I did. And I saw that there was really someone up there, and I even sneaked around so that I found the old Ford, steaming, run nose-in in a lot of shrubs.

"So I ran back to Jerry and told him to drive in town like hell and get the sheriff. But he told me I'd better do it because I knew the gang. And he'd watch, and he'd puncture the tires on the Ford or disconnect the battery and that he'd keep the guy from getting away if it was the last thing he ever did."

"Come on!" yelled the sheriff. "We'll dash down to the police station and get a couple more guns and lay siege to him. How far is it to the inn?"

I was already getting into my coat and tossing Father his. "Between three and five miles," I said. "About that."

"I'm coming, too!" said Jean.

"No!" said Father. "You—"

"I *am* coming!" she cried. And she came. And Miss Case came with her. They forgot their hats but struggled into their coats as we ran for the cars. Father got in with the sheriff and his man, I jumped in with Bill, and the women piled into my car, which Charlie drove. The sheriff led the way and at a tremendous pace we skidded around corners and down town past the dark campus to the little crazy wooden police station in Allen Street. The sheriff jumped out and disappeared inside, coming back in less than a minute. He handed a revolver to me and another to Bill and a third to Father.

"Now we're all armed," he said. "All the men. Let's go!"

Father knew the way. He told me he had often been to the old inn as an undergraduate, years ago. He directed the sheriff and away they sped. Charlie followed him and Jerry and I drew up the rear. We managed to keep up with the others fairly well, although now and then their tail lights disappeared in hollows ahead of us. It seemed only a minute before we reached the entrance to the old River Road.

Once upon a time it was the only road north from Hanover, and on it, in a clearing, which was level and grassy to the very brink of the Connecticut River, stood the old inn. It dated back to Revolutionary times, and now stood, dignified and ghostly, in gray old ruins. One wall was out entirely. The porch had fallen in, but old musty pillars still held the pediment up, and the stairs still stood, leading eventually to the only room in the place which was in any state of preservation at all—an arch-ceilinged ballroom under the roof on whose walls, in daylight, the faint gilt decorations could still be seen. Generations of students had scribbled their names and class numerals there, and I remember that a group of us, visiting it one day, had conceived a fantastic plan of buying the place and fixing it up, running it as a sanded-floor chop-and-ale house and calling it Prexy's Punch Bowl.

I have never seen anything look so huge and eerie as the inn when we came upon it that night standing in its clearing beside the narrow old road in the reflected light from our three cars.

The others had got out, and when Bill and I arrived, Jerry Dawes was running across the clearing to them.

"He's still in there!" he cried. "He's got a gun! He shot at me twice."

"Where is he?" demanded the sheriff.

"Upstairs," said Jerry, pointing. "Up in the old ballroom. I tore the battery out of his car and shouted to him that I'd done it, and told him that I had a gun, but I haven't, and that both ends of the road were guarded. He shot at me twice, but he's a rotten shot."

"Is he alone?" asked Father.

"I think so," said Jerry. "I haven't heard any voices. We couldn't see when we were chasing him, because his top was up. There might have been somebody waiting for him in the car on Tuck Drive, but I doubt it."

Something struck my mind that I hadn't thought of before! What if old man Meseraux were in this with him! Perhaps he found out the truth about the money and was egging the boy on! Perhaps he was with him!

The sheriff took charge. He ordered the women into the cars, but I knew they wouldn't stay there. I knew Jean wouldn't, anyway, as soon as we moved toward the inn.

"We can't merely raid him," said the sheriff. "He must have three shots left, even if he didn't bring a refill with him. He'd shoot us down as we came up the stairway."

Bang! There was a flash of fire from the broken window in the pediment and Charlie howled.

"He got me!" he cried, and Jean came running from the car. We crowded forward, foolishly, bunching ourselves together around Charlie despite the sheriff's order to scatter. "It's nothing," Charlie said. "Just grazed the back of my left hand." Jean was tearing her handkerchief up and wrapping it around the knuckles.

"Who has a flashlight?" called the sheriff.

"I have!" I cried, and ran to my car and got it from the pocket in the door.

"Bring it!" said the sheriff. "Hold it in your left hand and your gun in your right and come with me. The rest of you surround the house. You take charge of them, Mr. Harris. Shoot if he starts to run. There's another gun, Dawes, in the left-hand pocket of my car."

Jerry went and got it and Father barked out his orders, encircling the old building with Jerry, Charlie, Bill, the sheriff's man, and himself. I saw Jean slip into the dark with Charlie and Miss Case stand undecided for a moment and then follow Father. Nothing could happen to them, I was sure, so I said nothing.

The sheriff and I found our way over piles of debris to the inn door and set foot on the shaky timbers inside. "Look out for holes," I said.

"Put on your light," ordered the sheriff. "Find me the foot of the staircase."

My light clicked on and I moved it until the rays fell on warped and crooked stairs covered with fallen plaster. I could feel rather than see that against every paneless window one of the men outside was pushing, staring through the dark toward the circle of light.

"Are we going up?" I whispered. I don't know what I hoped the sheriff would reply.

"Not yet," he answered. "We'll try something else first."

He lifted his gun and pointed it up the stairs. It did no good; the staircase turned at right angles six steps from the bottom, but it seemed to give him authority, and an objective.

"You—up there!" he called.

There was silence from the dark above us.

"You—up there!" he called again. "Come down here!"

Still silence.

"You haven't got a chance," he went on, after a pause that was more exciting to me than his voice. My hand was trembling and making the light on the stairs dance crazily over the cracked and streaky walls. "The house is surrounded! And all my men are armed. You can come down peacefully and safely and submit. I give you that chance. Or we can raid you up there. You can shoot at a few of us, but we can overpower you in the end. Come down, now!"

We heard a movement and we bent forward, listening intently. It came to nothing, however, and soon all was silence again.

"You don't believe we're armed!" shouted the sheriff. "Take this!" He raised his revolver and fired dead upright into the ceiling. The shot echoed through the empty rooms. He motioned for me to fire as he had. "And this!" he shouted, as I, too, shot upward.

"Barker!" he called. "Fire up through one of the ballroom windows!" And a shot from outside banged in the blackness.

"Harris!" And my Father shot, from another side of the building.

"Penlon!" Charlie's gun spoke.

"Smart! Dawes!" Two shots in quick succession. There were movements now, upstairs, plainly heard.

"My God!" I said, "He's coming!"

But he wasn't. He had crossed the floor, but he had stopped somewhere. I pictured him crouching in some corner, with his gun trained on the top of the stairs and the fear of our sudden dash up them making his heart pound. My own was racing madly.

"Perhaps we'd better go up," whispered the sheriff. "Barker and I will lead." He turned toward the door.

But from somewhere outside came my Father's voice in a low tone. "Call his name, Kenneth. Show him we know who he is!"

I tried to steady the light. I tried to put power and threat into my voice.

"Meseraux!" I called. "John Meseraux! You're known and you're caught. Come down and surrender!"

We distinctly heard a whimper from above!

That touched him! And I had another idea!

"John Meseraux!" I shouted again. "*John Coates!*"

There were gasps of astonishment from the men outside the windows and the broken walls. But upstairs there was movement—a slow shuffling walk. He was coming down!

He was coming down indeed! We heard his feet on the stairs, uncertain, slow, but steady. One step after another. Down!

My hand shook unmercifully and the light danced again. The sheriff laid a comforting hand on my left arm and I steadied myself.

Two full minutes he took descending those complaining stairs, but it seemed two years. But at last the sheriff touched my arm again and we drew back a pace. And into the brilliant pool of light stepped John Meseraux. Under his gray cap a lock of his blond hair had escaped to hang down against a face as pale as death. Except for the colour of that hair he was Byron's ghost indeed, and I knew how Jean's heart was beating at the sight.

He was blinking wildly in the brilliant light and cringing back against the wall at the turn of the staircase, six steps above the floor. One hand was held tightly behind him. His right one.

"Throw your revolver to the floor!" commanded the sheriff. "Throw it down, now!"

Meseraux didn't move.

"There are seven guns trained on you. Drop that revolver!"

John's hand crept slowly from behind him until the light caught the gleam of the pistol. He held it out to drop it, and then suddenly raised it to point full at the light in my hand.

But just at that instant came a shot from somewhere in the dark behind me. And John's gun crashed to the floor while his hand spurted crimson. He howled.

"What do you want me for?" he cried. "What do you want me for?"

"For the murder of Byron Coates," boomed the sheriff. His voice was awful.

"No!" Meseraux screamed. "No! I didn't kill him! I didn't kill him! You can't accuse me of that!"

"And for the murder of Sam Anderson!" the sheriff shouted.

Meseraux's head dropped and he whimpered and held his wounded hand tightly in his other one.

"Yes," he sobbed. "I did kill Anderson. But I had to. I tell you I had to!"

I couldn't stand it any longer. "And Byron, too!" I yelled. "You killed Byron, too!"

He flung his head back until it lay against the cracked wall. "No! No! No!" he cried. "I did *not!* He was my brother! I did *not* kill him!"

Somehow his tone rang with truth, but it seemed incredible.

"Then who did, Meseraux," I cried. "Quick, tell me who did, or I'll shoot. Who *did* kill Byron? Quick!"

His head sank again and he seemed to shudder all over, but then he stared straight at us and his lips moved.

"Louder!" I shouted.

There was a shot—and John Meseraux crumpled before us and rolled down the six steps to our feet. I turned the light full upon him as the sheriff jumped forward and ripped open his coat.

The blood was welling from John's heart.

## CHAPTER XIX
## TUESDAY–WEDNESDAY: SILENCE AND A CRY

THE SHERIFF CAUGHT JOHN'S WRIST and held his pulse for a second or two. Then he looked up at me, standing above him.

"You fool!" he said, "You damn' fool!"

I stared at him in amazement. "But I didn't shoot, sheriff!" I cried. "I didn't shoot him. Someone else did."

The others were pressing around us and I turned the light on their blinking eyes. They were all there, stern and tense, with Charlie holding Jean to him and Miss Case standing rigid beside my father.

"Is he dead?" asked Bill in a hoarse whisper.

"Dead as a door nail," said the sheriff. He stood up and faced them. "Which one of you was fool enough to kill him?"

No one spoke, but I saw each one of them look at all the others.

"Come on," said the sheriff. His voice was rising in anger. "Which one of you was fool enough to kill him just as he was about to tell us Coates's murderer?"

"Sheriff!" cried Jerry Dawes. "You don't believe him, do you? You don't believe that he didn't murder them both?"

The sheriff was blunt and gruff. "I don't want to believe him," he said, "but I think I do."

"I believe him," said Father. "There was no object in his denying one and confessing the other. And besides, his voice rang true. He was scared out of his wits. He blurted it all out, and correctly, I'm sure."

"But who shot him!" demanded the sheriff. "Come now, speak up!" There was complete silence.

Was it another mystery? Was the one who fired that fatal shot in the dark going to hold his tongue? Was the guilty one the murderer of Byron Coates? Did he shoot to silence John Meseraux?

"Damn you all!" shouted the sheriff. "I'll soon find out. Give me that light!" He grabbed the flashlight from my hand and swept the group with it. Miss Case fell back a step and Charlie's arm tightened around Jean, whose face was livid as she followed the moving light with her eyes.

"Open your guns!" ordered the sheriff. "Break them and hold them at arm's length." There were a series of clicks. "You, too," he said, pointing his light at me. "Your guns should show one shot and only one shot fired from each."

He took my revolver, held the light to it, and then closed it and handed it back with a grunt.

"Next," he said. "Barker." Barker gave him his gun and it was handed back with the same grunt.

"Penlon." Charlie held his out. "You'll find two shots gone from mine, sheriff," he said. "I was the one that fired at Meseraux's hand when he raised the revolver."

"Good boy, Charlie!" I cried.

"Hm!" said the sheriff. "So you did that, eh? Mighty fine shot." He gave Charlie's gun back to him and stepped on to my father.

"I'm sorry, sheriff," said Father. "But I fired that shot at Meseraux's hand. At least I fired *a* shot. I don't want to doubt Penlon, but I *did* fire. Very likely we both shot at once. We would, you know. There was only a fraction of a second to do it in, and even if they weren't exactly together, these walls echo so that it might sound like one report. At any rate, I *did* fire. You'll find two shots gone from this." He gave him his revolver.

The sheriff grabbed it and cast one quick glance. "God!" he exclaimed. "Now I don't know what to believe." He turned the glare on Charlie's face. "Penlon," he asked, "did you hear another shot? Do you think you fired at the same time as Mr. Harris?"

"I didn't hear another shot," said Charlie. "But it's perfectly possible, as Mr. Harris said, that we fired together. I don't see why all of us didn't fire together. We were all watching, and ready for it."

"I was ready," said Bill. "I almost shot, but the others fired a fraction of a second ahead of me."

"Who saw flashes?" demanded the sheriff.

"I saw Charlie's," said Jean. "I was beside him. I didn't see any other, but I wouldn't, being beside the first flash."

"I was with Mr. Harris," said Miss Case. "He raised his revolver. I saw that. And then I shut my eyes. There was a report, and close to me. It must have been his."

"The rest of us," said Barker, "were on the other side of the house. We couldn't see. It was a loud report. There might have been two."

"Give me your gun, Smart," said the sheriff. He examined it, and then Jerry's. They evidently showed nothing, for he handed them back immediately. "Now," he said, "don't anyone move. We'll see what the wall behind Meseraux can show."

He leaped over John's lifeless body and up the few steps to the turn of the stairs. Holding the light close to the wall, he examined the cracked and falling plaster behind where Meseraux had stood. It took him a long time, but finally he stood up and faced us, turning the light on the ceiling so that it reflected down on us.

"There are only two bullets in this wall," he said. "One of you is lying, or else one of you is a damn' poor shot."

No one spoke but Jean. "Charlie shot," she said in a voice that was almost choked in tears. "Charlie shot. I know he shot!"

"What do you all say?" asked the sheriff, sweeping us with his eyes. "Is it my duty to arrest these two, Penlon and Harris, and hold them for further questioning?"

We all moved forward. "No!" we cried in chorus. "No!"

"You're presuming a bit too much, sheriff," said Father gravely. "I am telling the truth and I am quite sure Penlon is. The explanation lies in the fact that we both shot together. One of us hit. One of us went wide of the mark. That's all. Wait until daylight and I guarantee that you will find a third bullet somewhere in that wall. The plaster is so cracked and broken you've missed it. Besides, sheriff, we're all friends here."

The sheriff glared. "I doubt that like hell," he growled. "Three boys dead and two of these deaths a bloody mystery and this group over and over again involved. Killing for silence. It's a dirty business and one that doesn't pay." He shoved his revolver into the pocket of his coat. "However, until daylight I'll give you the benefit of the doubt. Barker, collect their guns and take them to my car." He followed Barker with his flashlight as the revolvers were taken from us and shoved into Barker's pockets until he was overstuffed.

"Dawes," the sheriff ordered, "you take one of the cars, please, and go up to the main road. Stop at the first house and phone the ambulance. Tell it to hurry. I don't want to stay here all night. Then you wait at the intersection of the road and direct it down here. You go with him, Smart." Then he turned to me. "You drive the others into town in your car. Penlon and Mr. Harris, I should like to see you both at Professor Bostwick's at nine in the morning. We'll try to talk this thing out."

With backward glances at John Meseraux lying still on the floor, we picked our way out of the room's debris. Bill and Jerry climbed immediately into my car, turned it around, and shot off down the road. I took Jerry's car, which would seat five. Miss Case climbed into the front seat beside me without a word, leaving the back seat for Father, Jean, and Charlie.

It made a rather awkward situation, for I felt that no matter how sure each of the men behind me might be, there were undoubtedly nasty thoughts flying back and forth; but no one spoke. A hundred things rose to my mind, but the atmosphere was strained, and I couldn't say them. As I remember it, the only sentence that was said at all came from Charlie calling attention to Jerry's car in the yard of a farmhouse that we passed after we had gained the main road and were speeding toward Hanover.

A plan was forming in my mind—a plan I didn't like to think of because it showed that suspicion of Father was growing stronger and stronger in my thoughts. I wanted to talk to someone about it.

Not the sheriff, for I feared he was too headstrong. Not Charlie, because he was, for the time being, Father's enemy. Not Jean: I felt that she would lie for Charlie's sake. I glanced sidewise at Miss Case. She was sitting bolt upright. Calm and confident. I would talk to her if I could get the chance.

At Bossy's house they all got out. Jean asked Charlie to come in and let her bathe his injured hand where John's bullet had grazed it. Father was grumpy. His dignity had been upset and he stalked into the house speechless.

"Miss Case," I said. "Why not ride down to the garage with me and I'll walk back with you. It'll help to take the whole business out of our nerves so that we can sleep."

"Good idea," she said. "I'll be back in a few minutes, Jean."

But I didn't drive to the garage. I turned down Tuck Drive and slipped under the pines below Bossy's house where Meseraux had hidden his car. I kept on to the end of the drive, and drew off the road onto the flat clearing beside the entrance to the great dark covered bridge that spans the Connecticut River and connects two states. There I stopped, turned off the motor and set the lights dim.

"Now," said Miss Case, "what is it? I knew you wanted to talk. I saw you glancing at me as we were driving down."

"I do want to talk," I told her. "I want to talk to someone, and all the others have become suddenly difficult."

"What is it?" she asked again. "I'm a good listener. That's part of my job."

I turned and faced her, resting my elbow on the back of the seat. "It's about Father," I said, and she nodded.

"It's a terrible thing to say, and I don't dare to think about it alone. But somehow, everywhere we turn, we run up against him. Never definitely. He hasn't done a thing, and I haven't got a single clue on which to base a definite suspicion. But there are little things."

She nodded again. "I have felt them. I wish I hadn't shut my eyes to-night when he raised his revolver. I might have cleared it up if I had seen the flash. But I didn't. And Charlie was so near. It might have been his shot. I don't know."

"That's not all," I said. "Miss Case, when I was down in Boston, I found his picture in Mrs. Coates's album. Years ago, of course, in Paris. It was signed 'Joe.' That's Father's name."

She looked me full in the face.

"Could he," I continued, "could he be—Joey Baird!"

"Heavens, man!" she exclaimed and stared straight before her toward the black river.

"It's awful to say!" I went on. "But you don't know how my thoughts have been running on it, ever since I saw the picture. And then to hear that letter. The two Joes. And the dates would be about right. And Father was out of sight when Jean was shot at. And now that mixup of the shooting tonight."

"I can't say a word," murmured Miss Case. "I can't say a word except that there's a place for suspicion. There's certainly that. But what are you going to do? You haven't said a thing?"

"That's what I want to ask you about. Do you think I could get Mrs. Coates up here?"

"Mrs. Coates!"

"Yes, by some means or other—even by telling her that John Meseraux is dead. Even by threatening her. Get her up here somehow—at once—to-morrow. And confront her with Father. And let her see!"

"It's a bold stroke," said Miss Case. "And he's your father, remember."

"I know it's bold, and I realize that he's my father. But By was my best friend, and it's one side or the other. And after all, it's not so much to accuse Father that I want to settle things, but it's just as much to free him from my suspicion. I have a right to do that."

"I think you have," she said. "Whether or not you can get Marion Coates to come is another matter."

"I hate to face her," I said, "but somehow I have a feeling that I could do it."

"She'd never take a train," said Miss Case.

"I don't intend her to," I answered. "I'll drive down to-night. It's almost one. If I started within an hour I could get there by six and probably snatch a bit of sleep and see her by nine. And get back here between one and two. I'd drive her up."

"That would be easier," said Miss Coates. She nodded her head. "Yes, I think it might work. And I think you're right in trying it. May luck go with you, and I'll back you up in everything."

"But don't say a word to anyone," I cautioned her. "Not even to Jean."

"I'll keep mum," she promised. "You can trust me."

I drove her home, shook her hand, and saw her disappear into the house. Except for the light in the hall downstairs, the lower floor was dark and I knew Charlie had had his hand cared for and was home by now. I was glad. I would go directly to my room and not see him.

When I got to North Mass. I found Jerry Dawes's door open, across the hall from mine, and had to talk with him for five minutes. The ambulance had come, he said, and he and Bill had driven back together. He had nothing more to tell and I left him as soon as I could.

I mussed up my bed and wrote a note to Father which I knew he would find in the morning. It said that I had a lot of things to do, about which I would tell him later, and that I'd see him soon after lunch. Then I changed my coat for a heavier one, took a final look around the room, and left.

The drive was cold and lonesome and endless. I went over and over again every step of the past three days, but trying not to piece them together because it was so confusing. I sped through sleeping towns and darkened cities, but I met with no adventure and stopped only once, at Keene, to replenish gas and oil. And it was dawn when I drove in over the Harvard Bridge and reached the Hotel Bellevue.

I threw myself down on the bed, leaving a call for eight o'clock, and slept that short while soundly and dreamlessly. When I was wakened the sun was bright and the day was crisp and cold, and I turned immediately to the telephone and got Mrs. Coates's maid on the wire.

Mrs. Coates was well, she said. She had rested all day yesterday and had slept all night. I asked if she would see me in half an
hour, that it was very important and that I had driven all the way
from Hanover. She said she'd inquire and left the 'phone for a long
time. When she came back she announced that Mrs. Coates would
see me, at a quarter of nine, and I hung up the receiver in triumph.

I drove to Chestnut Street after a quick shave and breakfast
and rang the bell. The same maid admitted me and let me at once
into the living room. Mrs. Coates, in a fluttering pale green negligee, was curled up in one corner of the sofa. She didn't look ill.
Her colour was good and her eyes were bright, but she didn't smile
when she took my hand—took both my hands.

"So soon again!" she said. "Hilda tells me you went back to
Hanover yesterday and then drove down again. Why?"

I sat down beside her and let her still keep my hands in hers.

"Mrs. Coates," I said. "I've come to tell you something and ask
you something. And it's not to upset you at all. It's nothing very
frightening, but it's so awfully important that I want you to take it
very calmly and then see if you can't think very clearly."

She looked at me closely, trying to read my eyes, but I kept
them firm and looked deep into hers.

"I'm better now," she said. "I think the hysteria is gone for good.
I think I can listen."

"I want you to come to Hanover with me—drive back with me
now, right away."

There was a flash of fright in her eyes, but it passed at once.

"Why?" she asked.

"Several reasons," I said. "In the first place, Jean needs you.
Last night—she isn't hurt, remember— she was shot at, and her
nerves are upset. Miss Case thinks you ought to come."

"Shot at!" Marion Coates cried.

"But not hurt, remember. I'll tell you why in a moment. In the
second place, Mrs. Coates, both my father, who is in charge of the
whole affair, and Miss Case, think we should have you there to keep
you away from the reporters. I'm afraid—I'm awfully afraid that
unless we are all together and can help each other to keep the

newspapers away that a lot of things will come out. You see, Mrs. Coates," I said as kindly as I could, "the letter you wrote to Byron has been found. And the authorities had to read it because it was on account of that letter that Jean was shot at."

I thought she was going to scream again, but she didn't. She merely freed one of her hands and held her handkerchief to her lips while her face went white.

"Take it calmly, please, Mrs. Coates," I begged. "You don't have to fear much if we're all together. Because John—John Meseraux he called himself—has been found. And now he is dead and there's nothing at all to fear."

She sat in dead silence for as much as a minute. And then she rose, firm and calm, but still white. "I'll come!" she said. "How much time will you give me?"

"Good!" I cried, and caught her hand and kissed it. "Can you be ready in fifteen or twenty minutes?" She nodded and swept from the room.

I was in high glee. Things seemed suddenly rushing to solution, and I even went, while I waited, into the music room and tinkled a merry tune on the piano.

It was quarter-past nine when she came down again followed by her maid with a small suitcase. She was becomingly dressed in a black suit with a black-and-white fur coat and a close little black hat with a splash of smooth white feather.

"Call the doctor and tell him, Hilda," she said. "And after that don't answer either the 'phone or the doorbell unless you look out first and see that it's a telegraph messenger. I'll wire when we're coming back. Jean will come home with me. See that her room is ready for her."

It was the most difficult ride I have ever taken. We did it quickly, for I went as fast as I dared whenever I had the opportunity. It kept us from talking, for one thing, and for another, I was in a great hurry to have my rather awful gesture over with. But we did talk some. And I told her the details—almost completely. Now and then she cried, but on the whole she was exceedingly calm. Naturally, I said nothing about Father. And, moreover, I let her believe, although I didn't say it outright, that John killed Byron as well as Sam.

And at last we reached Hanover. It was two o'clock and I thought I might still catch the group at Bossy's sitting around after lunch, so we drove directly there. At any rate, I thought, if Bossy didn't come home to-day, Father would move down with me or to the Inn and give Mrs. Coates his room.

We drew up before the house and I helped her to alight. I tried to be matter-of-fact about it, but heaven knows I was all of a tremble. I opened the door for her and asked her to walk in, and as she stepped over the threshold I heard Jean's voice from the living room.

"Mother!" she cried. "Of all people!"

I saw them rush into each other's arms, and Miss Case slipped by them and came out to me in the hall.

"I'll tend to this," she said. Your father is upstairs."

"I've told her nearly everything," I whispered. "You're supposed to have sent for her because Jean needed her. Nerves, you know."

"Leave it to me," she said, and went back into the living room.

I threw my coat and hat off and climbed the stairs. Father was in his room, seated at a desk, scribbling something. His door was closed, and I thought he might not have heard Jean's exclamation.

"Well," he said, looking up at me. "It's about time. Where on earth have you been!"

"Oh, round and about, Dad. Tell you later. Just now there's someone downstairs I want you to see. Will you come down for a minute?"

"Who is it?" he asked.

"Surprise," I said. "Come find out."

"I'll be down in a minute."

I ran down ahead of him and found Jean and her mother sitting on the divan with their arms around each other, and Miss Case standing in front of them. She turned to me as I entered.

"Jean's better already," she said, with a wink. "It was a lucky thought of mine."

I heard Father coming down the stairs and felt the colour leave my face, but I stepped back to the door to greet him. He came in briskly, smiling at me, and stood by the door glancing around wonderingly to see who the visitor might be. He caught sight of Mrs. Coates.

I tried to watch both faces at once. His filled with astonishment. Hers didn't change expression.

Jean rose. "Mother," she said, "this is Mr. Harris, Kenneth's father."

"How do you do," bowed Mrs. Coates.

Father crossed to her and took her hand and I stepped beside him. He was still staring at her, quizzically, I thought.

"Mrs. Coates," he said. "This is a delightful surprise." But he didn't drop her hand. He held it and looked into her eyes.

The pause became painful and Mrs. Coates felt it.

"Why do you stare so?" she asked, with a little laugh.

"I'm trying to think," said Father slowly. "I'm trying to think. Somewhere we've met before."

"Oh, no!" she said. "I'm sure we haven't, Mr. Harris," She drew her hand away and Father stepped back. "It's queer, too," she continued, "after Byron and Kenneth have lived together all these years."

"No," said Father. "It's longer ago than that. It's a long time ago. Wait—let me think." He put his hand to his forehead. "It was abroad. It was Paris. . . . Ah! Now I know. For heaven's sake—Marie Fleuron!" he stepped forward again and caught both her hands, drawing her to her feet.

She was bewildered. "Of course," she said. "That was my stage name, of course. But I don't remember you."

"It was just two or three times. I was a student and somebody took me to your dressing room, at the Casino, I think. And we went to supper. And then the next day I took you driving. We went to Auteuil! You lost your heel getting out of the carriage."

I saw recognition light her face. "Why *yes!*" she cried. "Harris, Harris. *Joe Harris*, of course! Why, I've still got your picture somewhere. I asked you for it. I was making a collection."

A wave of relief swept over me. If Father was involved, it was not in the way I imagined—unless these two people, the one so stern and straight, the other so soft and beautiful, were doing marvelous acting. But why should Marion Coates act? It couldn't be possible. I beamed my joy.

There were small talk and rambling reminiscences for ten minutes, and then Mrs. Coates went upstairs with Jean while Miss Case went to look us up some lunch. Father turned to me, elated.

"What a delightful coincidence, Ken!" he exclaimed. "She was a wonderful actress. How did it happen that her stage name was never mentioned to me."

"I have no idea," I said. "It was never mentioned to me until I went to Boston. It's forgotten, I guess, in her search for respectability."

Father shook his head. "I fear her respectability is gone now. We've had a devil of a time with reporters this morning, trying to tell facts and yet keep the truth away from them."

"What else has happened?" I asked.

"Only one thing of importance. I'll tell you that in a minute. The first thing this morning I went with the sheriff out to Sans Souci. Poor Madame Meseraux was almost distracted. She has come to consider John as her own child, although of course he was not. But I learned from her and from her husband that they had no idea who his real parents were. Mrs. Coates, it seems, saw to that. John was taken to them by a mutual acquaintance and secrecy was strictly maintained. We did not tell them the truth. It must be told them eventually, of course, and some recompense ought to be made them. Jean, when she gets her money, should see to that."

Jean, of course! All the money would be hers now! She would be a millionaire! Lucky Jean! . . . Lucky Charlie!

"The other thing was this," Father went on, gravely. "This morning Penlon and I met the sheriff here as we arranged. There was a lot more talk, but not a thing was accomplished. We stuck to our stories. It was a double shot and nothing more. And we proved it."

"How?" I cried.

"We went out to the ruined inn with the sheriff and in the full daylight found the other bullet hole in the wall. It was not where the sheriff had looked for it. It was down nearer the base board, not behind Meseraux's heart at all!"

"But that was probably your shot, or Charlie's which went wild. One of those two the sheriff found and thought crashed through John's hand was probably the one that got his heart."

"No," said Father. "John Meseraux was not shot from directly in front, but from the side. From the side and from above. The angle of the bullet entering the hole showed that. And the passage of the bullet through Meseraux's body showed it too."

"Then—"

"Then he was shot from the stairs above him—out of our sight—behind the turn of the staircase."

"God!" I cried.

There was a commotion at the door and the sheriff and his man entered.

"For Pete's sake," the sheriff exclaimed, "give me refuge from these reporters. They're everywhere, and damned if I know what to tell them!"

Father was looking out the door. "Here's a car of them now," he announced. "A taxi. . . . No, by heavens, it's Bostwick home again! Welcome home, Professor!"

"Hello!" called Bossy. He was beaming. "Hello, Ken. Hello, Mr. Harris!" Father held the door open and Bossy came in. "It's good to be home again!"

"Hello, Professor Bostwick," said Jean's voice. She was coming downstairs with her mother behind her.

Bossy turned to greet her, and then fell suddenly back against the sheriff who was closing the door.

"Who's that!" cried Mrs. Coates. "Who's that? *Joey Baird!*"

# CHAPTER XX
## THE END

Except for the glimpses I had of him during the short but notorious trial, I never saw him after that. I couldn't bring myself to visit him in his cell, and to my knowledge he never asked for me. But three days after that final scene in the hall of his own home when Father yelled, "Grab him, sheriff!" I read his signed confession, and it explained everything.

He was just a poor but fascinated student at the Sorbonne when he met Marie Fleuron. Already he had gone lightly into a few swindling schemes with other penniless students. And he skipped (he didn't attempt to justify himself here) when their child was to be born.

He was a musical adept, of course, and his life might have been, even after his disappearance, happy and honest and profitable. But he vagabonded around, taking various aliases, and every now and then studying more of the music which he loved. It was as Joseph Bostwick that he was respectably known—merely a using of the initials of Joseph Baird.

He *did* get the letter that Mrs. Coates sent him, telling of how she got rid of the child and who his foster parents were. And through friends of his he kept track of the Meseraux and watched their migration to America. He also watched the Coateses, saw Byron destined for Dartmouth, and by slow degrees, the plan already formulated in his mind, he gained teaching positions in this school and that, and eventually got his appointment on the Dartmouth faculty.

His plan was simple. To get rid of Byron, to teach John his identity, and to share the money with him. In the back of his mind was even a thought of doing away with Jean, and eventually with John himself.

The Meseraux family had settled in the suburbs of Boston, and it was Bostwick who, anonymously, got them the house at Etna and showed them the prospects of a roadhouse in the vicinity of a college town. He even advanced them money, and they arrived in Byron's sophomore year. At first he thought the similarity between John and Byron would be a point in his favour, that he could bring the two boys together, musically inclined by heritage as both were, and that John could work with him, unsuspected. The two of them could be close friends of the boy that was doomed. But the enmity sprang up, and Bossy had to foot it alone.

His liking of us both was sincere, however. Several times he almost gave up the plot but he called himself a coward. And to make the step irrevocable, he told John the whole story in the spring of our junior year. It was only John's tremendous admiration for Bossy and his own timorous poverty and under-doggedness which made him become a companion in the plot.

But time went on. Bossy couldn't seem to plan. The scheme was good but the means were difficult. He let it slide from day to day and month to month, enjoying the life he was leading and the friendships of us all.

And once again he almost threw the whole idea aside until, on the very eve of Byron's birthday, he heard the news, at his own tea, that I should be away until past midnight—that the dormitory would be practically empty—and that Byron, with "one of his moods," was sulking in his room alone.

He called on him. And from then on it was just as Father had so expertly imagined. Byron *was* in bed with the needle-gun beside him. He *did* get up and he *did* demonstrate it. And Bossy seized the opportunity of making Byron pose as model while the mechanics were demonstrated. It was hurriedly and in a panic, even after these years of planning, that he wiped away the traces of the blood and adjusted the inexpert rope. He knew he could delay matters a bit by locking the door, against its custom, but he didn't sleep a wink all night, expecting that I would call any minute with the horrible news.

He offered his house to us, partly for a blind, partly to enable him to watch every step of investigation and thus be ready to flee at the first sign of danger.

He was on the steps, of course, and heard Charlie's news to me that Sam Anderson knew the identity of Byron's night visitor, and in terror he formulated the plan for Sam's death. But he couldn't do it himself, so he called John in to do his part and protect his father's life. He told him at choir rehearsal, and gave him the gun. And then he sat in full view of the audience, at the console of the organ, and waited for the death he knew would come.

He was standing at his open window that night when Father and I, on his steps, talked about the possibility of a letter. And that night he ransacked Byron's desk. Until then he hadn't dreamed that Marion Coates would dare to tell the whole truth, but he knew that if the letter was found, John would be taken and would confess.

His next scare came just after I started on my first trip to Boston and Father mentioned the possibility of my bringing Mrs. Coates back with me. And Bossy lit out. He made up the engagement in Holyoke and let Charlie drive him to the train. In reality, he didn't take the train at all, but a taxi to Sans Souci where John hid him. Later he wired a friend of his at Holyoke to send a telegram to us.

It was Bossy himself, and not John, who was upstairs that night when Jean read the letter. He had let himself in the back way and had sneaked to the top of the stairs to listen and spy and learn what progress had been made. And when Jean came upstairs, he snatched an old cap and a handkerchief and his revolver.

John had stayed down on Tuck Drive in the darkened car, and they fled. They ducked down the River Road after they left Lyme, thinking that the pursuing car would take the upper road. John had hid in the inn that night when Father and I had chased him after the chapel episode.

John had a gun, too, but it was empty. Bossy was to get more cartridges in his house, but in the emergency he didn't have a chance. They were lighting matches in the upper room of the ruined inn, transferring one of the cartridges from Bossy's gun to John's when Bill and Jerry drove past.

They knew they were caught when we all arrived and when they had failed to hit Jerry in their shooting at him from the window. But Bossy was all for staying upstairs and getting raided, wounding or killing the assailants as long as the shots lasted. John, however, was for surrender, and when his name was called, and his identity made known, he broke down completely and came down the stairs. Bossy followed, still hoping there was a chance for a dive to safety.

And then John was ready to blurt out the truth—and Bossy fired and committed his second murder.

That's all there is to tell. I thought that Dartmouth would never quiet down again after the whole horrible affair was over. But before many months it did, and a new college generation is there now, and have dared to raise old ghosts by telling the tale.

# THE WAILING ROCK MURDERS

TO
BILL NORTH
*WHO HATES THIS SORT OF THING*

# CHAPTER I
## SPIDER IN THE WIND

I HAVE COME BACK to the scene of the crime—to the very room in fact—and the wind is still blowing. Far below me, below the foundations of this crazy house, the waves are dashing against the cliff on which these walls are built. I can hear their thunder, and I know how their gray tops burst into sizzling white and how the spray flings itself into the air in an attempt to reach the tangled juniper and bayberry that crown the rock.

I lay down my pen for a moment and walk to the complete circle of windows which surrounds this cupola room. Before me, for the whole southern half of the circle, lies the tossing ocean, clear to the far horizon, but gray and white under the November sky. Behind me, stretching toward the north, winds the gravel road that serves this house; its intersection with the highway is hidden by the scrub pines that clamber over the rocks and sands of this Maine coast. To the east, this brief, precipitous point on which the house is perched falls away to the long sands of Wells Beach with its dull parade of cottages. To the west, the point again falls away to another stretch of sand with its pounding, bursting breakers. But there are no cottages there; not many yards above the tide line stand the dunes, and behind them lie only the brown salt-marshes. The empty beach stretches for only a mile and then ends abruptly in a high and rocky point like this one. And similarly it is capped with a big house, the very copy of this, even to the cupola. I can see its ugly silhouette against the dull sky.

In that house Garda Lawrence died.

And in this house, its insane twin, I sit and try to tell the tale.

I am no writer; I am a detective. And I am an old man of nearly seventy-six—a very weary old man of nearly seventy-six. But I have no Watson to write for me. I have never had a Watson, lonely freelance that I have been for so long. Now and then some self-appointed chroniclers have gone to print with stories of my more, shall we say, fictional (not fictitious) exploits, and I have been content to let them reap their rewards of publishers' royalties. But never before have I touched pen to paper in the narration of one of my cases. Has any detective, I wonder? Has Holmes ever before been his own Watson? I seldom read mystery stories, so I don't know for sure. But if not, why not? Is it modesty, perhaps? Or is it ethics? Or is it, maybe, the convention which requires that tales of murder be given to the public in the guise of fiction, with action which rises, with the outcome concealed until the final, staggering revelation and the ultimate "There's your man!"—a method which would seemingly require the narration of the detective's action but not the step-by-step workings of the detective's mind. It is the credulous blunderer who generally tells the yarn, the impatient worshipper at the feet of the great man, the wide-eyed friend, skilled in suspense and versed in the art of apology. He knows his man's methods and his man's foibles; but he knows that he cannot penetrate one inch behind that impassive brow to reach the solution which is mentally forming within—until the great man speaks.

And that is why no Watson could touch this present case, the virtue and the interest of which lie in the manner in which people and events presented themselves to *me*, puzzling me, leading me on, making me sure, making me doubt, until the last slight clue came with the speed of lightning and with all its accompaniment of crashing thunder. No outsider could know that moment.

So—

I am Spaton Meech, detective, nearly seventy-six years old. They call me "Spider," and I know why. It is because I am slightly deformed from a spinal twist I received in a fall from a rope-swing when I was only five, and because my arms are very long and hang to my knees, and because my head is large and seems to lie on my chest when I walk, and because (on account of my shape) I prefer to sit cross-legged on tables or on the floor rather than to rest my hump against the unyielding back of a chair. . . . Hardly a pretty picture to have to paint of oneself. . . . But—please—I am not a sinister object. Strange children are, I've learned, more likely to laugh than scream and be afraid. And if what pictures you may have seen of me in the daily press seem forbidding, remember that I was always, at those times, the posing master mind. I can laugh. I have a wit. And I ogle all the arts and woo none—except the art of good-living, the art of good-reading, and the art of good-eating.

Naturally I am a bachelor. I have no family and I have no home. This hotel, that hotel, the house of this friend and that friend, these have been my dwellings for more than fifty years. And I own not one thing in the world which cannot be packed, with its fellows, into four or five suitcases. That is why I am in Maine.

That is why I was here on the night Garda Lawrence was murdered.

Garda Lawrence was my ward. Not legally, but by sentimental ties. It seemed useless, when her father died, to bind the poor girl to another stranger, knowing as I did (and as she did not) that she was taken from an orphanage by the childless Lawrences when she was a stringy-haired, black-eyed brat of two. The gracious lady who was her foster-mother died three years later, and with her totally inefficient, thoroughly charming foster-father, she roamed the world. And then, when she was seventeen, he was killed in the foundering of a racing sloop off Marblehead, and Garda came to me. It was natural; there were other relatives, but only distant ones, and they were all people she had seldom met during her globe-trotting life. And I was Stanton Lawrence's best friend and alternately "Uncle Spaton" and "Spider Dear" to Garda.

So I administered her estate—her very considerable estate—and I saw her through finishing school, and I picked her companions for European summers, and in general managed her life so that she not only did not have, but also did not need a home. And then, on a September day, I got this letter from her, from the White Mountains:

"Spider Dear,

"I think I'll spend the winter in Boston and putter
with music or something. But meanwhile I've met
some people up here, the Creamer Farnols (he's
funny and she's a peach) and they've suggested opening their house on the Maine coast at the end of the
month and doing October there. It ought to be cold
and swell. Their daughter Pat knows Phil Masterson
and thinks he should come. So do I. So, lest I be too
jealous, I've invited Victor Millard about whom you
have heard nothing until this moment, which is quite
your loss, and a loss you must remedy at once, because of various reasons. So, here enclosed, is a note
from Mrs. Farnol demanding that you join the party
and telling you where the house is—somewhere between Wells and Ogunquit I think. And you will write
me at once that you will come. . . ."

That is why, on a gleaming October morning, I left the train at
Wells and found the Farnol's car waiting for me. And that was only
a month ago.

No one met me but the chauffeur, and I know how carefully I
must have been described to him, for he came to the steps of the
train at once, and touched his cap and reached for my bags as if
|he had done the same thing for the same person every day of his
employ. He was in his forties, I should say, and he told me that his
name was Sutton. But he hadn't been told, evidently, that even
though I was in my middle seventies, I was still supple and spry
and agile, for he made motions toward helping me into the back
seat. (I thought for a moment he was going to stoop down and lift
me bodily.) But I shooed him away and climbed in front with him.

"Show me Maine," I said. "I've never been here before."

And, because what he told me is a bit important to this tale, I
must tell the same thing, as briefly as I can.

The Maine coast, from Portland down to the New Hampshire
line alternates between rocky points and broad, curving sandy

beaches, in regular, clockwork order. All the points are high, gnarled, exciting, visible one to another, and connected by those long, shining beaches. But almost without exception the beaches are backed by salt marshes extending away from the sea for a mile or two, so that the main highway from Boston to Portland must be inland, and the by-roads which connect the highway with the coast must either travel toward the sea over the rock-based ridges which lead to the rocky points, or else must cross the marshes at very infrequent intervals over man-made piers and causeways.

Thus, please note, it is not unusual at all for one habitable cliff to be only a mile distant from another, just like it, with a sweep of gorgeous sand between, along which, from point to point, it is a joy to walk. But should one care or require to drive from one to the other, it becomes necessary to ride directly inland the requisite mile or two, follow the highway, and turn toward the coast again only when the other seaward road is reached, thus making three sides of a square surrounding the inevitable marsh.

All this I saw with my own eyes as we were driving, for Sutton took the car down toward the sea upon one of the roads which led to Wells Beach, allowed us to follow the bending shore for a mile or more, and then headed toward the highway again. And shortly thereafter we turned for the last time toward the sea, drove through scrub pines, and came out upon the lonely point on which Creamer Farnol's house was perched.

Old as I am, and living as I have lived through the ugliest period of American architecture, I still can say I have never seen a house more scabrously ugly than the one I now spied, high on its rocks, with the unspoiled sea and sky beyond. It was like some horrible wart, some strange foreign growth, sprung from the cliff. And lesser warts sprung from the house itself, parasites on parasites in the shape of little turrets and dormers, leading the eye from one to another until it finally came to rest, high up, on the most important wart of all—a many-angled cupola topping the whole abomination. I changed my mental metaphor and decided that the entire house was the head of some underworld king, protruding from the rocky earth, and leering at the upper air. And on his head he wore the travesty of a crown, fashioned of rusty iron and set with blind isinglass.

I must have muttered something under my breath when the house came in view, for Sutton chuckled a bit and said, "Hardly what you'd call a beauty, is she now?"

I could only gesture feebly and make no reply.

"But Mr. Farnol knows it looks like hell," Sutton went on, "so you don't have to throw it compliments. He knows the reason for it, too, and he'll tell you."

And then I met Creamer Farnol himself. He was on the steps as we drove into the porte-cochere—a tall man, thin as a rolled umbrella, with a great pile of fluffy white hair. In fact, I can think of no better way to describe him than by having you imagine eyes, nose, and mouth painted just beneath the tangled head of a brand-new dish-mop. But they must be kindly features, with a twinkle in the blue eyes, and a little, sensitive, sidewise quirk to the mouth. He was an inch or two over six feet, and I had to look up at him as he shook my hand.

"Mr. Meech," he said, in a deep but smooth voice. "I'm very glad to welcome you. Sutton has your bags. Do come in."

I walked in—into the entrance hall which lay at the foot of a broad, bare, angular staircase of polished oak. And Mrs. Farnol was coming down the stairs.

Farnol turned to her. "Vera, dear. Garda's Uncle Spaton has arrived. This is Mr. Meech, dear."

She was coming down briskly when he spoke, but then, as she raised her eyes and saw me, she stopped, fully and suddenly, and something flashed over her face. I know now what it was, but I didn't know then whether it was surprise or fear or disappointment. But for a second, and only for a second, her foot moved on the step as if she were going to turn and run up again. Creamer Farnol didn't see it; he was looking at me and smiling after the introduction. And in the next moment she was coming down again as if nothing had happened, and smiling as he was, and extending her hand to me.

"Welcome, Uncle Spaton," she laughed.

I wish my powers of description were better so that I could make you see her beauty. She was nearly as tall as her husband, but despite that fact she wore her thick, dark hair dressed high with little waves running across an almost colorless forehead. In her youth, I thought, she might easily have been a Gibson Girl, or, better, one of the tall beauties that Sargeant loved to paint, save that she had more vivacity. She was, I guessed, about forty; and I remember thinking that she would be perfection itself in a green Empire gown, commanding the prism-sparkling drawing-room of a Continental diplomat.

She and her husband together showed me to my room, a large one on the second floor, and told me that Garda and the other youngsters were off swimming but would be back in an hour for lunch. And then they left me alone and I turned to the windows and discovered what I have already mentioned, the second architectural abomination of this amazing coast. I looked eastward, along the curving beach, and saw the twin of this house in which I stood, perched on its rock a mile away with nothing but the sandy desolation between me and it. And I saw something else—the graying of the early Autumn day. Subtly and slowly, although it was almost high noon, the blue was going from the sky and the sun was fading. There was no apparent fog, there were no discernible clouds. It was, as I think back, as if the heavens, with my arrival, caught a hint of impending tragedy to someone dear to me and were starting to dim their blazing blue to a more suitable shade.

We lunched together, nine of us: Garda and I, the two Farnols and their daughter Patricia, Victor Millard and Phillip Masterson, and a married couple, Richard and Helen St. John. But I don't intend to stop to describe them now. They will be met later, in great detail. I merely wish to record one or two of Garda's remarks and hurry on to the late afternoon, the evening,—and the night.

Garda wasn't looking well. The mountains had given her a slight coat of tan, but although it was covering what I was sure was essential paleness, it didn't hide a slightly drawn look. And once, during the meal, she drew her hand across her forehead with a weary gesture. I was seated beside her, with Mrs. Farnol on my left, and I spoke to Garda in a low voice.

"What's the matter, girl? Anything wrong?"

"I don't know, Uncle," she said. "I guess I've just got a little headache." She smiled—a bit wanly, I thought.

Vera Farnol heard us and bent forward. "You probably stayed in the water a little too long, Garda. We didn't swim at all in the mountains, Mr. Meech, and she probably isn't used to it—particularly at this late date."

Garda shook her head. "I wasn't in more than forty seconds. I've never in my life felt such cold water. Victor says that the water's cold enough in July and August to satisfy a polar bear, and that when it comes to be October, you might as well crack ice and jump in that."

That was all, then, but at four o'clock in the afternoon, Garda took to her room and her bed. She went willingly enough in the end, but for a long time all of us had to argue that it was simply no use for her to drag herself around so listlessly. Patricia went up with her; Mrs. Farnol said she would bring dinner up on a tray to her with her own hands; and I said, "If you want me, Garda dear, let me know. I'll come up after dinner, anyway."

So she left us, and when Patricia Farnol came downstairs again and reported Garda safely tucked in bed, the eight of us fell to bridge, a game which I abhor and at which, paradoxically enough, I excel. And again there is only one remark which I have to record. It was made by Vera Farnol.

"By the way, Mr. Meech," she said, "when you want to go up to Garda, she's in the cupola room. The stairs go up from the northern end of the upper hall. We always put our most favored guest up there; the view is magnificent."

And that is why, after dinner that evening, I took my walk in the wind.

Vera Farnol left the table before we did, to carry Garda's tray up to her, saying that she would stay for a few moments and then come down to the living room, adding that she hoped we would

have the bridge tables all set up again and the drawing and dealing all completed. But in three minutes or less she returned, while
we were still at dessert, and she had a little slip of paper in her
hand.

"I guess she's asleep, poor girl," she said. "Her door was closed
and she had pinned this note on the outside of it, asking me to put
the tray down, and that she'd get it when she woke up and wanted
it. It's better, I think, to let her rest."

So there was more bridge, but I am glad to say it lasted only
about an hour and a half, and by nine o'clock we were finished.
Then it was that I stepped out of the seaward door onto the broad
veranda. My plan was merely this: to look up and see if there were
lights in the cupola room. If there were, I should go up and talk to
Garda. If not, I should finish my second and last cigar since dinner, and then go back and hunt for a book to take up to my room.

But I hadn't realized the luring power of the coastal night, nor
its glorious wildness. In the Farnols' living room the great fire had
been burning high, and the heavy, upholstered chairs and the
shaded bridge lamps had made the place a haven of comfort. And
the windows that looked toward the sea, I had noticed, were broad
and high and heavy, of sheer plate glass, thoroughly able to with-
stand without rattling the force of wind roaring across the water. . . .
I met it when I first opened the door, and it set my cigar furiously
glowing and the curtains behind me streaming horizontally into
the room as I struggled with the latch to keep havoc out of the
house.

Practically leaning against its strength I went down the veranda
steps to the small plot of grass which was all that separated the
house from the edge of cliff and the sharp drop to the water. And
there, on the very brink, I stood and looked up. The cupola was
inky black—nothing but a flat silhouette against what little light
there was in the sky. Garda was still asleep. She would probably
sleep now until morning.

But oh, the night! I was inland born, and I was unused to this.
It fascinated me. I never realized how a wind like this, coming from
an ocean which must be boiling mad but which was totally invisible

in the blackness, could appear to have body, substance, definite tangibility as if it itself were water. It rushed past me, but it enfolded me. It almost thrust my arm down when I raised my cigar to my lips. And finally it wrested the cigar from my very fingers and threw it back toward the house. But I got it again and put it out, and then tossed it into the wind's mouth; and the wind spat it out again, over my head, and I heard it thump on the veranda steps.

Then I turned and skirted the house and found the path that I had noticed during the day, one which wound through the grass, juniper, and bayberry on the top of the rocks, and then slowly descended to the deserted eastward beach. I followed it, moving cautiously, until I felt the sand under my feet, and then, as briskly as I could, I turned my back upon the rocks and the point and the house, and started off into the darkness.

Now I could see the ocean. The tide was past the full and there was about twenty feet of hard-packed, damp sand between the loose, deep sand and the lapping, foaming, gurgling wash of the waves. And on that I walked, and further down was the roaring white line which marked the great breakers themselves, roaring even above the wind, and bursting with a sound which was almost metallic. It was cold, but not too cold, and I pushed on into the darkness, leaving the Farnol point behind me. Only once did I turn, and then I could make out the black bulk of it, with the house on top, brilliantly lighted in its lower floors and silently dark above. And so on again.

And then, suddenly, there loomed up before me the silhouette of the other house, identical with the Farnols' save in one particular—the lower floors were pitch black, unlighted, empty. But there was a light in the cupola, blazing against the sky. I stopped and looked and wondered who lived there and determined to find out from Creamer Farnol at my first opportunity the reason for these twin monstrosities, and who owned and occupied this eastern one. And as I looked, the cupola light went out and there was nothing but the dark.

I turned, then, and started back with the breakers booming on my left this time, and the wind pouring around me and whistling through the coarse grass on the top of the dunes. And, pressing toward the Farnols', I suddenly saw something which made me pause for a second and then break into that scuttling run that people say I have—with my little bowed legs and my top-heavy hump.

I saw that in the Farnols' house the lower lights were out and the cupola was lit. Garda was awake! As I say, I ran.

I ran, if you please, from no fright and no worriment. I ran only because I wanted to see the girl before she went to sleep for the night. But as I ran, there came some sort of premonition—not of danger to her, but of, perhaps, a sudden more severe illness. And as I continued to run the premonition grew. And, to the great detriment of my mental comfort, I remembered other hunches and premonitions of mine which had proved accurate and which had caused my colleagues in the detection of crime to accuse me again and again of possessing a morbid clairvoyance. I can actually recall instances when I have waked in the dead of night in my hotel room and stayed awake, breathless, waiting for something and being unable to sleep until, in less than ten or fifteen minutes, the telephone would ring and summon me to take a hand in the solving of some ghastly crime.

So on I ran, and reached the end of the beach. I found the path and scrambled up it, through the grass and over the rocks to the porte-cochere. The hall light was on, left for me, I supposed, although I had been unable to see it, in its dimness, from the beach. I opened the door and paused inside, with the door closed behind me, to catch my breath, spent by the running, the climbing of the path, and the force of the sea-born wind. And as I paused, I heard footsteps above me, and the closing of a door, and up the stairs I went.

There was a dim light in the upper hall, too, and without difficulty I found the cupola stairs, turning sharply upward from the hall's north end. I climbed them, and found they twisted twice and ended in a closed door, outside of which, on a broadish landing, still rested Garda's supper tray, its dishes swathed in napkins.

I knocked on the door.

"Garda," I said softly, "may I come in?"

There was no answer.

I bent down and put my eye to the keyhole. The cupola room was in darkness. Strange! Two minutes ago, just as I started the scramble up the rocks, the lights had been blazing. She must have been awake then, and she could hardly have fallen asleep in that short time.

I knocked more loudly and called more loudly, "*Garda!*"

Still there was no answer, and this time I put my ear to the keyhole, hoping, I suppose, to be able to catch some sound, even the regular breathing of her sleep, to show me I had nothing to fear. But what I heard was the rush of wind, telling me that the cupola windows, some of them, were open.

So then I banged on the door—banged with all my force, to beat the wind and raise my voice above it.

But it didn't waken Garda. It wakened, or aroused, the others. And one by one they came in their negligees or dressing gowns to the foot of the winding stairs, and pushed up the steps, talking to me all at once, and asking the reason for the racket—Creamer Farnol first, and then the two St. Johns, and the others following.

"I've got to get in!" I cried. "I'm afraid she's very ill. I'm afraid she's fainted. The light was on a moment ago, and now it's out and I can't rouse her."

And all at once it struck me that I might not have been seeing through the keyhole at all, but had had my vision blocked by the key from the inside. The light still might be on, which doubled my anxiety.

"Then break the lock," said Creamer Farnol. "It's a light one. If you're worried, break it."

And I broke it. I did it with three sharp, heavy kicks, drawing back my leg as Farnol supported me on the landing, aiming directly under the knob and hearing the wood splintering. And with the third, the door burst open, and a rush of wind came hurtling out against us. The room was dark.

I stumbled in, calling at the first breath, "Garda!" and at the second, "Where's the light!"

Farnol came in behind me, and I felt him fumbling around. And just then something brushed my face.

"Here it is!" cried Farnol, and the room burst into light.

Around me, in the air, a dozen sheets of paper, tossed by the wind, were whirling. They confused me as the light dazzled me, and for a fraction of a second I didn't realize I was facing the bed, and that on it was lying Garda, bathed in blood, with her throat most horribly, most hideously slit.

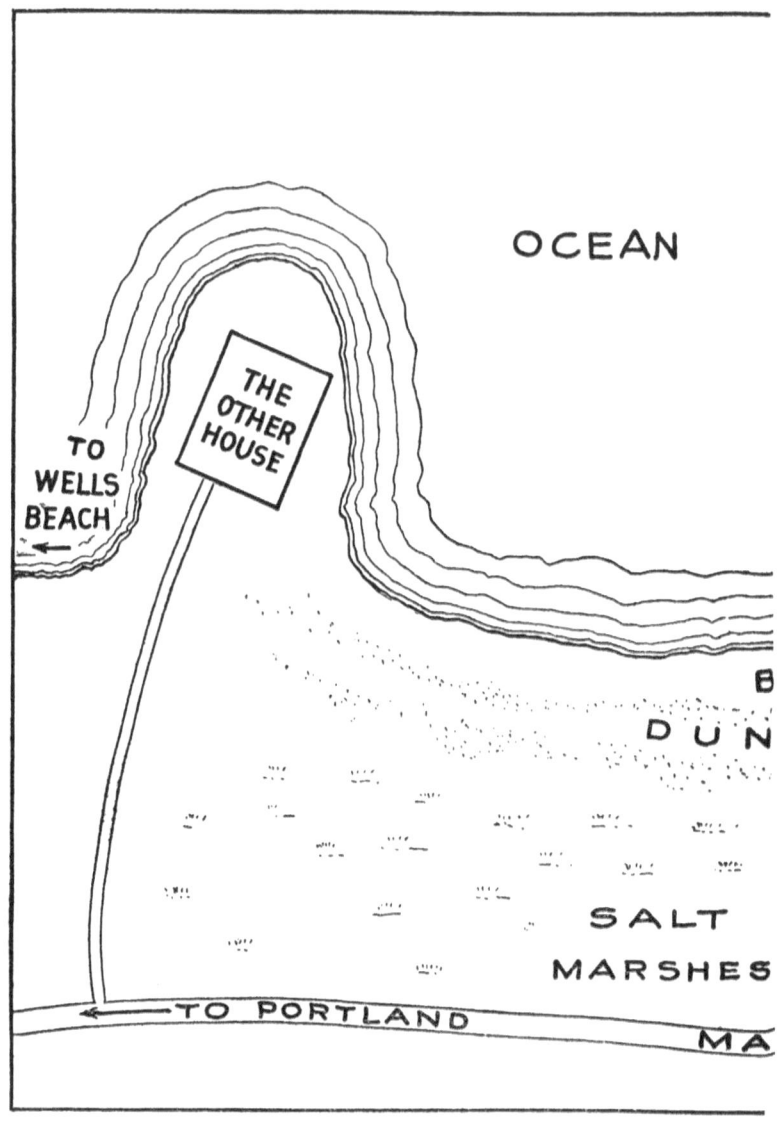

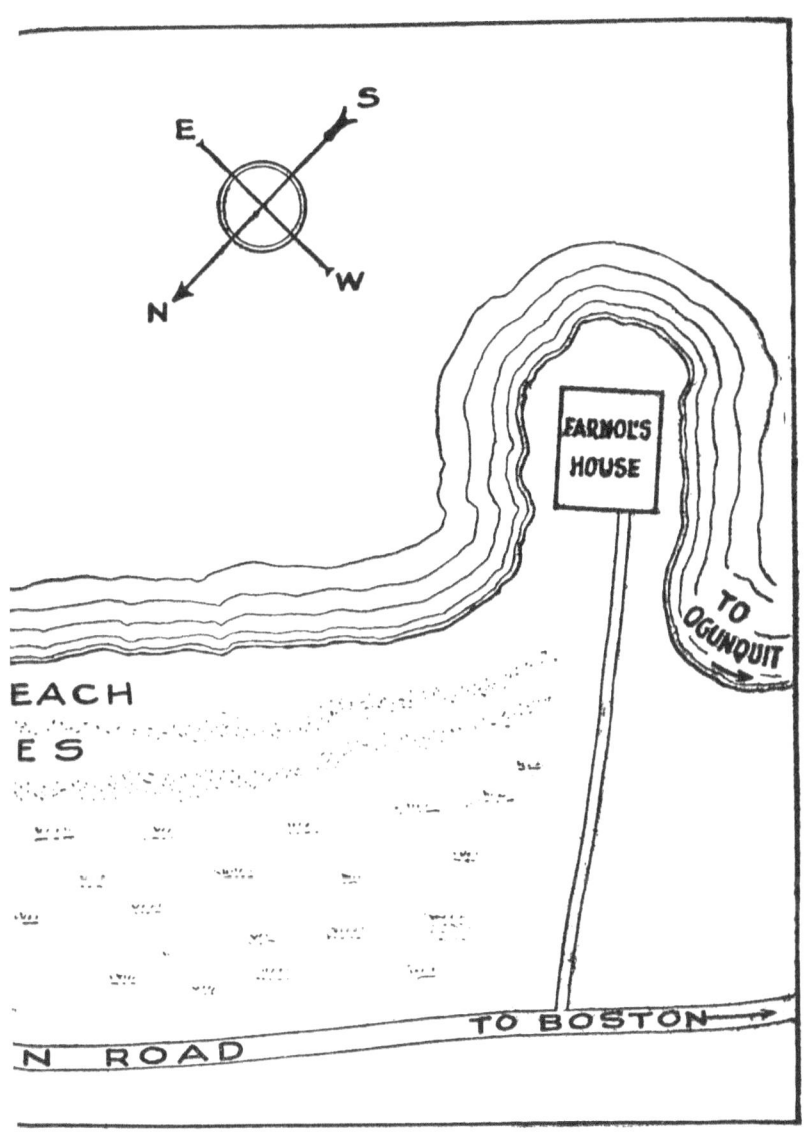

## CHAPTER II
## TOWER BLOOD

I HAVE ACCESS to a very long and very detailed account of the entire case written by Creamer Farnol, and from it I shall quote several times during the course of my own narrative. Such quotations will help present a more objective picture of me; as, for instance, the following:

"Spider Meech stood there, staring at the bed, with the most horrible look on his face that I have ever seen on any man. His legs were spread and his great head hung forward, chin pulsating, eyes blazing. I couldn't tell whether it were terrible anger he was feeling, or enormous surprise, or sheer terror. I only know it was awful and that the sight of him was more morbidly fascinating, even, than the gory figure of the girl. And add to this, as background, the roar of the wind, the whirling and fluttering of the papers around his head, and the ghastly white faces of my house guests huddled at the door, and you have some slight idea of the awfulness of the moment."

Such a description is hardly flattering to me, I admit, but that it is true I have no doubt at all. I can tell Creamer Farnol, however, that it was anger that made me look like that—not terror. I have seen too many murdered men and women to have it affect me like that. But this was Garda—a daughter by chance only, but my sole remaining interest in the world of people as distinct from the world of myself, which is work. And she was a young woman, and a lovely one. And even in that first moment of realization of what had happened, it was brain-piercingly clear that almost positively—

within nine chances out of ten—one of these people with whom I had dined that night had drawn the knife across her throat. That was why my anger overtopped any other possible emotion and blazed out in my face.

At length I moved. I did three calculated things, and did them rapidly. First, needlessly, I stepped forward and laid my hand on Garda's arm, feeling it starkly cold. Next, I took out my watch and noted that it was exactly five minutes after ten. Thirdly, and swiftly, I walked across the room to the door and looked at its inside key-hole. It was empty.

My anger rose again, and turning to the crowding spectators, I cried with all force, "Who did this!"

There was not a sound from any of them but Creamer Farnol, and he stepped forward and laid his hand on the hump of my back.

"Meech, Meech," he said soothingly, "pull yourself together, man. This is the most awful thing that any of us has ever seen, but we must take it as coolly as we possibly can, and we must keep our heads clear. You most of all. Please, please, calm down. And please take the lead and tell us what we're to do."

His words accomplished what he had intended, and I felt my head cooling and something of my own sanity come back to my brain.

"Very well, Farnol. Very well," I said. Then, without any plan whatsoever, or without any knowledge of what I was going to do, I motioned toward the stairs. "Please, will you all go down into the living room? And will you all please wait there, together, until I come down? I shall only be a very few moments, but I should like to be alone for that length of time." But then I realized that, in their eyes at least, or in the eyes of the police when they should enter the case, I had no more right to stay alone in a room of mur-der than anyone else. "No," I added, "not alone, but only one com-panion, if one will stay with me."

"I will, Meech," said Farnol, "gladly."

There was a faint cry from his wife, tall, pale, by the door, regal even in her negligee, which was of black and gold and which she held tightly about her with one hand holding it together at her throat, clutchingly.

"Creamer—please no!"

I looked at Farnol. "Thanks," I said, "but perhaps you'd better go downstairs with your wife and the others. Suppose we say that you're in charge of them, and that the responsibility is yours of keeping them together."

He nodded. "Very well."

Then I pointed to young Victor Millard. "What about you, young man? Will you stay?"

He stepped forward, not eagerly, but certainly without any hesitation. "Of course, sir," he said.

The others turned to go immediately, and there was definite relief in the swiftness of their movements and the carriage of their shoulders. Only Farnol spoke.

"What about the— Shall I send for—" I knew he was thinking of the police but not wanting to be the first to mention them, and I interrupted him.

"Do nothing," I said. "We shall be down in five minutes."

He nodded and reached the door.

"Oh, Farnol," I said in a low voice. "Beside keeping them all together, please do one other thing. Keep the conversation general. Don't let anyone talk to anyone privately. The way to do it is to take the floor yourself."

Again he nodded, and I watched his bushy white hair going down the staircase into the dark.

"Now, young man," I said to Victor.

Victor, as far as I knew him then, was any nice boy. He was, I judged, about Garda's age—that is, twenty-two or twenty-three, of average height, of average fresh good looks, blond and pleasant. During the afternoon and evening I had found him to have an amusing line of collegiate chatter, a quick, ready, infectious laugh, and a careless way of wearing excellent sport clothes. I had put him down as a well-to-do young graduate, destined for good, moderate success in bonds or advertising. Now, of course, there was no smile on his face, and there was anything but bubbling good humor shining from his eyes. He was in dark green pajamas with a tan silk dressing gown over them, and soft leather slippers that matched the gown. And he was standing facing me with his eyes wide. One little detail I noticed at once. His hair was unruffled, save as the wind caught it. He obviously had not yet been to bed.

"Now, young man," I said again. "Let's move quickly. You are here only to watch and to see that I touch nothing, just as, if you were playing the role of detective, before the police came, I or someone else should watch you. The only thing we'll actually do is close the windows."

We did that together. They were the swinging kind which locked with iron clamps at the bottom, and I found it necessary to use the locks to keep the wind from flinging the casements open again. But once the wind was shut out, the room lost its wild horror and assumed an atmosphere that was almost peaceful. There was still tragedy, of course, but it was tragedy in the classic manner, and one felt that the howling, cackling furies had been banished. I found my wits entirely restored, and I fancied a slight straightening of Victor's shoulders.

"Come," said I, touching him. And we moved to stand beside the bed.

I knew what must be passing through the mind of a healthy youngster unused to the sight of death, so I talked, and talked steadily, keeping my voice as calm, as steady as possible, speaking truly whatever came into my mind.

"We're not to disturb a thing, you understand. We're just to stand here and look and see what we can see. And what do we see? We see that her throat has been cut and that she is dead. And what comes into our mind first is that someone else has done it, and not she herself, because we know Garda well, and of all people in the world, we think, the carefree, happy Garda would be the last to take her own life. But then we remember her illness, or what we thought was illness, of the afternoon, and we wonder if that was not really despondency, put by her into the form of a headache. And we wonder if—after all— So then, standing here, we can readily see that death was caused by a knife, or something very like a knife. Surely either a knife or a razor. And we know that if she used a knife or a razor on herself, it would be right here near her.

"We know that it would be near her, because we can see that the actual cutting of the throat took place right on this bed, because here and here only is there any blood. Naturally we can't see, from here, whether or not there are any little flecks of blood anywhere else, but we know that such a wound as that, cutting the most important vein in the body, would immediately pour forth a terrific flood. And the light grey rug would show it up at once.

"Now, let's look carefully, everywhere on the floor near the bed, leaving not a place unsearched. I can even, I think, move these slippers of hers without violating anything important, noticing, of course, that they are placed side by side, and neatly, in a perfectly natural manner."

So I chattered on as both of us searched every inch of the floor about the bed, going even farther afield than, in any realm of possibility, it could be necessary. Unless of course, and this I also mentioned, she had hurled the knife from her—an action which I have found from experience is almost unknown to suicide. We could rule out, I was sure, the thought that the knife could have been thrown, by her own strength, out the opened windows, fifteen feet away from the bed.

There remained, then, the bed itself. It was perfectly obvious that it was not lying upon the outer covers. It was not in the dead girl's hand. It was nowhere in sight.

"I think," I talked on, "that we shall do one thing that very possibly we should not do. I think we shall raise the covers from her. But we shall do it very carefully, Victor. I shall go in here behind the bed and take hold of the top blanket like this—and will you take it on your side? And we will lift it from under Garda's arm. . . . That's it. . . . Now we'll lay it carefully over the foot of the bed, and take the next blanket and the sheet, and replace them as nearly as we can the way we found them."

All that we did, slowly and carefully, and no trace of a knife was found. I don't know whether I was glad or sorry. I don't know whether I preferred to have my Garda dead at her own hands, or at the hands of another, and I laugh at myself for even mentioning here so finicky a choice.

Victor's lips were set as we were working, and as I talked, and from the moment we had been left alone in the room, he hadn't said a word. Now, however, he spoke. And he said exactly what was in my own mind, and he said it the very same second it flashed into my own mind. We had replaced the covers until they were exactly as they were before, and we were again standing side by side, gazing at the bed.

"She's been dead a long time, hasn't she, Mr. Meech?"

I nodded. "Yes," I said. "How do you know?"

He warmed to my question. Youth, I've found, always warms to me when I let it "help" me thus. Age, contrarily, puts its head in the air and looks down at me from a newly discovered height of superior knowledge.

"From the blood," he answered. "It's pretty dry."

He was entirely right. Every bit of the blood, and there were quantities of it, was drying indeed, and the clothes it was spread upon were becoming stiff and hard.

There, very definitely, was something to start upon. The light in the cupola which I had seen from the beach, the light which started me hurrying home, was not turned on or off by Garda's hands. It was not even turned on by the hands of the murderer at the time of the murder.

The cupola, in other words, had been visited again, long after the thing itself was done!

By the murderer himself? I didn't know, of course, but it was highly probable, else the second visitor would have given an alarm.

And how long afterward? I didn't know that. But as I realized the state of the blood, and as I leaned forward again and felt the joints of the fingers and the flesh of the bared arm to determine the progress of rigor mortis, I knew that she had been dead a span of hours. But how many? Five—six—seven. Only the medical examiner, in autopsy, could tell that.

None of this I spoke aloud, so that Victor had to ask me, "How long, do you think, Mr. Meech?"

"I don't know, Victor."

"Before dinner time, do you think?"

"Very possibly. Almost probably."

"Then you think she was dead when Mrs. Farnol brought her dinner up to her, and found that note?"

"Yes. I think I do."

"Oh."

I looked up at him and saw that sudden tears had come into his eyes. He dashed them away with the back of his hand.

"I loved her, Mr. Meech," he said simply. "Did you know that?"

I shook my head, still watching him. "I don't know anything— yet," I answered. "Very very soon, we'll talk, and try to find out everything." I moved toward the door. "Just now, son, we must go and join the others. We know all we need to know in order to find the police—which is that she has been murdered. Now—action!"

He came after me. "Shall I leave the light on?" he asked.

"Yes," I said. "It's too bad the lock had to be broken, for we should seal the room up. However, the latch will still work, so we'll just close the door after us, and trust in heaven. You first, Victor."

We went down the stairs briskly, in thorough silence, and made our way to the living room. They had lighted it completely, I was glad to see, and they had built the fire up again. Hastily I cast my eyes around the room as I entered, and I saw exactly what I expected to see. Creamer Farnol was standing by the fireplace, with Vera seated close beside him in a big wing chair, Patricia Farnol sitting on the arm of it and holding her mother's hand. The two St. Johns were together on a sofa, and young Masterson was back by the veranda doors, alone, leaning forward in a straight chair with his elbows on his knees and his chin in his hand. The eyes of all were dead, expressionless, and I pitied every one of them.

I turned directly to my host. "Now, if you please, Mr. Farnol," I said, "we will telephone the police."

"I'm sorry," he told me, "but there isn't a phone in the house. Since this is the only house on the point, we've never had a line run down from the main road, and of course you couldn't carry it along the beach either from Ogunquit or Wells. And then, you know, we're here so little."

"I see." I thought a moment. "Then the nearest telephone is on the main road?"

He nodded. "There's a farm house right at the top of this road, and we pay the farmer for the privilege of breaking in on him and using it." He moved toward the door. "I'll put some clothes on and take the car right up."

"Don't bother," I said. "I'll go. I'm the only one that's dressed, and go right away if you'll trust me with your car."

"Of course."

"I shall want the sheriff, I think. Do you know where he is or where he lives?"

"No," Creamer answered. "I only know that the county seat is Alfred. That's about twenty or twenty-five miles away. And this address, by the way, is merely Farnol's Point. Everyone knows it. Merely tell him that it's the house on Farnol's Point, near Ogunquit, and that there's a sign on the main. road."

"Thank you," I said. "Don't bother to come out with me. I'll find the car." Then I turned and spoke to everyone in the room in general and to no one in particular. "People," I began, "I've sort of assumed authority here, partly because it's my line, and partly because it's Garda. And I know that Garda has been murdered, and the police must come at once. But until they do, because I very much fear that suspicion will fall almost at once upon someone in this room, I'm going to ask that not a soul leave this room until I get back. I'm going to put each one of you in the charge of each other one, and merely request mutual cooperation. And I'm going to add one little word of advice. All of you who are innocent should try to lift your spirits up. You can't think clearly unless your spirits are high—and clear thinking is what both the police and I will want. I'm going now." And I left the room.

I didn't wait to find a hat, but walked at once out the heavy oak door into the porte-cochere.

And still the wind was blowing, as wildly as before, and below me the sea was dashing. I felt my way around the house to the rear, keeping my hand trailing on the wall to guide my way. I knew where the garage was, and I made for it.

It was eerie. It was ghostly. It was cold.

But, as I reached the garage door, I couldn't suppress a desire to cast one last look up at the cupola. And I did look up, seeing its windows gleaming, and realizing how falsely cheerful it looked, shining against the tossing sky.

And as I looked, I suddenly fell back against the door of the garage in indescribable terror.

For out of the night, filling the night, came a tortured, shrieking cry. It was all about me, rising to an unearthly climax, wailing, dying again. It was the most awful sound I have ever heard.

## CHAPTER III
## THE LEGEND OF THE ROCK

THERE WAS ONLY ONE THING TO DO, and I did it. I couldn't investigate; that would be like a blind man roaming a desert in search for the source of heat. For the cry, which ceased as suddenly as it came, was nowhere and everywhere, surrounding me, beating at my ears. I ran back into the house, fumbling with the door, and came at once into the living room again.

Vera Farnol had fainted. She was in a tumbled heap on the floor before the fire and her husband and daughter were standing over her. And in a moment I had scuttled out through the dining room and found the kitchen light-switch. The big room jumped into brilliance and revealed Sutton, in a curious bathrobe, coming down the short passage which evidently led to the servants' rooms.

"Water for your mistress, quick!" I called to him, and dashed back to the others.

They had raised her now, and Farnol and St. John had carried her to a divan, where Patricia was rubbing her wrists.

"Sutton is coming with water," I said.

"She'll be all right," Farnol remarked. "She's rather given to fainting."

And in a moment Sutton had come in, and the water he brought was rubbed on Vera's forehead and forced between her lips; and her eyes opened.

"I'm sorry," she said. "I'm all right now. Pat, dear, sit down beside me. Creamer," she went on, with a voice suddenly petulant, "I can't stand that noise! I simply can't stand it again!"

I burst out with my question to Farnol. "What on earth *was* that noise? Where did it come from? It's the most unearthly—"

There was just the faintest flicker of amusement playing about Farnol's eyes before he answered, but it disappeared immediately.

"So it got you too?" he asked. "It's just the Rock, Meech, that's all."

"What rock, for God's sake!"

"This one," he said, pointing down through the floor. "The one this house is built on. There's a deep cave down near the water line, on the side toward the sea—curiously constructed, with a cavern inside which is larger than the cave's opening. Whenever the wind blows across the opening in a certain way, there's a slight humming which we can rarely hear from up here. But every now and then—very, very rarely, and only on such a night as this with such a tremendously heavy wind—the angle and the force are just right and we get that awful wail. 'Wailing Rock' the natives have always called it."

"Well," I said again, "of all the unearthly sounds I've ever heard, that was the worst. I'm not easily frightened, but I admit it struck terror to me."

"Tell him the legend, Mr. Farnol," said Victor, coming forward.

Farnol shifted on his feet and ran his long fingers through that white hair. "Why, it's nothing," he began, "but we've always heard— my family, I mean—and we've always repeated it because it sort of adds an atmosphere to the place—fun, you know—that every time it wails it's a warning of death within twenty-four hours."

My head shot sharply up and I looked at him closely.

"Is there any basis in fact?" I snapped at him.

"None that I know of."

"How often, on an average, does it wail?"

"Oh, very, very seldom. I don't suppose I've heard it more than four times in my life—but of course we're here very little."

"But," I pursued, "were there any circumstances at all in connection with the other wails that make you think that the legend has any excuse for existing? I understand, of course, that they would be entirely coincidences."

Farnol glanced at his wife, and I saw her nod at him. "You might as well tell him," she said faintly.

"Why," said Farnol, turning to me again, and again running his fingers through his hair, "yes. There are two. As you say, coincidences of course. But some twenty years ago, on just such a night as this, we heard the Rock. My father was here then, and he took the late train from Wells Beach back to Boston. He died on the way, from heart failure."

I nodded. "Go on."

"Then," he continued, "one night, during a terrible storm, we heard the rock along about daybreak. This was eight or ten years ago, wasn't it, Vera?"

"It was when I was eleven," said Patricia. "Eleven years ago."

"Yes. That's it. And in the middle of the morning," Farnol went on, "when any of us ventured out, we found the drowned body of a man flung up on the beach beside the cliff!"

He paused.

"Who was it?" I demanded.

"Oh, no one!" he exclaimed hurriedly. "No one, I mean, that had any connection with us. It was just a fisherman whose boat foundered outside here somewhere."

"I see," I said. I forget what I was thinking. "And that's all? Those are the only times you've heard the wailing until tonight?"

There was complete silence in the room. Outside, faintly, we could hear the wind still straining at the heavy windows, and far up the chimney above the blazing fire, the draughts were humming. But inside, no one and nothing made a sound. And the only movement was the sinking back on the pillows of Vera's head.

I couldn't stand it, and my temper flared.

"Answer me!" I shouted, and banged my heel upon the floor.

The reply came from the back shadows of the room, from young Phillip Masterson, still in his straight chair by the door. He tossed his black hair and spoke in the slowest, calmest, most expressionless of voices.

"*The Rock wailed last night*," he said.

Sutton, after all, drove me to the telephone. Immediately after Masterson had made his announcement, I sent the chauffeur from the room to pull a pair of trousers over his pajamas, and to put a coat on. And then together we left the house and found the car.

The wind was dying. It was as if it had done its work and given its two warnings—last night's warning of poor Garda—tonight's warning of what? I tried to think what conclusion I should reach if I were superstitious. Would I actually consider it the prophecy of another death, or would I decide to call the second wailing nothing but a howl of accomplishment and triumph at having forecast, upon the rock's very back, the most horrible of all deaths—murder?

"Sutton," I said, as we turned our backs upon the house and started through the scrub pines, "do you know what has happened in the house tonight?"

"No, Mr. Meech," he replied. "Something, that's sure enough. I know there's been a lot of running around, because I heard it, but it's sort of early and I thought you were all having fun or something. I got up when I heard that god-awful noise because—well, because you can't sleep after a thing like that. Not right away, that is. Not without a little snifter of whiskey or something."

"What other servants are there, Sutton?"

"Only Bessie," he answered. "She's the cook and everything else. Sometimes there's a maid, but not this year, we're here for so short a time. You noticed I serve the meals. I do that when there ain't a maid."

"Sutton," I said (by this time we were out of the pines, off the point, and were speeding over the causeway that picked its path across the inky marsh), "Miss Lawrence is dead."

The sudden, impetuous increase in the car's speed showed that, in complete surprise, his foot had involuntarily pressed harder upon the throttle. He checked it at once.

"Dead, sir? I'm sorry."

"Murdered, Sutton!"

This time his foot left the throttle entirely and he turned to me in blank astonishment.

"Murdered?" he echoed. "God! Whoever done it, sir?"

I searched his face in the faint light from the dashboard. His surprise and his ignorance were real; I instinctively felt that. I instinctively felt that I had no cause to think otherwise.

"We don't know, Sutton," I replied as we resumed our speed.

He turned to look at me again.

"One—one of *them?*" he asked, his hand leaving the wheel for a second and jerking back over his shoulder toward the sea and the house.

"Almost surely," I replied.

"God, sir!"

"And the devil," I added. And then, after a slight pause: "Sutton, how long have you been with the Farnols?"

"About ten years, sir."

"You're sure it's not eleven? Weren't you here eleven years ago when there was a shipwreck just outside and the body of a man was washed up?"

"No sir. I came the next summer. I remember hearing about it."

"Then the first time you ever heard the cave in the rock make that noise was last night?"

"Yes, sir."

"Positively?"

"Yes, sir . . . . Here's the farmhouse, sir. They're still up. I can see a light."

The telephone operator, an incredibly stupid young lady with a perfect Maine twang, knew nothing about the residence of the sheriff, but after much haranguing, gave me a constable in the village of Ogunquit. From him I learned that the sheriff's name was Gallant and that he lived in Kennebunk, some nine or ten miles up the coast. And by many wrestlings with the hand-crank on the side of the telephone, I reached Sheriff Gallant at his home.

Wonder of wonders and by the grace of heaven, he had heard of me. Accustomed as I am to having city officials in whatever town know my name and my reputation, and piqued as I am when they do not know me, this was my first experience at being recognized as rather prominent in my profession by a country officer. I warmed at once to Mr. Gallant.

I told my facts and gave the location and most certainly did not have to urge his immediate presence. One thing, however, I did urge, and that was that he bring a man or two with him. And the reason, of course, is entirely clear. Unsuperstitious as I am, there was most definitely a net of coincidences about the wailing of the Rock which I could not ignore. There was most definitely, by the laws, of analogy, the possibility of another death, following the Rock's second wail. Not—please don't let it be misunderstood—not by any power of the wind against a salty cavern; but because—and rapidly this conviction was shaping itself in my mind—someone in the company had had the idea of murder planted in his mind by the awful legend of the place. Someone, perhaps, who had a grievance against Garda, however slight, and who felt, when he heard the tale and heard the cry of wind and rock, that here was the prophecy of his own action, and that here was the solution of his real or fancied difficulties. I knew I was probably romancing, and I knew that I was too old in my profession to be a psychologist. But, as I have said before, I always play my hunches.

Sheriff Gallant informed me that he would summon the medical examiner who lived still farther away, in Biddeford. And that he, himself, would come within the hour, as soon as he could round up a couple of men. And then I left, waving away with a dollar bill the thousand questions which were rising to the moustachioed lips of the farmer, who had heard it all, and who stared, fascinated, at my ugly form, and who (I knew) would rush to the bedside of his wife and tell how a horrible hunchback, looking half spider and half ape, had come into his kitchen and reported murder down at Farnol's.

In the drive back, Sutton and I spoke hardly a word. There were many things I wanted to ask him, principally about the Farnol family, but I wanted first to give Creamer Farnol himself an opportunity to answer them. All I said, therefore, was: "Sutton, I don't think you'd better go back to bed just yet. Stay up, will you, in the kitchen? I doubt if we'll need the car, but we may."

"I couldn't think of sleeping, sir," was his reply.

It was during the drive, then, that instead of talking I laid a few tentative plans, and these I give you in my own words as I announced them to the group around the fire when we got back to the house. They had hardly moved—the people sitting there—save that young Masterson had come out of his shadows and was crouched by the hearthside, and that the two St. Johns were not occupying the wing chair before which Vera had fainted.

"The police are coming," I began. "Now, people," I went on, "I've worked on many and many a murder case, and my status in such cases widely differs. Sometimes I'm chief investigator; sometimes I'm merely unofficial adviser to the bereaved family; sometimes I'm expert assistant to the police detective in charge. I don't know what I'll be here as regards Sheriff Gallant, but I fully imagine I shall be in charge. I certainly intend to request that I be put in charge, and I think he'll let me have my way. In which situation, I suppose I become, automatically the personal enemy of every one of you. I shan't feel the enmity, but you will unless I plead with you against it—plead, that is, with everyone except the guilty one. Let him consider me his enemy if he chooses, for he will be quite right. But from the rest of you, I do beg friendliness, and cooperation."

Mr. St. John spoke. He was tall, and thin, and violently red-headed, with a slight goatee, and he was holding the arm of his mouse-like little wife.

"You have definitely decided, then, I take it, that Garda Lawrence was killed by one of us?"

"Quite," I answered, as calmly and as kindly as I could. "There is really no other possible decision—probable decision, I should say. Little as I confess I know about Garda's affairs, I am quite certain that she has no other acquaintances, let alone enemies, in this out-of-the-way spot. And none, we can rest quite assured, who would care to penetrate an occupied house to do a thing like this—in the full knowledge of the placing of her room and the way to get to it.

"No, I am going to proceed on the supposition that one of you seven has killed my ward—until I find a sign which shows me I'm on the wrong road. Furthermore, that is the supposition I shall tell the sheriff. And furthermore, I am going to begin now to exert the authority I fully believe the sheriff will vest in me. . . . I'm going to call for a confession, and I will wait three minutes."

I have mentioned a thing I do which has caused comments in the press and in reports of my cases. It is just a personal idiosyncrasy, but it seems to have caught the fancy of the reporters in their ever-watchfulness for the unusual and the grotesque. It is my habit of sitting, in moments of drama or intensity, cross-legged on table-tops. The habit comes, as I have said, from the shape of my legs and back and from the consequent difficulty I have of finding a chair which gives me even a slight degree of comfort.

Here, then, I swept aside an ashtray and a few magazines from the end of the heavy table near the center of the room, and climbed upon it. And there I sat, watch in hand, surveying my little group.

"Three minutes," I repeated, "for any one of you to say a little word or make a little sign—before I give my first order. . . . Ready— we begin now!"

Of course no one spoke. I knew for a certainty that no one would. When first, after a crime like this, the guilty one has kept his silence and has, apparently with nonchalance, taken his place and his part in the events of the next few minutes or hours, it needs far more than a simple call for self-betrayal to make him take the blame upon himself. But still, it's a good trick. It starts things off. It shows the weight of authority, and it proves to the innocent majority that business is meant, and that their aid is needed.

No one spoke, as I say, and with the dying of the wind and the fading of the fire, the silence was heavy, absolute, impressive.

Promptly at the end of three minutes I put away my watch, hearing the increased breathing and the slight shifting in chairs as I did so. Then I began my speech again:

"Very well. The war is on. . . . Now these are my plans. The sheriff will want to talk to me first; he will want to go into the cupola and spend some time there; he will want, eventually, either to talk to each one of you separately, or have me do it. Therefore, it is entirely unnecessary for you to stay here together. It will be much better, I think, if you go to your rooms. Mr. Farnol, has each bedroom door got a lock and key?"

"Yes. I'm very sure."

"Then," I said, moving off my table, "I'm afraid we shall use the locks. The reason is obvious, of course. May I take you upstairs now—two by two?"

And that was what I did. Again it was really a useless procedure, but again it gave that little touch of authority and drama, so often infinitely valuable at the opening of an investigation. I took the St. Johns up first, saw them safely in their room, and transferred the key from the inside to the out, turning it swiftly. And then the dark young Masterson and the blond young Victor Millard, each to his separate chamber. And then the three Farnols.

It was amazing to see Vera Farnol ascending those stairs. She was badly shaken, I knew; she was even, I feared, on the verge of hysterics, but she walked like a sainted martyr, and I pitied her and admired her. Patricia, glowing with pale beauty, went by her side, and Farnol walked with me, more stooped, more haggard than the rest of his family. I shook him by the hand as I left him at his door, and said, "I'm more than sorry, Farnol, to take the ruling of your house from your hands. But do you see the necessity?"

He clutched my hand with a real warmth. "Of course, Meech. Of course. Let me know if you want anything," and he closed the door behind him while I turned the key.

Then, from the top of the stairs, I surveyed my row of prison cells. There were four rooms on each side of the upper hallway as I looked the length of it toward the circular staircase that led up to Garda's cupola. On my right, in order, were the rooms of Patricia, first, then of the St. Johns, then Victor Millard, and finally my empty one. On my left the row began with Vera Farnol's, followed by Creamer Farnol's and Phillip Masterson's. But beyond Masterson's was one more to which I had conducted no one. Rapidly I traversed the length of the hall and tried the knob of its closed door. It was locked. I put my eye to the keyhole, but it was dark within. And even by the most careful listening, I could hear no sound.

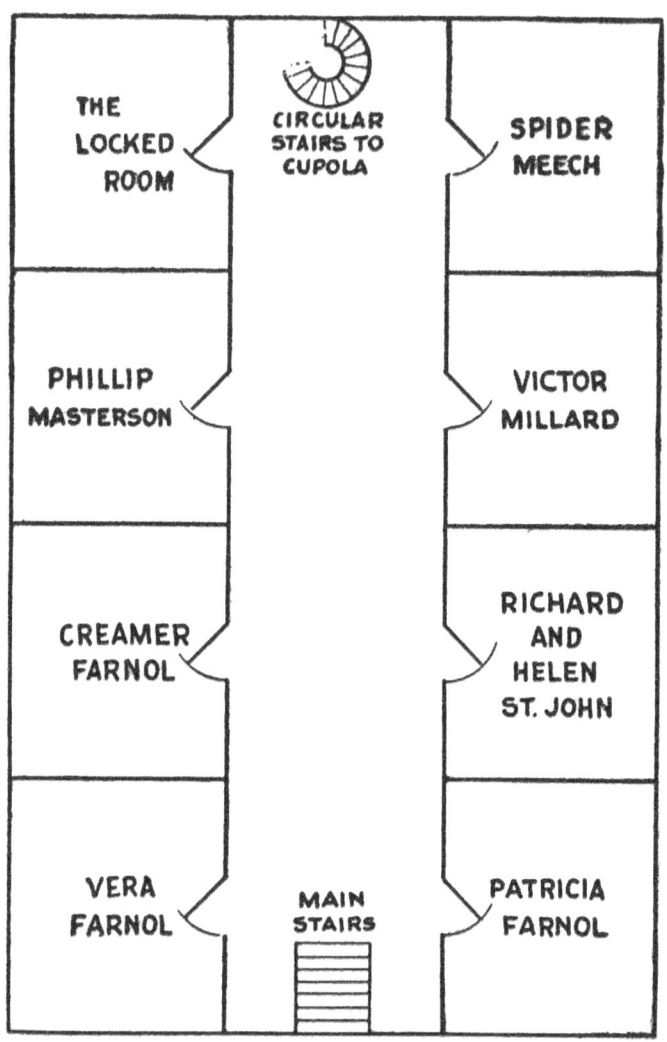

**SECOND FLOOR OF CREAMER FARNOL'S HOUSE**
**SHOWING DISPOSITION OF CHAMBERS**

So back I went to Creamer Farnol's room, tapped upon his door and unlocked it as I heard him move inside.

"Oh, Farnol," I said, as he came in response, "what room is that at the other end of the hall—the one on this side of the house, just opposite mine? It's locked."

"Nothing, Meech," he said. "We've never had occasion to fix it up. It's just a store room now. On account of the cupola, you see, there's no attic space in the house, and we throw everything in there. Don't let it worry you."

"Thanks," I said, and turned his key again.

Down the stairs. I went, took one turn around the living room, and looked at my watch. It was just eleven o'clock.

I stepped out on the veranda with another cigar, and leaned on the eastward rail, looking out and over the black and curving beach with its dark, dark sands, toward the other house, and realizing that it was only two hours ago that I had been walking there, and seeing the two cupola lights—first that one—and then this. And I marveled, too, at the change in the night. Only the slightest of quiet breezes was coming from the ocean now, but the air had chilled, and there were no stars.

I leaned over the rail and flicked an ash down at the rock.

The latch of the door clicked behind me, and I turned with a sudden start as a figure emerged from the door and came toward me.

"Who's there!" I cried, and I'm afraid my voice was raised.

"It's only Sutton, sir," the figure said. "I heard it all quiet and I just stepped into the living room to see if you had all gone off to bed—not that I want to go. And I saw the light of your cigar out here. Can I wait with you, sir, until the police come? It's a bit spooky in that kitchen."

"Of course, Sutton," said I, relieved, and even glad of his company. So he took a cigar, and together we leaned over the railing, staring into the darkness, waiting for the sound of the sheriff's car, and thinking our own thoughts.

Finally I spoke to him. "Sutton," I said, "who owns that other house that's just like this one—up on the next point?"

"Why—Mr. Farnol, sir."

"Creamer Farnol?"

"Yes, sir."

"Who occupies it?" I pursued.

"No one, sir."

"No one, Sutton? What do you mean?"

"Just that, sir. It's been locked and shuttered tight for many years now."

# CHAPTER IV
## THE SANDS ARE DARK

SHERIFF GALLANT WAS A SMALL MAN and a very alert one with a head going rapidly bald in front and a little black moustache. He had the Maine accent—that curious up-and-down sing-song with the stresses coming on unexpected words. As he and his two men got out of the car, he treated me as deferentially as if I had been the governor of his state, and he shook me by the hand and said, "More than glad to meet you, Mr. Meech. And more than proud to be in on a case with you."

And in five minutes we had my status settled: I was to be the chief investigator exactly as if I were the entire Homicide Bureau; he and his men were to be my ready and willing aids—the force and the authority of the law, ready to guard, to assist, to watch, and to arrest.

Before we began our work—before we even began to lay any plans about the beginning of our work, he gave me one slight tip. "Take it or leave it, Mr. Meech," he said, "but it may help you to start your thinking. It's just this. Maine, you know, has no capital punishment, and it isn't unknown to our records to find killings done in this state just to escape hanging or the chair. Instance not far from here where a man took care to get only a few hundred feet over the border before he done his work. Now, this here's a summer resort pure and simple, which generally means out-of-the-staters, and the summer resort season closed a month ago and practically every other house around here is shut as tight as a drum. So it might help you to start thinking that it isn't impossible that some

233

of these folks deliberately chose the State of Maine to do their dirty work in—just in case they *did* get caught! We're less than twenty miles from the New Hampshire line, you know, at Portsmouth. Think it over, and if it's worth anything, you might try to find out if every one of these people had a good, clear, vacationing reason for coming into Maine at this time of year."

It was a good point and I thanked him heartily. And then I suggested that if he wanted to start in helping me, he and his men could go up into the cupola and begin finger printing. He told me he knew all about it, had taken a course in it at Augusta, although he had no apparatus with him. I had—a pocket set which is one of my prize possessions and which goes with me, like everything else I own, everywhere I go. I told him that the prints of the people in the house had not been taken, and I told him it would be of advantage to take those of Garda and, in his report to me, to eliminate all of hers.

"The outer door knob of the cupola," I went on, "will unfortunately be useless. I've messed that up myself, trying to get in. The light switch may be of value, but difficult to take clearly. Mr. Farnol turned it when we first entered the room, but he touched it only once. It may possibly be that at least part of another print will be discernible under his. If you can find one, a fairly fresh one which is not Garda Lawrence's, we will have gone a long way toward our first step. The woodwork of the bed ought to be gone over very carefully. The windows, I think, will be valueless; it's unlikely that they were touched after Garda opened them, when she went to nap, until young Victor Millard and I closed them. But the inside doorknob should be the best of all. Make very sure that neither of your men touches it before you've got it fixed. I can't see how anyone could have used it since the door was locked after the murderer's second visit to the room—a very few minutes before I found the body. Certainly neither young Millard nor myself. In our inspection of the room we didn't close the door, and when we left and shut the door behind us, we used only the outside knob, of course."

All this was told to him, naturally, together with a resume of the events as I had witnessed them, a narration which I omit here, but which was factual, true, and complete. The only thing I omitted was my discovery of the light in the cupola of the other house, and I omitted that for two reasons: one was that I had no real conviction that it concerned this case at all, and the other was that I was rapidly forming a plan to visit that cupola before the night was over—perhaps almost immediately.

"Don't you agree with me, sheriff," I said, "that it will be better in the long run if you and I and the coroner do our preliminary work alone tonight, leaving the suspects, if we can call them that, to face us in the morning after they've had what sleep they can get, poor souls?"

"I certainly do, Spider," he answered. And then in a rush of embarrassment accompanied by a violent reddening of his face, he stammered, "Oh, I'm sorry! Damn, if I'm not sorry, Mr. Meech. But you see—we—I—I've got so used, in reading about you, and talking about you, to calling you S-s-s—"

I laughed at him. "Think nothing of it, sheriff," I told him. "I've never had a colleague yet who didn't call me Spider, and you'd better begin now instead of later. . . . Let's get to work."

I took them upstairs and got them the print apparatus, and then showed them into the cupola. There, I stayed less than a minute, merely asking the sheriff to note and to jot down any details he cared to or thought would be of value later, and then to cover Garda up until the coroner should arrive. Then I left them and descended to the second floor.

I was thinking hard and thinking fast, phrasing the little interview I was planning to have at once with Creamer Farnol on the subject of the other house up the shore. I wanted to go in it, and I wanted to find out the means of entrance without letting Farnol know that I suspected a single thing in connection with it. If he betrayed any worriment at my request, well and good, if not—well and good.

And so, as I say, I was thinking hard and phrasing my questions and his possible answers, and I had, at that moment, one of my absent-minded lapses which I am, unfortunately, prone to have at such times of concentration. And down the long, dim-lit hallway I went, treading lightly, stooped in my thinking—past Creamer Farnol's door, and on, in my stupidity, to the next and last one.

It was my intention to unlock his door, push it open, and call softly, "Oh, Farnol!"

And I did unlock the door and push it open. But back in the shadows of the room, a few feet beyond the inward swinging of the door, so that the light from the hall fell upon her only faintly, stood Vera—tall, all in clinging white, motionless, staring at, through, and beyond me.

I think I murmured an apology. I know I made some sound or some movement before I realized that she didn't know I was there— that she was coming toward me—that her lips were moving. And then I saw that she was sleep-walking, or doing something very akin to it, and immediately every bit of romantic literature from Lady Macbeth on down flashed into my mind and I fell back. Self-betrayal! was what I thought. Watch her! Don't disturb her! Listen to her! What is she mumbling, and does she seek something stronger than the perfumes of Arabia!

On she came, so very, very slowly, the soft folds of her silk gown rippling ever so slightly in the pale light. And not a word could I catch, nor could I, from the moving of her lips, see the forming of any definite word.

And on she came, step by step, with feet that were bare and white under the low hem of the silk.

But then she stopped. She reached the door-sill and stopped, swaying slightly, forward, then back, and shuddered and closed her eyes and reached her hands out.

I knew it was all over and I caught her hands, calling her by name and rubbing my thumbs over the backs of her fingers as I held them.

"Mrs. Farnol; Vera Farnol—come, come! Wake up!"

And she woke, her eyes opening and breaking into a light of recognition, but with that recognition she recoiled a step or two, suddenly, almost pulling me with her, and giving a cry half of despair and half of shame.

"It's all right," I said. "It's all right. You were just walking in your sleep. It's all right. Come, let me put the light on." And I pushed past her into her room and found the light, turning it on and spying immediately her black and gold negligee thrown over the back of a chaise-longue. I took it and went to her by the door, throwing it over her shoulders and leading her as best I could back to the chaise-longue where I made her sit down.

She was fully awake now, and ready for tears, so I crouched on the top of a little bench beside her and held her hand, patting it and being soothing.

"How awful!" she said. "How perfectly awful!"

"Awful?" I ventured. "Nonsense. Don't think anything about it. Put it out of your mind altogether that there's anything unnatural at all about it. Just think of it as a good joke. As a matter of fact, it's probably lucky I discovered you or you might have hurt yourself falling against something. You see," I lied, "I was going by your door when I heard you moving inside. And I called to you and got no answer. And because, as you realize, I'm very interested in everything my little band of unwilling prisoners does," I forced a smile, "I took the liberty of opening the door. It was nothing. It was less than half a minute." I patted her hand again, and I watched carefully to see if she gave any sign that she knew I was lying, for very naturally the suspicion of fake had come to my mind. But she gave no sign at all.

"I don't know what makes me do it," she said. "And it's only in the last few years that I have done it."

"Often?" I asked softly.

"No," she answered. "Not really often. Once or twice a year, so far as I know—times that I catch myself, I mean, or someone else catches me."

She was silent for a moment while I studied her beauty and searched her proud, patrician face for whatever I might find. The hand that lay in mine was still and warm.

"And it's not only when I'm asleep, you know," she suddenly added, looking at me.

"What do you mean, Mrs. Farnol?"

She drew her hand away and interlocked it with the other on her lap.

"I get funny lapses." I watched her closely. "Oh—nothing serious, but sudden little times when I'm reading, or writing, that all at once I realize that I have been actually unconscious or far away for a few seconds. It's nothing unpleasant. It's more like fainting without any of the falling or the dizziness. I simply come to with a start, knowing that between the second when I read the last word on the page and the second when I read the first word on the top of the next one, there has been a tiny little interval when I thought of nothing and knew nothing. Silly, isn't it?"

"Yes," I said, "rather silly. Have you ever told it to a doctor?"

"Oh, yes," she answered. "Several times, but they've never seemed to help me any. One said that it was my eyes and another my digestion, and one told me to stop smoking for a while. But nothing seems to help. And please don't think," she went on, rapidly, "that it's really very bothersome or that I worry about it. It's only this rare sleepwalking that's at all humiliating, such as tonight with a stranger. The waking times are such tiny little intervals that I'm sure no one in the room would ever notice it. In fact, I've never even told Creamer, he's so finicky about such things as health."

"It doesn't sound very serious to me," I told her, "so long as these—shall we say, unconscious intervals aren't of any great length. So long as you don't walk, or do anything during them. You don't, do you?"

"Never," she said. "Never at all."

I left her shortly after that, sure that she was entirely herself again and more calm and unafraid than I had ever thought she could be, considering the events of the night. Not once did she ask me any questions concerning the progress of the case. Not once in any way did she even by remote implication refer to Garda. . . . I regretted having to turn the key in her lock as I left the room.

Then, immediately, I went to the next door, unlocked and opened it, and called inside, "Oh, Farnol!"

"Come in, Meech," he said, and as there was a dim light burning, I walked directly into the room and found him sitting up in his bed, reading. "How are things going?" he asked. "Is there anything I can do for you?"

Because of the heavy doors and walls of this sturdy house, and because of the fact that his wife and I had talked in extremely low voices, I hoped he had heard nothing of the little scene we just had played, and I determined not to mention it to him.

"Things are going as well as we can expect," I answered, perching on the foot of his bed. "There's nothing we can really do tonight, and nothing that we want to do until the sheriff has made his few preliminary examinations and the medical examiner has come. The sheriff is here now, with his two men, and he agrees with me that all talk shall be left until the morning.

"And that's what I want to talk to you about. I want the sheriff and his men here tonight—the sheriff to get his normal sleep and the men to take their turns at guard, 'round the house. Now, I take it there aren't any empty beds, are there?"

With one long finger marking the place in his closed book—it was Spenser, I noticed—he thought a moment. "No," he said, "except for the extra one for the maid when we have one, and that's in Bessie's room. There's the sofa in the living room. Couldn't—"

"I'd like to have the man who's not on guard use that," I broke in. "And I'd like to have the sheriff sleep in my room. Now, as for me—I don't want a lot of sleep, but I do want a place alone, where I can walk up and down and think, if need be, and fall into a chair and doze when I feel like it. . . I'm wondering if you'd mind if I walked up the beach to that other house—Sutton tells me you own it—and find an old chair or a blanketless mattress or something."

Farnol gazed at me in astonishment. "Why, that would be absurd!" he cried.

"Why so?"

"Why, it's been closed for years. It's shuttered tight—nailed shutters, you know, and you couldn't get a breath of air anywhere."

"What about the cupola?"

"Well," he admitted, "that's open. But I don't believe the electric current is turned on, and I forget whether there's any furniture there or not. The rest of the house is furnished, but all covered with dustsheets. No, no, Meech. I couldn't think of it!"

I looked at him long and hard. "It's only my discomfort you're thinking of, isn't it, Farnol? There's no other reason, of course."

He returned my look quite unflinchingly, but I knew it was a searching gaze. "There's no other reason why you want to go, except to think and sleep, is there, Meech?" he asked with a slight laugh, conscious that he was giving me as good as I sent.

"Certainly not," I replied.

"And certainly not to your question too."

"Then I think," I said, "that I demand your hospitality as an honoured guest, and I think you'd better let me decide my own comfort. Oh, come, Farnol! It's just a crotchet, and I want the walk and the solitude, and if I find the house impossible, I can do no worse and no better than to turn directly around and come back here."

He sighed and laid his book away. "You're incorrigible, Meech," he said, moving from the bed to a heavy desk. "But one thing you must promise me: that you'll confine your wanderings to the stairs and the cupola and not go wandering around those rooms. As I say, I doubt if there are lights, and you'll hurt yourself, sure as fate, if you go stumbling among the furniture. As a matter of fact, I think most of the rooms are locked, and I most certainly will not tell you where the keys are."

"Very well," I returned. "I promise." There was no harm in that.

He found, in a pigeon-hole of the desk, an ordinary key of the Yale type, marked with a little tag, and tossed it to me. "Now for heaven's sake, be careful, Meech."

"I will be," I assured him. "And thank you heartily. I'll wake you early in the morning. Goodnight." But at the door I stopped and asked a question. "Oh, Farnol, who on earth built these houses and why?"

"My grandfather," he replied, "back in the eighties. He was an eccentric old codger with what he thought was a flair for design. It was, all right, but it was a flair for grotesque design. He built these two marvelous creations for his twin sons, one of whom was my father. My uncle's branch of the family has all died out and both of them are mine now. We still occupy this one because it's a grand location and we've become used to the awfulness of the house. But the other one is a white elephant. I can't rent it, and I haven't got around to selling it. Five or six years ago I simply boarded it up— some of the furniture is fairly valuable, I suppose, although I've never had it inventoried—and I don't believe I've been in it half a dozen times since."

"I see," I said. "Goodnight again."

At the foot of the cupola stairs I called softly to the sheriff and he came down to meet me.

"I'm going out for a while," I told him, "on a little tangent of my own. Whenever you feel like it, get a wink of sleep here in my room—this is it." And I told him he'd better arrange a patrol round about the verandas and grounds as soon as he could spare a man, letting the two men spell each other as the night wore on. "I'll be back," I said, "but I shan't want any sleep."

On the back of an envelope I drew him a rough design of the second floor, labeling each room with its occupant's name so that if any of them called to him, or if any emergency arose, he would be slightly informed.

Then, as he climbed the cupola stairs again, I found a flash-light in my room and slipped it into my pocket, replenishing my matches and refilling my cigar case. After that, there was but one thing left to do before I set out. I had determined to make a quick and silent inspection of my seven prisoners. And this I did, passing in the hall one of the sheriff's men going downstairs to take up his guard.

Creamer and Vera Farnol I had just seen. There was no use looking in on them again. But I made the rounds of every other room, softly opening the door, softly calling the name of the person within, merely making sure of each one's presence. Masterson and Patricia Farnol failed to answer me, and I let a quick beam of light flash upon their beds and their huddled, sleeping forms. St. John didn't answer me, but his wife did, assuring me that both of them were all right. Victor Millard's light was on, and I entered his room. He was sitting at his desk, writing, still with his dressing gown on.

"Not in bed, Victor?"

He looked up with a slight grin. "Hell, I can't sleep. How do you spell 'autopsy'?"

I laughed and told him. "What are you doing, bringing your diary up to date?"

"No, a letter. Telling my ex-roommate all about this mess. Say, will it have to be censored?"

"I hardly think so," I answered. "We'll see. But I may ask to read it tomorrow, to help correlate details, you know. Ex-roommate? College roommate?"

"Yes," he said. "I left Amherst last June and I'm just going to putter around for a year before I go to Harvard Business next fall. I'm sailing in a couple of weeks, you know. Bud—this ex-roommate of mine—is going with me."

"Europe?"

"Yes. And northern Africa."

"Fine. Well, try to get some sleep. Goodnight."

Poor kid, I thought, as I locked him in his room and started down the hall. He doesn't realize that there are great chances that he may be forbidden to leave the country for some months yet, if by any chance the mystery should drag on. And if there should be a solution and an arrest, the chances would still be that his presence would be required as a witness. How much more deeply, I have often thought, crime and its consequences bite into the lives of youth than age. The most stolid, conservative, middle-aged man or woman is less wounded by the snapping jaws of violence and the law than is the careless youngster with his head in the air, looking at the happy future. This was really more Victor's tragedy, and Patricia's, and Phillip Masterson's, than the St. Johns', the Farnols' or mine.

I took a brief look in on Sutton, in his bed at last, heard Bessie snoring heavily, and then, remembering the growing cold, took my topcoat, gloves, and stick and started out. The sheriff's man, on his watch, spoke to me, and I told him to guard well, to keep moving, and to let no one out of the house and no one in it but the medical examiner when he came and myself when I should return. He asked me the time and I told him.

It was just midnight.

So again upon the sands. The tide was four hours or more past its full and the line of breakers, still high, but much less forceful than before, was far down the wet, pool-ridden beach. It was very cold indeed and I walked as briskly as I could.

It is amazing how deceptive a beach can be at night—how so flat, empty a place can seem full of slopes and hills and shadows. A dozen times my eyes and the atmosphere of mirage played tricks upon me and I thought I was about to step up a precipitous hill or step off the edge of a bottomless pit. Each time, of course, my feet proved to me that all was even, straight, monotonous, smooth, but I couldn't rationalize away my illusions. There was no star-shine to glitter in the pools and rivulets left by the departing tide, and no echo of the sun or moon in the sky to fix an horizon and make an objective. And there were shapes, too, fancied human shapes about me with whom, it seemed, I was about to come face to face, forming, vanishing, flitting, dying. Had the beach been a rocky one, I thought, with crags and boulders jutting from the sand, a thousand more phantom humans would have been dancing around me thus. And they, being rock-dwelling folk and therefore known to be derisive, would have laughed and jeered at me as I went my bent, ungainly way.

Seriously, though, I thought, how simple and how easy it would be for anyone who chose to hide, to lie, simply and starkly, on such a beach as this, on such a night. For despite the flatness, despite the absence of any place of concealment, one could lie unobserved by a person—even a person on the alert—passing within twenty feet. He could be a log, if noticed at all, or a more deeply shadowed pool, or one of a thousand creations of the wanderer's brain.

Take Mr. X., now. Some sinister Mr. X. in whom I did not believe—who wished Garda's death—who, egged on by the second awful wailing of that ungodly rock, lay here in wait for me, to rise and run and kill. Or to stay until I passed him and then to creep to the house, escape the guard, and somehow kill again. Easy. Not to be thought of, but easy.

And what should I find in the house that lay somewhere before me? It was dark, and there was no light in the cupola now. I could see that, even though the silhouette of the house itself was still lost in the distance. No one, probably. But the traces of someone, I hoped. Still, one never knew.

And so musing, I came to the mile's end and after a little search found the path up the cliff, and thereupon I scrambled. And as I reached the house I saw, dimly, how heavily shuttered the windows were, and I ran the beam of my flashlight over two or three of them on the ground floor. My key, I assumed, fitted the main door under the porte-cochere, and there I went, fitting it into the little lock—so small for such a door, and giving it a lusty turn. It clicked, easily, naturally, and well, and the door swung inward without a complaint from its hinges.

I stood and listened, but from the blackness beyond there came not the slightest sound.

Into the hall, then, I shone my light, moving it over the stairs and around the walls. Detail by detail the room was the same as that in Creamer Farnol's house. In I stepped—and it was a strange sensation, to be entering thus a house which I felt I knew so well and yet which was so vastly different. For that house, peopled as it was, had a soul—no matter how tragic that soul might be—and this had none. It had only echoes and a blackness so thick that I had a fanciful thought my flashlight beam might not be able to get through. And the mustiness of the air added to the imaginary thickness of the gloom. It was not unpleasant, but it was real and strange.

In the living room to my left, as the glow from my light fell inside the arched opening before I turned the direct beam within, were a dozen squatting ghosts, sitting on their haunches in midnight conclave—heavy chairs, of course, in their death shrouds—waiting. There was no sign of human habitation. There was no sign, even, of their having been disturbed for heaven knows how long, for when I entered the room and flashed my light around, I saw the dust lying heavy and undisturbed on the graying covers. The dining room was the same, and the kitchen, and the chambers down the servant's passage, identical with those of Sutton and Bessie.

So back to the hall I came, and up the stairs. Here—ah! here were footprints discernible in the dust on the varnished oak steps— coming up and going down. Not clear, but easily recognized as being of man's size. I chose one of the clearest of all and, setting down my flash on the steps beside it, I drew a piece of typewriter paper from my pocket—an old letter—and laid it carefully over the print, pinning it down into the wood as securely as possible with four pins from my lapel. So onward and upward I went.

At the top of the stairs I stopped and turned the light switch, but its metallic click produced no light in the wall brackets down the upper hall.

And still there was awful silence as I moved down the line of doors, zigzagging from one side of the hall to another as I tried each knob and pushed against the panels. Every one was securely locked.

And so I reached the foot of the stairs to the cupola, and with my light held straight before me, I climbed them slowly, around two bends, up into the copy of that ghastly other room where Garda lay. And here the mustiness ended, for here there were no shutters and some freshness and coolness had penetrated the cracks of the storm-worn casements. But here again was emptiness—emptiness, I think, even more noticeable because of the invisible, black night outside, pressing at the panes.

My light, traveling around, showed two faded wicker chairs, a cot bed with a mattress but no blankets, a table desk with a few drawers and a straight chair before it. And it was to the desk that I went, and opened the top drawer. It contained only a few scattered tacks and screws and a rusting hairpin. Nor did any of the other drawers show anything at all but tiny remainders of a former habitation—save one—and in that one drawer was an assortment of papers—old letters, mostly, some in their envelopes, some loose. And a quick glance showed me they were addressed to various Farnols.

Were they useless? Were they worth the trouble even of a hasty reading? I decided to give them five minutes, and I pulled them from their drawer and threw them onto the table top, drawing the chair close and sitting in it, keeping my light full on with my left hand.

I chose one at random and began to read. It was undated:

> "Dear Solomon:
> "I am writing to you upon that subject which is always uppermost in our minds but never on our tongues. What is going to become of her? What are we going to do? Vera says—"

Far, far down in the depths of the house I heard a noise.

A step. A most decided step on the main staircase. And then another—and another—and another—and somebody was coming up! Slowly, but without hesitation.

I didn't wait to think. I didn't stop to wonder whether he had come from within the house itself and possibly knew nothing of my presence, or whether he had come from outside and had seen my light. And whether he wished me harm or not, I didn't stop to decide. I flashed my light out and I stood in the center of the room, some few feet from the open door at the top of the stairs, and I raised my stick over my head and kept it there, in my right hand, while my left still held the light pointed at the door.

And I waited.

On came the footsteps, now reaching the top of the main stairs, now slowly, steadily, as if they had no light to guide them, going the length of the hall. Now—now! Reaching the foot of these very cupola stairs of mine, and coming up, and up, and up. One—two—three—and the sound of heavy breathing. And he was here—paused on the landing at the door.

"Who's there!" I cried, and pressed the button of my flash.

# CHAPTER V
# THE KNIFE

PHILLIP MASTERSON STOOD at the end of my beam of light, his black hair all awry, his face drawn and pale, his eyes wide and staring and reflecting back, in two flaming points, the glowing lens of my flash.

"Masterson!" I cried. "Masterson!"

He nodded and clenched his fists. "Please turn that light away. *Please* turn it away!" he pleaded, with his voice curiously hollow.

I turned it, letting it fall on the wall beside the door so that its reflection lit the room with a dim radiance.

"Oh, not even *that!*" he cried petulantly, and stepping to the wall bracket near the bed, he turned the switch. To my astonishment the room broke into brilliance.

"Why," I said, "I thought—I thought the current was off!"

He gazed at one of the bulbs in complete blankness. "I didn't know," he said, "but evidently not."

I snapped out my flash, tossed it onto the bed and then turned and faced him.

"Masterson!" I cried, my voice rising in excitement. "What on earth are you doing here! How did you get out!"

The faint shadow of a pitying smile began to play around his thin lips. "Easily, Spider Meech. And not more than fifteen minutes after you locked me up, over an hour ago."

"But *how!*"

"Out the window and onto the roof of the veranda. It's not much of a jump from there."

"But why—why!" I sputtered. "Oh, you fool! Why did you come here? How did you get here?"

"I saw you on the beach," he replied. "I was sitting there, and thinking and thinking, and I saw you pass. You passed within a dozen feet of me, and I knew you by your ugly little shape that I wish I'd never seen!" He blurted it out, his fists suddenly beating the air in front of him.

"But why— Why!" I persisted, with all the vehemence that was in me. "Why, you fool!"

*"Because I killed Garda Lawrence, that's why!"*

"What! What's that you say!"

Up within me, pouring, so it seemed, from every portion of my body, there boiled and bubbled a flood of anger, and (heaven help me!) I sprang upon him, throwing my stick from me with such force that it shattered the entire pane of the cupola window and went hurtling out into the night. I sprang upon him, grabbing him around the neck and bearing him backward upon the bed with me on top of him, pushing and strangling.

But I fell back—of course I fell back. After all, I'm a comparatively sane individual and know the law. I left him lying there, choking and spluttering, with his hands feeling for his bruised throat. I stood before him and cursed, letting my anger out as well as I could in what I fear was a tirade of profanity.

"For God's sake, Masterson," I concluded, "are you telling me the truth!"

And through his breath-catchings he mumbled, "Wait—wait a minute—and I'll tell you—I'll tell you everything."

I waited, for a full five minutes, I think. And while, during that time, my anger far from died, it faded somewhat; it lost its violent aspect at least, and I drew a wicker chair close to the bed and sat in it, watching him.

He was a good-looking boy—I had noticed that before, but there was nothing of Victor's healthy ruddiness about him. He was about the same age, I judged, but taller, and his face was the face of the sensitive youth, the artist perhaps, possibly even the sensualist. His eyes were gray and his hair was coal black. Now, of course, there was blood in his eyes, and his hair was a snarled and tangled mat.

He had crept into Garda's letters now and then, as in the letter I had last received from her, inviting me to witness this tragedy, but I knew little about him. And I must confess that during the afternoon and evening he had faded most definitely into the background before the more definite if not more attractive radiance of young Millard. Still, I remember having told myself at dinner, there was probably more intrinsic worth buried in this shyness and this silence than in Millard's open frankness.

"Come—come, Masterson," I finally said, as his breathing quieted and he raised himself on his elbow.

"Will you let me talk—then?" he panted. "Will you let me talk without interrupting me?" And as I nodded, he buried his face in the mattress and sobbed, "Oh, why didn't you kill me! Why didn't you shoot me when I came up the stairs, or strangle me when you had the chance!"

So I had to soothe him again, raising him once more on his elbow and pleading with him to tell his story straight and clearly. And slowly, often incoherently, but steadily his story came out.

"I've known her for years—for three years. We met on the boat and I saw her in Paris. And I loved her. I did! And you don't know what that meant to me who hadn't ever loved anyone at all before. Not anyone anywhere, because that's how I am. I hated the world, and you know what the world does to you when you hate it. . . . And she told me she loved me, and I believed her. And it went on and on. . . . You don't know how things can go on and on. . . . Oh, what's the use of telling it! You can't understand what it means when the only girl—the only *person*—you've ever known or ever could possibly know who loved you, or said she did, went out of your life—like that! . . . Now listen . . . Are you listening? . . . She's in love with Victor. . . . She said she is. . . . I mean she said she was. . . . And I saw she was, and I accused her—and she laughed when she said she was. It was on the beach and I got mad—oh, more than mad. Because, you see, I'd often pictured such a possibility and I'd often thought that I'd be sad instead—you know how you picture things when you try to get to sleep. But I wasn't—I was mad. And I told her then that I was going to kill her!

"But of course I didn't think I would. That was yesterday afternoon. And last night we heard that awful, awful noise in the rock, and old Farnol told us that story, and I *knew* it was meant for me—for me to kill Garda, because that Millard—that smug, good-looking, good-for-nothing, happy Millard—he couldn't have her!

"And you came today—like a little frog, getting Garda's kisses! And Garda knew! She knew that every time she raised her eyes or opened her mouth, she was making one more move that would start me flaming. . . . A dog did that to me once. A dog that bit me when I was a kid, and I ripped his belly open. . . . With this same knife. Look at it!"

He reached in his pocket and threw a long folding knife, curved in its blade, with a sheaf of chased silver, etched with his monogram. I opened it, and found it almost as sharp as a razor, but its blade was shining clean.

"Oh, I wiped it!" he cried. "I washed and scrubbed it, and then I came down to dinner in peace. In perfect peace, after I'd written a little note, in Garda's handwriting as well as I could, telling Mrs. Farnol to leave the tray outside. Yes, it was while the house was quiet, just before dinner I did it. And Garda was asleep. It was easy. It only took a second, and it was worth it—and then I came downstairs."

Again my anger boiled, and it was only by the sheerest will power that I could keep from leaping at his throat again. But again I forced it down and demanded: "Why did you go back? Why did you go up there again just before ten o'clock!"

"I didn't," he cried. "I never went near the place again. I didn't have to."

"You swear to that!" I thundered.

"I swear! I couldn't have gone—except with all of you when I had to, to keep my—my face up. Because all night long—all the evening I mean, things began to get worse and worse and worse, and when that rock howled, if you had been there, I should have howled too, and told you everything. But then Vera Farnol fainted, and that took the attention off me. And then I decided that at the first chance I should run away—get away from there—get a ship. And when you locked me up, I got out at once.

"But I couldn't go away! I didn't dare to take the road, any road. I huddled my clothes up in the bed so that you wouldn't notice that I was gone if you just came to the door. But I knew that wouldn't fool you for long, and you'd have the roads covered. . . . So I just stayed on the beach, and wandered and wandered. And hid in the dunes—I dug a hole. . . . And oh, how awful the darkness was! You don't *know!* I wished there was a wind to make a noise. And I had to go out on the open beach. And then I saw you—scuttling along there, like a little crab. And I knew I had to tell you. And I followed you—and why, why, why didn't you shoot me!"

I don't know what I expected to happen to me when I finally did discover the murderer of my Garda, but I certainly didn't dream that, with my experience with confessions and final fixing of guilt, I should consider it vastly different from the usual satisfactory, scientific, workaday ending. But here I was, trying to force myself to think clearly through the blood that boiled in my brain. But finally I stood up, stood over him, and said:

"I shan't say a word to you now. You know what's going to happen to you. I'd like to take you by the hair and drag you back along that beach to the sheriff. But I don't want to be within the sound of your voice that long. . . . See—there's a key in the lock to this room, and I'm going to lock you in here until I get back to Farnol's and send the sheriff's car for you. Half an hour you've got to yourself, and if you've got spunk enough to jump out one of those windows, I shan't care a bit. The sheriff will—but not I!"

And I left him, his head down on the bed now, covered by his arms, sobbing into the dust of the mattress.

I put his ghastly knife into the pocket of my topcoat and with it, when I had closed the door behind me, I put the key. And then, like lightning, leaving my pocket flash behind, I dashed down the stairs and through the halls, mindful of no obstacles, seeming to see clearly through the darkness which was so oppressive before.

I didn't stop even to pull the outer door closed behind me, but ran through the porte-cochere, found the path, and scuttled down it. And just as I reached the bottom of the rocks and felt the soft sand under my feet, I felt something else, too. I felt something catch between my legs and nearly trip me up, and I saw that it was my heavy knobbed stick, fallen from the cupola. I bent to pick it up. I raised it.

But someone else had it too!

A figure beside me—suddenly—out of the darkness. He wrenched the stick from my grasp and I shouted in sudden terror.

And something came crashing down on the back of my skull and I fell forward on the sand.

\* \* \* \* \*

Consciousness comes slowly. There are voices first, and strange lights—these buzzed across my brain. I heard someone say, "Look at him!"

I was lying in the living room of the empty house, on one of the divans with its dust-cover thrown back, and over me, in very dim light, the sheriff was standing. He had his hat and coat on and a sponge in his hand. It was dripping on my face. And one of his men was there too, also in his hat and coat.

Sheriff Gallant was speaking to me. "Meech," he said. "Meech, are you all right? Can you speak to us?"

"Of course," I said. There was a biting pain at the back of my head, but the weakness and the dizziness were going fast, and I strained to get up.

"What happened, Meech! For God's sake, who hit you?"

"I don't know," I said. "I couldn't see a thing, and it was all so sudden."

The sheriff sat down on the divan beside me and laid his hand on my knee. "Then listen, Meech," he said. "Here's how we happened to be here and find you. . . . We've got work to do as soon as you can get up. . . . Soon after you'd gone, my man down stairs thought he heard people shifting around in the house. He wasn't sure. But I'd told him to call me at the slightest thing out of the ordinary. And I didn't know—until Millard told me—that you'd made a final round of the rooms anyway. So I made one. And what did I find but that Masterson had skipped—clean skipped out, leaving a heap of clothes in his bed! And old Farnol told me you'd gone up here to this house, and Mike and I drove right around to get you—you have to go way up to the main road to get across."

I nodded, a little wearily. "I know, sheriff," I said. "And he's the one who did the trick."

"Crashed you like that?"

"No—no—sheriff, you fool," I cried. "Killed Garda Lawrence!"

"Of course," said the sheriff, "but he's—"

"He's upstairs!" I cried triumphantly. "Locked in the cupola! Here's the key. See for yourself." I drew the key from my pocket and handed it to him. "And here's the knife he killed—"

There was no knife!

And something came to my mind that made me jump to my feet and start running up the stairs. Could he have got out, broken the door, followed me down stairs, brained me, and made away with the knife—the evidence?

Behind me, treading as heavily as I, came the sheriff and his man, round the turns in the staircase, down the long hall. Up—up the little stairs as fast as my short legs could carry me, stretching out my hands before me to feel the door—to feel whether it would be there or not.

It was there—sturdy and whole. I rattled the knob.

"The key, sheriff!" I cried. He pushed behind me, handing me the key, thrusting it into my hand as I felt for the keyhole with my other one.

I found it, pushed in the key, turned the lock, and kicked open the door. The light was on, bright—and the sheriff howled no louder than I.

Phillip Masterson's throat was slit, and the silver-handled knife was still in the gaping wound.

# CHAPTER VI
## SPLINTERING GLASS

THE SHERIFF, I SAY, howled no louder than I, and together we made the cupola room ring and echo with our sudden cries. What we said, I have no idea. In fact, the first recollection I have of any definite speech is of the sheriff's man calling out, in that moment of ghastly silence which followed our exclamations, "He's killed himself!"

"Killed himself! Killed himself!" I sputtered, feeling the muscles of my face jerking spasmodically. "Killed himself—hell!"

Sheriff Gallant strode toward the bed, and I could see how his fingers, one after another, were tapping the sides of his trousers as if they were nervously playing a wild tune. I followed him, hardly a step behind, stopping when he did, a few feet from Phillip Masterson's body. And seeing the familiar folding knife, with its unmistakable chased handle, I had involuntarily to thrust my hand in the pocket of my topcoat again and to make sure that it was no longer there, even though my eyes told me, more surely than I wished, that it stood before me, plunged into the boy's throat.

"That's the knife, sheriff," I said as calmly as I could.

"You're positive?"

"As I am of my name."

"And you're positive you carried it downstairs with you?"

I gestured impatiently. "Gallant, I know what I did!" I cried, pettishly, I fear. "He tossed it to me, and after I had examined it, I slipped it into this pocket. It was there when I left the room and it was there when I left the house. It was there when that unknown devil crashed me on the skull with my walking stick."

The sheriff, who had been bent over Masterson, looking intently at the knife, now straightened up and glanced around the room. "Excuse the questions, Spider," he said, "but I want to start that brain of yours working. There's no way, is there, that this young man could have got the knife himself?"

"Emphatically no," I answered. "I locked this cupola door behind me. I put the key in the pocket with the knife. I *ran* down the stairs, and it wasn't more than two or three minutes at the very most before I got banged on the head, down where the path hits the beach."

"It's impossible, of course," said the sheriff, musingly, as if he were merely thinking aloud, "that this boy could have clambered down outside and met you at the foot of the cliff—even if he had any call to, I mean. That broken window, now. . . ."

"I broke that, sheriff. When he told me what he'd done, I lost my temper, and I hurled my stick away from me. It crashed through the window, and it's that that I was hit with. . . . No, sheriff, use your reason. If it were suicide Masterson wanted, he could get it easily enough by a simple little jump from here onto the rocks. Messy, but effective. As a matter of fact I half suggested it to him. Or, rather, I told him that if he wanted to, I couldn't do anything to prevent him. I was mad, I tell you, sheriff, and then I didn't much care. Now, damn it, I do care!"

"But why—"

"Don't ask me things not just now, sheriff. Because I don't know! I want to get back to Farnol's as quickly as I can. There's nothing to do here but this." I took my handkerchief from my pocket, and grasping the knife with it, as near to the blade as possible, I drew it from the fresh wound. And while I did so, I examined young Masterson's face. It is not my belief, nor is it in my experience, that the expression of the face, in death, is the same as it was in the last moment of life. At least I have never seen, frozen on a countenance, the terror, the horror, or the pain that legend and the fiction writers place there. To me, all dead faces are alike (save, of course, in their features), gaping, expressionless, lacking everything that makes the faces of us living beings, even the homeliest of us, things to watch with fascination and profit. Phillip Masterson showed nothing—nothing at all, save the already apparent fact that he was very lately dead.

But as I bent over him, I found my emotions strangely complex as rival theories of the motive of his murder went whirling through my mind. Setting them on paper makes them seem much more deliberate and coldly calculated than they really were, for actually they passed like lightning. . . . I loathed him. For the death of Garda, I still could take his throat in my hands. . . . Suppose, for the death of Garda, someone had thirsted for, and had taken, revenge. Victor Millard, perhaps, who had murmured to me, in that other cupola, "I loved her, Mr. Meech." Could I, after the actual, blind attempt I had made on Masterson's life, springing at his throat on this very bed, find anything to condemn, emotionally, in the completion of the act by another? I found I could, slightly. I found, to my surprise, that Masterson's confession and the sudden, apparently sincere baring of his tortured and twisted mind, had made a deeper impression on my sympathies than I had supposed. I found I could *understand* the murder of Garda; and although understanding is far from halfway toward forgiveness, it is a step.

But suppose that for some unfathomable reason, Masterson had made, to me, a false confession, under youth's heroics, taking another's blame upon himself because his over-sensitive mind thought it the thing to do in some complicated situation I knew nothing about. Suppose, in that case, the actual murderer misunderstood Phillip's midnight interview with me in the cupola as being tale-bearing. Suppose, hiding, he saw me leave the empty house, anger on my face, and obviously hurrying toward Farnol's across the beach, bent on reaching the sheriff and making an arrest. He would knock the information from me with my own stout stick, and still it forever in Masterson's heart with a thrust of the boy's own knife. In such a case, of course, I would have nothing but pity for the blundering, well-meaning fool that lay before me.

I presume the momentary, twisting emotions showed slightly in my expression as I bent over Masterson, for the sheriff asked, "See anything, Spider?"

I straightened up abruptly, handing him the withdrawn knife, loosely wrapped, now, in the handkerchief. "Not a thing, sheriff. Here—use your apparatus on this as soon as we get back to the other house. You'll find Masterson's prints on it, of course, and maybe mine. I really forget whether or not I had my gloves on during the scene with him up here." I felt, then, in the inside pocket of my topcoat, where I always keep my gloves, and found them not there. But another gesture located them in a side pocket, and a word from the sheriff explained their presence in an unusual place.

"You had them on when we found you," he said. "We pulled them off and rubbed your wrists."

"You put them in this pocket?" I asked.

"Yes."

"The knife, naturally, was not there then? The key, of course, was. But you wouldn't have noticed either, merely pushing a pair of gloves in. Let's look at the key and then be off."

We moved across the room, all three of us, to the door at the top of the cupola stairs where, in the outside keyhole the key was still resting. I withdrew it and held it up.

"Ordinary, old-fashioned lock. But slightly intricate. Listen, sheriff. You'll agree with this, won't you? One of three things happened. The person who entered this room used a skeleton key. Or he used a duplicate key. Or he used this key and then returned it to my pocket while I was still unconscious. The last seems, at present, perfectly absurd. The second, we know nothing about. The first, I can, after a fashion, test."

I own and always carry with me a skeleton key made from my own design by the best locksmiths in Connecticut, and very few indeed are the locks of ordinary type that it has failed to open. On spring locks such as Yale, Seigel, etc., it is naturally useless, but this door was not of that sort. I detached my key from my pocket-ring (how few keys a homeless bachelor owns!) and tried it. It failed. I tried again, using less pressure, working it this way and that, slowly and delicately. And eventually it worked, but I had convinced myself that any modern, commercially designed skeleton would have been useless in this antedated mechanism, and so I told the sheriff.

Then, locking the cupola door behind me, leaving the lights full on, and Masterson undisturbed on the bed, I motioned for the two men to precede me down the stairs. And immediately that the door was closed, the darkness of the stairway enveloped us for the few seconds which elapsed before the sheriff turned on his flashlight. It gave me a thought and I remembered my own flash.

"Go ahead down," I told the sheriff and his man. "I'll be with you in a moment." And, unlocking the cupola door again, I re-entered the room.

This I remembered clearly, even though, following the first excitement of the discovery of Masterson, my head was beginning to ache again: that immediately after young Masterson turned on the lights in the room, I had, as I have already narrated, thrown my flashlight on the unmade bed. And there it lay all through my interview with him. Furthermore, I remembered absolutely that when I dashed from the room, locking him in, I left the light behind me in my haste, for I recalled missing it and needing it in my hurried descent of the stairs, but my impatience to be off down the beach toward Farnol's kept me from returning to the room to get it.

Now, as I say, I re-entered the room to get it. And it was not there.

It was not on the bed; it was nowhere in the room. I knew from my own observation that neither the sheriff nor his man had taken it from the cupola. Obviously, then, either Masterson had thrown it from the window, which was most unlikely, or the murderer had taken it with him when he left, which was highly probable and very natural. The finding of the light, then, on someone's person or with someone's belongings would be the first piece of tangible circumstantial evidence that the case afforded, particularly as my light was a unique one, English imported, covered with artificial maroon leather.

I locked the door again, leaving, as before, the cupola lights full on, and, feeling my way down the dark stairs, joined the sheriff and his man in the lower hall.

"Sheriff," I said, "I think with your permission, I'd like to leave your assistant here for a short while."

"That's all right, Spider."

"It won't be long, for I shall send the medical examiner over as soon as possible." I gave the man the front door key and suggested that he stay in the vicinity of the lower hall, either inside, or directly outside, and I promised to have him relieved within the hour.

Directly, then, in the sheriff's car, Gallant and I started off toward Farnol's, and as the car started I looked at my watch. It was twenty-five minutes past one. I sank back in my seat and thought:

The last time I looked at my watch was just as I was leaving Farnol's house on my second and last trip across the beach. The sheriff's other man, on guard there, had asked me the time, and it had been exactly midnight. From that, then, I could reckon roughly. The walk of a mile across the dark beach to the empty house on the other cliff must have taken me approximately fifteen minutes. After I arrived, I could allow ten minutes for my prowl through the corridors and lower rooms, including the covering of the footprint in the dust. Fifteen and ten is twenty-five.

Five minutes, surely no more, I spent in the cupola, starting on the letters in the drawer when Masterson came up the stairs. Then, that wild session with Masterson, about twenty minutes. Twenty-five and twenty-five is fifty.

From the moment I had come to my senses on the living room divan until the sheriff and I started off in the car, couldn't have been more than twenty minutes, I reckoned. And I corroborated my reckoning powers by asking the sheriff for an estimate. Twenty minutes was his guess, too. Fifty and twenty is seventy.

Seventy minutes after midnight makes ten minutes past one. But my watch showed me twenty-five minutes past. That extra fifteen minutes, then, must mark as nearly as it could be approximated, the time that elapsed between my rushing out of the house and my awaking on the living room divan. Slightly less, then, than fifteen minutes was the period of my unconsciousness—the period in which the murderer, after crashing me on the head with my own stick, mounted to the cupola, did his work, and made his getaway.

Mentally, then, I made a time-table and placed it before my eyes as clearly as if it were in print on a page:

12:00 mdt.—I leave Farnol's.
12:15 a.m.—I reach the other house.
12:25 a.m.—I reach the cupola.
12:30 a.m.—Masterson arrives.
12:50 a.m.—I run from the house.
1:05 a.m.—I recover consciousness.
1:25 a.m.—The sheriff and I drive away.

By the time I finished my calculating, we had covered the road over the marsh, had sped our mile along the main highway, and had turned once more toward the ocean on the marsh-road that led to Farnol's. It was still clear, and still very cold.

"Sheriff," I said, hunching nearer to him on the seat, "tell me, rapidly, exactly how you found me and what you did."

"Why, it's this way, Spider," he began. "I told you that the moment we discovered Masterson was missing and that you had gone up the beach to the other house, we jumped into the car. The moment we got in sight of the house, I grabbed Caswell's arm and yelled, 'Look, there's a light up there'—"

"Did you see anyone moving in the cupola?"

"Not a soul, just the light on bright."

"Yes. Go on."

"We jumped out of the car and started toward the house, and then Caswell grabbed my arm, and yelled, 'The door's wide open!' and we went up the steps onto the little porch. I whispered to Caswell, 'Quiet,' I said, 'let's go quiet,' and just as we were about to walk inside the house, I heard, from somewhere, someone groaning. Really groaning, loud."

"That was I?"

"Yes. And I yelled, 'Caswell, my God, it's Spider Meech!' and I—"

The sheriff never finished. From Farnol's house, a hundred yards or so down the straight, dark road before us, there came cries—a shot—and the sudden sound of splintering glass.

# CHAPTER VII
## A SPOT

"STEP ON IT, SHERIFF!" I CRIED, and the car fairly leapt from the road and shot that final distance through the air. And while the brakes were still screaming with pain, I jumped from the running board and ran toward the house.

There was turmoil inside. Above the sound of my own footsteps, over the ringing and pounding of my aching head, I could hear heavy feet running down the cupola stairs. Every window on the second floor that I could see as I reached the front steps seemed to break into light at the same second with all the others, as if the shot had been the control of a master switch. And when I stepped inside the wide open door, I could hear, it seemed, a voice in each bedroom above, calling in terrified tones to know what the matter was.

The footsteps which had run down the cupola stairs crossed the long hall of the chamber floor, and began to descend the main stairs. I drew my revolver at once and called "Halt!"

Two men in their shirt-sleeves stopped at the bend in the stairway, and their hands flew over their heads with a rapidity which must have amused me had I had time to think. But surely I was an ugly sight, with my legs spread apart like that, and my loose topcoat hardly concealing my hump.

"Who are you!" I demanded, and one of them replied instantly.

"Dr. Forrester, medical examiner, and my assistant, Dr. Bock."

I lowered my gun. "Come down, doctor," I said. And at that moment the sheriff's man, the one who had been left on guard, came dashing into the hall from the darkness behind, bare-headed, wild-eyed, his revolver in his hand.

"Mr. Meech!" he cried. "Who was it? Which way did he go?"

"Who!"

"Someone broke in! Just a minute ago! I shot at him. Look— look in here!"

He stepped inside the living room and snapped the wall lights on, and immediately I could see that a large pane of glass in the door that led to the veranda was shattered, and that the door itself was standing open. The sheriff joined us, then, and together, in less time than I can write it, we heard his man's story.

He had patrolled the house as I had told him to, making a complete circuit of it every few minutes, and being more than particularly watchful since the sheriff had reported the escape of young Masterson and had driven off up the coast in search of me. He had left the front door wide open (he had no key to it) and every time his circuit of the house brought him to the door, he mounted the steps softly and listened inside. A minute or two ago, while so listening, he heard an approaching car, and as he went toward the road to watch for it, he heard a sudden sound behind him, as if someone were crossing the veranda. He ran, then, straight to where the noise was coming from, and called to the figure there to halt. He could see, only very dimly, as there were no lights to stream out from the living room, the faint silhouette of a man. It moved rapidly toward the glass door, and, still running, our guard fired. The glass of the door shattered, and at the same moment the figure hurled something over the veranda railing which caught our guard in the chest, knocked his gun from his hand, and sent him falling backward, perilously near the brink of the cliff.

Indeed, he actually slipped over for several feet, but the spot was not one where the cliff dropped sheerly away, and he had managed to save himself from the final descent by grabbing some sturdy (if prickly) shrubs of juniper. By the time he had climbed up again and found his revolver, the intruder had disappeared, and we were standing in the hallway.

"You didn't recognize him?"

"No."

"Was he fully dressed?"

"So far as I could see."

"What did he throw at you?" I asked. I thought I knew, but I wanted to make sure.

"A club," said the man, "or a heavy stick of some kind."

Exactly! It was my knobbed walking stick, and thrown without doubt by the same hand that swung it over my head—in other words, by the murderer of Philip Masterson. In still other words, by some member of the household upstairs who had escaped, as Masterson had, who had done his work in the other house up the beach, who had walked back down the beach while the sheriff and I were discovering Masterson's body, and who had just endeavored to get back into Farnol's house, and into his own room, undetected.

Well. . . . Was he clever enough to lock himself into that room again and present an unsuspicious appearance to me, two minutes after he was shot at on the veranda? For I repeat that hardly more than that time had elapsed since the sheriff and I heard the beginning of the uproar.

I turned at once and requested the sheriff and his man (whose name, I presently learned, was Hackett) to go carefully through the lower rooms, the dining room and kitchen, and to look in on Sutton and Bessie in their beds. I suggested also that Hackett try to find, as soon as possible, the stick which was thrown at him, and then I asked the two doctors to accompany me upstairs.

They came with me eagerly enough, and when we reached the top step and the long, dim hallway, we were in the midst of the turmoil. Every chamber door—save mine, save Masterson's open one, save the one to the room that Farnol had told me was an unoccupied storeroom—was being rapped upon, and all the voices within were calling to me, to each other. A quick glance down one side of the corridor and up the other showed me that every key was in its lock, as it should be.

"Be quiet!" I shouted. "Be quiet, *please!* No one has been shot, and I'm opening your doors in a second."

The turmoil ceased.

I motioned to the doctors to help me in unlocking the doors, and I told them in a low tone to make sure that each key turned and that none was merely closed and not locked. Dr. Forrester attended to the doors of Victor Millard and the St. Johns, Dr. Bock to Patricia Farnol's, and I myself to Creamer Farnol's and to Vera's. And, calling down the corridor, I asked each one to step directly into the hall. They all appeared at once, and I looked at them, walking slowly from door to door and talking as I went.

"There is no need, no need at all," I said, "to get excited and alarmed." (Vera was pale as death and in her long, sweeping negligee.) "The shot that you heard fired was fired by one of the sheriff's assistants at a person who was entering the house—re-entering, I choose to believe." (Farnol, with his white hair on end, and a close-fitting dressing gown of colorless linen, looked more like a dish-mop than ever.) "It happens to be in my mind that someone in this house has been on a little midnight adventure of his own and has recently come back to his own room." (Patricia was calm—pale, but lovely in green chiffon with her red hair glowing above it.) "Who it was, I mean to find out, although exactly how I don't know yet." (The two St. Johns had their arms around each other and she, I saw, had been crying again.) "I must say that I half hoped to find that one of you was not yet in his room, or at least that one of you was a bit slow in stepping into the corridor. But even you, Victor—"

He was fully dressed.

The last time I had seen him, I recollected, was when he was sitting at his desk in his own room, writing that letter about the crime to his partner in foreign travel. Then, he was in pajamas and dressing gown. Now he had on the same informal tweeds he had worn at dinner, and his hair was freshly combed. Vainly I tried to remember whether the momentary, insufficient flash I had caught of my assailant as both of us reached for my walking stick carried any hint of light tweeds to my mind, but I found that even the attempt to force my memory failed miserably. I had seen practically nothing.

"Even you, Millard," I said, "seem to be on hand."

He didn't wince, and I'm very sure that I was glad he did not. Instead, his fresh young face took on the shadow of puzzled disappointment.

"Why do you say that that way, Mr. Meech. Why *even* I?"

I was about to answer when he raised his eyes and stared over my head at the open door of Masterson's empty, unlighted room.

"Where's Phil Masterson?" he blurted out. "He doesn't seem to be here!"

I didn't turn toward Masterson's room as he expected me to. Instead I kept my eyes glued on Victor's face, not even removing them to follow the faint gasp of astonishment that passed from lip to lip, down the corridor.

"Are you bearing tales, Victor?" I asked, in mock reproach.

He blushed, and gave a quick glance along the corridor, I thought, to his left, as if he wanted to see if Patricia Farnol's eyes were on him.

"Certainly not!" he cried. "But it's just as fair for me to call your attention to the fact that Phil isn't in front of his door, as it is for you to stand there and insinuate that you're surprised I'm here."

If he were ten years younger, I remember thinking, he would have burst into tears.

"Oh come now, Victor," I said. "I insinuated nothing of the kind."

"You did too! You said, 'I half hoped to find that one of you was not yet in his room, but *even you*, Victor'—"

"But even you, Victor," I interrupted him, "should know that these people here are much too clever for that." I waved my hand down the corridor. "I'm very sure that one of them has been out on a little adventure of his own, and very, very recently. In fact, that he came upstairs just a minute before I did. Yet look at them, Victor. They're all here, and all undressed—except, of course, yourself."

His brow clouded. "Oh, now I see!" he exclaimed. "That's the reason for all these damn suspicions of yours—just because I'm dressed! Well, do you want to hear the explanation of that now or later?"

I folded my arms. "Now is as good as any time, if it won't embarrass you."

Again he shot that sidelong look down the corridor toward Patricia, but I knew he could be getting no satisfaction from his glances. The St. Johns, still standing together, were between him and the girl.

"It certainly won't embarrass me," he said, "except that it'll sound foolish. . . . I'm dressed because I got dressed right after the sheriff made his round of the bedrooms, after you'd made yours. I couldn't sleep—I told you I couldn't—and I'd written the only letter I wanted to write. And there weren't any books in my room. So I just had a slight idea if I got dressed, and were completely dressed when you came again—whether you came in, or whether I merely heard you go by in the hall—I'd ask you if I couldn't come out and help you. You know, the way you let me help you with Garda up in the cupola—just go around with you, if you kept me in sight all the time and knew I couldn't escape or do anything harmful or anything like that. You see," he concluded, lowering his head at me slightly, reproachfully, "I had an idea you'd decided to trust me."

Trust him! God knows I wanted to. God knows I wanted to trust them all and believe every word they told me. And most particularly I wanted to believe the apparently simple, straightforward story of this lad that stood before me, looking as far removed from the popular idea of the criminal type as it is possible for a young man to look.

And even that, of course, was a point. Your fiction stories all aside, it is most definitely not the handsome young juvenile, hiding a murderer's heart behind his blond innocence, who commits the crime. True enough, our juvenile courts are full of young delinquents, justly charged, staring with wide, blameless eyes; and our criminal courts have a surprisingly large total of prisoners-at-the-bar whose regularity of features and whose publicly expressed devotion to home and mother set the shears of the nation in action clipping their pictures. But court reporters know their stuff, and half-tones are notorious in their inability to be subtle, and anyway—

damn it all—Victor Millard was the very personification of normality, good breeding, frankness, and honesty.

That was surely in his favor, despite the fact that the edge was slightly taken off it by analogy with Phil Masterson. Yet only slightly, for Masterson, as well-bred no doubt, and probably as honest, was a confessed neurotic. But also a confessed murderer! There lay another point: your normal, intelligent, high-bred youth *seeks* confession, for he kills (when he kills at all, which is almost never) only for two major reasons, because of sudden and uncontrollable passion, or because he is momentarily convinced that his crime is justified. Of the first he is promptly ashamed; of the second he is temporarily proud. And in either case, because he is not the permanent enemy of society, his instinct and his innate good sense prevent him from being the fugitive. The unsolved murders, the real-life mysteries—these, we may be sure, are seldom committed by the young men who are born in, brought up in, and taught the code of the families who live on this side of the railroad tracks and take the *Literary Digest*. Kill they may, now and then, but they pay for it.

What else was in his favor? The fact, it seemed to me, that he was wearing light tweeds. They're comfortable, surely, but hardly the things to put on if the escaping of detection is any factor. The fact that he looked as smooth and unruffled as if, indeed, he *had* merely dressed himself leisurely and waited to hear my voice. The fact that the key to his door was apparently securely turned from the outside, locking him in. The fact that he (or whoever it was) had violently attacked me with a club merely, it seemed, to relieve me of a key (which was returned) and a knife. And however wildly romantic his murderous plans might have been, it was hard to conceive that this boy would have been quite so dramatic and would have gone to quite such lengths merely to make the same knife kill twice.

But what in his disfavor? The fact, of course, that he was fully dressed, despite his explanation. The fact, which I promptly noticed, that instead of wearing the excellent tan brogues he had worn at dinner-time, he had on a discoloured pair of canvas tennis shoes—the best thing for swift running on the beach and quiet sneaking about the house. The fact that, next to myself, he was the logical one to avenge the death of Garda Lawrence, if avenging must be done. The fact (hardly to be considered) that he had, in a rather unsportsmanlike manner, called attention to Masterson's absence from the corridor line-up.

"Why," I said, "it's not really a matter of trusting you, Victor."

There were two little things I wanted to do immediately, and I did them. First I bent down swiftly and touched one of his shoes.

"I suppose you put these on in order to be able to gum-shoe around the house with me."

"Yes," he said quietly. I don't know yet whether he realized I was ragging him.

There was sand, plenty of it, caught in the crevice between the rubber and the canvas. But that might have remained there since earlier in the day. They *had* gone swimming, I remembered.

"Do you own a skeleton key, Victor?" I asked.

"No I don't, sir."

"This is one," I said, taking mine from my pocket. I stepped behind him and drew the key from his bedroom door, inserting my own. It turned and locked readily. Then, replacing the original key in the outside of the lock, I tried, by stepping inside the room, to lock the door from that point with the door-key filling one side of the keyhole. It could not be done. Some modern locks, notably those used in up-to-date (if suspicious) hotels, can thus be tampered with.

"All right, Victor," I said, putting my key-ring back in my pocket and standing before him again. "I'm through being nasty to you for the moment, and I'll reply to a little suggestion you gave me a minute ago—about Phillip Masterson."

I looked down the half-light of the long hall. Before each chamber its occupant was still standing, silent, watching, listening, and at the top of the stairs were the two doctors, one against each balustrade like the guardians of a dungeon descent.

"Phillip Masterson, Victor, is dead!"

I spoke, ostensibly, to him alone, but in reality I watched them all, so far as the light allowed. Victor, the only one whose expression I could see clearly, lost all the colour in his face immediately, set his lips as if he were trying to suppress a cry, and inhaled sharply, raspingly. In her far corner, tall Vera swayed on her feet, and I saw her hand go out to touch the wall and steady herself. Creamer Farnol didn't move a muscle, nor did the St. Johns, unless it was to creep more closely into each other's arms.

Patricia, in her corner, was the only one who made a sound. Pressing her hands, palms flat, against her cheeks, she cried, "I knew it! Oh, I knew it!"

I walked rapidly down the corridor toward her, asking as I went, "How do you mean, Miss Farnol? How did you know it?"

She turned toward me as I approached her, catching the molding of the doorway with one hand, and holding her negligee to her throat with the other.

"I mean," she said, with a voice that nearly had tears in it, "that I knew we weren't through—after we heard the rock again."

"I didn't realize you were that superstitious," I said, reaching her side and standing there.

"How can I help being—now?" she asked.

I considered a moment, watching her beauty and watching the faint colour come and go under the unruly glory of her hair. "Tell me," I said, "if you half suspected another death, did you in any way suspect that it would be Phil Masterson?"

She shook her head vigorously, and now there really were tears in her eyes and in her voice.

"No! No!" she cried. "Least of all!"

"Do you really mean that?" I asked.

From some inexplicable and invisible source, she drew a handkerchief and held it against her mouth.

"No! I mean that I thought—" She pressed the handkerchief more firmly and was silent.

"Please, Miss Farnol," I continued, as gently as I could, "just what do you mean? Is there someone you thought was in danger of being killed—more danger than Phillip?"

I thought she started to nod, but whatever she started she checked immediately, withdrew the handkerchief from her face, and said, "Please don't make me answer that question—not now, Mr. Meech."

That's a plea which I have run up against a hundred times in my life of official question-asking, and almost every one of those hundred times, I have said the same thing, and I said it now:

"That means 'yes', doesn't it, Miss Farnol?"

Her eyes shifted rapidly from my face to her mother's, to her father's, and then to mine again. "If you'll let me talk to you alone sometime—not now—but later—I may—I'm not sure, but I may answer you," she replied.

At that moment the sheriff came up the stairs and, seeing that there was an interval of silence—as there was, for I was standing motionless, searching Patricia's face for things I did not find—he made bold enough to speak.

"Sutton and the cook are downstairs, Spider," he said. "They were in their rooms all right. The cook was crying and Sutton was getting dressed. Neither of their rooms was locked."

"No," I said, "I know that. I didn't see any cause for it." Then I paused. "Sutton was getting dressed, was he? How nearly dressed?"

"He had everything on but his shoes and his shirt. I waited while he put those on."

I thought a moment. What would I do if I were a well-trained servant? If I were in bed, on a night like this, and I heard cries outside the house, and a shot, and the running of feet upstairs and down, would I, before appearing to offer aid or to see what things were all about, stop and dress myself? I thought not. If I wore a night-gown (which I do, but I doubt if Sutton did) I might pull a pair of trousers on over it, but nothing more.

"Farnol," I asked, turning toward the tall figure so straight and silent by his door, "in a few minutes I shall have to ask your man Sutton if he thinks a good servant should wait to dress before attending to an emergency. Whatever he thinks, he will say yes. Have you ever issued any orders on the subject?"

Farnol smiled rather ruefully. "I've hardly prepared the servants for emergencies," he replied. "But, knowing Sutton, I should most certainly say nothing short of—of—well, I was going to say murder—would keep him from showing himself any other way than fully dressed."

"You can't cite any instances?"

"No. I'm afraid I can't."

Then Vera spoke, and it was curious to see how every face in the hallway turned toward her at once, at the first sound of her voice. While I had been speaking, while Farnol was talking, eyes were wandering, cast down, cast upward, looking wherever they pleased. But it was impossible to hear Vera's smooth, lovely voice without focusing upon her, as if you listened through your eyes as well as your ears.

"I can," she said. "Just last night I couldn't sleep and I wanted some hot milk. I called Bessie—it was very late, after two o'clock—but I couldn't rouse her. So I called Sutton. And when he brought it to me, he was not only fully dressed, but dressed in exactly the uniform he uses to serve all the informal meals—black trousers and white coat."

It was hardly an analogous case, I thought to myself, but I asked her an entirely different question.

"You say you called him. Have you bells in their rooms?"

"Why no," she answered. "House phones."

"Oh!" I said, actually surprised, for I had certainly seen none in my room. "I hadn't noticed them."

"We've never had them put in the guest rooms," she said (as I hoped she would). "They're in mine, and Creamer's. That's all."

"Connecting only with the servants' rooms, I suppose," I pursued. I don't know why.

"And the kitchen," she said. "That's all."

Abruptly I turned on my heel and walked, I fear, the length of the corridor and back. I say "I fear," because I'm afraid it was not only brusquely impolite but falsely dramatic. In reality, I was merely trying to think for a moment. I had no ideas in my mind which have not been put down here in black and white, but there were a dozen things that cried to be done. I wanted to have a word with the medical examiner about Garda. I wanted to send him over the beach to Masterson. I wanted to talk to each one of these people separately. I wanted to talk to all of them together. I wanted to fingerprint them. I wanted—well, there was no time like the present.

"After all," I said suddenly, "after all this extra excitement— and a thousand thanks to everyone for not asking me about Phil Masterson—I doubt if there's any use in any of us trying to get sleep tonight." I pulled out my watch. "It's quarter of two. I think I'll ask you all to come down into the living room and we'll have that little joint talk that I was going to postpone until tomorrow."

I was amazed, I remember, at the equanimity with which my suggestion was received. But guilty or innocent, poor souls, I can see now that they must have been ready to welcome anything as a blessed relief from the solitary confinement in their rooms with the noises about them, and the merciless beat of the ocean on the cliffs below. I motioned to the sheriff to accompany them down, and I signaled the medical examiner to remain behind, and at the top of the stairs I waited and watched them pass. St. John asked permission to go into his room and get a package of his own ciga- rettes, and I gave him that permission, being fully able, from where I was standing, to see that he got the package and did nothing else. His wife went down with Patricia, and I couldn't resist the impulse to press Patricia's hand as she passed me, or to clap Victor Millard lightly on the shoulder. But neither of them smiled at me, nor showed in any way that they felt and appreciated my affection. . . . The investigator is the enemy of them all, the innocent as well as the guilty. . . . Farnol and Vera descended the stairs together, look- ing as if they were the last of their line, on their way to the tum- brels.

For two minutes, then, Dr. Forrester and I had a conversation in the corridor which it is useless to relate. He had, of course, per- formed no autopsy as yet, and until then, until he had seen the actual progress of digestion in the girl's stomach, he could make no closer guess than I had made as to the definite time of death.

He would remove the body, with my permission, to his own place. Yes, he had a car with ambulance accommodations. Yes, he knew the other cupolaed house up the coast, and he would go there at once and get Phillip Masterson with the cupola key I gave him, and he would drive back here and deliver the key to me. No, Maine did not have the formality of the coroner's inquest. Yes, Garda was certainly a lovely girl; might he offer his sincere sympathy?

I went downstairs to the assembled group, still not knowing exactly what I was going to do, and I surveyed them, from Bessie—plump, tear-stained, in a wrapper that looked as if it had come off a gigantic box of candy—around the room to Mrs. St. John, sitting with Patricia on a settee that backed against a window onto the veranda, back again to Sutton, standing near me at the door, completely dressed in his olive chauffeur's uniform, his hands clasped behind him.

Gaining time, thinking, I crossed the room to the veranda door with its shattered pane of glass, and from there I spoke.

"Perhaps Bessie will get a dust-pan and brush and sweep up this glass," I suggested, "and then make some more black coffee. And perhaps you, Sutton, will find a piece of cardboard or something and tack it over this opening."

And as I said the words, and as the two servants moved toward the kitchen to obey them, I noticed something.

The broken pane was next to the door's hinges, slightly more than waist-high. And on the woodwork, smearing the inside of the molding that held the glass, was a splash of blood.

Turning quickly, I looked at the carpet near the door. I followed with my eyes the only possible route across the room, straight to the only exit—the arched doorway into the hall. The light, fawn-coloured carpet showed no spots.

Just as quickly, then, I stepped outside the door, onto the veranda. To the people within (I hoped) it seemed as if I merely bent toward the house to light a cigar and shelter it from whatever breeze might still be coming from the ocean. In reality, from the flame of my match I saw the splotch of blood outside as well, and I saw a few spots on the gray paint of the veranda floor. And I re-constructed as follows:

That the man, whoever he was, had been feeling his way along the wall of the house, had had his hand—a bit more than waist high—near the door's hinges when Hackett fired. The bullet had grazed his wrist, broken the glass. Or the flying glass had cut the wrist or hand. And it had been sudden pain as much as anything else which had made him turn at once and fling the heavy walking stick toward the sheriff's man. Thus came the moment's pause that made those blood spots on the veranda. And a wrist or a hand could be held, without shedding more blood, until his own room was reached.

I paced the veranda for a moment, past the row of heavy, plate glass windows, puffing my first cigar in more than two hours.

Someone inside there should have a wounded hand—one, in-deed, which could hardly have stopped bleeding, unless it were very tightly bandaged. And who had had time to bandage a hand? Whose hands had I not seen?

I paced, thinking, while the ocean rolled and crashed below me, against the rock walls, in and out, with a deep and ominous gurgle, of the strange cave whose wind-born voice had twice sounded the warning of death.

And then I stopped, and my cigar went flying in a red parabola over the rail. For, looking in at the window against which sat Patricia Farnol and Helen St. John, I saw all I needed to see.

On the back of Mrs. St. John's lavender negligee, under the right shoulder, was a definite stain of fresh blood.

## CHAPTER VIII
## THE RINGING OF A BELL

When I say, "I saw all I needed to see," I don't mean it quite so fully and completely as that, of course. I certainly didn't know all I needed to know, and I most certainly hadn't proved anything at all.

Obviously, very obviously, little Helen St. John was not the person, disguised in man's clothing or not, who hurled my walking stick at the guard, receiving a bullet nick in the shoulder for her pains. And just as obviously she didn't know that blood stain was there, smirching her fresh, otherwise spotless negligee. And the blood was fresh, very fresh. The color showed that; and even through the window I was sure I could catch a glimpse of the sheen of dampness.

I had guessed that the blood by the veranda door had come from someone's hand or wrist, and it now seemed more than reasonable to suppose that that same hand had been laid across Helen St. John's shoulders. And during the very few moments which had elapsed since the intruder was fired at, only one hand, to the best of my knowledge, had been so placed. And that, of course, was her husband's.

That was easy. Throughout my little sentimental scene with the inhabitants of the upper corridor, St. John, as I persistently related, held his little mouse of a wife close to him. And, I remembered, with his right arm. Was that, perhaps, more to hide the guilty wound from my eyes, despite possible damage to Helen's clothes, than to express husbandly protection? It mattered little. But what did matter was the presence of such a wound on St. John's hand, and that had to be verified at once.

Through the window I could look across the room and see him, and note that his left hand which hung by his side seemed to be unharmed and whole. He was standing by the fireplace, his entire right side hidden from me.

Thankful for an immediate definite problem to hold me on the veranda for a moment to light a fresh cigar, I determined not to enter the living room until I had decided exactly what to do when I discovered (as I expected to discover) that Richard St. John had injured his right hand. . . . I should speak of it, most surely, and ask for an explanation, and I should undoubtedly get a very plausible one, true or untrue. Such an explanation, still true or untrue, would require the corroboration of his wife—and that he would get, for it seemed impossible that he could be out of his locked room without her knowledge. And certainly the presence of the wound alone would be no evidence upon which I could order an arrest.

Indeed, really, before even stating my suspicions, I should have to look into the means of his leaving, and re-entering, his bedroom. It seemed a totally impossible thing to do, to manipulate the lock so that by the time the medical examiner and I arrived, it should not only be securely locked, but should have a key sticking in the outside. Even with two keys; even with a confederate, Helen St. John, in the room, I could not see how it was possible.

There was another point: there was always in the back of my mind that faint shadow of a possibility that Masterson had made a false confession and was taking the blame wrongly upon himself. It was only the faintest of shadows, but it was worth watching. Would it be better, then, to tell these people what Masterson had confessed, or to leave them with the idea that the mystery, as well as the tragedy, had merely doubled? The former way would have this possible advantage: it would perhaps put courage, dare-devil courage, into Garda's murderer if he were still alive, and lead him to self-betraying rashness. But the latter way would have this advantage: it would keep Garda's case still very much open (a thing I earnestly desired) and it would keep hovering over the group that sense of further disaster still to come which is often important in hastening confidences. Moreover, however Garda died, Masterson must have been killed either for revenge or silence. And if it were for the latter, it might be very well indeed for the murderer to believe that Masterson died without speaking to me, in as much as he told me nothing at all which involved any other member of the party.

So, with my cigar half-burned, I came to two conclusions. To locate the wounded hand, but to make no accusations on the strength of it; and to keep silent about Masterson's confession, at least for the time being. Once again I threw a cigar away and stepped into the living room.

And once again the room looked cheerful. So cheerful, in fact, that I'm afraid I committed the sin of looking cheerful myself. Indeed, of smiling a trifle. But alas for this face of mine, and this twisted shape of mine—for I find at this point in the chronicle of the case written by Creamer Farnol to which I have referred before, the statement "Spider Meech entered through the broken door from the veranda, a crafty grin on his lips."

Crafty! Heaven help me! I felt far from that!

The only "craftiness" which was in my mind at the moment was the decision that the very best way to examine the hands and wrists of the assemblage (and particularly St. John's) was to make everyone at once submit to having his fingerprints taken, and accordingly I called the sheriff for my apparatus and asked young Victor to set up a bridge table under the standing light by the fireplace.

Talking in as pleasant a voice as I could assume, to make what is not particularly an enjoyable ordeal in the best of circumstances more easily and willingly undergone by these people with their frayed nerves, I said, to the company at large, but looking at none of them: "There's no one here, of course, who objects to having his prints made, is there? Not, I'm afraid, that it would do anyone any good to object, because I believe that not even Quakers and Christian Scientists are immune. I mean, they seem to have the handy little whorls and ridges like the rest of us."

"Isn't it awfully messy?" asked Helen St. John, from her seat near the window. And then she gave a nervous little giggle as if she had caught herself speaking out of turn, and added quickly, "Oh, you mustn't think that I'm objecting, because I'm not, and wouldn't think of it. But the stuff, you know —the black stuff that might get on your dress."

"I'm very sure, Mrs. St. John," I replied at once, still not looking at her, "that we can wipe your fingers right off and not soil a spotless negligee."

And again she giggled, and I knew for a certainty that she had no idea there was a blood-red spot on her shoulder. But, I suddenly decided, I didn't want any of the rest of the company to know it either—not just at this moment. So I left the card table at once and crossed to where she was sitting and took her by the hand.

"Come," I said, "you be first and let me show you how easy it is, and you can show the others how clean it is, and how I can restore you to your seat in a cat's wink, as unsullied as before." And I led her around the edge of the room, conveniently and naturally, but calculatingly, so that never once did she turn her shoulder to any part of the assemblage. And I placed her with her back to the fireplace, and deftly and quickly rolled one finger after another on the inking pad and on the ruled paper, and then dipped them lightly in alcohol and wiped them lightly and spotlessly on a fresh cloth.

I had determined to ask each one of the people a brief question or two as I worked, and the one I asked Helen St. John was, "Tell me, Mrs. St. John, when did you first meet Garda?"

She answered readily enough, and the quaver in her voice which was accompanied by the trembling of her fingers as I held them and worked with them, was caused, I knew, merely by the fact that she was in the limelight and that all eyes were upon her.

"Why, in the White Mountains, Mr. Meech," she said. "Just a couple of weeks ago, in Dixville. It was on the seventeenth that we got there, wasn't it, Richard, and Vera introduced us that very day."

I looked up at her husband, standing near, in time to see his answering nod, and I noticed that still I could not catch a glimpse of his right hand. It was in the pocket of his dressing gown and he was smoking with his left.

"But you've known Vera—pardon me—I mean Mr. and Mrs. Farnol longer than that?"

Again she gave her little nervous giggle. "Oh, yes. That is, Richard has known Creamer for some years."

"Thank you," I said, more for her fingers than for her information, and I led her back, circuitously, through the outer shadows to her seat beside Patricia. "There you are, and you may show Miss Farnol that you're unsullied and unstained."

Then, going back to my table again, and jotting Helen St. John's name on the paper with its ten dark blobs, I looked up at St. John himself, anxious to have my suspicions over with, and stretching out my hand to him, said, "How about you now, sir? Will you follow your wife's excellent example and submit to this 'messy' operation with the same willingness and grace?"

"Most certainly," he said, and tossed his cigarette into the fireplace. "With all the willingness in the world, and with as much grace, if you mean physical grace, as I can manage with rather stubby and acid-stained fingers."

"You're a chemist?" I asked, taking the left hand he tendered me, and rolling the fingers on the pad.

"Yes," he said. "I'm employed by the Luxall people in New Jersey, for pure research."

"I take it, then, that this is your vacation."

"Yes, but a rather extended one. I've been on a leave of absence since February, and Mrs. St. John and I have only recently returned from abroad. Two weeks in the mountains and a month here, and I go back to the job on the first of November."

"I see. . . . Now may I have your right hand, please?"

He drew it from the pocket of his dressing gown with a quick movement, but at the same time he drew out, presumably by mistake, his package of cigarettes and they went falling to the hearth. Immediately he said, "Sorry," and stooped to pick them up, but I had caught his hand and held it fast, and now I said rapidly, "Let them go for a moment," and I pulled his hand into the light, and at the same time, as if to keep the cuff out of the ink, I pushed the sleeve up.

His hand and wrist were whole and unscratched.

There was nothing at all to do but bear my disappointment without expressing the least surprise, and to finish with his prints as quickly as possible, and write his name on the record, thank him, and let him go to the recovery of his cigarettes.

Then I called for a volunteer to be the next one at the operation and got Victor at once, extending both hands, and revealing at a glance that no bullet had grazed them. As I took them in my own, I said, "You shouldn't bite your nails, Victor."

"I know it," he replied, without a trace of expression in his voice, and I glanced up at his face.

"Still furiously angry with me, Victor?" I asked.

He made no reply whatsoever, and I finished my work as quickly as I could, and when I had done, I snapped one of his knuckles with my forefinger and said, in a low voice, "Don't be," and let him go. He went at once to one of the windows, turned his back on the gathering, and stared out at the night.

Creamer Farnol, who presented his long hands at my table next, crossed the room to the accompaniment of the tapping of Sutton's hammer as he began to close the opening of the broken pane in the veranda door. I expected to find no blemish on my hoot's wrists, and I found none, but I admired the length and grace of his sensitive fingers, and as I worked, I said, "Tell me about your books, Farnol. I know you write but—"

The tapping ceased.

"—but I'm afraid no one has ever told me just what."

He gave a short laugh. "Nothing, I'm afraid, that you'd ever run into. Literary history, for the most part. Brief things, primarily for scholars. And I've done an anthology of pre-Shakespearian verse which is used in a few colleges. And articles, of course, for the Modern Language Association, but nothing at all that's so-called popular."

"You must have—excuse my asking—an independent income, then?"

"Yes," he replied. "I've been, as they say, retired for ten or twelve years. My father left me a bit, and my uncle, and I gave up teaching to do what I was more interested in."

"I see. Other hand, please. Now would you mind telling me how long you have known Garda and where you—"

"*OW!*"

There was a sharp, loud, sudden cry of pain from the distant shadows, and all of us, nerves on edge, jumped in our chairs, and Vera gave a faint little cry.

And from where he was working by the door, Sutton straightened up, holding one wrist with the other hand, and saying—it seemed as if he were saying it directly to me rather than to his master—"I'm afraid I've cut myself on this glass, sir. Rather badly, I think."

I ran across the room to him, calling as I did so, "Warm water at once, sheriff! Bessie is in the kitchen. . . . Here, Sutton! Come here!"

I pulled him to the table and caught up one of my clean cloths, holding it in the palm of my hand and laying the wrist on it, upturned. It was a straight cut, quite deep and about an inch long, and the blood from it was flowing freely, streaming down each side of the wrist and reddening the cloth underneath.

"How did it happen, Sutton?" Creamer Farnol asked, bending, as I was, over the wound.

"Why, sir, I thought I—" he winced under a spurt of pain—"I thought I had the glass all out of the frame, sir, but I reached out through to straighten the cardboard from the outside, push it in a bit where it had slipped out, and I ran onto a jagged piece."

Oh, clever Sutton! That was all I could think, but what I said was, "Have you some blue mercury tablets, Farnol?"

"Yes," he said. "In the cabinet in my bathroom."

"Get them, Victor!" I said briskly, over my shoulder, and I could feel rather than see the animation come back to the boy.

"M—may I?" he asked, and I snapped out, "Of course!" and knew I had won him back.

Out to the kitchen, then, I took Sutton, asking Farnol to stay in the living room with the others, and I found Bessie standing by the stove, chewing a corner of the gingham apron she had most unattractively put on over her candy-box wrapper. And while I was waiting for the water to heat and for Victor to return with the bichloride, which he did almost at once, flushed with the brief exertion and with his restored importance, I said to Sutton, casually, "Too bad, my man, that you had to open this cut again."

His wrist jerked as it lay in my hand, but that might have been from another spurt of pain. "What, sir?"

Of course, with the flowing blood, I could see nothing at all, but I bent over the wrist. "I thought it looked as if you had cut yourself a while ago, almost in the same place, and had had the misfortune to reopen it, deeper this time."

I was not mistaken; he *did* hesitate a moment before replying, "No, sir. I've never cut myself there before."

I was sure he was lying, but I didn't see anything that I could do or say without accusing him of being grazed by the shot on the veranda, which would be the same as accusing him of being my assailant on the distant bluff, and which would therefore entail the accusation of him as Masterson's murderer, a thing which I was not ready to do. Furthermore, I could not see, from guarded inspection, that there were any spots of blood on his tan uniform sleeve, or on the cuff of his white shirt, which looked any older, even by the scant thirty minutes which had elapsed since the shot was fired, than those just made by the glass. And when the mercury solution had been made, and I had helped him plunge his hand and wrist into its blueness, and had withdrawn them once and wiped away the still flowing blood, I could not see any evidence at all of two cuts.

But that was easy, I knew. If he had, as I was very sure, deliberately taken a piece of glass and slashed himself with it, it would be a simple matter, to be performed with plenty of time and care, to cut himself directly over the former, still fresh wound while he was working in the corner and while the eyes of all the rest of the company were focused on Farnol and me at the fingerprint table. And what's a bit of self-inflicted pain? He probably had no idea that I already knew that the shot had grazed him, or that I had found the smear and drops of blood, but he did know that when I came to fingerprint him, I should find the wound and ask him about it. Therefore, before it was too late, the wound must be fresh and logical and received in the presence of all.

I said nothing, therefore, but "Perhaps you're right," and left the sheriff in the kitchen with him to help bandage his hand when the soaking process was over, and I took Victor back with me into the living room.

And there, as quickly as possible, I took up the fingerprinting where I had left off, receiving, by a repetition of my question to Creamer Farnol, the simple information that he and Vera had met and liked Garda during September at The Balsams in Nixville Notch, and that she and Patricia had become such close friends, that it was only natural to invite her to Maine when they decided to open the Wailing Rock house for a month and have an autumn party.

I asked Vera nothing as she came to the table, and I asked Patricia, who came last, to tell me how she came to know Phillip Masterson.

"I didn't know him awfully well," she said, "although I had met him at several house-parties here and there, and we had a few grand times together in Paris. But when Garda and I were talking about male prospects to invite down here—you know October isn't a very easy time to get hold of people—she suggested both him and Victor, and as it happened I had no better choice."

It is needless to mention, of course, that there were no wounds on the hands and wrists of Patricia and her mother.

Just then the outer door opened and Hackett, the sheriff's man came in from the outside, asking if he could speak to me for a moment, and I went to him in the hall.

"Can't find it high or low, Mr. Meech," he said, and I knew he meant my knobbed walking stick. "When it caught me on the shoulder and knocked me over the bluff, it must have kept right on. I've been all over the place with a flashlight—"

You may be sure that I glanced at the flashlight in his hand and saw that it was not my missing one.

"—and I've come to the conclusion that it's fallen down the cliff into the water. I've even been down on the beach at the foot, hoping it might have been washed up, but there isn't a sign."

I thanked him and asked him to look again as soon as the dawn should come, and then I went back to the living room. With only a hazy idea of what I was going to make the people talk about until the sheriff should have time to make careful comparison of the prints on the records with those he might have found in the cupola room and on Masterson's knife, I climbed once more to the top of the heavy table and, after asking and receiving permission from Vera Farnol, I lighted a cigar.

And the room, save for the scratching of my match and the slight snap of the fire, was in dead silence. I knew that still everyone's nerves were at high tension, and that they were waiting, waiting, to see what I would do next. . . .

And then, without warning, from somewhere in the house came the sharp if somewhat muffled ringing of a bell!

# CHAPTER IX
## "THERE'S SOMEONE—"

I THINK IT IS IN THE NOTE-BOOKS of Thomas Bailey Aldrich that the sentence occurs something like the following, as the suggestion for a fantastic mystery, and it has always seemed to me to be one of the most breath-taking ideas ever conceived: *You are the last person left on earth. . . . The door-bell rings!!*

Something of Mr. Aldrich's breath-taking thrill descended on us, I am very sure, at the moment when we heard the bell. At least it descended on. me, and I could not move and I could not speak. Immediately and vividly, the present whereabouts of everyone in our group flashed into my mind: the three Farnols, the St. Johns, and Victor were here before me; Sheriff Gallant, Sutton, and Bessie were in the kitchen; Hackett, the sheriff's assistant, I had just left in the hall, going to join the sheriff; the sheriff's other man was guarding the house up the beach; and Dr. Forrester and Dr. Bock had taken Garda's body and were by now at the other house to get Masterson.

There was no telephone in the house, save the house phones which merely connected upstairs with downstairs, and there was no one upstairs to call down, or to be called up to. There was no doorbell, I had noticed, but only a massive bronze knocker. And this bell was distinctly not an untended alarm clock, for its ringing came in three short sharp jerks and then was still.

Vera's hand, as the sound came, found her other hand on her lap and the fingers intertwined; the blood seemed to leave her lips. At the same moment, with no expression on his face whatsoever,

Creamer Farnol's head came sharply up, and his ears actually seemed to prick. Patricia caught the arm of the settee and strained slightly forward. None of the others moved.

For twenty seconds, perhaps, there was no other movement in the room. We were all, I knew, waiting for a repetition, but nothing came.

Finally—"What was that?" I demanded of Farnol.

"I—I don't know," he faltered.

"You *must* know!" I cried. "What bells are there!"

His hands moved in his lap, but he answered me calmly enough. "There are no bells, Meech, except on the house phones. Perhaps someone in the kitchen—"

Br-r-r-r-r-ing!

It came again, one long insistent note, and scrambling from my table before it ceased, and reaching the door of the hallway, I could place the sound definitely as coming from up the stairs, almost surely in one of the rooms on the chamber floor.

"Sheriff!" I cried as I ran through the dining room. "Sheriff! Who is touching the phones?"

The scene in the kitchen was natural enough as I pushed open the swinging doors and crossed the pantry. Bessie had the coffee tray ready and was standing with it in her hands. The sheriff had one end of Sutton's bandage between his teeth and was still winding the other around the cut wrist, and Hackett was leaning against the sink watching the operation.

I could see the miniature wall-phone with its little ringing crank, hanging by the pantry door, untouched.

"Did anyone touch that phone?" I demanded.

Gallant, surprised, shook his head with the gauze still in his mouth.

"Did this phone ring?"

"No, sir," said Bessie, and the sheriff, untangling his teeth, said, "Why no, Spider. What's happened?"

I didn't answer him, but ran at once down the passage to the servants' rooms and glanced in each. There was, of course, no one there. So immediately I ran through the pantry and dining room again, and paying no attention to the group in the living room, who had risen to their feet and were huddled at the hall door, I dashed up the stairs and into the first room I came to on the left—Vera's. The door was open and the lights were on, and I found the phone at once, bracketed to the wall beside the closet door. I looked at it and wished (as I have wished of a score of other phones) that it could look as if it had recently rung.

I examined it, and saw at once the working of its mechanism. There were three little black buttons under its mouthpiece, and a little crank or handle on the right-hand side, opposite the receiver hook. One rang by turning the crank. The buttons controlled the location in which the caller wished it to ring, if they were pressed simultaneously with the turning of the crank, and although they were unlabelled, I thought that one rang the phone in the kitchen, one in Bessie's room, and one in Sutton's. All phones on the line, I knew by experience with such contraptions, could listen in on the same conversation. It was only the ringing which was controlled.

Therefore I lifted the receiver and held it to my ear.

I heard nothing, but I called into the transmitter: "Hello! . . . Hello! . . . Is anybody there? . . . Hel-*lo!*" But there was no answer. Not even a buzzing or a click to show that anywhere the apparatus was in use.

Experimentally, then, I pressed the first button on the left, and keeping my finger upon it, gave the crank a short turn with my other hand. I could fancy a buzzing sound in the depths of the house, although I could hear no definite ring. And in a moment the sheriff's voice came over the wire.

"Hello, there!" He barked it out.

"Gallant, this is Meech, trying the phones. Which one rang down there?"

"This is the kitchen."

"Good. Hang up and listen. I'm going to ring twice more, each in a different place. After the second ring, pick up the receiver and tell me where they rang."

I pressed the central button and gave the crank a turn, waited a moment and did the same with the right-hand one, and then I lifted the receiver again. Presently I heard the other end of the line click, and the sheriff's voice came over. "Meech?"

"Yes."

"The first one was in Sutton's room, down the passage. The second was in the cook's."

"Thanks. Now listen, Gallant. How many buttons are there on that kitchen phone?"

"Two."

I thought a moment. Yes, there would be. It would be unnecessary to connect the kitchen with the servants' quarters so near.

"Well, Gallant. Hang up again, and press first the left-hand button, turning the crank as you do it, and then the right-hand one. That's all. I won't talk to you again." I replaced the receiver.

Almost at once, from Farnol's room next door came the sharp if distant ringing of a bell. And right upon its heels the bell before me rang. So far as I could judge, the tones of the two were almost exactly the same. And so far as I could judge, *the tone was the one we had heard from downstairs.*

There was now but one thing left to try, and I went to the top of the stairs.

"You people down there!" I called, and they all rushed out into the hall—all, that is, except Vera, and she must have stayed in the living room.

"You heard those two bells. Which one, the first or the second, sounded most like the ringing we heard?"

There was a confused answer, from which I caught "first" and "second" indiscriminately mingled, and I started down the stairs.

"Come, come," I said, "one at a time. . . . Farnol?"

"They were very much alike, Meech," he said. "But I think I favor the second." (The second was Vera's room.)

"Patricia?"

"Oh, the second, I think."

"Victor?"

"The first." (That was Farnol's room.)

"St. John?"

"The first, almost certainly."

"Mrs. St. John?"

Her same giggle burst out. "Why, if you ask me, I'd say the same as Richard: the first."

I had reached the foot of the stairs, and now pushed through the group and entered the living room. "Mrs. Farnol?"

She was sitting in the big wing chair before the fire, looking at nothing, but as I spoke she gave a sudden little start and met my eyes.

"What?" she asked.

"Which do you favor, Mrs. Farnol, the first or the second?"

She looked at me without blinking, in a complete air of ignorance and innocence.

"The first or second what?" she asked.

"Bells, Mrs. Farnol. Do you mean to say you didn't hear the two rings just now, or our conversation out here by the stairs?"

I turned my head for a moment and looked at her husband. He was scowling at his wife with his head lowered and his brow wrinkled. I remembered suddenly that she had told me that her husband knew nothing and had been told nothing of her "tiny intervals of unconsciousness" she had mentioned to me earlier in the night, and I presumed that his scowl meant displeasure at the stupidity she was showing for trying to bluff me so patently. Well, I reasoned, I had no proof that she was not faking, that she wasn't actually stalling because of her reluctance to answer "Second" and make the opinion of the three Farnols unanimous against that of the rest of the party.

She shook her head and showed me the faint flicker of a pitiful little smile. "Why no," she answered. "I didn't hear anything. I must have been absolutely lost in my own thought. I do that sometimes, you know," and I realized she was attempting to draw my memory back to the earlier scene upstairs.

"Very well," I said, turning my back on her, resolving to waste no time puzzling over the truth or falsity of her "spells." I went at once to the kitchen and asked the sheriff to wait a few seconds more, and to repeat the calls, and then I went back into the living room and took up my position beside the table on which I had previously been perched.

"Now listen carefully," I said, holding up my hand.

The rings came—first in Farnol's room, and then in Vera's. Vera's was the loudest. Farnol's, I felt very sure, was the one. But still I held up my hand and made them listen without moving, and the rings came again. Now, there was no doubt in my mind. It *was* Farnol's. The distance muffled it exactly right. Vera's was the same note, but being nearer it was louder and more shrill.

In a buzz of voices Victor and the St. Johns corroborated my expressed idea, and Farnol, with the downward lines from his nose to the corners of his mouth showing more clearly than ever, nodded and said, "I guess perhaps you're right. But they're so very much alike that it was hard to say at first."

Patricia said nothing at all.

"But how *could* it ring, Mr. Meech?" asked Victor, thrusting his hands into his trouser pockets and shifting on the hearth-rug. "The wind, do you think? Could it have crossed some wires?"

"The wind has gone, Victor," I told him, "and these machines need hand turns, not just button contact. And besides, going back to the wind, if Mr. Farnol is right and these are only house phones, there should be no outside wires."

"That's quite right, Meech," said Farnol.

"You're telling me the truth, aren't you?" I shot at him. "Your phone connects only with the kitchen and the servants?"

"That's all," he replied, looking me straight in the eye.

"Creamer, dear," said Vera suddenly, "perhaps Mr. Meech would let you go upstairs and get me something more to throw over my shoulders."

"Why—" began Creamer, but I interrupted him at once.

"I'll get it," I said. "Here's Bessie with the coffee. Drink some, Mrs. Farnol, while it's hot," and without offering them any more explanation, I again left the room and went up the stairs. This time I passed Vera's door and went directly to Creamer's beyond, and at once found the wall instrument.

It had four buttons under its transmitter!

"Meech!" called a voice from halfway up the stairs. "Oh, Meech! Is it all right if I come up? My wife wants a particular—"

"Farnol!" I cried. "Come in here. In your room. At once."

He appeared at the door, the lines on his face deepened still more, and his mop of hair appearing, if possible, more awry.

"I'm worried about Vera, Meech," he began, "She—"

I interrupted him without any compunction. "Look at those, Farnol!" I demanded. "What is that fourth button for?" I touched the one at the right, feeling perfectly sure that that was the odd one and that the others were arranged in the order of Mrs. Farnol's phone.

He ran one hand through his hair and I could fancy that he was trembling slightly. "Why—why that?" he said. "That's nothing. That's not used."

I'm afraid I stamped my foot.

"But what is it *for?*" I cried. "What is it *there* for? What did you *plan* it for?"

Again that hand in his hair.

"I'm trying to remember. . . . Oh yes. Originally we intended to put the chauffeur's room out in the garage, and I had my phone made so that I could call from here—I didn't think the others particularly needed it. But we changed our plans, and there you are."

I peered at him, having no idea whether or not he was telling the truth. I watched him closely and then turned abruptly away as he made a little despairing gesture with his hands as if to say, "You see, it's all as simple as that."

"I hope you don't mind," I said, "that under the circumstances I must doubt your word—experimentally—for the moment. Or, if you like, call it proving your word," and I reached my finger for the button on the right.

"There's no need!" he fairly cried. "On my honor, Meech, you're wasting your time, and there's so very much to do!"

"I can spare a moment," I said tersely, and I pressed the button and turned the hand crank— turned it hard and long so that the bell on the other end—if there were an other end, would cry out into the night harsh and shrill.

And then, lifting down the receiver, I clapped it to my ear and listened intently.

There was no sound at all over the wire. If by any chance this instrument were arranged differently from Vera's and I had rung any of the phones downstairs, the sheriff, I knew, would answer at once. Or if it had rung anywhere in the house, someone would have heard it, scattered as we were within hearing distance of the whole building. But, as I say, there was no sound.

The only sound I heard was Farnol's breath trembling—yes, that's the word—trembling behind me. And, feeling more and more certain that he was involving himself in a colossal lie, I pressed the button and turned the crank again—even harder this time, and even longer, until I could well imagine that other phone, if such there was, fairly shrieking in its agonized insistence.

But still there was no sound. And reluctantly—very reluctantly—I replaced the receiver and turned toward my host. His lips parted in what was the beginning of an attempt to smile at me, and he spread his hands again, and this time said aloud, "You see?"

And by my ear, loud as a steam whistle, piercing to my eardrums, the telephone bell rang out!

I whirled like a flywheel and grabbed the receiver and cried at the top of my voice, "Hello! Hello!"

And I heard someone strange, someone very out of breath, call back, "Hello! Hello! Who in hell is this!"

Farnol's hand suddenly came to rest upon my shoulder, forcibly, but I wiggled and thrust it off, and cried, "This is Meech! Meech! Who is *this?* Where are you?"

Behind me Farnol grasped my shoulder again, and I heard him whisper, "Meech, for God's sake, I beg of you—"

But again I shook him off and again strained to listen, closing my free ear with my other hand this time.

"It's Forrester," the panting voice said. "Dr. Forrester. Can you hear?"

"Forrester!" I cried. "Where in heaven's name are you?"

And the reply came more clearly now: "In the cupola of the other house."

"Yes," I shouted. "Yes, go on!"

There was a quick movement from Farnol behind me.

"There's someone—" Forrester's voice began, clearly enough, but trailing off into something I couldn't catch.

"Someone—*where!*" I demanded.

And something made me cast a hurried glance over my shoulder—a glance just in time to see Farnol, half a dozen paces behind me, grab a heavy brass candlestick from his dresser and thrust it behind him. And in much less time than I can write it, I yelled "Hold it!" at the transmitter, dodged—scuttled—past Farnol, and was outside of the door, facing in, but calling over my left shoulder down the stairs, "Victor! Victor! Sheriff!"

Called? I shrieked, and my voice can rise to heights you wouldn't dream of. And as I faced Farnol, with my hands holding each side of the door jamb, I heard Victor spring to action in the living-room below, and heard him waste not a moment in crossing the hall in one stride and calling through the dining room toward the pantry door, "Sheriff! Sheriff! *Quick!*" and then start bounding up the stairs.

Farnol had not moved. His face had gone dead white, and his hand—both hands now—still held the candlestick behind him. But as he heard the footsteps coming up from below, he whirled around quickly and with a hollow thump banged the candlestick back on the top of the dresser, and then with just as swift a motion, he turned toward me again, and in a hoarse whisper said, "Meech! I beg—"

Victor was beside me, and the sheriff was not far behind, and at the foot of the stairs I heard all the rest of them, pushing, crowding up, with Vera's voice frantically screaming her husband's name. But despite the fact that Farnol had relieved himself of his weapon, I cried to Victor and the sheriff, "Grab him! Hold him! He threatened me!"

And I hardly waited to see the sheriff dart forward and pin Farnol's hands to his side, or to see Victor, after pausing momentarily in shocked and embarrassed surprise, spring to his assistance, before I leapt across the room to the phone again and yelled into it.

"Forrester! Forrester! Hello!"

"Meech!" came the reply. "Can you hear me!"

"Yes. Yes, Forrester. Go *on*, please!"

Behind me at the door, I could hear Vera, screaming at the sight of her husband, and I heard a thump on the door panels and on the floor as I knew she fainted and fell, but I didn't turn from the phone, but closed my free ear again.

"Go on!"

Now Forrester's voice came clearer than ever, and with more control, and I heard plainly every word he said, and he said them slowly.

*"There's someone—locked in one of the bedrooms here—moaning and groaning something awful!"*

## CHAPTER X
### ELEVEN YEARS AGO

IT WAS A GHASTLY TABLEAU that I faced as I turned away from the telephone. Farnol's wall lights were shaded in blue and added neither depth nor warmth to the grim and silent picture before me, and as, for the briefest possible moment, no one in my sight moved a muscle, the whole scene was like some poorly lighted and awful snapshot thrown by a stereopticon on a screen.

The blue-white faces of six people were straining toward me. Farnol was still in the center of the room, one of his arms in the grip of the sheriff, the other clutched tightly by Victor's two hands. Helen St. John had again crept into her husband's protecting embrace, and they had inched into the far shadows. And over her mother's inert form, crumpled on the threshold and for the moment unheeded, Patricia was standing, leaning against the doorjamb with her hands crossed on her breast.

I broke the silence by demanding of Farnol at once, "Who is locked in that other house!"

The fire that had shone from his eyes a moment ago had entirely gone now, leaving them not even smoldering, but dull and lustreless.

"No one," he replied in a dead voice.

My old impatience came back to me and I stamped my heel upon the heavy floor. "But Forrester has found some one! Who is it?" I cried.

He didn't answer at once, but looked at me with such a woebegone air of a penitent dog that I felt momentarily ashamed of myself.

"May I be let go?" he asked at length. "Will you allow me to see to my wife?"

"Leave him alone," I said to Victor and Gallant, "and lift Mrs. Farnol to the bed. Patricia will get water or a smelling bottle."

And immediately, as if the stereopticon had been a cinema after all, and my words were all that were needed to start the wheels turning, the picture sprang into action, and the figures flitted through the shallow light. Patricia, with the slightest of sobs, half stumbled out of the doorway and disappeared up the hall; Victor and the sheriff without a word dropped Farnol's arms and moved to where Vera lay, and lifted her, and rested her gently on the bed. And as Farnol went at once to her side and took up her hands, placing the bed between himself and the door, I abandoned my momentary project of moving toward the door myself in case my host should make the slightest attempt at a race for freedom, which I doubted he would do, and instead stayed where I was. Even the St. Johns moved a few steps towards Vera, but their embrace did not relax.

Patricia was soon back, holding a stopperless crimson bottle to her mother's nostrils, and I saw Vera quiver and flutter her lids. Faint color mounted again into her cheeks and she breathed regularly. Her eyes did not open, nor did she speak, but I knew she was now all right and I motioned her daughter aside, but allowed Farnol to remain where he was, still stroking her wrists. He too, I presume, saw that his wife was no longer in a faint, but either in conscious repose or else in a natural sleep, for he raised his head to me and spoke.

"Will you believe me, Meech?" he asked, in almost his natural voice.

"When you say there is no one there? No!" I replied.

"When I say," he continued, as if I had never said a word, "that no one is locked in that house who has, or can have, the slightest connection with these—these murders?"

I frowned. "That," I answered, "I cannot take your word for."

He dropped Vera's hands and faced me directly, drawing himself up to his entire height.

"I'm willing to swear," he said.

"I cannot even take your oath," I countered. "Nor can I forget that if I had not seen you first, you would have done everything in your power to prevent me from hearing the end of Forrester's message."

"Oh no!" he cried, suddenly, "I wouldn't have—"

"In fact," I interrupted him, "I'm going to show you right now, if only technically, exactly in what position you've placed yourself, actually, and by suspicion." The sheriff, divining my purpose, stepped forward and placed his hand lightly on Farnol's shoulder. "I ask the sheriff," I went on, "to place you under arrest on my charge of attempted assault and of attempted hindrance of an investigator appointed by the law." I looked at him more sternly from under my brows. "The charge can be changed to one much more severe at any time."

"I arrest you," murmured the sheriff mechanically, feeling himself, I'm afraid, slightly the fool, and hardly warming to my melodrama, "for the charge as read."

There was a sudden moan from the bed, and Vera sat up, her face flushed and her eyes glowing deep and dark. "You can't do that!" she cried. "Creamer had no more to do with the murders than—than I did," she finished weakly, and laid her head down again, shaking it from side to side and saying, "He didn't, Mr. Meech. He didn't, really."

"Hush, darling," said Patricia, bending over her.

"It's all right, Vera," spoke Farnol, showing more calmness than I knew he felt. "I'm not accused of murder, because I couldn't be. They've merely mistaken me because I lost my head for a moment and did something foolish that they've put a wrong interpretation on."

"Farnol," I demanded, breaking in on this little family scene, every bit of which I knew was for sentimental effect, "do you know who is in that locked room?"

What he was going to reply, I have no idea, for he paused just long enough so that Vera spoke first.

"What! Doesn't he know all about that yet?"

"Ah, then you *do* know!" I shot out to Farnol.

He nodded his head.

"Do you care to tell me or shall I go and see for myself?"

"Meech," he replied, "again I beg you with all the sincerity I can to believe that whoever is there has nothing whatsoever to do with you or with what has happened here tonight."

"Do you care to tell me or shall I go and see for myself?" I repeated.

"I shall not tell you, because it in no way concerns you," he answered simply, and his words were punctuated by a sharp intaking of Patricia's breath and by the faintest cry of "Creamer!" from the bed.

I hardly, even now, know why he made that decision; indeed, he hardly knew himself why he made it, for I find in his chronicle the following statement:

"I refused, I suppose, more because postponement seemed sweeter than anything else at the time, than because I had any idea that his projected visit to the other house would result in anything favorable to me. I was wrong, of course. I should have told him what he was about to find, and attempted to prepare him for it, fairly, and without prejudice. But I couldn't think clearly, and I didn't know his reputation for mercy."

But to go back to my own thoughts at the moment, I knew that I must waste no time making demands on him, but must see for myself who was there, and whether that person had any bearing on the case or not. Certainly, whoever it might be, that person was important enough, in Farnol's view, to arouse him to violence. And already he had shown me that he could stoop to violence if sufficiently aroused. Therefore, I must go at once; and turning to the telephone again, and making connection with Forrester without delay, I shouted that I was on my way over and that however far along he was with his own work there, he should wait my coming. And then I gave my orders to the sheriff.

"You will stay here, Gallant," I said. "And keep Hackett here, using your own judgment as to how you will guard these people and—and restrain your prisoner. Sutton is, I suppose, still in the kitchen with Hackett and the cook. I shall leave him here and ask

Victor if he will drive with me. And while I'm gone, I suggest that you get to work on comparing the prints you've found with the sheets downstairs. Now we know there's a phone, we'll keep in touch."

I said nothing else at all except "Come, Victor," and without even a backward glance at the faces that were staring after me, I turned directly away and left the room. But once in the hall, a thought struck me, and motioning Victor to stand and wait, I went toward the north end instead of toward the stairs, and stopped before the locked door of the room across the hall from mine. For the first time an actual suspicion about it had crossed my mind, and I fumbled at its lock with my skeleton key. It yielded and I pushed it open, groping for the light switch inside.

The clicking on of the lights revealed a room differing in no respect from any of the chambers I had been in. It was fully and completely furnished in every way, and even the bed was made.

Turning the lights out then, and locking the door once more, I headed for the stairs, but I couldn't resist stopping for a second at Farnol's room as I passed it, or calling in to him, "Oh, Farnol! I like your store room. I shouldn't mind being stored there myself." But I got not even an answering grunt.

But before I left the house, I learned one more thing—something that gave me plenty to think about during the drive up the coast. I delayed a moment in the lower hall and the living room, finding my hat and coat, and I looked out into the kitchen for a second, long enough to satisfy myself that Hackett, the chauffeur, and the cook were still there, and then, as I came to the foot of the stairs again, some of the people were coming down, with the St. Johns in advance. The sheriff, I presume, had suggested that they gather in the living-room again.

As Helen St. John was halfway down, her little foot, with its absurd high-heeled bedroom slipper, caught on the edge of a step and she very well might have fallen if she were not still being held by her husband's arm.

She gave a little squeak. "Oh!" she cried. "These shoes! That's the second time. I fell once before, Richard, when we came down last time, when you went back to get your cigarettes."

I stood quite still and listened, suddenly realizing what was coming.

"But it was way down on the bottom step," she continued, "and Sutton was there, and he caught me."

\* \* \* \* \*

Victor had the headlights on and the motor running when I climbed in the front seat beside him.

"You know the way, boy?"

"Of course, Mr. Meech." He touched the throttle and off over the marshes shrouded in their deep dark velvet we went.

So Sutton *was* the wounded man in all certainty. I remembered now how Helen St. John preceded her husband down the stairs while I watched him disappear into his room for the cigarettes, and how, when I reached the bottom of the stairs Sutton was still there, standing in the hall. So he had played the cavalier and saved a woman from falling—catching her, I didn't doubt, by her left hand with his left as she slipped on the bottom step, and letting his wounded right rest for a moment around her shoulders as he steadied her on the hall carpet. Well—many cavaliers had hanged before now!

Seriously, though, beyond a shadow of a doubt that proved that Sutton's cut on the wrist by the glass was self-inflicted to hide the earlier wound. Seriously, too, it was the bullet which did it. And more seriously still, if it was my walking-stick he threw, then he was my assailant. But why—why in the name of heaven should he kill Phillip Masterson!

"Thinking, Mr. Meech?" asked Victor.

And all at once I had it!

Leave out for the moment that Sutton did kill Masterson, why did he attack me? Because, of course, I was headed, by Farnol's knowledge, to that other house. Because, very likely, the moment I had left Farnol's house, Farnol had called Sutton on the house phone (Sutton, the only one in the place who was not restrained) and told him to follow. Because, perhaps, Sutton, not knowing that

Phillip had followed me too, had heard me talking with someone—
and probably with this person whose secrecy seems to mean life
and all to Farnol—and had, either in anger or by instruction attacked me. Did he see, I wondered, the struggle I had had with
Phillip in the cupola with its subsequent crashing of the windows
by my stick and conjecture that the unknown and I were at grips?
Or were Farnol's definite commands to him to strike me down when
we first met? Or did he construe my wild exit from the house—
running, I remembered, and probably incoherently muttering to
myself—as an emergency to be met with force? Whatever the exact
explanation, I felt absolutely sure in my own mind that it was
Sutton, and that he was acting as the agent of his master.

"Yes, Victor," I replied. "Thinking quite a bit."

"Mr. Meech," he asked, "will you tell me how Phillip died?"

"Yes, Victor," I answered. "He was murdered in exactly the same
way that Garda was."

I could see by the dashlight how he set his lips and bit them
until they were pale. But presently he asked, "By the same person?"

"I don't know," I said. "Phillip confessed to me, before he was
killed, that he murdered Garda." It was curious how, at the bare
mention of the fact, my blood rose angrily again and set the bump
on my head, quiet and practically painless the past hour or so,
throbbing and aching again.

"I thought so," said Victor simply.

"I don't know yet whether to believe him or not," I said.

"I should," Victor said. "He was capable of it. He was a funny
mixture, Mr. Meech. Quiet and rather queer most of the time, but
when anything went against him, he'd fly into the most awful rages.
Not just outbursts of temper, but sort of crafty anger. I remember
once seeing him pick up a brick and throw it at the back of a fellow's
head—a fellow he was suddenly angry with, just because he kidded him—but a good half hour had passed since the little quarrel
and we thought it was all over. . . . I suppose this time he was furi-
ous at Garda and me."

"Hardly at you, I think, Victor. At least, according to what he told me, he resented you your health and normality, but he flew into murderous rage at Garda because, so he said, she was the only person he had ever loved, and she turned her back on him for you."

The great house loomed before us and we rode the intervening hundred yards to it in silence, but as Victor turned off the motor and switched the lights dim, he said, more as if he were speaking to himself:

"What an awful thing to kill for! Besides, I only kissed her once."

Once more, then, I stepped inside this eastern house, into its dim and echoing hall. But it was not empty this time. On its stretcher laid upon the floor was the body of Phillip Masterson, covered, of course, from our sight. And I knew that in Dr. Forrester's ambulance outside in the dark, Garda was lying on her identical stretcher, waiting for the long ride up the coast. Victor, I noticed, would not look at the shrouded figure, but kept his head lifted and his eyes directed up the stairs, down which at once came the sound of footsteps.

Dr. Forrester appeared round the turn of the stairs, and hailed me.

"Damned glad you've come, Mr. Meech. We *did* get a turn, all right, when we heard that man in there."

"Come down," I said, "and tell me all about it. Everything exactly."

I sat, for the moment, on the lowest step while he leaned against the heavy newel post; and Victor, his back turned resolutely toward the white-shrouded stretcher, faced us both. A form came suddenly up the outer steps of the house, looked in for a second through the open door, and silently went away again.

"The sheriff's man," explained the doctor. "My man, Bock, is still in the cupola, cleaning up."

"Why, it was this way," he went on at once, "we came right over, made ourselves known to the sheriff's man, and brought the stretcher in the house. We found the body in the cupola, and the door locked, as you said, but the cupola lights were on. Did you leave them that way?"

"Yes," I answered, "go on."

"It was my assistant, Bock, who found the telephone. There's a small empty closet up there, with the door open, and the door was hiding the phone on the wall behind it."

"You didn't use it right off, did you?" I asked.

"No. Not then. But it was when we were carrying Masterson down stairs on the stretcher that we heard a noise in one of the rooms. There aren't any lights in the hallway of the second floor—at least none that I can make work—and it was rather frightening, I can tell you, to hear sounds coming out of a room you're sure is empty—in the dark."

"What sort of sounds?"

"Well—first just the noise of a chair or something. And we stopped dead in our tracks and Bock said, 'What was that!' and we stood there listening, still holding the stretcher. We didn't hear anything for a minute, and then we heard the chair, or whatever it was, move again, and some footsteps cross the room."

"Just a moment," I interrupted. "Which room is this?"

"On the right as you come down the cupola stairs. The first room."

I nodded. It corresponded to the locked room in Farnol's house, the one he had lied about.

"Well," Forrester continued, "when I heard the steps, I shouted 'Who's in there!' But I didn't get any reply at all, not just then. So after listening a moment I motioned to Bock to put the stretcher down, and I went right up to the door and knocked. And this man inside said, in the queerest voice I've ever heard, 'You'd better not knock on that door!' . . . Well, Meech, you know that that was a pretty funny thing to hear, and I didn't know what to make of it, and I couldn't think of anything to say, so I just stood there—oh, for quite a while. And I can't deny that I was pretty scared. But soon I called in again and said, 'Who's in there? Who are you?' And the voice answered me, and said—well, Meech, you can imagine how I felt—said: *'One person who's still alive!!'*

"And then he didn't say another thing, but burst at once into a sort of laugh which changed into groans, and then sort of grumblings, and all the time there was a noise in the room as if he were moving chairs about, or even shifting the bed."

"What about lights?" I said. "Did you try to look through the keyhole, or did you see any light through the door-crack?"

"No," Forrester replied. "I mean, I didn't see any lights through the crack, and I didn't try the keyhole. But there are lights in the room, very faint, though, and with the shades pulled down, because just a few minutes ago, while you were on your way over, I went around outside and looked at the windows. . . . Well, to go on, I knew you ought to be told right off, so I ran up into the cupola and tried the telephone. I had no idea, of course, where it led, whether it was just a house phone or whether it went through central. But I tried it, twice, and didn't get any answer. And then, thinking that what we'd have to do would be to drive over to you, we went on downstairs with the stretcher, and put it here in the hall. And then I thought I'd bring Miss Lawrence's body in, so that I could make better time on the run over to you, but while we were outside by the car, I heard the phone ring up in the cupola. And then ring again. But by the time I could get to it, someone had hung up. And so I rang it myself, and got you. That's why I was so out of breath, from running up those stairs."

That was the end of his story. Now it was up to me.

"Will you come upstairs with me, doctor?" I asked, rising from my step. "Will you, Victor?"

They both expressed all eagerness, and with myself in the lead and the others following abreast, we climbed the stairs in the half light into the darkness of the upper hall. Not total darkness, though, for some illumination, faint and yellow, was twisting its way down the circular stairs of the cupola. Without a word we crossed the full length of the hall, and I stopped before the door at the end, on my left. Raising my head to Forrester, I received an answering nod and bent to listen.

I could hear no sound inside.

I stooped and laid first my eye and then my ear against the keyhole, but I could see nothing and hear nothing.

So then I knocked briskly and loudly on the panels, and waited for a reply.

It came slowly, but it came at length, spoken loudly in a curious throaty voice: "You'd better not go knocking on that door."

"Who are you!" I demanded, as Forrester had done, but, I am sure, in a sterner voice.

And the same answer came that Forrester had heard: "One person who's still alive!"

"But what is your name!" I cried.

And the answer, the last thing in the world I had expected, came at once:

"Vera!"

I must admit that I was taken aback and that I couldn't move or speak for a score of seconds. But when I did, it was to rattle the door-knob, and call in, "Will you open the door for us?"

"No," said the voice.

"Why not?" I demanded.

"Because I haven't got a key. I'm locked in."

"Who locked you in?" I persisted.

"*A murderer!*" was the reply.

Again I had to pause, but again I moved and spoke, reaching for my skeleton key and fitting it in the lock. "I'll open it," I said. "I'm coming in!"

"You'd better not!" cried the voice, but the lock had yielded to my turning of the key, and I pushed the door wide open as Forrester and Victor crowded onto the threshold beside me.

In the center of the room, which was lit by one lone candle on the dresser, a candle whose flame wavered crazily as the draughts came in, was standing the most hideously ugly old woman I have ever seen, her aged lips drawn back in a toothy grin, and her back burdened with a hump larger than my own. And as I stood there, she spread her antique, muddy brown skirts, and sank before me in a curtsey.

It was travesty—sheer, diabolic travesty, but what could I do but remove my hat and bow from the waist toward her!

"What is *your* name?" she asked, in that voice which was as deep as a man's, but without a man's resonance.

Again there was nothing to do but reply. "Spaton Meech," I said.

"How do you do?" she said. "You're quite as ugly as I am. In fact, I think we're quite a pair," and she went off into a short fit of horrible throaty laughter. And instinctively I felt that I knew why Vera Farnol had paused on the stairs when she first caught sight of me in the door. I reminded her of this terrible creature!

"What is your whole name, Miss—" I asked as soon as I could speak.

She shook her hand in the air in front of her. "Mrs.!" she corrected me. "Mrs. Vera Darlow. Mrs. Hannaford Darlow, but my husband died forty-three years ago December, before my daughter was born."

"You have a daughter?"

"Yes. And a son. But my son is dead. He was murdered."

How comforting it is when dawn, even though it be false dawn, begins to break after a dark, dark night. Dawn was breaking in my mind, and rapidly I fired my final questions, and just as rapidly came the replies.

"What is your daughter's name?"

"Vera. She's Vera Farnol now."

"When was your son murdered?"

"Eleven years ago."

"Who murdered him?"

"The man who locked me up. My son-in-law."

"How did he kill him?"

"He pushed him off the cliff. I saw him from the cupola, and it was in a storm, and when the body was washed up it was all battered and you couldn't recognize him, and Creamer said it was just a poor drowned sailor from a sinking ship, but I knew the truth, but no one would listen to me because I'm insane, you see, and so is Vera, a little."

"But why did he murder him?"

"Ha! For his money, of course. That his father had left to him, but not to Vera because Vera wasn't born when her father died."

"How long have you been locked up?"

"For eleven years."

"I mean here—in this house?"

"Since yesterday."

"Who brings you your food?"

"Sutton did tonight, about quarter of ten. But I didn't eat much of it because they put things in it."

"What do you mean—things in it?"

"Things to make me sleep. So I won't go around saying things I shouldn't. And moaning and groaning. I moan and groan, you know, because I'm insane. But so is Vera, too, a little."

"But you can always say things to me," I told her, gently, "because I'm here to help you, and because, as you say, I'm uglier than you are." I tried to laugh. "So I want you to tell me about tonight. You must have heard people going up and down stairs, and I want you to tell me about them."

But I had lost her, for suddenly she set to her "moaning and groaning" and she shook her head and waved her hands aimlessly in the air before her, and try as I would, I could get absolutely nothing coherent out of her. Not by wheedling and begging, not even by approaching her and taking her old hand in mine, not even by stern demands. But when, by a stroke of luck, I mentioned that I would take her home, back to her room in the other house, she stopped her noise immediately and turned at once and began to pick up a few pitiful toilet articles from the dresser, and would have blown out the candle if I hadn't restrained her.

"You'll talk to me when we get home, won't you?" I said, as I would to a child.

She laughed, deep in her throat—I might almost say (for so it seemed) deep in her hump. "If you're a good boy," she replied.

So, turning to Forrester and Victor who, with their eyes fairly popping from their sockets, were still in the doorway, I asked them to help her prepare to move, and then I ran up the stairs to the cupola. Dr. Bock was still there, but I paid no attention to him and went at once to the telephone, pushed its single button, and gave the crank a heavy turn.

The wait seemed endless, but in reality it must have been less than half a minute before the sheriff's voice called "Hello."

"Gallant," I said. "On some pretext or other, put all the people back in their bedrooms. I'm bringing someone in I don't want them to see for the moment."

"Right," he answered.

"That's all, I guess," I continued. "How's everything going?"

"Fine," he said. "I'm working on the prints and I've got a thing of beauty for you."

"What do you mean?"

"Shall I tell you now?"

"Yes," I answered, "if you can."

"Well, sir," he said. "Would you care to know who was the last one to take hold of the inside cupola doorknob—and with bloody fingers?"

"Yes!" I shouted, with so much vehemence that Bock straightened up suddenly from his work on the red-splotched mattress.

"Well, sir," said the sheriff, with exasperating slowness. "It was Miss Patricia Farnol."

# CHAPTER XI
## PATRICIA'S TALE

I AM GOING TO PAUSE A BIT in my narrative for a page or two and attempt, in some slight fashion, to show just where I was, mentally, at this point in the night's proceedings. I have gone over the whole thing enough, in the past month, to know clearly just where I stood, so far as the ultimate decision was concerned, at practically every point. I have made notes, copiously, since then, and I can give the reader the advantage of them now, although naturally at this point in the action I had not put pencil to paper. And it must be remembered that there had hardly been time for any very deep reflection. Indeed, thinking of the length of time it has taken me to write this, it really rather astonishes myself to think back, and jot down, and discover how little time had actually elapsed and how fast events had moved. And it may tickle the fancy of the amateur detective if I set down here and now my reconstructed time-table of the whole night, beginning with the moment when, standing beside the bed of the murdered girl, I started the whole thing off, as I have related, by looking at my watch. It was then five minutes past ten. From that time, then:

10:05   I discover the murder of Garda.
10:15   Victor and I join the others in the living room.
10:20   The Rock wails.
10:30   Sutton and I start for the farmhouse to phone.
10:55   I lock the people in their bedrooms.

| 11:00 to | |
|---|---|
| 12:00 | I hold my little scenes with the sheriff, with Vera about her sleepwalking, with Farnol about permission to go to the other house, and with Victor. |
| 12:00 | I start my walk up the beach. |
| 12:15 | I reach the other house. |
| 12:30 | Masterson arrives. |
| 12:50 | I run from the house and am attacked. |
| 1:05 | I recover consciousness. |
| 1:10 | I discover the murder of Masterson. |
| 1:25 | The sheriff and I drive back to Farnol's. |
| 1:35 | We reach the house and hear Hackett's shot. |
| 1:45 | I discover the blood-stain on Mrs. St. John and start finger-printing. |
| 2:00 | Sutton cuts his wrist. |
| 2:15 | The bell rings. |
| 2:45 | Victor and I reach the other house again. |
| 3:00 | I meet and talk with Mrs. Darlow. |
| 3:15 | We start for Farnol's again with Mrs. Darlow. |

Hardly much leisure, anyone will agree, for sitting down and attempting to figure things out. Indeed, my only moments of peace had been during the few drives, and during my lone walk up the sands. But after each one of those periods, something further had happened to add to the complications. But because I fear that often I have rushed too fast in narration, let me think back now, and think back fairly and see exactly where, up to this point when we started home with Mrs. Darlow, my suspicions lay with regard to the guilt or innocence of each one of the party. And for ease, I'll list them all in table form.

*Creamer Farnol*: Proven desperate and hot-blooded in emergency. Probably guilty of his brother-in-law's death eleven years ago. Perhaps personally or by proxy through Sutton guilty of Masterson's death, though why, not yet clear unless still protecting his old secret which they might have learned. Certainly under enough suspicion to be arrested.

*Vera Farnol*: Undoubtedly in cahoots with her husband concerning her mother's virtual imprisonment. Perhaps, though, only because of shame for her mother's appearance and insanity. Doubt any connection with Masterson's death except as she might have been in knowledge of Sutton's following me. Very possibly shamming her sleepwalking and unconscious moments. Also possibly not. Absolute puzzle to me, with all sorts of suspicions in the back of my mind, but nothing at all definite. The most shadowy figure in the case.

*Patricia Farnol*: Another puzzle. Up until the sheriff's last phone call could have sworn her innocence with the reservation that she knew more than she seemed to know. Now, with the sheriff's news, know she visited the cupola. When? Was she the one who went there just before ten o'clock and whom I saw turning out the lights? If so, was it a revisit? If it was not a revisit, why didn't she give the alarm?

*Victor Millard*: Undoubtedly exonerated. The only thing in his disfavor is his being completely dressed. Doubt very much if he is clever enough to act so well the innocent, ingenuous boy.

*Phillip Masterson*: Until the news of Patricia's being in the cupola I was practically ready to accept his confession as true. Now must reject it until Patricia has explained the finger-prints. But if her visit there was a late one, after the crime, would she keep silent to shield Masterson? See no reason for it. Must still hold open mind on his confession, although still think I'm enough judge of human nature to feel that he spoke the truth. But he was capable of acting where Victor was not.

*Richard St. John*: Don't like the man very well, but must write "exoneration" since learning that it was Sutton who was wounded in the wrist.

*Helen St. John*: Never thought of connecting her in any way except as possible confederate of her husband in leaving the locked bedroom, which now I am sure he did not do. Exoneration.

*Sutton*: Undoubtedly my assailant. Undoubtedly shot by Hackett, still holding my walking stick. Undoubtedly faking the cut on the glass. Working probably under Farnol's direction. Probably the instrument in the murder of Masterson. But if so, Farnol's must be the mental guilt. Certainly under enough suspicion to be arrested. Certainly, above all, the most to be suspected.

*Bessie*: Exoneration.

*Vera Darlow*: Probably actually insane with moments of probable lucidity. Her story of the death of her son perhaps an hallucination but to be believed for the time being as a working point. Save for her being presumably locked in her rooms, could I suspect her of being a homicidal maniac and doing both murders? In each case her room was at the foot of the cupola stairs. Until yesterday afternoon she was in Farnol's house. Was she there when Garda was killed? Certainly she was in the other house when Masterson was killed. Can't say anything yet. Suspect is all.

And that, fairly and truthfully, is all I knew at the moment. How to proceed with that knowledge was another question, but I wanted to do certain things before the night was over and, with daylight, the hubbub of newspapers and publicity would begin. And those things too, for clarity, I shall list in table form.

> 1. Arrest Sutton and accuse him directly, at least of his attack on me.
> 2. Question Mrs. Darlow further.
> 3. Confront Creamer Farnol with his mother-in-law's tale.
> 4. Accuse Patricia of her presence in Garda's room after the death.
> 5. Learn more about the fingerprints, particularly on the knife.
> 6. See if the note Masterson said he forged is still in existence.
> 7. Find my flashlight if possible.
> 8. Find my walking stick if possible.
> 9. Find the key to Garda's room.

It must be remembered that all these things were not arranged in my mind in as orderly fashion as I now set them down. I knew vaguely, of course, my method, but heavens! every time I started to do something, the gods of these rocks dropped another thunderbolt and shattered my plans and created new chaos to try to bring order out of. But one thing I was immediately and definitely sure of, and that was that I must get us all back to Farnol's at once, and so my orders were given.

I told Forrester that he might as well proceed at once to Biddeford with the bodies, and asked him to lock the cupola door behind him and give the key to the sheriff's guard below. Autopsy on Garda, I knew, would begin as soon as he got home, and by early morning I could, if I rode up to the farmhouse and telephoned, learn as nearly as medical science can place it, the time of Garda's death if I still appeared to need it. He told me that in the case of

Masterson the means of death was so apparent and the time of death so definitely placed by observation as between ten minutes of one and five minutes past, that autopsy would not be performed unless I requested it, which I did not.

Then, bidding him farewell, I bundled Victor and the old lady out of the house and into the car. It wasn't difficult. She found a crazy brown bonnet with all the old-fashioned paraphernalia of wrinkled strings and cotton roses on it, and clutching her little toilet articles unpacked in her bare hands, suffered herself to be led down the hall. And perhaps suffered is too strong a word. Trotted eagerly is better, following behind me with uneven little steps. But at the top of the stairs she stopped and raised her elbows.

"I'm to be carried," she said.

I paused with what I'm afraid was a shade of annoyance.

"Why?" I asked.

"Because I'm always carried up and down stairs."

There was a point! Was she incapable of going up and down them herself? If so, that did away with any suspicions I might have that she had anything to do with either of the murders.

"Oh come, now," I said. "That's a little silly, isn't it? Why, you're a perfectly spry woman, and I guess if I can do it, you can."

She lifted her chin with almost a touch of pride. "Yes," she answered, "but you haven't been locked in a room for eleven years."

"Did someone carry you up here?"

"Of course."

"Who?"

"Sutton. That's who did. Sutton."

That explained, then, why I had found no trace of her footsteps, and probably also why the set of footprints were so deep in the dust. That print that I had covered, and which I could see was still covered, was undoubtedly his.

"But won't you try it this once, to please me?" I begged. "I'm afraid I'm not strong enough to carry you—you know what a burden these deformities are. And Mr. Millard here—Mr. Millard sprained his back this afternoon, at tennis."

She glanced us up and down, with scorn, I thought, and then replied, "Well, anything to please a couple of weaklings," and went down the stairs as easily and well as if she did it twenty times a day. But when she reached the bottom and I attempted to congratulate her and express pleasure at her accommodating us, she relapsed into silence and would say not a single word. Nor did she speak at all during the whole drive, or at our arrival before Farnol's house, nor while she was mounting the stairs there (which she did without a sign of suggestion from me, or without the slightest hesitation). I went up stairs behind her, and saw that she headed directly for her door by the cupola stairs. I unlocked it for her, and switched on the lights, and she went immediately to the dresser and began to lay out her toilet articles in exactly the same order as they had lain on the other dresser.

"Now you'll talk to me, Mrs. Darlow," I said, "won't you?"

She took off her bonnet and began to press and pat it into greater shapelessness. "In a little while," she said. "But first I must make a few notes."

"Notes?" I asked. "What sort of notes?"

"Just notes," she answered. "In ten minutes, if you happen to be passing this way, drop in and we'll have a chat. But just at present I must make a few notes." And she shut her lips so resolutely that I knew I had no other choice than to bow to her wishes, and leave her for the time being. And bow I did, literally, receiving in response a spreading of her skirts and the same absurd, grotesque curtsey. Then I locked the door behind her and went downstairs.

The sheriff, who had met us at the porte-cochere was now in the living-room with all his apparatus and "exhibits" arranged on the same card-table I had set up, and Victor was with him. I knew that in all fairness, if I had ordered the St. Johns locked up, I should do the same to the boy, even though I trusted him almost completely. But I hesitated to lose his confidence again, not, I must admit, that his presence had been of any material help to me, although I liked his company. However, I asked him, as nicely as I could, if he would mind going to his room, as the sheriff and I had some things we wanted to talk over. "I won't lock you in, Victor," I said. "It isn't that."

"All right, Mr. Meech. But you'll call me if you need me, won't you?" He covered his disappointment so well that I answered. "I'll call you soon, whether I need you or not," and he left us. I heard him ascend the stairs, and shortly I heard his door open and close.

The sheriff at once showed me the drawings he had made of the prints on the inside doorknob of the cupola, and explained them to me.

"The only fresh ones," he said, "are these, and it only takes half an eye to see that they're Miss Patricia's." He held up beside his drawings the sheet of prints that I had taken from the girl's fingers. "Look at them. You don't even need a magnifying glass. See that funny reverse whorl, on all her fingers. None of the others have got them. And, Spider—the index finger had blood on it, very definitely. Furthermore, her prints are on top of all the others— the newest. And there aren't any other discernible prints at all, except for a mess of Garda Lawrence's, new and old. If I had to say, I'd say that no one else but Patricia and Garda had been in that room the last day or two."

"Oh, no!" I cried. "You can't say that. Say: no one else opened that door from the *inside* the last day or two. Anyone might have gone in and come out, leaving the door open behind him. All of us did."

"Yes, of course, that's true."

"All right. What about the rest of the room?"

"Nothing, I found one of yours on the window catch, and one of what I think is Farnol's on the light switch, but it had blurred with someone else's underneath. Besides, you've explained both of those. None on the woodwork of the bed."

"All right," I said. "Now what about the knife?"

"Masterson's mostly," he began, "and one—"

"Masterson's!" I interrupted. "You've never taken his prints!"

"I know," he said. "But these on the knife are so clear—look at them—you don't even need powder, really—that I used them as the original and then went up in his room and found specimens all over there that corresponded. Particularly on his cigarette lighter. He had left a silver one, and you know how silver will take prints."

"Good work," I said. "But you started to say something else."

"Yes," he went on. "There's one other print."

"Mine, of course," I said, remembering how Masterson had tossed me the knife as he lay on the mattress in that other cupola, and forgetting for the moment that I had had gloves on.

"No," he said. "Victor Millard's!"

I bent over the table with my heart suddenly pounding against my ribs. "Where! Show it to me!"

He opened, not the blade with which Masterson's throat had been cut, but the small blade at the other end, larger than a penknife's blade, but smaller, perhaps, than the blade on the ordinary jack-knife, and showed me his prepared print. And using my glass on it, and comparing it with one of the sheets, I could see that it was unmistakably, so far as first judgment was concerned, the print of Victor's right thumb.

"I don't believe it!" I cried.

"But you can see for yourself, Spider!"

"I know. I know. I mean—wait a minute." I left him and ran out into the hall and up the stairs, going directly to Victor's room and throwing open the door.

He was not there!

The lights were on but they revealed no sign of him: and I remember now how, momentarily, my heart seemed to stop its beating as the double vision of Victor's guilt and my betrayed trust flashed across my mind. But as I stood there, incapable for a few seconds of any coherent thought, the slightest of noises came to me from the further end of the corridor, from, indeed, the cupola stairs. And as quickly as I might, and as softly as I could, I went to the foot of them, and just as softly but less quickly, I climbed their steps, rounding the first turn and then the second until I could see Garda's door.

And Victor was before it, fumbling with its lock!

He didn't hear me and I didn't speak, but watched him and saw that he was turning a key. Why do that! We had broken the lock hours ago.

And then he straightened up, withdrawing the key from the lock and putting it in his trousers pocket, turned and saw me.

I got in the first word. "Victor!" I cried. "What are you doing?'"

"Oh, Mr. Meech," he said, thrusting his hand into his pocket again and pulling out what he had just put there, "look! I've found the key!"

There was not a hint in his voice or his manner that I had caught him doing anything he shouldn't he doing. For the moment, at least, I could neither scold him nor accuse him.

"What key, Victor?"

"The one to this room. I just came up to try it, and it fits. It's the one, right enough. Aren't I lucky?"

I climbed the remaining stairs and stood on the landing beside him. "Where did you get it?" I asked, as I took it from his hand and myself fitted it into the keyhole and saw how easily it turned.

"Right in the hall," he said, "just now. Right spang in front of the door to my room. It was close up against the threshold, so sort of in the shadows, and I suppose it could have been there all night long without our seeing it. And when you had us lined up in front of our doors, it must have been behind my feet where you couldn't see it. Not even, do you remember, when you bent down and felt of my shoes. But this time, as I was going in, I kicked it. Of course I thought at first it was my own door key, but no, because there it was still in the outside of the lock. And then I had an idea, and came up to try it."

I put it in my own pocket. "Thank you, Victor," I said. "Now before I put you in your room again, I'm going to ask you a question. When did you last use Phillip Masterson's knife and why?"

There was not the slightest hesitation in his answer. "If you mean his silver-handled one, it was this morning—or yesterday morning according to what day or night you figure this is. Anyway, the last morning there was. We were playing tennis and one of the strings of my racquet broke. It left a loose end and I borrowed Phil's knife and cut it off."

"Do you remember which blade you used?"

"Yes. The little one. I supposed it would be sharper."

"Thank you," I said. I had to be satisfied, and of course I wanted to be satisfied. One can do nothing in the face of simple, natural, and logical explanations. So I said no more but took him down the stairs with me and saw him into his room. But something made me turn the key in his lock very softly, I must admit. Strange that I should have qualms about it and find the need to justify my action to myself.

Down I went, then, to the sheriff again, and told him what I had learned and that I was willing to abide by Victor's explanation. Then I asked him about Farnol and Sutton and where they were, learning that Farnol was locked in his own room and Sutton (to keep him off the first floor) in Masterson's empty one. But this time, because of the ease with which Phillip had escaped from it, Hackett was confining his patrol to that side of the house.

So once more I climbed the stairs and went to Patricia's door and knocked softly on it.

"Who is it?" she asked, from within.

"It's I," I said.

"Mr. Meech?"

"Yes. May I come in?"

"You've only got to turn the key," she said, a trifle bitterly I thought.

The room was lighted only by the shaded reading lamp on the bedside table, and Patricia was propped up against her pillows with a book in her hands which she laid aside as I entered. Her hair was shining and unruly against the white of the linen, but her face was colorless.

"I'm glad you've come at last. You found her, of course."

"Your grandmother?"

"Yes. And I suppose you've heard her tale about father?"

I nodded.

She sat up a bit higher on her pillows.

"And I suppose you believed it?"

I threw out my hands. "Why," I hesitated, "for the time being—as something to look into—yes."

"In spite of the fact that you could see at once that she's insane?"

"Why—yes, again. . . . But look here," I interrupted myself, "I shall want to talk to you about your grandmother in just a moment. But right now, Patricia, I want to talk about *you*."

I went to the foot of the bed and took hold of the carved wooden footboard, leaning over it and staring her directly in the eyes. "What were you doing in the cupola?" I demanded.

She didn't shift her gaze in the least degree, but she held her breath and was silent for a long moment. Then, while one of her fingers plucked at an ornament on her negligee, she said, calmly, "I suppose you've found my fingerprints."

"Yes," I said, and leaned farther forward. "Bloody ones, Patricia!"

She nodded. "I know," she replied.

And then, as a pause followed, I said as sternly as I could. "Do you care to give me an explanation?"

Again she nodded, still with infinite calm, but calm which seemed to be merely covering a seething nervousness.

"Yes," she replied. "But I should like to give you my explanation in my own way, and not have you cross-examine me until I am quite through. Will you do that?"

I relaxed my hold upon the footboard and straightened up. "I'm willing to let you start, at least. But it's very difficult for me to keep from asking questions."

"I'll try to be clear enough so that there won't be much need for questions. . . . Will you come around and sit on the foot of the bed? You see, Mr. Meech, I've got something to tell you and I've got to prepare your mind for it."

This was all very curious, but I could see no harm in letting her take her own course. If I were about to receive a pack of lies—well, I might as well have them all at once and have them over with. Furthermore, as I have previously said, I'm greatly influenced by a pair of clear eyes. And Patricia's were very clear, very steady, deadly in earnest. I perched on the side of her bed and held my knee in my clasped hands.

"Mr. Meech," she began, "I was in the cupola at ten o'clock tonight,—it was the first time I had been in it all day. I undressed as

soon as I came up stairs when you went to take your walk. But
before I went to bed, I thought I would go upstairs and see how
Garda was. And that was what I did. The dishes were still outside,
and the door was closed but not locked. I didn't rap, but went in.
The light was out, and I didn't turn it on—not just then—but went
over to the bed and spoke to her softly, to see if she were asleep.
She didn't answer me, and I put out my hand to touch her gently."

She paused, and shuddered, and drew in her breath and held
it. Her left hand found and rubbed the fingers of her right. "You
know what happened. . . . I touched her throat!"

"Well," she continued after another tiny pause. "I didn't realize, even then. I guess I thought that—that—it isn't very pretty—
that she had been sick. So I went and turned on the light. . . . Now
don't ask me what I did, because I don't remember that I did anything but stand and stare. And don't ask me what I thought, because I don't remember when I began to think—what I thought
later. But I do know that it was some little time—perhaps, perhaps
two whole minutes before I put out the light and went downstairs."

I started to speak, but she halted me with a raised hand.

"You want to know why I locked the door and why I didn't give
the alarm. Why I went back to my room and closed the door. I heard
you or someone come into the front hall down below and I started
to run and dropped the key somewhere. . . . Well, I can tell you
that. But that's what I want to prepare your mind for."

She bent away from the pillows behind her, folded her hands
in her lap, and leaned toward me.

"Mr. Meech," she said. "I've got to tell you about something
else now. And I've got to ask you a question."

I looked in all readiness.

"What would you do—what would you have to do if you ran onto
the truth about a murder that happened many years ago?"

"What do you mean, 'what would I have to do?'"

"I mean, officially, so far as the law was concerned."

"Officially, nothing, save as the duty of a private citizen. I have
no official connection with the police, except as I am appointed
for a particular investigation."

"What—what would you do as a private citizen?" Her eyes seemed to beg me.

"Why, I think it would depend—"

She interrupted me with a little "Yes, exactly" and then hunched herself even nearer to me, and spoke again.

"Mr. Meech. Grandmother Darlow is dead, dead wrong about my uncle's death. My father did not push him off the cliff."

I still stared at her, drinking in her words and her earnestness.

"*But my mother did, Mr. Meech!*"

"How—" I began, but again she cut me short with a wave of her hand in the air.

"How do I know?" she cried. "Because I saw her!"

# CHAPTER XII
## "DIE GEISTESUNTERSTRÖMUNG"

"You think it's pretty awful, don't you, Mr. Meech, for a daughter to accuse her mother of such a terrible thing?" she said, after I had stared at her for a long time, stared not in surprise but in admiration for her audacity and in complete inability to understand where she was leading me.

"I think it depends," I said at length, "on the circumstances." It was the vaguest thing to say that I could think of at the moment.

"Of course," she replied. "And I've had several hours tonight to think it over—to say nothing of eleven years! But now I'm going to say something else which may be a bit startling to you. And this is it: My mother does not know she pushed her brother off the cliff!"

"What!" I cried.

"She thinks he was killed—lost—somewhere up near Hudson's Bay."

"But how does she think that? Wasn't it he that was here?" I demanded.

"Oh, yes," she replied. "It was my uncle all right. But later, to explain his absence, my father concocted the tale of an expedition— my uncle was a great hunter—and the story that it ended in disaster."

"But still I don't see

"Of course you don't." Without taking her eyes from my face she fumbled on the bed covers and drew the book she had been reading into her lap. "Can you read German, Mr. Meech?" she asked immediately.

"Why, yes. A little."

"Have you ever seen this book?" She pushed it forward, with its title turned so that I could read it. "Read me the title," she said.

"*Das Verbrechen and die Geistesunterströmung*," I read aloud.

"Can you translate it?"

"'Crime,'" I said, "and—well, literally, I suppose, 'the under-current of the mind, or spirit'."

"Yes," she said. "Or, as Dr. Bernd, the author, uses it, it's almost the same as 'the unconscious'. Not exactly, but near enough. 'Crime and the Unconscious'. . . . Do you see what I'm driving at?"

I did and said so, and the picture of tall Vera in her clinging gown as she stood in her dark doorway came before my mind. And that other picture of her sitting in her chair by the fire, calm and serene, while all around her we chatted excitedly about the order of the ringing bells.

"You're trying to imply," I said, "that your mother pushed your uncle off the cliff deliberately, but didn't know she did it?"

"Well," she replied, "hardly deliberately if she didn't know she did it. But I do mean that she *did* do it, and that it was an unconscious act of which she has no memory at all—and two minutes after she did it she was conscious, and had no memory of it. And I know because, as I say, I saw her. From the window of my father's room. And I ran out to her. It was a terrible windy day, and I remember how I grabbed the skirts of her raincoat and cried out to her what I had seen her do. And in the most incredulous way she laughed at me and told me I was a little goose and that she had just been saying goodby to my uncle—which was true—and that he had turned and gone away, to walk to the station and take the train for Boston. And nothing that I could say could make any difference, of course, because she *knew*, you see, that she hadn't done it. It was just a blind impulse of a moment of total unconsciousness, when her unconscious wish was doing what her conscious will forbade. She hated him, you see, as we all did, except Granny."

"But what about your grandmother?"

"She saw it too, from her cupola window!"

"But then why does she think it's your father who did it?"

"She didn't, at first. It's awfully hard to explain and I'm not sure I can do it, because I don't understand it completely myself. But at first—her mind was just beginning to go then,—she knew she had seen the same thing I did. But when father learned it all and realized what had happened, he began working on my mind and on Granny's to get it out of us—almost hypnosis, continued suggestion—and while he practically did succeed in making me believe I had been mistaken, he never could get out of Granny's poor weak mind the picture of what she had seen. But what he did do was what he hadn't expected:—because he would not listen to her, because he kept up that everlasting denial, her poor shaky mind began to make one of those strange transferences, and it put father in the place of mother and made him the actual villain. . . . Then, well then there was nothing to do but keep Granny out of the way once father had begun his tissue of lies about the Canadian trip. And he had to do that because to let mother know the truth would have been to break her mind completely. You see, there's that strain of insanity—Granny's awful appearance is really only mental; she didn't look like that when she was apparently sane. . . . So Granny has had to be kept hidden, and it wasn't awfully hard because we have no relatives. Uncle Solomon—that's my father's brother—was alive at the time, and he knew everything. And then—I've never actually been told all this, you understand, but I've dug it out by myself—I believe father got hold of Sutton who was a Canadian, and down and out, just released from a penitentiary for something minor, and used him, by doing some big favor for him, as the one to swear at law that he had guided my uncle through the north woods and had seen him die.

"Oh, I know you're finding all this awfully hard to believe, but I want you to understand that it's the truth!"

I was finding it hard to believe and just as hard to understand. And I didn't see—

"Patricia," I said, "why are you telling all this to me? I'm glad you are, but why, if it's been a secret all these years—"

"Because you've met Granny. Because you might not actually believe her story but you'd begin to follow it up, and because I'm afraid that an actual investigator would find father's deceit not entirely holeproof. And besides, with suspicion on him already because of his actions about the telephone, you'd follow it through to the end. And that was just unguarded temper that made him raise his hand to you, I know. That, and guilt. But he's wholly sane and wholly normal. He's just, from protecting mother and trying to keep her with us, got himself into a terrible hole. And mother is too lovely and too normal herself all but one-ten-thousandth of the time to put her away. But of course such things do get worse and perhaps sometime there'll come a day when something will have to be done. . . . and I thought—" she lowered her eyes and clenched and unclenched her hands in her lap—"I thought I'd tell you all, first hand, and ask for your mercy."

I said absolutely nothing for there was absolutely nothing that I could say. But my silence never had time to become embarrassing because almost at once she raised her head and began to talk again.

"Do you see now, Mr. Meech," she asked gently, "why when I had had a moment to think, I didn't report what I had found in the cupola?"

"You mean—you think your mother killed Garda?"

"Oh no!" she cried, clasping her face with her hands. "Don't accuse me, please, of saying anything like that! But don't you see what flashed into my mind—*that*, of course! And don't you see why I'm telling you all this—aside from the reason of father's safety—to make you begin to see that you're dealing with—with unresponsible people—so that—so that," she began to falter and hesitate, "if you *should* come to suspect—or find—" Her voice trailed off into silence.

"Ah, Patricia!" I exclaimed. "Then you do—you really *do*—deep in your heart suspect your mother of Garda's death."

She shook her head furiously and tears began to stand in her eyes and she felt for her handkerchief under one of the pillows.

"No! No!" she cried. "I'll never say that. No! Never."

"But my dear girl," I said, as tenderly as I could, "you're really implying it. And I'm not criticizing you, or thinking that it's cruel

and unnatural. . . . Instead, look! . . . I'll say that I don't believe
you, and that I've found proof that it wasn't your mother. Never
mind for a minute, whether I'm speaking the truth or not. But I
think that if we talk this out for just a little while, it may prove to
help you in your mind, just as much as it will help me. . . . And see,
my dear, if it should ever possibly be true that your mother did
this, why now we would *know*, wouldn't we, that it's time she went
somewhere where she could be—helped? . . . And besides, Patricia,
you know so much more than I do about these psychological
things."

She dabbed at her eyes and her breathing quieted.

"Listen, Patricia," I went on. "Tell me some more about Dr.
Bernd's *Geistesunterströmung*. . . . You say that this unconscious
crime can be committed when there's a suppressed wish down deep
in the unconscious mind."

"Yes," she said, "if there's something that brings it out, such as
a split personality—which mother's really is. Those little things that
she calls unconscious moments are really *conscious* moments of
that second Vera which is really there, but which the regular Vera
knows nothing about. All she knows is that time has elapsed—a
tiny little interval of time."

"But what can split a personality?" I asked.

"Oh, lots of things," she answered. "A sudden shock can do it,
or hypnotism sometimes, or moments of great emotion, or little
things that suddenly start something working down deep in your
unconscious. That is, if the split personality is there already, these
things can bring the sleeping one to life."

"I see," I said. "But if one's other personality does come to life
and commit a crime, mustn't that personality already have the definite *wish* to do it. It wouldn't just kill blindly, would it, without
logic?" I was actually asking for information.

"No," she said, "not usually. Not according to Dr. Bernd. Oh,
Mr. Meech, I see what you're getting at all right. You think that
mother couldn't have done it to Garda because she had no enmity
at all for her!"

"That's what I mean," I said. "She liked her, didn't she?"

"Oh, mother loved Garda!"

"Well, then." I spread my fingers. "Where's the *wish!*"

"I don't know," she answered slowly. "But the mind does awfully funny things. . . . Oh, Mr. Meech, doesn't it sound as if you were defending my own mother from my accusations!"

"Not at all. Not at all, Patricia," I soothed her, "we're just talking together and trying to get somewhere."

"Don't think I haven't thought about it," she began again, suddenly, "all night long. And even if I do seem to be accusing, it's good to talk it over with some one. . . . I've been wondering about the Rock."

"Yes, Patricia, and so have I."

"But I mean—in—in—mother's connection. You remember father's saying that it wailed that night eleven years ago. The night before the body of a man was washed up. Well, of course that was the storm I mentioned. And the body was my uncle, but it was unrecognizable, and father, I feel pretty sure, found it first—sat up all night for it—and removed all identification. Well, actually his death had occurred before the Rock wailed, but we couldn't mention that, and so far as the legend and the natives were concerned, it seemed like a prophecy of the finding of the body. . . . And of course, to mother, too. To mother's *conscious*, that is. But do you think—that's why I've been reading Bernd again tonight do you think that last night when the Rock wailed again, for the first time in mother's hearing for eleven years, that it could have started something deep down—by analogy you see—and have brought back something of that other day that had lain dormant all the years? Do you think she could have been doing the same thing all over again?"

"No, I don't," I replied at once with utter conviction in my voice but none in my mind. I didn't understand these things. I knew I didn't.

"Thank you for saying it," said Patricia softly.

Oh, what a state my mind was in! To attempt to write fairly of my whirling thoughts at this distance of a month's time, is to find myself looking back at a shifting mass of cog wheels with fog and mist blowing through it. But one thing stood out. If Patricia were right in what I felt was an actual suspicion in her mind, actual if only half-formed and shadowy, of her mother's guilt, then why in heaven's name should Phillip Masterson take upon himself the burden of the crime. He was no protector of Vera Farnol. He was no protector of the Farnol family. It was Garda he was in love with, not Patricia. . . . Unless—oh, the devilish eddies of thought—his whole story were one huge fabrication and he cared nothing for Garda after all, but were crazily in love with Patricia. Enough so to shield her whole family from disgrace by taking the blame upon himself and doing the foolish and false-heroic act of self-blame. It was very hard to believe.

"Patricia," I said, "a, few hours ago, when I had you all lined up outside your doors, you intimated to me, when I told you Phillip was dead, that you half expected another death, but didn't expect his. Will you tell me now whose you did expect?"

"Oh, that was foolish of me," she replied. "But while I had been in my room here, I'd been thinking about exactly what I've just told you. And if it were true that the Rock had started mother off again, why then, the wail tonight might do it again. And I—oh, you see, don't you, that I didn't have anything definite in mind. I was just groping, and trying not to believe anything. But Phillip, of course, least of all!"

"I see. Now, one thing that I'm afraid I don't quite understand. What does your mother believe about your grandmother's insistence that she saw your uncle murdered? For I suppose your grandmother talks about it every chance she gets."

"Just that it's an hallucination, Mr. Meech. That's all. Father has insisted on that. He has made her understand that it was just a trick of the wind and fog which both Granny and I misconstrued. And as I never mention it, and as Granny has made that funny transference, it seems perfectly natural to her. Particularly as father has told her that, driving home, he met my uncle walking to the station and stopped and talked with him and offered him a ride which he refused."

I rose and took her hand. "Now, Patricia, I'm going to tell you something which I hope will put your mind a little bit at rest and set you at your ease, and I think you'd better sleep a while. It's this. Phillip Masterson confessed to me and told me that he had murdered Garda!"

Closely I watched the effect on her, and I saw the muscles of her face relax as if they had been tied up in hard little knots which were suddenly released, and I felt her hand go limp in my own.

"Oh, if that's true!" she cried. "If it's only true!"

And I knew that she was wishing no stain on Phillip's memory so much as she was expressing relief at her mother's vindication.

"Could you believe it?" I asked. "So far as his nature is concerned, I mean."

She compressed her lips and nodded seriously. "Yes," she said. "Oh, certainly yes. If he was aroused. From awful jealousy, or anything like that." It was practically what Victor had told me.

"Then goodnight for a while, my dear," I said, and moved toward the door. "I've left you, I hope, with something more pleasant to think about."

"Oh, you have! You have!" she cried, "Goodnight."

And as I closed the door behind me, I stood for some moments in the hall, fighting with myself as to whether or not I should lock the door.

And finally I locked it—softly. I hoped she didn't hear.

I hoped also that she didn't hear me go directly across the hall, around the stair well, and knock gently on her mother's door. I didn't want her to think that I was immediately going tale-bearing.

Vera answered me, and as I turned the key and opened the door, she rose from her chaise-longue and came toward me, holding out her hands to me and speaking in a voice that was so high-pitched that I closed the door behind me at once.

"Mr. Meech! You found her! And she talked to you! Oh, Mr. Meech, please let me tell you that my mother's mind has been gone for years, and that she doesn't know what she's saying. There's not a word of truth—"

I tried to stop her by raising my hand and starting to speak, but she kept right on.

"There's not a word of truth in what she says about Creamer and my brother. He died quite naturally—I mean he died far from here, in northern Canada when Sutton was acting as his guide."

I finally was able to speak.

"Hush! Mrs. Farnol. It's perfectly all right. I can see that she isn't responsible for anything she says, but, please, let's not talk about it just at this moment. I disturbed you for another reason. . . . Do you happen to remember what you did with that little note you found outside Garda's door when you took up the supper tray? I admit I haven't looked for it, but I thought it might save time if you remembered what you did with it. Did you destroy it?"

She showed definite relief, and then she put her hand to her mouth and thought.

"Why, no, I don't think I did," she answered.

"Let me think. You were still at coffee in the dining room when I came down. Let's see. . . . Why, if I remember correctly, I simply crushed it up and threw it in the dining-room fireplace."

There was, I remember, no fire in it, so I thanked her and turned to go.

"Please, Mr. Meech," she cried, coming to me and catching me by the arm, "you don't believe a single word of what my mother—"

As gently as I could I released her grasp and pushed her away.

"Mrs. Farnol, I haven't thought a thing about it. Just now I'm working on something else. If you'll let me go now, I'll come back quite shortly and talk to you."

And, abrupt as it may seem, I left the room at once and locked the door behind me. I went directly down the stairs and turned on the dining-room lights. The fire in the fireplace was laid but never lighted, and I found the paper at once, crumpled, it's true, but not torn, nor the writing obliterated. It was scrawled in pencil, in what was at first glance, almost anyone's writing, Garda's as well as another's.

Please don't disturb me. I'm going to try to sleep. If
I need anything I'll call.

And with only one thought in my mind, I went rapidly up the stairs
again and to the door of Masterson's room. Without the ceremony
of knocking, I unlocked it and entered. As in all the others, the
lights were on. Sutton, fully dressed, stood up in a cloud of cigarette smoke from the easy chair by the bed.

I gestured at him with my hand and said, "Don't say anything,
Sutton. I'm after something."

And I went at once to the desk between the windows. A quick
glance showed me that there was nothing there but unused stationery and the usual writing equipment. And so I turned my attention to the wardrobe, and found inside it one of Phillip's suits still
hanging. And as I hoped, I felt a little address book in its pocket,
and took it out and carried it to the light, and spread Garda's note
beside it.

I am no handwriting expert, although I believe I know a little
about it. But even to the unpractised eye I am sure that the similarity between Phillip's entries in his book and the writing on the
note would have been almost immediately apparent.

Phillip had spoken the truth. He had written the note.

And I—I was back where I was before.

# CHAPTER XIII
## DAWN

IT IS WITH A CURIOUS MIXTURE OF EMOTIONS that I begin the writing of this final chapter. As I take up my pen, I realize that in—how long does it take me to write a dozen pages?—in three or four hours I shall have done with the tale. Yet there is so very much to tell! But looking back to that night a month ago, it is more than curious to realize that, despite the crowding of events, it was less than an hour in actual time between the moment when I straightened up after bending over Masterson's address book, until the moment when, almost simultaneously with the coming of the dawn, came the revelation to my mind of the whole mystery. I didn't know and couldn't know that the truth was so near. In all honesty, I thought, now and then, that I had made some progress, but I didn't realize how simply and logically, despite the seeming chaos, things were falling into their correct places so that when the final truth had been revealed, all the little complexities and minor mysteries should no longer be complex or mysterious.

But why! oh why! did I have to go trafficking with what I didn't understand—a human mind? Why didn't I accept at face value from the moment it was made until the very end the confession that Phillip had made to me? Why must I go probing around in locked, dark recesses?

But I must tell my story. . . .

It was four o'clock—six hours after the moment when I first battered on Garda's door and called her name and heard the wind whirling through her cupola windows. An hour to dawn. And in my hands was proof enough that Masterson had written Garda's note, as he had said. It seemed easy enough to believe his whole story as the simplest and the best, and yet—well, I suppose it was Patricia's teaching me that I was dealing with abnormal minds that made the doubt persist. So I stood and held the paper and the little book and thought. And I suppose it was while I was standing there that the first faint idea of my course of action came to my brain. But it didn't develop—not then. And that's why I leave it, for the moment, unrecorded, and hasten on to my little scene with Sutton. Certainly it was not more than half a minute before I turned to him.

He had not moved from beside his chair, but he had put his cigarette out and the cloud from it was forming a gray tent in the conical light from the shaded lamp.

I stuffed both paper and book into my pocket and went and stood beside him. The bandage was still on his wrist, and as I looked down at it, I saw that his fingers which were held against the side-seam of his trousers (as a good servant's ought to be) were ceaselessly in motion, rubbing against each other in little, quick movements.

"Sit down, Sutton," I said.

"I'd just as lief stand, sir," he said.

"Sit down," I ordered. I certainly didn't expect any violence from him, but still, it was safer to have him off his feet. He obeyed me, but sat stiffly, with his hands on his knees and his fingers still moving.

I stood with my head bent forward toward him, my feet spread, and my hands clasped behind my back. He has told me since that if I had swayed back and forth, or suddenly chattered and leaped with my long arms for the chandelier, he would hardly have been surprised.

"Sutton," I demanded. "Why did you kill Phillip Masterson?"

His eyes never for a second ceased to watch my face.

"I did not kill Phillip Masterson, sir," he answered in a voice that was only slightly more husky than his normal one.

I gestured his words away with a quick shake of my head, and then in the same tone, I demanded, "Why did you attack me on the path down the cliff?"

And again he answered, "I did not attack you, sir."

"Oh, now look here, Sutton," I exclaimed. "Lies for your own good are of absolutely no use. And loyalty to your employer has no place here, now."

"I don't know what you mean, sir."

I shifted a bit, and took a step nearer to him. "Very well," I said, "I'll tell you a story. It may not be absolutely true in all details, so I hope you'll correct me if I'm wrong. And let me start off by saying that I believe you to be absolutely and completely innocent of anything in connection with the murder of Garda Lawrence. That is solved, and you're out of it." (I might as well say that anyway.) "And then I'll go on to tell you that you took Mrs. Darlow's food over to her by car, shortly before ten tonight. Didn't you?"

He was silent.

"Oh, there's no need trying to deny things like that by silence. Or to deny anything in connection with Mrs. Darlow, for I know all about her. . . . Now come—why did you go into the cupola during that visit?"

He started with silence again, but evidently thought better of it, and spoke. "I went up to telephone Mr. Farnol. I always did that when she was over there, telephone back that she was all right and that I'd given her her food. . . . How did you know I was up there, sir?"

"I was walking on the beach, you remember, Sutton, and I saw the cupola light. . . . But that's a small matter. Let me go on with my story. . . . You drove back, reaching the house before I did, before ten, that is, and you went to bed. I believe you when you say that you heard all our tramplings around upstairs after we had found Miss Lawrence's body, and that you didn't get up until the Rock wailed and I came after you to drive me up to the farmhouse. When we got back, you merely stayed around the kitchen and your room until you joined me on the porch. We talked a bit, you remember—that was about eleven o'clock—of the other house, and you attempted to divert my interest from it by saying that it was locked and shuttered tight for many years. Now, what I want to know is, when the sheriff came and I left you, did you go to your room and telephone Mr. Farnol upstairs that I was asking about the house?"

"Oh, no, sir. He—"

"Exactly!" I cried. "He telephoned you, about an hour later. And he told you that I had wheedled the key out of him and was already on my way up the beach. Didn't he?"

The perspiration was beginning to stand out on his forehead, and his answer came hesitatingly and slow. "Y-yes, sir."

"And he told you to follow, and to brain me if I discovered the presence of his mother-in-law!"

"Oh no, sir!" he cried. "He didn't say any such thing! He told me to follow, yes. But I told him that the old woman would be sound asleep, with those powders we put in whenever there's guests, and that all the bedrooms are locked anyway, and you wouldn't know there was anyone there, even if you did go roaming around."

"Then why did you attack me?" I demanded.

Again I thought that he was going to keep silent, but again the silence was only temporary. And this time he broke it by standing up and making a half-swing with his head and body as if he were look-ing for some mental way out, and saying, "Oh, I guess I'll tell you!"

"I guess you will," I responded.

He sat down again and put his hands back where they were upon his knees, and leaned slightly forward.

"How much do you know about me?" he asked. "I mean, about what I'm here for?"

"Enough," I replied. "Enough, that is, so that I can understand that you had yourself to protect as well as Farnol."

"That's what I mean," he went on. "Well, sir, when I got to the house—I was a good ten or fifteen minutes behind you, I think, and I walked like you did, up the beach instead of taking the car which you would see arrive. And you were already up in the cupola."

"Wait a minute," I interrupted him, wanting to time his arrival more definitely. "Did you see me break the cupola window with my stick? Did you see it fall?"

"No," he answered. "I saw the broken pane when I got there, and I tried to remember whether it was already broken when I was there a few hours before. And I decided that the big wind had done it."

Then Masterson had come in before he got there—that was clear. And when Sutton arrived, Masterson was telling me his tale in the tower room.

"Go on," I urged.

"Well, I just waited on the path, out from the house so that I could see up, and tried to plan what to do. I knew that as long as you were in the cupola, there was no harm done. I guess I waited about ten minutes."

"Didn't you hear any voices?"

"No. The breakers were making such a noise I couldn't have heard anything unless it was near me. . . . But then—you must have got up from a chair, or something—I saw you up against the light, and I could see that you were coming downstairs. And I crouched down in the bushes near the foot of the cliff and waited again. But in just a second—of course it was longer than a second, but it seemed like a very short time—you came running out of the front door and started right at me, down the path. And you were talking to yourself. Did you know that?"

"I often do," I said rapidly, "but I don't particularly recall that I was then. Go on."

"And when you came near me I heard what you were saying. You were saying—you were really growling it—'He'll hang for this! He'll hang for this!'"

"Sutton!" I cried, "I was speaking of Masterson. He had just told me he had murdered my ward."

"Oh, God!" cried Sutton. "I didn't know that, of course. I thought you had seen the old woman and that she had told you that Farnol had killed her son, and that you were running back to arrest him. And like a flash I could see him swinging and myself in the coop for perjury or something worse. And just at that moment you stumbled, and I thought you saw me, because you stooped and picked up a stick—and I tell you that it was just sort of blindly and what you call mechanically that I got it out of your hands and crashed you with it.

"And then when I saw what I'd done, I just turned and ran a few hundred feet, right away from you, over the beach. And then when I stopped and tried to think again, it seemed the safest thing to do, whether I'd killed you or not—and I didn't know—to get right back and tell Farnol. And that's what I did, though I took it slowly, because every little while I had to stop and wonder what would happen now, and decide to go back—and even *start* back once in a while—but change my mind and keep on home." He paused, a little breathless.

"Sutton," I demanded, after a moment, "if you believe in any god at all, do you swear to him that you're telling me the truth and that you didn't enter that house after you hit me with the stick?"

"Oh, I swear! I swear I didn't do anything but come right home! I swear to God! . . . I came right here, and had to hide in the bushes to watch my chance to get into the house, because that sheriff's guard was there. I suppose I had to hide fifteen minutes or so, and I'd almost given up hope when I heard a car coming down the road."

"That was the sheriff and I."

"Yes, but I didn't know it. . . . The guard heard it too, and walked a few steps toward the road, with his back toward me for a minute, and I made a dash for the piazza steps. But he heard me, and ran too. And before I could get the door open he shot at me. It got my wrist, as you know, and I threw the stick at him—I was even surprised to find that I still had it in my hand, my head was going around so."

"And you went in the house and made believe to be just getting dressed?"

"Yes. . . . Oh, I hope you believe me, Mr. Meech. Because whatever I've done, I've never killed anyone—yet."

My hand went to my head in a pitifully humorous gesture. "You came very near it, my son. . . . Yes, I do believe you, for the time being."

Talk about Sutton's head going around—certainly mine was doing nothing else at that moment. Was everything I learned merely going to clear up seemingly important points and leave the really important ones as closely shrouded as ever? I left him, locked him in again, and once more stood in the twilight of the hall, leaning against the paneling and trying to think. And perhaps I muttered to myself and was nearer Vera's door than I had imagined, for very shortly there came a little tap from the inside of her room, and a low voice, calling from inside the door.

"Mr. Meech! Mr. Meech! Is that you? Mr. Meech!"

I roused myself and went to the door. "Yes, Mrs. Farnol."

"Won't you please come in?" she begged plaintively. "Can't I talk to you?"

I didn't feel like talking to her. I knew I should have to some time, but I didn't want to just then. However—

"Yes," I said finally, unlocking the door and opening it. "But I think there's very little to say."

She was still in her black and gold, and she was still pale almost to death with her hair loosed from its high piles and falling in a black wave over her shoulders.

I stopped at once the begging questions she began, and took her by the arm and led her to her chaise-longue, sitting beside her on the same bench I had sat on five hours before.

"Please, please, Mrs. Farnol," I said, "don't ask me anything more about your poor mother. I have seen her, and I have talked with her, and of course I give no credit to her tale about your husband and your brother. It's out of my mind. It's out of my mind entirely."

"Oh!" she cried. "Oh!" and burst into a flood of weeping, induced by relief and gratitude, I knew, but so much more violent and uncontrolled than the usual tears of joy. Her shoulders shook with her sobs and her face was buried in the black handkerchief in her hands.

I murmured things like, "Please, Mrs. Farnol," and "Come now, Mrs. Farnol," but I could do nothing with her until the crying had spent itself and she was lying back on the cushions in exhaustion, limp and weak and in complete relaxation. Her eyes were half shut and her breath was long, deep, and slow.

And so she lay, and so I sat, with one of her hands in mine, for five endless, motionless minutes while she, I suppose, thought of nothing, and while I thought of—

Oh, where is the justification for what I did then! I need it, I know. I need it more than I ever needed anything! But at the time, it seemed such a little thing to try—large in its possible consequences, of course—but not so awfully out of the ordinary. Not really at all out of the realm of logic. But blunderer—double blunderer that I am!

I decided to try to hypnotize her!

I have fooled with it a little. I know a bit about the technique, and there was a time, during Munsterberg's heyday, when I was rather a champion of its use in the courts. But I was and am far from an expert. Still—what if, by some stroke of good fortune, I could sink the conscious Vera into unconsciousness and bring into consciousness that other Vera who slept there, the one who, if Patricia is to be believed, pushed her brother from the cliff. If I could, I could question her. I could find out if she had climbed the cupola stairs—

What possible harm if I was very very careful and held myself ready to stop at the slightest sign of anything going wrong.

Oh, blind, blind fool!

"Vera." I bent over her and spoke very low.

"Vera." Her eyes, calm, and quiet, opened and looked at me.

"Vera. Vera, my dear. I want you to rest." I kept my voice as even as possible, and in a low monotone. "I want to help you get out of your mind everything that has happened. I want you to sleep—not a real sleep, Vera, but a perfect, perfect rest. . . . I want you to give me all your troubles, and I'll give you just rest . . . real rest . . . wouldn't that be nice?"

She expressed a nod more than actually doing it.

"Then just look at me. Just look at me. . . . just look at me and don't think of anything but rest . . . rest . . . rest."

Her little silver clock on her dressing table began to tick more slowly, it seemed, and much, much more loudly as I fitted the rhythm of my voice to the rhythm it was beating and counted out its minutes with continued repetition of soothing words. Over and over again. Over and over again.

Once or twice she stirred under my gaze. Once or twice her eyes closed, but I did not want them closed in natural sleep and opened them again by a word and continued, over and over again, my soothing sing-song with the clock.

The master's mind, I presume, should not wander during hypnosis, but mine was wandering. It began to lose, now and again, the picture of the woman lying so quietly before me and go flitting around among other pictures. There was one it saw, I remember, of Patricia sitting against her pillows, reproaching me with her clear eyes for putting to uses which she might consider nefarious the information she had so trustingly given me. There was a shadowy picture of Vera with the form I know so well, but with the mind of someone I did not know at all, ascending the cupola stairs toward the room where Garda lay ill. There was a picture, too, of Phillip Masterson doing the same thing, and the two pictures blurred into one until I had to blink my eyes.

And I mustn't blink my eyes! I must keep them fixed on Vera's. I must never for a moment cease my monotone. I must let that clock take the lead and beat my rhythm for me. But then, as so often happens when one strains every nerve to hear a certain rhythm in a constant sound, I lost it and began to hear not a regular monotonous beat, but a silly, syncopated tune, jumpy, irregular, and maddening. I had to shut my ears to it and search the world about me (which seemed so very far away) for something else to keep my time. And the world came to my assistance, bringing, slowly, into my consciousness the regular, low ceaseless pounding of the waves against the cliff.

Beat. . . . Beat. . . . Beat.

"Rest. . . . Rest. . . . Rest."

I fell in with their slow time and the clock's sound faded, died, and passed out of my mind.

And finally—ages after I had begun—I started something new. "Vera is gone. . . . Vera is gone. . . . The Vera that we know is all gone. . . . The other Vera is waking. . . . The Vera that has been asleep is waking. . . . The old Vera. . . . The Vera that we don't see is waking. . . . She is waking and will talk to me. . . . The Hidden Vera is here. . . . She is here. . . . She is here. . . . She will not move but she will talk to me. . . . She will say am here.'"

"I—am—here," said the parted lips before me. And, I swear, in a lower voice than Vera's own.

I had done it!

I bent lower over her.

"Listen, second Vera," I began again. "Eleven—years—ago. Eleven—years—ago. . . ."

Her whole frame on the sofa shuddered.

"Eleven—years—ago. . . . You hated your brother. . . . You pushed him off the cliff. . . . The real Vera doesn't know. . . . The real Vera doesn't know there's another Vera. . . . But you're the other Vera. . . . You pushed him off the cliff. . . . Didn't you? . . . You pushed him off the cliff?"

And over and over I said it, as the minutes passed and as the woman lay before me, shuddering now all the time—the faintest of shudders, but perceptible—still, however, with her eyes on mine.

And finally she spoke. Very faint. Very low. "Yes."

Oh, the hot surge of triumph that flooded up within me! Out of the land of shadows I had brought that half-woman who had real existence only momentarily, who lived in subordination to another Vera entirely. I hadn't created her; I had reached down into the dark and brought her to the light where she could speak and where she could remember that wild day on the brink of the cliff.

Now I could know! Now I could ask about this very afternoon and the gloom of the stairs and the figure on the bed. . . . It was a moment when, so far as my mind was concerned, clock and ocean stopped together and the air about me congealed into breathless, solid silence.

I bent again over the woman. . . .

"And this afternoon—this afternoon, second Vera. . . . This afternoon you went up the cupola stairs. . . . You went up the cupola stairs . . . didn't you . . . ?"

Again a long, low-breathed "Yes."

"And you killed—you went up the stairs—and killed Garda Lawrence!"

Oh—!!

I wish I could spell—I wish I could write and make you hear the shriek that rang out through that room, or see Vera as she sprang to her feet before my very face and clutched at her hair with her fingers and screamed until the walls rang, "No! No! No!"

I fell back. I couldn't do anything. I was seized in a grip of ice with burning hot fingers poking through and prodding, pounding my brain.

What had I done! Oh, God, what had I done!

"No! No! No!" she kept on screaming, tearing, clutching at her hair. "Oh, no! Oh, I didn't do that! I didn't do that!"

And as I found my voice at last and started to speak to her—to do anything to stop her noise, she suddenly shouted to me in a voice gone harsh, "You thought I was asleep! You thought I was. . . ."

"Vera!" I shrieked. "Vera!"

And from the room next door came a violent pounding on the walls and above the racket I could hear Farnol's voice, shouting my name, shouting his wife's name—calling, "Let me in!"

"My brother!" she cried. "Did I kill my brother!"

"Vera! Vera!" I could only say.

"I did! I did! You were telling me the truth!"

"Let me in! Let me in!" Farnol was insisting, from a distance which did not muffle his anguish.

And in a panic I turned toward the door, and threw it open, and ran into the hall, turning first in the wrong direction, blindly hitting my hand upon the wall, turning again in the right direction and fumbling, fumbling, with Farnol's lock, crying, I think, "Farnol—what have I done! What have I done!" and getting it unlocked at last, and seeing Farnol yank it open from the inside and rush out—rush into me, nearly knocking me from my feet—and whirl through the hall and into the next door.

And I heard him cry, mingling his voice with her, "Vera! Vera! Stop! Wait!"

And suddenly, even above the hubbub of the house, for now the others were beating on their doors, filling the hall with thunder and with cries, I heard outside the house the voice of a man crying warning, and finding my wits again, I ran through Farnol's room and to his window. And leaning out, was just in time to see Vera standing on the farthest edge of the veranda roof, her white arms moving against the sky. And just in time to see Farnol spring out of the window behind her and leap across the intervening space toward her.

But he was too late.

* * * * *

I have heard the soldiers who knew the trenches say that sometimes the silence was more awful than the noise, and I can well believe them. I know at least that for me the comparative quiet of the next few minutes is so impressed upon my mind as sheer horror both in actuality and retrospect that I cannot bring myself to write about it, or to pick from my disordered memory any of the details. I still can see the crumpled body lying on the rocks below with the long waves moaning their dirge; I still can catch flashes of white-faced Farnol bending over her, and of Patricia and Victor, with terror in their eyes, speechless with the gravity of youth; I can still feel the touch of Farnol's hand across my shoulders, and I can experience again the despairing movement with which I thrust him away. But beyond that, I do not care to go.

At this point in my tale, I want to be alone, even as I wanted to be alone then—to get out where there was air, and dark, and solitude. To walk, in other words—to walk the sands again, as fast as my little legs would carry me, and try to leave behind the thoughts of my folly. And that's what I did do, when my first opportunity came, and when I knew that Farnol was no more in condition to hear my story than I was to tell it. I wanted to walk, and walk I did.

Down the same old path. Out across the beach I had begun to know so well—pressing into the morning. For it was morning! Overhead the sky was graying—lighting. The sea was beginning to glow, far down underneath, with light that was the color of ice, and the great waves, still piling high upon the shore, were bursting into white glory. I saw three gulls wheel up from the water's edge, and I smelt the bitter freshness of the waking ocean.

And I had killed a woman! I had driven a woman to her death by blundering with what I had no right to touch! How, I didn't know. Was she shamming all the time, to see what I was going to say and see what I was going to do? Or was there really a second Vera, who came momentarily to say, "I am here" and then went away again—a second Vera of which the first knew nothing, so that I spoke of her brother to the real Vera and impressed it into her consciousness? But whatever I did, why did I do it? Why did I meddle with something further when so patently before me lay the guilt of Masterson, satisfaction enough? Didn't I know myself sufficiently to let well enough alone, or was I getting old—too old for this sort of thing?

So the sands went by me, and the waves rolled in, and all around me the sky and sea and land grew brighter.

And my head cleared as I breathed the bitter air. And a voice called my name!

I stopped short. I hadn't realized I had come so far, that I was already at the foot of the other cliff and that the other house was looming before me. On the path Caswell, the sheriff's other guard, was standing, waving to me and calling my name.

"Mr. Meech!"

I suppose I waved in return, for he came down the path and met me at the foot. I waited for him. After all, I still had duties to perform, and I couldn't be solitary for ever.

"Good morning, Mr. Meech," he said.

"Good morning, Caswell," I returned, cordially enough. "Any news?"

"No news at all, Mr. Meech. Quiet as a grave since the doctors went. Any news over at the other place?"

Any news! Great heavens!

"Some," I said. "Not much, but some, and I guess I won't talk about it right now." I raised my face away from him and saw the windows of the deserted cupola, and the broken pane, a dark blotch set in silver—memento of my outburst of anger against the murderer of my ward.

"Say, Mr. Meech," Caswell went on, "is there any chance of my getting spelled off? I'm getting sort of hungry, and I thought that if you'd shift me over to Farnol's and put Hackett over here, I could get a little something to eat."

"Why yes," I said. "In fact, now that it's light, there's no need of anyone's being over here. You might as well go over there now, if you want to, and you can tell Gallant what I said. That is, if you don't mind the walk."

"Oh, no," he said. "Thanks, Mr. Meech. I'll start right off."

He gave me a wave of his hand, and started along the beach, thrusting his hands into the pocket of his coat as he did so. But as I watched him he stopped suddenly, and turned, and held something up to me.

"Oh, Mr. Meech," he said. "Here's something I forgot to give you. It's your flashlight, isn't it?"

I sprang forward, reaching out my hand for it.

"Yes!" I cried. "Where did you get it?"

"Why, I've had it all the time. Just slipped it in my pocket, and forgot about it."

"Yes, yes. But where did you get it? Where did you find it?"

"Why," he said, blankly, "we took it out of your hand."

"Who did!" I demanded.

"The sheriff and I."

"But where! When!"

"When you were unconscious, after you'd got knocked out. When we found you on the stairs and carried you into the living room."

"*When you found me on the stairs!!*"

"Yes. You were all sprawled out on the first landing of the big stairs as if you were coming down. That's where he hit you, wasn't it?"

Oh no, you fool! No! my mind was crying. I was hit on the bluff, not in the house, with my flashlight safely up in the cupola, not in my hand! I had moved after my head was battered! I had got my flash! I had, in blind unconsciousness, climbed again to the cupola—

Oh, curse this fresh air that was making me think so clearly! Oh, blinding flash of light that made me see for the first time— that I myself had avenged my Garda's death!

# CHAPTER XIV
## WAILING OF THE ROCK

"I HAVE COME BACK to the scene of the crime, and the wind is still blowing."

With that sentence I began my story, and with that sentence I begin this little afterword, letting the legend of the murderer's return live up to life itself. And again from this eastern cupola, from the room in which the dagger entered Masterson's throat, driven by the blindness of anger and revenge, I survey the coast, and I see the waves in all their fury beating against the beach. And I see that house, down the sands, and wonder if the diabolical hands who fashioned its diabolical shape knew what it was to hold.

A month has gone. I have been here; I have been away; I have done everything I can think of to try to make up my mind and reach a decision of what I ought to do. And meanwhile, God help me, I have let the case drag on—and on—and on. Getting nowhere, reaching nothing. Asking Farnol for this room to think and work in, asking him to write his memory of everything out completely, as a supposed help to me.

But what on earth or in heaven can I do! Give myself up? Tell the truth? Take whatever consequences come to a man who has murdered another while in the grip of "the under-currents of his spirit?" Or just wait—wait and live out my few last years, thinking, perhaps, how many other men I have sent to the gallows because of the grip of those same under-currents.

At least, whatever happens later, I can record now, as truthfully and (I think) as fairly as if it were my last testament, the ultimate facts, so that whatever I decide to do, the mystery shall some day be solved.

But now that I've finished, somehow there's a greater peace, and I begin to feel as if shortly I may come to some conclusion.

Meanwhile—there was a storm last night, and the ocean seemed to open its mouth and belch forth, endless, a terrible wind. We were sitting around the fire at Farnol's, just three of us. Farnol had gone to town, and the St. Johns have gone home. And while we sat there, talking of I don't remember what, the Rock wailed—shrieked—died, and Victor held Patricia close, while I sprang to my feet and shut my ears against it.

I wonder what that foretold.

COACHWHIP PUBLICATIONS

COACHWHIPBOOKS.COM

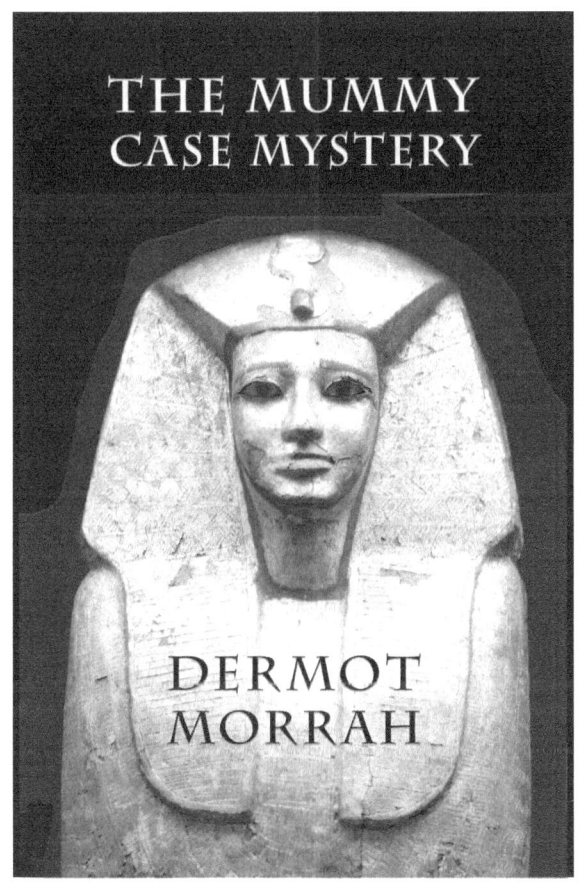

THE MUMMY
CASE MYSTERY

DERMOT
MORRAH

ISBN 978-1-61646-250-5

COACHWHIP PUBLICATIONS

COACHWHIPBOOKS.COM

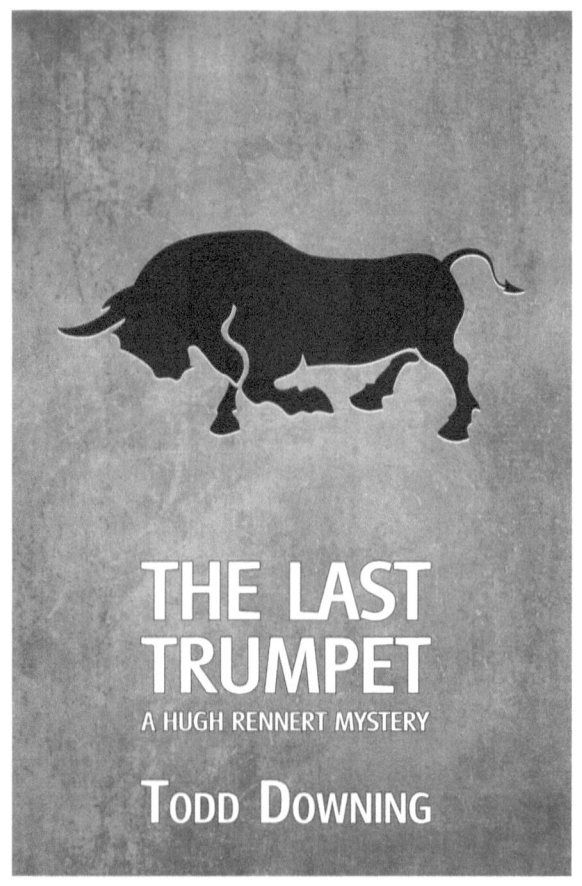

THE LAST
TRUMPET
A HUGH RENNERT MYSTERY

TODD DOWNING

ISBN 978-1-61646-152-2

# COACHWHIP PUBLICATIONS

## COACHWHIPBOOKS.COM

BLOOD ON HER SHOE

MEDORA FIELD

ISBN 978-1-61646-275-8

COACHWHIP PUBLICATIONS

COACHWHIPBOOKS.COM

THE
DEATH
OF A
CELEBRITY

HULBERT
FOOTNER

AN AMOS LEE MAPPIN MYSTERY

ISBN 978-1-61646-263-5

THE QUINNY HITE
MYSTERIES
CHINESE RED · HERE LIES THE BODY

RICHARD BURKE

ISBN 978-1-61646-247-5

www.ingramcontent.com/pod-product-compliance
Lightning Source LLC
Chambersburg PA
CBHW020529020726
47494CB00006B/1684